First of State

Other Books by Robert Greer

The Devil's Hatband

The Devil's Red Nickel

The Devil's Backbone

Limited Time

Isolation and Other Stories

Heat Shock

Resurrecting Langston Blue

The Fourth Perspective

The Mongoose Deception

Blackbird, Farewell

Spoon

First of State

ROBERT GREER

North Atlantic Books
Berkeley, California

Published by
North Atlantic Books
P.O. Box 12327
Berkeley, California 94712

Cover photo by University of Colorado
    Department of Medical Photography
Cover and book design by Brad Greene
Printed in the United States of America

First of State is sponsored by the Society for the Study of Native Arts and Sciences, a nonprofit educational corporation whose goals are to develop an educational and cross-cultural perspective linking various scientific, social, and artistic fields; to nurture a holistic view of arts, sciences, humanities, and healing; and to publish and distribute literature on the relationship of mind, body, and nature.

North Atlantic Books' publications are available through most bookstores. For further information, visit our Web site at www.northatlanticbooks.com or call 800-733-3000.

Library of Congress Cataloging-in-Publication Data

Greer, Robert O.
    First of state / Robert Greer.
        p. cm.
    ISBN 978-1-55643-915-5
    1. Floyd, C. J. (Fictitious character)—Fiction. 2. Vietnam War, 1961-1975—Veterans—Fiction. 3. African American bail bond agents—Fiction. 4. Bounty hunters—Fiction. 5. Denver (Colo.)—Fiction. I. Title.
    PS3557.R3997F57 2010
    813'.54—dc22

                                                                    2010020235

        1 2 3 4 5 6 7 8 9 SHERIDAN 15 14 13 12 11 10

Dedication

For who else but Phyllis

Author's Note

The characters, events, and places that are depicted in *First of State* are spawned from the author's imagination. Certain Denver and Western locales are used fictitiously and any resemblance between the novel's fictional inhabitants and actual persons living or dead is purely coincidental.

Money is the last thing a wise man will hoard.

—*Will Durant*

Acknowledgments

I remain grateful for the support and dedication of my editor, Emily Boyd, and the very professional staff at North Atlantic Books. As always, I owe a special debt of gratitude to my secretary, Kathleen Woodley, who completed the final typed draft of *First of State* while burdened with a terrible cold and the recent death of her mother. I am appreciative of the help of Kathleen Deckler, who stepped in to help with the typing of the manuscript, while trying at the same time to decipher my cryptic handwriting. As always, Connie Oehring and Adrienne Armstrong both did first-rate jobs of copyediting.

My final heartfelt thanks are reserved for Jim Gummoe, whose knowledge about the world of collectible, and not so collectible, license plates is unsurpassed.

Portions of *First of State* appeared in much abbreviated form in the following copyrighted short stories by Robert Greer: "A Matter of Policy," first published in *Shades of Black: Crime and Mystery Stories by African-American Writers*; and "Something in Common," first published in the *Rocky Mountain News* in the collection of stories *A Dozen on Denver*.

AN ORDINANCE CONCERNING MOTORIZED VEHICLES

Be it ordained by the Board of Trustees of the Town of Monte Vista, Colorado

SECTION 6: Every owner of an automobile used in the town of Monte Vista, except persons visiting with such machine for a period not exceeding one (1) week, shall register his name and address with the Town Recorder, and shall obtain from him a number, which shall be displayed from the rear of his automobile in a conspicuous place. The said number shall be furnished at the expense of the town of Monte Vista, and be composed of figures not less than three (3) inches high, and over or near the number shall be placed the initials "M.V." Upon such registration the Town Recorder shall collect a fee of Two Dollars ($2.00), and shall issue to such owner a license to drive said automobile within said town, and shall also furnish such owner with a number to be displayed from his automobile as hereinbefore provided. Upon the transfer of ownership of any such automobile, the transferee shall likewise register with the Town Recorder, the same as the original owner, and shall pay to said Recorder the sum of Two Dollars ($2.00) for such registration, which registry shall include the name of the owner and the number and name of such automobile.

Passed and approved this 4th day of March, 1909, James H. Neeley, Mayor Pro. Tem.

Part 1

Something in Common

AUTUMN 1971

Chapter

1

The mid-October Mile High City air was dry, crisp, and rich with the home-again smell of burning leaves and the barest hint of ponderosa pine. It was a scent that at least momentarily suppressed the lingering smells of napalm, machine-gun oil, and jungle rot that CJ Floyd had lived with for the past two years. Hours earlier, after rising from another sleepless night, the decorated Vietnam veteran had decided to retrieve something he'd left behind before going off to war. Something from the past that he hoped would help him build a bridge to the future and outrun his demons.

Three weeks earlier he'd returned to Denver after serving back-to-back one-year tours of duty as an aft-deck machine gunner on a 125-foot navy patrol boat in Vietnam. Like so many of his generation, he'd seen far too much of the dark side of life, even though he was barely twenty years old. He'd killed people and watched people being killed. He'd had time to think about what it would be like to die, had eaten more C rations than he cared to remember, and more than once, in the middle of some humid Mekong Delta estuary, had washed the U.S.

Navy's canned mystery-meat delicacy down with roasted swamp mushrooms and river rat.

While on R&R in Saigon he'd made love to delicate, beautiful, war-numbed women for less than the cost of a car wash in the States, often wondering as he did whether he would be the GI to finally crush what remained of his paid lover's spirit. He'd thrown up at the horror that was war, and every day of his two years in country he'd prayed that he'd somehow make it home. Now at least the physical side of his ordeal was behind him. There would be no more search-and-destroy missions for one-time gunner's mate Calvin Jefferson Floyd.

As he stepped off the number 15 RTD bus at the intersection of Colfax Avenue and Larimer Street to head for GI Joe's, a Lower Downtown Denver pawnshop, he took a long, deep breath. When the word *home* briefly crossed his mind, he broke into a nervous, uneasy smile, teased a cheroot out of the soft pack he'd taken out of the pocket of his peacoat, and toyed with the miniature cigar. He hadn't been a smoker when he'd left for Vietnam in the fall of 1969. Now he was. Slipping the cheroot loosely between his lips, he thought about the rare antique license plate he'd pilfered from a GI Joe's display case two years earlier and hidden behind three loose wall tiles next to the groutless seam of an electrical box. He'd uncharacteristically acted on this impulse three days before he'd shipped out for Vietnam, and he wondered if his hidden treasure would still be there.

He couldn't be certain that the Larimer Street pawnshop would even still be standing; many Lower Downtown buildings and dozens of neighboring structures for blocks around had been bulldozed as part of Denver's ongoing Skyline Urban Renewal Project while he'd been gone. But if the pawnshop was there, he had the feeling that the valuable porcelain license plate he'd stashed would still be there as well. There to soothe his fragile psyche, to offer him a belated welcome home.

There's undoubtedly substantial truth to the saying that you can tell a lot about a man by what he reads. However, you could learn much more about a man like CJ Floyd by taking a long, hard look at the things he had little or no use for and the things he saved. CJ saved ticket stubs from plays and movies and every manner of game. He still had his ticket stub from the Denver Rockets' inaugural ABA basketball game as well as two unused tickets to the 1969 Denver premiere of *Butch Cassidy and the Sundance Kid*. Tickets he'd won by being the tenth caller to a local radio sports talk show but had never used because three days before the opening, and ten days before shipping out for his first tour of Vietnam, he'd come down with a flu that had kept him bedridden for a week.

The more than half-century-old Victorian home on Denver's famed Bail Bondsman's Row where he'd been raised by his alcoholic uncle had an earthen quarter-basement that he'd filled with coffee cans full of cat's-eye marbles, jumbos, and scores of rare and valuable shooter steelies. Stacks of mint-condition 45s and pristine, unopened LPs stored in dusty-sheet-covered tomato crates filled every corner of the musty underground room.

For most of his teenage years CJ had been a gangly, standoffish, six-foot-two-inch black kid with closely cropped hair and the merest hint of a mustache. A kid with a strange inner sadness and seemingly nowhere to light, an oddly out-of-place young man who spent most of his free time checking out estate liquidations, antiques auctions, and an endless string of garage sales.

A collector in the old-fashioned sense, CJ considered himself a guardian of precious things from the past. Conspicuously missing from his collectibles, however, were report cards, family-oriented board games, and those all-too-human, follow-the-leader possessions that required interacting with other people instead of going it alone. For CJ Floyd, there were no albums filled with Pop Warner football pictures, first swimming lessons, or photographs of grade school field trips to the zoo. No yearbooks or kindergarten finger paintings for relatives to gush over at holiday gatherings. No mementos from debutante balls or long-forgotten souvenirs from the senior prom. CJ's collectibles were the ghostly, precious treasures of a loner, artifacts assembled by someone who'd spent his short lifetime honing a party-of-one image and running against the wind.

CJ's collection of antique license plates, his equivalent of Olympic gold, said more about him than any of his other collections. He'd begun the collection during his early teens, when his Uncle Ike's drinking had reached its peak and street rods and low riders had taken the place of family in CJ's life.

The pride of his collection were his 1917 New Hampshire plate and his prized 1919 Denver municipal tag. Both had been fabricated using the long-abandoned process of overlaying porcelain onto iron. Although his collection was impressive, it remained incomplete, and Ike, one of the few people who'd seen it, suspected that like CJ, abandoned by his unmarried teenage mother just a few days after he turned two, the collection would remain forever less than whole.

Most of the buildings in the 2100 block of Larimer Street, including GI Joe's, had escaped demolition during CJ's absence, but scores of buildings to both the east and west had been leveled, leaving behind a landscape that looked almost war-torn.

The long-established pawnshop shared a white, two-story brick building, erected in 1893, with Lucero's Furniture Store. The second-floor windows of the pawnshop had been bricked over and painted white, giving the building the neo-Gothic look of a mortuary. Harry Steed, a returning World War II veteran, had started the business in the late 1940s, and the shop, along with Pasternack's, a pawnshop next door, had a reputation for selling everything from college scholastic honorary keys to microscopes for medical students.

World War II veteran Wiley Ames, a recovering alcoholic, former Denver skid row derelict, and Salvation Army reclamation project, had helped Harry Steed manage GI Joe's for nearly two decades. Ames's left arm, a casualty of the war, was nothing more than a ten-inch-long stump. Over the decades, with the help of Harry Steed, he'd exorcised his war demons and strangled his alcoholism. Now, at age forty-six, he was a teetotaling, nearly psychologically whole physical fitness devotee whose street reputation was that of a no-nonsense straight shooter with a soft spot for hard-luck stories.

The wind kicked up out of nowhere as CJ entered GI Joe's. Uncertain exactly how to proceed with his mission of retrieval, he stood silently inside the entryway of the dimly lit establishment, thinking and waiting for his eyes to accommodate to what could best be described as a giant, larger-than-life-sized box of clutter.

Moving purposefully into the musty bowels of the store, past glass-topped display cabinets and row after row of shelves chock-full of everything from slide guitars to roller skates, he had the sense that he was back in the Mekong River Delta, cruising through enemy territory well beyond the safety of his 42nd River Patrol Group's operations base.

His heart sank when he stopped to glance across the room for his remembered landmarks—the electrical box and a bank of loose tiles. Feeling suddenly defeated and, surprisingly, a little cheated, he sighed and took a hesitant step in the direction of what was no longer a wall of failing tile and cracking plaster but instead a whitewashed alcove, the back wall of which was filled with hanging art.

Hugging a photo album to his side with his stump, Ames, who'd watched his young customer's every move since he'd entered the store, surprised CJ by calling out, "Help you with somethin', son?" and quickly closing the gap between them.

"No. Just looking," CJ said.

The seasoned veteran, who now stood just a few feet from CJ, nodded and took a long, hard look at his customer. Recognition crossed Wiley's face as he took in the strangely vacant look in the young black man's eyes.

"Well, look all you want, and let me know if you need some help. Been in before?" he asked as an afterthought, his eyes never moving off CJ.

"A couple of times," CJ said quickly, fearful that anything but the truth might expose his motives.

"Well, go on with your lookin'. I'm around if you need me."

CJ continued staring at the wall of art, taking in the simple beauty of the black-and-white photographs, watercolors, and pastels, most of them depicting classic Western themes. There were scenes of rodeo cowboys, a photograph of two ranch hands on horseback chasing a steer, a painting of an angler shaded by a cottonwood canopy fishing in a remote mountain stream, and near the center of the collection a photo of a startled hunter, shotgun at the ready, mouth agape, watching half-a-dozen sage grouse flush. Once again the word *home* wove its way through CJ's subconscious. Remembering his purpose, he walked over to the spot where the electrical box and loose tiles should have been. As he reached out to adjust one of the photographs, as if to make certain he wasn't looking at a mirage, Wiley Ames, ghost-like and silent, reappeared.

"So, whatta ya think?" Ames asked, beaming.

"Nice."

"I like to think so. I call it my Wall of the West. The boss let me do it. Said it gave the place a sense of character, and wouldn't you know it, the damn wall even faces west." He watched CJ's eyes dart from photograph to photograph. "They're not for sale if you're lookin' to buy. All of 'em are by local artists, most of 'em down on their luck. Mostly they're here for the enjoyin'. Sorta like life."

"They're great. How'd you get the idea?" CJ asked, thinking primarily about the missing license plate and electrical box.

Wiley chuckled. "DURA, them urban redevelopment folks, gave the idea to me a year or so back when they blew the Cooper Building over on Seventeenth Street to smithereens. The explosion nearly took down that wall you're eyein'. Had to just about rebuild the sucker. Bricks, mortar, a hell of a lot of tuck-pointin', and of course new drywall and electrical."

"I see," said CJ, imagining the hidden license plate flying out from behind the tiles and crashing to the floor, its delicate porcelain face cracking into a hundred pieces. "Find anything behind the wall?"

"Not really." Ames cocked an eyebrow and looked CJ up and down. "Least, not anything of importance. Sure you don't need my help with anything?" he asked, a sudden hint of suspicion evident in his tone.

"Nope."

"Well, then, admire my wall as long as you like. After a while it sorta grows on you. I'm around if you need me." Wiley sauntered back toward the store's only cash register on the counter up front. Halfway there, he glanced back at CJ, eyed the spot on the sleeve of CJ's peacoat where the first-class gunner's-mate stripes had once been, and thought, *Boy's got damage for sure.*

Realizing that the license plate was lost to him forever, CJ locked his gaze on a painting of two cowboys branding a calf. One cowboy had the calf's head pinned to the dirt with a knee while the other, smoke rising from his branding iron, seared the calf's right hindquarter. Thinking that all some people might see in the photo was brutality, unless of course they'd been to war, he turned to leave. As he pivoted, he caught a glimpse of a grainy black-and-white photograph near the bottom of the wall. Bending to take a closer look, he realized that the strangely out-of-place photo was the image of a World War II–vintage Sherman tank. Three American soldiers stood beside the tank's turret, one smoking a cigarette, one staring aimlessly into space, and one drinking coffee. Even after more than two decades, there could be no mistaking the face of the man staring into space. It was a slightly thinner, gaunt-looking Wiley Ames.

CJ stared at the photo for several more seconds before shrugging and walking toward the front of the store. When he reached the checkout counter, where Ames stood organizing a handful of receipts, he asked, "That you in that tank photo on the wall?"

"Yep," Ames said in response to a question he'd been asked hundreds of times.

"Thought so."

"Long time ago," said Ames.

"Bet it never goes away."

"Not really. But you move on."

"Guess so," a suddenly glassy-eyed CJ said, offering Ames a hesitant two-fingered, mission-accomplished salute and heading toward the door. "See ya around."

CJ was six blocks away when Ames left his post behind the cash register and headed toward a glassed-in display case near the center of the store. He wasn't certain why he'd made a bee-line for that particular case except that CJ's words, "Find any-thing behind the wall?" continued to resonate in his head. As he stooped to open one of the case's misaligned rear doors, intent on retrieving the 1918 California porcelain license plate that had been coughed up from behind his Wall of the West the day DURA had blown up the Cooper Building a year and a half earlier, he found himself shaking his head. Eyeing the flawless antique license plate, he had the strange sense that he and the young black man who'd just left were somehow connected. He couldn't put his finger on exactly why or how or for what rea-son, but he knew it had something to do with his wall of art and the look he'd seen in the young man's eyes when he'd first walked into the store. A lost, hollow look yearning for expla-nation. A look identical to the look in his own eyes all those years ago when he'd stood next to a tank turret, oblivious to the falling snow in a German forest, just hours before losing his left arm in the Battle of the Bulge. A look that told him he and the young black man had something very much in common.

Chapter

2

After a fitful night's sleep that included waking up drenched in sweat just before 3 a.m. to the sounds of what he thought was small-arms fire dinging off the hull of the *Cape Star,* the patrol boat he'd served aboard in Vietnam, CJ stood red-eyed and rest-broken in front of GI Joe's the next morning, a few minutes before nine. The sleep-sapping noises he'd heard the previous night had turned out to be several loose roof shingles rat-a-tat-tatting in the wind against the roof of the turn-of-the-century home he still shared with his bail bondsman uncle, Ike Floyd.

He'd grown up roaming the old painted lady's dimly lit halls and high-ceilinged rooms. Played cops and robbers in its musty earthen basement and felt safe and secure in its arms during sweltering summers and subzero winters. As a child, he'd shared the first floor's generous quarters with Ike—two bedrooms and the building's bail bonding offices, which Ike had carved out of the original parlor and kitchen.

Ike Floyd had been a trailblazer in the Denver bail bonding game, the first black bail bondsman on the city's notorious Bail

Bondsman's Row. It had taken him years filled with harassment by cops, threats from criminals, and a decade of being black-balled by the other bail bondsmen on the Row to establish himself as the city's premier bail bondsman.

During CJ's teenage years, Ike had given CJ the run of the building's unused second floor, which now housed CJ's apartment. Ever the loner, CJ had turned the then largely open space into his own separate world. The cherrywood-floored and vaulted-ceilinged getaway afforded him the chance to escape the sometimes harsh realities of the first floor. He'd tacked old cowboy-movie posters and a dozen or so Rio Grande & Santa Fe Railroad posters to just about every second-floor wall and covered the floors with threadbare Indian rugs that he'd picked up at garage sales for pennies on the dollar, using his *Rocky Mountain News* paper-route money or occasionally simply begged old ladies out of. However, none of those past comforts or the newer comfort of the apartment Ike had refurbished just before CJ's return home were a match for the ghosts of Vietnam.

Sleep-deprived, cottonmouthed, and busy watching two city workers inspect a curbside storm drain several doors down from GI Joe's, CJ didn't see Wiley Ames remove the crayon-colored, dog-eared, yellow-and-green cardboard CLOSED sign from the front door of GI Joe's and replace it with one that read OPEN. When Ames, raspy-voiced from a night of mouth-breathing and snoring, swung that door open, stepped outside, and said, "See you're back," CJ spun around and offered a startled "Yes."

Ames, wearing a faded yoke-backed black-on-white cowboy

shirt with two full sleeves, his armless left one flapping in the breeze, simply nodded, slipped the business end of the broom he was holding in his right hand down onto the sidewalk, and began sweeping. "First job of the day, every day—sweeping," said Ames, moving briskly down the sidewalk in front of the store. Suddenly stopping his sweeping, he stared at CJ and said, "By the way, I'm Wiley Ames."

"CJ Floyd," came CJ's clipped response.

"Initials stand for anything, Mr. Floyd?"

"Calvin Jefferson."

"Well, it's a pleasure, Calvin Jefferson. You back to have another gander at my wall?"

"Nope. Looking for something more specific this visit."

"And that would be?"

"A license plate."

Ames cocked a suspicious eyebrow and continued sweeping. "We've got quite a few sittin' around."

"The one I'm looking for would be porcelain."

"Got a few of those rascals, too. You a collector?"

"Since I was a kid. But the hobby sorta got interrupted by a war."

Ames stopped sweeping and tucked the broom handle under his stump. The look on his face said, *Knew it*. "War tends to do things like that." He eyed his armless shirtsleeve. "Come on in the store. I'll show you what we've got in the way of plates, and you can decide if they're up to your standards. How long you been home from 'Nam?" he asked, pushing open the pawn-shop's front door.

"A couple of weeks," said CJ, wondering how Ames had been able to peg him as a Vietnam vet so easily until he remembered that he'd been wearing his navy peacoat during his previous visit. "Did my peacoat give me away?"

"Nope." Ames twisted the broomstick around beneath his armpit. "Wouldn't say it was the peacoat at all."

"What, then?"

Turning and staring directly into CJ's eyes, Ames said, "The look on your face. It was the kinda look you see on the faces of folk who've been through hell. Yep, I'd say that look pretty much told me your tale." He nodded and set the broom aside. "Enough about that though. Come on and let me take you through the shop."

During the hour they walked the store together, and, uncertain exactly why he was doing so, CJ opened up to Ames. Told him about growing up on Bail Bondsman's Row, about his passion for collecting antiques, even shared a few bits and pieces about his two gunboat tours of Vietnam with the antique-savvy amputee. Occasionally reflective and seemingly all ears, Ames said very little about himself.

In workman-like fashion, sometimes sounding like a docent at a museum, Ames walked CJ through the pawnshop's eight hundred square feet of floor space, space often filled to the rafters with unclaimed possessions and the collateral of people's lives. As they talked softly and undisturbed, CJ felt more and more at home, relaxed and amazingly in sync with a man who quite obviously shared his passion for collecting.

They spent several minutes at the Wall of the West, where Ames explained the history behind every photograph and painting. The artist who'd painted the branding scene, titled simply *Property Tag,* had enjoyed some degree of artistic success, according to Ames. Rights to the use of the image had been bought by a New York advertising agency that had for a time marketed the custom-made cowboy boots of a bookmaker client using the image. Problem was, Ames said dolefully, "the young man who painted the thing was pretty much a hippie strung totally out on weed. Died over on Arapahoe Street in the middle of winter a few years back from hypothermia. Shame. A god-awful shame."

When CJ asked, "Who took the tank photo?" hoping to find out a little more about Ames, a mournful sounding Ames answered, "A friend of mine. He's dead. So are the other two fellows up there on that turret. All of 'em killed just a couple of days after that picture was taken." Ames eyed his shirtsleeve and shook his head. "Least all I lost was a partial piece of redundant equipment."

CJ nodded understandingly. "Ever wonder why you got to come home and your buddies didn't?"

"For a good long while I did. Don't much matter now, though. Life's ups and downs tend to make a man forget about the past."

"Ever have night sweats and problems sleeping after you came home?"

"I had 'em, sure. Flashbacks, nightmares, and whatever else I suspect a man's mind is capable of conjurin' up. They lessen with time. Yours will, too," he said, patting CJ reassuringly on the shoulder.

"What did you do about the flashbacks before they calmed down?"

"Drank myself silly, for the most part. Don't advise doin' that."

CJ swallowed hard and eyed the floor. "You ever go to the VA for, ahhh ..."

"Professional help?" said Ames. "Nope, but I probably should've. What I did mostly was drink. Drank enough to float a boat to China, I'd guess. And I would've gone on drinkin' if I hadn't met the man who owns this place. Turns out he was a World War II vet, just like me. Never turned himself inside out the way I had, though, thank God. Name's Harry Steed. He got me hooked up with the Salvation Army. Started me to dryin' out, servin' folks in a lot worse shape than me meals, and hangin' out in, of all places, a damn soup kitchen. More important than all those things, though, he gave me a job. Let me know that he trusted me and that he cared." Ames eyed CJ thoughtfully. "Hope you got people around you like that, too."

"I've got an uncle and a bunch of friends."

"Then stick with 'em, the way I've stuck with Harry Steed. Set some goals for yourself, and maybe even dream."

Thinking, *Easier said than done,* CJ simply nodded.

Sensing from the look on CJ's face that he'd made his point, Ames shifted gears. "Whatta you collect besides license plates?"

"Just about anything to do with the West," CJ said, glancing up toward a dust-covered skylight. "Spurs, bits, cattle-brand books, chaps."

"Got a favorite among any of those that you'd never part with?"

"My 1906 Colorado brand book, I suppose," CJ said, continuing to eye the skylight.

"Good," said Ames, aware that turn-of-the-century brand books from just about any Western state were not only collectible but quite valuable. Smiling and nodding to himself as if he'd discovered a much-needed piece of a puzzle, he said, "Then you've got yourself a cornerstone for one of your passions. Somethin' to help move you ahead. You tuck that brand book away in the safest place you can, then go out and find yourself another brand book. One that's older and rarer. There're rarer ones out there, aren't there?"

"Sure. The first one issued in Colorado was in 1883."

"Then look for that book and every one in between it and your 1906 cornerstone. Make it your life's quest if you have to, but keep on lookin' 'til you find every book out there from A to fuckin' Z. It's a little mind-occupyin' trick that Harry Steed taught me."

"That could take years."

"That's my point. More than anything else, a man needs a mission in life. No different from the missions the navy assigned to you durin' Vietnam, except this time around there's no killin' involved." Noting the quizzical look on CJ's face, Ames said, "I know what you're thinkin'—*Old Wiley's a little touched.* But look at it this way. I'm twenty-five years or so down the road from where you're standin'. Give my methods a shot. Won't hurt one bit to try."

"Okay," CJ said with a shrug.

Sensing that he needed to gain the young black man's full trust if he expected to move him ahead, and uncertain why he was about to take someone he'd met only twice into his confidence, although he'd realized the first time they'd met that they had something strangely in common, Ames said, "Why don't we have a gander at some license plates and a few other things I think are worth your seein'?" Moving to lock the front door and placing the CLOSED sign back in place, he waved for CJ to follow him toward the rear of the pawnshop. "I think you'll like what you see."

When they reached the back of the store, CJ noticed a doorway he hadn't seen the previous day. Framed in white and just barely set back into the wall, the five-foot-high, three-foot-wide door had a security lock and a large wood screw in place of a doorknob.

When Ames pulled out a key, slipped it into the lock, turned the key, and pushed the door inward, motioning for CJ to follow him, CJ had the sense that he might be stepping into some kind of lost world.

Grunting as he stooped, Ames flipped on a forty-watt lightbulb and stepped down into a catacomb-like space no more than three feet high. "You gotta squat a bit at first, but it opens up," he said, moving deeper into what CJ suspected might once have been a crawl space. A few seconds later Ames stood erect in a twelve-by-twelve-foot room framed by cinder-block walls.

Realizing as he also stood up in the dimly lit, confined space and stared at Ames that the World War II vet's head seemed far too large for the rest of his noticeably slender body and that his broken-veined drinker's nose seemed even more bulbous than it had earlier, CJ found himself thinking he'd stumbled into the land of Oz.

When he caught sight of three four-foot-long display cases similar to those in the main store hugging the walls, each stocked to the gills with antiques, he whispered, "Damn." A padlocked, drab green wooden army footlocker with the name *Ames* stenciled in orange on its face hugged the fourth wall.

As their eyes adjusted to the light, Ames pointed at the footlocker. "Dragged that government-issued piece of kindling across most of Germany and half of France back in '44." He knelt and ran a hand across the footlocker's badly splintered, dusty top.

A look of amazement crossed CJ's face as he tried to imagine how something so fragile-looking could have been transported across half a continent during a war and survived intact.

Ames dusted off his hands. "Never really brought anyone back here before except for Harry, the electrician Harry had do the wiring and lighting, and a couple of women, of course." He winked and smiled.

"Your inner sanctum?"

"You might say that. I come back here to think off and on, but mainly it's just a place where I keep my important stuff."

"I've got a place like that myself," said CJ, feeling more and more convinced that he and Wiley Ames had a lot more in common than the killing fields of war.

Nodding as if he'd half expected CJ's response, Ames slipped a key out of one of his pockets, inserted it into the footlocker's padlock, removed the lock, and lifted the lid.

CJ was so busy looking at the contents of one of the display cases that he missed the fact that Ames had started laying antique inkwells, spurs, bits, miniature Indian pots, and even a few license plates out on the tiled floor. As he continued eyeing what was in the display case, he could hardly believe his eyes. There were rare books by the dozen, including pristine-looking hardback copies of *Nineteen Eighty-Four, Brave New World, Fahrenheit 451,* and *The Postman Always Rings Twice.* "Are the books in the case first editions?" he asked.

"Every one of 'em. And every one's signed."

"Damn," said CJ, counting off titles on the spines of an additional twenty rare books.

"Nice collection, don't you think?" Ames said proudly.

"Absolutely." It was the only word CJ seemed able to dredge up right then. When he turned away from the display case to see what Ames had spread out on the floor, he asked, "How long did it take you to collect everything?"

"Most of my life," Ames said with a wink. "Took me forty years, drunk and sober, to collect the spurs." He pointed at several sets of rare August Buermann spurs he'd lined up on the floor. "Not another six pair like 'em in the world."

"Hell of a stash."

"Not many license plates here to show you, but I've got a few," Ames said, handing CJ a 1958 Colorado plate, the only Colorado plate to ever feature a downhill skier.

Admiring the plate, which was in reasonably good condition but not nearly as good as the one he owned, CJ said, "Nice."

"Got a lot more here for us to look at," said Ames, digging back into the footlocker. Eyeing the display cases, CJ said, "Let's do it, then."

For the next hour and a half the two war veterans examined most of Wiley's collection of prizes, with Wiley recounting in detail how he'd hunted down the rarest of them.

They also talked about war. About their close shaves with death, about friends who'd died, and about the luck involved in making it home. They spoke in hushed, almost reverent tones about burning Vietnamese villages and destroying German towns, and when it was clear to both of them that there was no more right then to talk about or tell, Ames packed everything he'd taken out of the footlocker and display cases back into its proper place. Snapping the footlocker's lock closed and moving over to one of the display cases, he said, "You take what I've said to you to heart, you hear me, son?"

He didn't wait for CJ's response but instead slid the back door to the display case open and reached deep inside. "Got one last thing for you to look at. Ain't really that rare, but it is one of my favorites." He slipped a porcelain plate that had been pretty much hidden off the shelf, rubbed the dust off on his shirtsleeve, and handed the plate to CJ. "Rare but not so rare, as they say in the trade."

He watched CJ study the plate for a good half minute before saying, "It's a Colorado municipal plate from the town of Monte Vista. Issued around 1909."

The plate, which clearly wasn't mint, had several nicks in the porcelain near the top right-hand corner, but in CJ's eyes it was absolutely flawless. The number 87 sat squarely in the middle of the plate, flanked on the right by two small letters, an M over a V.

As CJ continued to stare at the plate, Ames said, "It's the equivalent of that brand book of yours from 1906. My cornerstone of sorts. I come look at it from time to time, generally when I feel like I've been runnin' against the wind."

Handing the Monte Vista plate back to Ames, CJ said, "I'll remember that the next time I'm up against it."

"You do that," said Ames, putting the plate back in its place on the shelf. "Now, how about we go?" he said, flashing CJ a final satisfied wink. "I'm thinkin' we've had ourselves enough fun for one day."

Chapter

3

"You're a stubborn man, Ames. Stubborn, above it all, and when you get right down to it, just plain funny-acting. And you're a thief." The person talking long-distance to Wiley Ames checked the clock on the wall. "Should be just about sundown there in Denver. Sunset in the Rockies. Pretty as a postcard, I bet. So how about it, Ames? You playing ball or not?"

"I've told you before. The only thing I'll be playing as far as you're concerned will be 'Taps,' or maybe 'Swing Low, Sweet Chariot' at your funeral."

"Funny, Ames. Real funny. Now, here's a little something less rib-tickling for you to think about. Deliver the goods you and your Chinese buddy Chin promised, or you'll both be too dead to be sorry you didn't. And remember, I'm never more than a few minutes from your doorstep, old chap."

"Go pick your nose and look for your brains in the snot, asshole." Ames slammed down the receiver, gritted his teeth, and nervously rubbed the end of his stump. His lip quivered as he rose from the pressback wooden chair behind his desk and walked from the small study in his Congress Park condominium to his living room, where he stared out the bay window.

He loved his neighborhood, a place filled with Denver and Colorado political history, tree-lined streets, and a healthy mix of old wags like himself and energetic young people. He never could have afforded the remodeled, always shady northern half of what had once been a three-thousand-square-foot, craftsman-style home if it hadn't been for his boss, Harry Steed, who'd lent him the money for the down payment. The only downside to the deal was that Steed, who understood more than any person he'd ever met about how to make money, had gotten to take the principal and interest stemming from the deal out of Ames's paycheck every month.

Angry and shaking, Ames thought about having a drink, knowing full well that he couldn't. There was no way he'd let Harry or himself down by jumping off the sobriety wagon he'd ridden on for so many years. His dealings with Chin, unfortunately, would eventually come out. There'd be no way of stopping that, and as the voice on the phone had said, he was, in fact, in a roundabout way, a thief. Even so, he'd been in worse straits before, and he expected he'd be able to weather the current storm. During his days as an alcoholic he'd slept beneath bridges, lived in taped-together cardboard refrigerator boxes, and once worn the same filthy clothes for a full winter. On top of that, he'd survived a war, and if push came to shove he expected that he'd be able to outrun allegations of being a thief.

From his bay window overlooking the park he could see people jogging and a woman pushing a stroller. Just to the right of a towering maple tree he loved to watch, especially during the change of seasons, were several young men, college boys, he suspected, playing Frisbee.

He watched the activity in the park for several more minutes before walking back to his bedroom. Stepping inside and kneeling beside his bed, he thought about the advice he'd given young, war-damaged CJ Floyd earlier that day and wondered whether that advice would be enough to sustain the young man through the bumpy readjustment period that was facing him. Hoping it would be, he stretched an arm beneath the bed to grab hold of the duffel bag. Grunting as he pulled it toward him, he let out a truncated sneeze triggered by the thick layer of dust that covered the long-undisturbed bag. He sneezed again as he unzipped the army-surplus bag, fumbled around inside, and extracted two boxes of shotgun shells and a 12-gauge sawed-off shotgun. Laying the shotgun aside on the floor, he reached back inside the bag and pulled out a .38 long-barrel, the kind big-city police departments had been so fond of in the 1940s and early 1950s. He set the .38 aside and zipped the duffel bag back up. It had been a long time since he'd held a weapon. Longer still since he'd killed someone. But if forced to kill, he knew he still could.

Shoving the duffel bag back beneath the bed, he rose with both weapons cradled securely under his amputation stump, then released them onto his bed. He thought about returning to his bay window to catch a final glimpse of the sunset, but when he craned to look beyond his bedroom doorway, he could see that it was already too late. Congress Park was on the downside of darkness. He'd have to enjoy the sunset view another day.

CJ hadn't had as restful a night's sleep as the one he'd just awakened from in weeks. Uncertain exactly what had precipitated the full night of slumber, free of the flashbacks and energy-expending tossing and turning, he simply thanked his lucky stars. He thought the luxury might be in part due to the fact that he'd gone to bed earlier than usual after passing on a trip to Trundle's Pool Hall for some eight ball with his best friend, Roosevelt Weeks. He suspected that the uninterrupted night of rest was also linked to the fact that his Uncle Ike had informed him as they'd polished off a dinner of ham hocks, French-fried sweet potatoes, cornbread, and collard greens the previous evening that he wanted CJ to join him in the bail bonding business.

It wasn't a job CJ had lobbied for. In fact, he'd been toying with the idea of starting college, but by throwing in with his uncle, a man whom CJ idolized in spite of his imperfections, he'd at least have an immediate paycheck and some job stability.

The one thing he was certain had sparked his night of unbroken rest, however, was his encounter with the positive-thinking Wiley Ames. As Ames had said succinctly during their discussions the previous day, whether he became a bail bondsman, a teacher, a lawyer, or a mechanic, he'd never again have to start each day knowing that his mission would be to seek out and kill his fellow man.

Wiley Ames watched a street sweeper swish its way south down Larimer Street before turning west on Twenty-first Street and heading toward the mountains. It was just past 5:30 a.m., and only quietness was left in the sweeper's wake. Letting himself in the front door of GI Joe's, Ames tugged at one of the straps on the backpack he was wearing, then walked in the semidarkness toward the rear of the pawnshop. Glancing briefly toward his Wall of the West, he jiggled the backpack off, catching it one-handed before it hit the floor.

Frustrated and sleepy-eyed, he was responding to a 4 a.m. page. He'd been carrying the doctor's-style pager for nearly a year, and although he often cursed the device, he'd come to realize that it helped with his business dealings. He'd been the one who'd initially set up the pager-first communication system with his business partner, Quan Lee Chin, telling Chin that he was never to contact Ames by phone without paging him first.

Ames had known the gangly, six-foot-six-inch, sunken-cheeked Chin, a refugee from the homeland that he doggedly insisted Ames call Taiwan, not Formosa, since Chin had first appeared at GI Joe's one winter afternoon two years earlier, looking for old movie posters. Three visits later and after considerable probing from Ames, Chin had admitted that from his very first visit to the pawnshop, he'd been looking not for movie posters but for rare Chinese artifacts. What could only loosely be described as a friendship grew between the two men, and when Ames somehow learned that Chin was a concert cellist who, during his first visit to GI Joe's, had been in Denver unsuccessfully auditioning for a seat with the Denver Symphony, he had Chin bring in his cello and play for him.

Once, after Chin had rummaged around the pawnshop for over an hour before finally leaving without making a purchase, Harry Steed pointedly said to Ames, "Your Chinaman friend sure looks around a lot to never spend a dime. What's he after, anyway?"

"A big score," Ames responded.

In the sixteen months since then Ames and Steed had sold the man who they now knew to have been a musical prodigy everything from Chinese sewing baskets to badly carved imitation-ivory elephant tusks. Only once during those visits had Chin shown up with anyone else. It had been a snowy early-spring visit when he'd purchased an 1899-vintage Oliver "standard visible" typewriter while the woman who had accompanied Chin never moved from just inside the pawnshop's front door.

Grunting and kneeling, Ames unzipped his backpack and nervously fumbled through it. His hand shook as, clutching his .38, he called out in a surprisingly loud voice, "That you, Chin?" in response to three knocks at the back door.

"Yes," came the barely audible reply.

"Step back from the door and I'll let you in," said Ames, walking to the back door, his .38 firmly in hand.

He swung the door open to a sudden burst of sunshine and the startled-looking Chin, who stood a few feet from the door clutching a toaster-oven-sized cardboard box under one arm. "What's with the pistol?"

Ames ignored the question. "Move back a few steps and let me check out the alley."

Chin took three steps backward into the alley as Ames stepped through the doorway. Scanning the alley and eyeing the box Chin was carrying, Ames said, "First time, last time, Chin. I don't know how I ever let you talk me into this deal in the first place. Now, let's get the hell back in the store. You can never be too careful. Besides—"

A single shot from a semiautomatic handgun cut Ames's response short. Collapsing to his knees, he fell face forward into a pothole near the alley's edge. The jagged asphalt edge cut a three-inch-long gash in his forehead as blood oozed from the pencil-eraser-sized entry wound in his neck and his lower jaw twitched. Eight seconds later both of his eyes rolled back in his head, and Wiley Ames gasped a final truncated breath.

Clutching the cardboard box like a football under his right arm, Chin had sprinted twenty-five yards up the alley when the shooter squeezed off a second round. The bullet found a home a little higher and more to the right than the shooter had expected, severing Quan Lee Chin's right pulmonary artery. Chin took three final steps before he fell onto his side, grabbed his belly where the tumbling bullet had lodged in his duodenum, and expired in under a minute.

All in all, the killings had taken less than forty seconds. In less than another minute, the killer had Chin's cardboard box securely in hand and had vanished from the alley, swallowed by an archway that framed the narrow passageway between two buildings that fronted Larimer Street's neighbor to the west, Market Street. The day had become a little brighter, and the morning was silent once again.

"You lookin' as spry as a cat on midsummer highway asphalt," Ike Floyd said, looking up at CJ after stabbing his spoon into the wedge of cornbread he'd just plunked into a buttermilk-filled mason jar.

"I feel pretty good, for a change." CJ stared at the piece of dry toast he'd just shoved aside on the kitchen table, then eyed the thick, grainy mixture in the mason jar. Stirring his spoon around in the unappealing concoction, Ike, a wiry-haired tree stump of a black man with salt-and-pepper hair and dark brown sunken eyes that matched the color of his skin, said, "You slept better 'cause you knew you had a job to look forward to?"

CJ simply nodded.

"Even so, it's still awful early for you to be up." Ike glanced across the room at the hand-carved school clock he'd brought back from Korea. The clock was the only souvenir he'd returned to the States with after serving fourteen months as a sergeant in the all-black 159th Field Artillery Battalion during the Korean War. "Ain't but eight o'clock. You generally been sleepin' in 'til ten."

"Not today, and hopefully not tomorrow or the day after that," said CJ.

"Good. 'Cause you're gonna need all the rest you can muster when I put you out there on the street. I'll start you out slow, hitchin' up nickel-and-dime bonds and handlin' baby skips— nothin' too serious at first."

"Fine by me," said CJ. He was well schooled in the jargon, if not the nuts and bolts, of the bail bonding business, and he was aware that nickel-and-dime bonds were everyday postings that involved first-time petty offenses such as DUIs, minor property-damage cases, and thievery a notch or two above petty larceny. CJ figured he could handle those.

Bond-skip cases, whether the baby variety or not, were another matter, and contrary to his uncle's assessment, as far as CJ was concerned, "baby" skips didn't exist. He knew enough about the bail bonding business to know that bond-skip cases of any sort could turn deadly. Ike had even developed a ranking system for bond-skip cases. Baby skips involved arrogant first-time offenders, well-heeled drunks, or doped-out college kids without the street smarts to know they'd be hunted down by a pro if they skipped out on their bond. Smartmouths, no matter how minor the offense, always moved up a notch on Ike's list.

"Yearling" skippers, a term Ike had borrowed from the cattle industry, were Ike's equivalent of troublesome, rambunctious year-old cattle. Included in that category were people who had either the gall or the stupidity to skip out on bonds for more serious transgressions, including everything from minor assault to aggravated robbery.

Ike reserved his "senior" skipper status for career criminals, repeat bond skippers, murderers, arsonists, and any of the tangle of thugs, regardless of their transgression, whom he considered a menace to the cherished, mostly black Five Points Denver community he'd grown up in since moving to Denver from Cincinnati at the age of ten. There was a fourth category Ike had no name for, and one he rarely mentioned. It was well known around the Mile High City that Ike Floyd never posted bond for pimps or skip traced suspected rapists. The rationale behind that choice, according to those who knew him, was that the love of his life had once been a prostitute, and he was afraid he might kill anyone capable of crushing a woman's soul.

Spooning up a generous helping of gooey cornbread and buttermilk, Ike asked, "Where you headed this early, anyway?"

"Downtown to that pawnshop I told you about last night."

"To have another shot at findin' that mysterious missin' license plate?"

"If it's there."

"Hope that one-armed guy don't peg you for a thief."

"I don't think he will," said CJ, dusting off his hands.

"Why not?"

"Because, just like you, for one reason or another, he's in my corner." CJ flashed his uncle a quick wink, grabbed an apple from a nearby bowl, offered Ike a clenched-fist salute, and rushed out the kitchen door into the sun-drenched autumn day.

Ike smiled and spooned up a large dollop of cornbread and buttermilk. He'd been in CJ's corner since the day CJ's California-bound mother, Ike's drug-addicted baby sister, had dropped the boy on the drafty old Victorian's doorstep with only a five-word note: "Take care of him, Ike."

Neither CJ, who'd been just a few days past two at the time, nor Ike had had any idea that they would never see Ida Floyd alive again. There was a generous piece of his beloved sister in CJ, and for Ike, who'd been fighting a losing battle with alcoholism and arthritis for more than a decade, his nephew and a former prostitute named Marguerite Larkin were pretty much the only things in the world that mattered to him.

Chapter

🦎 4

The first things that caught CJ's eye and let him know something was wrong at GI Joe's were the two black unmarked but unmistakable police sedans blocking access to the 2100 block of Larimer Street. He'd driven over, feeling relaxed behind the wheel of his two-tone, cream-on-red, drop-top 1957 Chevy Bel Air, a car that he and Rosie Weeks had lovingly spent a year restoring and finished just weeks before CJ had left for his initial tour of Vietnam.

That relaxed feeling suddenly disappeared. A uniformed cop stood in front of the two black sedans, waving traffic east onto Twenty-second Street toward Lawrence Street. Neither of the two drivers ahead of CJ asked the burly, thick-mustached cop why they were being diverted. They simply moved on as directed, but, ever inquisitive, CJ pulled the Bel Air to a stop a few feet from the cop, rolled down his window, and asked, "What's going on up ahead?"

"Police business. Move it along, cowboy," the cop said, eyeing CJ's Stetson.

CJ ignored the directive and pointed down the street. "Have a robbery or something further up Larimer?"

"Move it along, son," the increasingly irritated cop said.

CJ craned to see past him and glimpsed a third police vehicle parked just beyond a couple of barricades that blocked access to the building next door to GI Joe's. "Something happen at GI Joe's?"

Frowning and with his right hand inching toward the butt of his holstered service revolver, the cop bellowed, "Get the hell moving, buster, now!"

CJ smiled and called out, "Have a nice day, officer," shaving the Bel Air as close to the fuming policeman as he dared while he turned onto Twenty-second Street.

Unlike Ike, CJ had no deep-seated hatred of policemen. But, also unlike Ike, he'd never had a rogue bond-skipping, drug-dealing cop on the run try to kill him; in fact, he hadn't had to deal with much along those lines except the occasional racial slur tossed his way by some insecure redneck authority figure in blue. He was pretty much neutral when it came to the police, but lockstep-obedient he wasn't. There'd been trouble at GI Joe's or Pasternack's next door, he was certain—trouble enough to warrant cordoning off an entire city block, and he intended to have a close-up look at the problem.

Removing his signature Stetson, which he'd been wearing since the tenth grade, as much to set himself apart from the sheep-like long-haired white kids and their Afro-coiffed black counterparts as anything else, CJ set the hat on the passenger seat. He'd taken to wearing cowboy boots and a gambler's vest by the time he was a high school senior, and the boots, vest, and hat had become his youthful trademark by graduation. He'd carried that tradition to Vietnam, and as far as most of his shipmates knew, the boots, vest, Stetson, jeans, and a couple of Western shirts were the only civilian clothes he owned. Only Henry Bales, a kindred-spirit white shipmate who'd been raised on a Durango, Colorado, cattle ranch and who was now a premed student at the University of Colorado in Boulder, knew that CJ had a stateside closet filled with silk pajamas, custom-made shirts and robes, and a half-dozen tailor-made suits that he'd purchased on R&R in Thailand during his first tour of duty.

In CJ's mind, there was no need for most people to truly know him. And one unfortunate taunting gang-banger from high school had learned when CJ had fractured his jaw with a powerful right jab—a punch that Ike, a onetime amateur boxing champion, had taught him—that it was possible to end up in the hospital with his jaws wired shut for making fun of the wrong person's clothes.

CJ was comfortable in his own skin. So comfortable, in fact, that Henry Bales always claimed that, given the urban cowboy that he was, CJ had been born one hundred years too late.

Glancing into his rearview mirror, CJ caught a final glimpse of the traffic-directing cop before turning into a vacant lot at the corner of Twenty-second and Curtis Streets. As he slipped out of the Bel Air, he thought about something that he and Henry Bales, who'd been a corpsman, had had drilled into their heads by an old navy gunnery chief: *Knowing the lay of the land's always an advantage. Use it.* That was exactly what he planned to do. As a teenager, he'd scoured Denver's Lower Downtown pawnshops and thrift shops, most of which sat in the heart of what had been skid row before urban renewal came along. He'd visited them so often, in fact, that he knew every nook, cranny, archway, and crevice within a ten-square-block area. Even in the face of Denver's current massive Lower Downtown redevelopment project, he had an advantage. He knew how to weave his way between buildings, down alleys, and around rubble to get to GI Joe's with only the remotest possibility of detection.

Although he suspected that the cops were investigating a robbery at GI Joe's or Pasternack's, he knew he could be wrong. The one good thing, he told himself as he started his trek back toward Larimer Street, was that since he hadn't seen an ambulance, likely no one had been injured.

He quickly headed west, threading his way between empty old buildings that hadn't yet been bulldozed by DURA, past archways and sagging facades, from one protective building corner to another on his way back to Larimer Street. It took him the better part of five minutes to work his way down side streets and west beyond cordoned-off Larimer and Market Streets. When he finally reached a passageway that he knew led into an alley between the two streets, he let out a sigh of relief.

His heart started racing when, from the end of the passageway, he caught sight of a man dressed in hospital scrubs pushing a gurney top-heavy with a body bag toward the open back door of a Denver coroner's wagon. Only after the gurney's legs collapsed and he watched the body slide into the wagon did

CJ notice the yellow chalk outline where a body had once lain. His mouth turned dry when he spotted a second outline twenty yards or so farther up the alley.

With no cops in sight and in the absence of the technical crime-scene people he knew typically managed a homicide scene, he reasoned that the man in scrubs was merely a driver. Boldly and without hesitation, he stepped out from the protection of the archway where he'd been hiding and headed toward the man.

"Hey, man, I live just up the alley here," he said, flashing the startled man his very best concerned-citizen look. "What's going on?"

Looking as if he wanted to ask CJ, *How the hell'd you get here?* the man in scrubs instead nodded toward GI Joe's. "Some one-armed guy who worked at a pawnshop and another guy, some Asian, bought it. Already carted the first guy off."

"Robbery?" CJ asked dolefully.

The driver shrugged, slipped behind the wheel of his vehicle, and cranked the engine. "Real likely. Now, if I were you, I'd head back home. The cops are gonna come outa the back door of that pawnshop hungry for suspects any second. Don't think you wanna end up bein' one."

Aware that being in the wrong place at the wrong time was all too often what Ike liked to call *the black man's penalty point,* CJ was prepared to heed the driver's advice. However, he stood listless and dumbfounded for a few seconds as the coroner's wagon pulled away. Only when he heard voices from just inside GI Joe's did he sprint for the protection of the archway.

"Hell of a way for Wiley to buy it after workin' for me all this time. Real sad," CJ heard a man whose voice was clearly cracking say, a split second after he slipped into the shelter of the archway.

"You're right, Mr. Steed. Pretty damn sad. But that's the world we live in," a second man said.

CJ didn't hang around to catch any more of the conversation. There was no need for him to end up being the cops' initial murder suspect. He'd gotten what he'd come for. Wiley Ames was dead, and no matter how much he might want to, he couldn't change that.

The rest of CJ's day was a sour-tasting dog of a day. One that carried with it a strange, sorrowful, missed-opportunity kind of hurt.

He'd known Wiley Ames for less than two days, yet it seemed as if he'd known the crusty, one-armed World War II veteran for years. When he found himself thinking about what it was that made people friends—like him and Rosie Weeks, the man now sitting across the table from him—he couldn't put his finger on anything specific. What he did know was that he and Rosie both loved cars, appreciated the same kind of music, and enjoyed the same kinds of food. All pretty superficial connections in the end. He realized that the roots of true friendship, like those that linked him to Rosie or Henry Bales, sank much deeper than that.

Perhaps he and Wiley Ames would never have become true friends, but someone had stolen that opportunity from them, and perhaps more than anything else, that was what had made CJ not simply sad but angry. Sitting forward in an old straight-backed kitchen chair and planting both elbows on Ike's kitchen table, CJ sighed.

"You sound put-upon, brother," said Rosie. Six-foot-four with an enormous head, no neck, and shoulders that made it appear as if he was permanently wearing football pads, Rosie was even-tempered and slow to anger. Even so, he could intimidate just about anyone with his size and legendary ice-dagger stare.

"Yeah." CJ stared blankly past his hulking 250-pound best friend toward the door that separated the Victorian's business offices from Ike's living quarters.

"Well, spit out your problem."

"Have you seen the news?"

"Nope. No need to listen to all the problems in the world when I've got problems enough of my own."

"A guy I knew got killed."

"Damn! Did I know him, too?"

"No. He managed a pawnshop down on Larimer."

"What happened?"

"He and another guy got shot. From what they're saying on the news, the cops think it was robbery."

"Bad shit. Did he serve with you in 'Nam?"

"No. He was a World War II vet."

"Old guy, then. A brother?"

"Nope. He was white," said CJ, smiling at his best friend's old-age take on a man who'd probably only been in his late forties.

"You're worried about what happened to some white guy left over from World War II? Shit. After what the Man just put you through? Come on, CJ. Get real."

Since *the Man* had once shipped Wiley Ames's young white ass to the same kind of hellhole where he'd shipped CJ's, CJ found it hard to buy in to Rosie's take. In no mood to debate the issue, he simply said, "I'm gonna find out who killed him, Roosevelt."

"That serious a deal?" Rosie asked, knowing CJ would never otherwise have called him by his full name.

"Yeah, that serious."

Rosie, who understood CJ's tenacious nature better than anyone except perhaps Ike, shook his head. "Don't pay to get involved in some white man's murder case. Only thing worse would be gettin' dragged into one involvin' a white woman." When Rosie realized his words were falling on deaf ears, he said, "You better listen to me, CJ."

"I'm listening," said CJ, who suddenly found himself pondering the issue of friendship once again, knowing that in spite of Rosie's protest, he wasn't about to change his mind.

For most of the next week CJ moped around feeling sorry for himself, telling himself that had Wiley Ames lived, he would have had a mentor to help guide him in the right direction.

A week to the day after his and Rosie's kitchen discussion, as Rosie helped him sort through a basement stash of more than a hundred handblown glass bottles that CJ had amassed over the years, the two lifelong friends found themselves on different sides of the same argument once again.

When Rosie suggested to a morose-looking CJ that what he needed to get his head straight was less time on his hands to worry about Wiley Ames, CJ shot back, "What I need is folks who support me, Roosevelt."

Rosie's assessment had come after CJ had interrupted what they were doing to show Rosie three hanging Pendaflex folders filled with newspaper clippings, handwritten notes, and xeroxed copies of a local Denver talk-show host's interview with a panel of experts about what was now being called the GI Joe's murders.

"Come off it, CJ. You got Ike, me, and Etta Lee, Henry Bales when he ain't busy studying, and most of the folks in Five Points pullin' for you."

CJ's response was a snort. "Pulling for me? None of them helped me babysit that .50-caliber of mine in 'Nam. None of them shouted from their rooftops, 'CJ's had enough. Send him on home.' None of them suffered through foot rot or endless days of one-hundred-degree heat. To the best of my knowledge, none of them fought off disease-carrying bugs the size of small birds, and Lord knows, not a one of them, including you, ever had to put up with the smell of rotting flesh or the cries of wounded men dying."

Rosie's jaw muscles tightened as he tried to stave off his gathering anger. "You can stop, CJ. I get the picture. Don't matter, though, really. You been through what you've been through. The issue now is, where the shit are you headed from here?"

"For a life full of lots of nothing it looks like!"

Rosie had had enough. He'd held CJ's hand all week, let him cry on his shoulder, assured him that things would work out, promised him the cops would find Wiley Ames's killer. For weeks before that, he'd sat up with CJ, sometimes all night, calming him down when he screamed at the sound of nothing, reassuring him that things would be okay when CJ sometimes sat for hours in a corner. He'd sworn things were getting better until the killings at GI Joe's. Uncertain what to say or do next, Rosie said, "Hate to say it, my man, but you're actin' more and more like a scalded dog on the run. Maybe what you need is professional help."

Fighting back tears, CJ yelled, "Get outa here, Rosie. Right now. Go on home to Etta Lee and that precious gas station of yours."

Sensing that he needed to do just that in order not to damage their lifelong friendship, Rosie said, "I'm goin'. But you better get help, CJ, and quick."

"Go, Rosie. Please!"

Rosie shrugged, turned, and headed for the musty earthen basement's stairs, leaving CJ staring at a fifty-year-old wooden tennis racket he'd picked up for a dollar at a garage sale just before leaving for his first tour of Vietnam.

At the top of the stairs, Rosie ran into Ike. Brushing past him, he whispered, "CJ needs help real bad, Ike," before quickly heading down the hallway and out the drafty Victorian's front door.

Ike paused and took a deep breath before heading downstairs. When he reached the bottom step, he called out, "Now that you've sent your best friend runnin' for cover, am I next, CJ?"

When CJ didn't answer, Ike called out in a tone an octave higher, "I asked you a question, boy."

"Nope," CJ said somberly.

"Who is, then? Etta Lee? Henry Bales? Those halfwit ne'er-do-wells who hang out at Rosie's Garage, talkin' all the time about you bein' a war hero and all? The paper boy? The mailman?" Ike walked over to CJ and placed a reassuring hand on his trembling nephew's shoulder. "Have you reached the point where you're needin' to see a shrink, CJ?"

The way Ike said the word *shrink*, so forcefully and straight into his face, caused CJ to take a half step back.

"No. What I'm in need of is a future."

"We're all in need of that, son," Ike said, removing his hand. "But you gotta imagine one before you can have one. And even then you gotta have the gumption to go after it."

"I was thinking I was on the road to having one until Wiley Ames got killed."

"Horseshit! You're just usin' those GI Joe's killin's as an excuse. Just like you been usin' most of your wakin' hours this past week mopin' and spinnin' your goddamn wheels. Clippin' articles outa the papers about them killin's, talking to that pawnshop owner and Ames's niece on the phone without ever once goin' to see 'em, hoverin' over the radio and TV, playin' like you gonna investigate two murders when you don't know what the shit you're doin'."

"I've dug up some things," CJ said defensively.

"Like what?"

"I know a lot about Quan Lee Chin, that Chinese guy who was killed. I know for certain he was a fence."

"Okay." Ike looked unimpressed. "Do you know anything about the weapon that was used to kill 'em? Got any insight on a motive for the killin's besides robbery? Have you talked to any eyewitnesses, to the cops?"

Looking puzzled, CJ said, "Word on the street is that the murder weapon was a .44 Mag; and the papers say—"

"The papers, my ass. All newspapers are good for is gossip-mongerin' and wrappin' fish. What you wanna know is why Ames and that Chinaman were there at that pawnshop so early in the mornin', whether somebody had set up a meetin' with the two of 'em, and if so, who? You need to know if either one of 'em was followin' somebody else's orders. Was Chin at that pawnshop makin' a delivery, or was he there for a pickup? Most of all, you need to find out what coulda been valuable enough inside that place to murder two men for, or if maybe Ames and Chin were packin' what the killer wanted on 'em. Those killin's didn't have to be over money or goods like the media's been busy claimin', neither. They coulda been over nothin' more than a minor insult. Now, have you looked into every one of those things?"

"No."

"Well, if you haven't, them folders you been fillin' up with newspaper clippin's and God knows what else all this past week ain't worth dogshit. No offense, CJ, but I'm gonna do somethin' that needs doin' here—a little investigatin' of them murders on my own. I need you to agree to do somethin' for me first, though."

"What's that?"

Ike's response seemed prepared: "I'm gettin' older and slower and flat-out more arthritic by the day. Can't run this bail bondin' business of mine much longer on my own. Sorta been countin' on you to step in. Now, I offered you this job before, and you been puttin' it off while you moon around over these murders."

"I'll have to think—"

"Ain't no thinkin' involved. I'm tellin' you I need your help, CJ."

CJ found himself at a loss for words. He couldn't recall hearing Ike ask anyone for help more than three or four times in his life. But as he stared up at the man who had raised him and caught a whiff of the ever-present alcohol on Ike's breath, he couldn't help but notice the increasing stoop of his uncle's shoulders, his gnarled, arthritis-ravaged hands, and his constant wheezing. Realizing that Ike could no longer do all the heavy lifting required to keep a bail bonding business afloat, CJ said, feeling instantly guilty, "And you'll help me find out who killed Wiley Ames?"

"I'll do what I can."

"So when do you need me to start?" CJ asked. There was more trepidation than enthusiasm in his voice.

"Right now'll do just fine. And you can begin by puttin' away them hangin' folders of yours and openin' your ears and eyes a damn sight wider." Ike draped his arm over CJ's shoulders.

"Somethin'll come down the pike here soon enough concernin' them killin's. And when it does, you're gonna have to learn to sniff out what's important and discard what's not. I can help," Ike said with a wink. "But murder-sniffin's a lot like wine-tastin'. You gotta develop your palate pretty much on your own."

Chapter

5

For most of the next two days, with Ike pushing and shoving him all the way, CJ felt as if he was back in school again. He'd always been a decent though reluctant student and except for the time he'd spent in navy gunnery school learning the importance of coordinate couplings, backdrop sight-ins, and projectile slump compensation, most things that smacked of formal textbook learning tended to rest a little uneasily with him.

Recognizing at Ike's insistence that what he needed to learn about the investigative end of the bail bonding and bounty hunting businesses was very much akin to his gunnery training, CJ found himself more often than not hanging on Ike's every word.

Although he'd lived with Ike all his life and had an overall general understanding of what his uncle did for a living, he'd never paid much attention to Ike's day-to-day business dealings. He did know that the majority of the bonds Ike wrote were underwritten by agents of the Pioneer Insurance Company and that Ike referred to every bond he posted and every bond skipper he had to track down as simply a *case*, never calling the people he represented or pursued *clients*.

CJ spent hours learning how to size up potential cases in the quiet dimness of Ike's office with his chair pulled up to the left of Ike's desk, listening and learning. Occasionally he found himself staring at the wall behind Ike's desk, where a portrait gallery of the more than sixty bond skippers Ike had brought back to face justice hung. More often than not, the tutelage took place with CJ rolling an unlit cheroot from side to side in his mouth while Ike, outfitted in bib overalls, an always freshly laundered, heavily starched white shirt, and a bolo tie, chewed on a toothpick as he talked.

CJ learned quickly. In order to, in Ike's words, *tenderize a case,* Ike always kept his office overly air conditioned in the summer and excessively hot in the winter, claiming that the temperature extremes tended to make belligerent, ill-tempered, and sometimes even psychotic cases worry more about their comfort than popping their top.

The temperature gambit, at least according to Ike, also tended to scoot cherry-pickers looking for a cheap bond straight out the door. Ike's MO whenever he sized up a case was to have the *case* ushered into his office by his next-to-incompetent secretary, Nordeen Mapson, while he remained seated in his high-backed red leather chair behind an oversized, 1950s-vintage, solid oak classroom teacher's desk, staring at the two barrel-shaped imitation suede chairs where the *case* was obliged to take a seat. A Tiffany floor lamp, the only nonceiling lighting in the room, tended to give the massive floor-to-ceiling bookcase to the right of Ike's desk, a bookcase filled with the writings of Louis L'Amour, Zane Grey,

Elmore Leonard, and Langston Hughes, plenty of light, but never the *case*.

Years earlier Ike had sawed three inches off the legs of the room's suede chairs, claiming that when negotiating business, *height offers its own advantage*. Thus, any case who came to negotiate with Ike Floyd, unless he or she happened to be six-foot-five or more, always sat below Ike's eye level.

Halfway through the week of CJ's crash bail bondsman apprenticeship, Ike invited CJ into his office to watch him negotiate a bond for an arsonist whom Ike had bonded out of jail once before. The arsonist's brother, a pudgy little clear-eyed Spanish man with a Benedictine monk–style hairdo and a goatee, sat nervously in one of Ike's barrel chairs to negotiate on behalf of his incarcerated sibling.

Aiming his words down at the little man as CJ looked on, Ike said, "Your brother don't seem capable of learnin' his lesson."

"He can't help himself, Mr. Floyd." The brother sounded as guilty as if he'd been the arsonist himself. "He just likes lookin' at fires. Can you help him?"

"Yeah. But it'll be the last time. Firebugs got too many screws loose for me to keep dealin' with."

A few minutes later the deal that would allow the arsonist to walk the streets of Denver once again, free on bond thanks to his brother offering up his house in North Denver as collateral, was done. Ike showed the brother to the front door with one arm draped encouragingly over the man's shoulders. "He'll be out by midday tomorrow," Ike said, watching the little man with the monk-style haircut leave.

"Awful nice brother," CJ said, watching from the Victorian's porch as the man slipped into a late-model Cadillac DeVille.

"That's what I thought the first time around, too," Ike said, shaking his head. "That was before I found out that our polite goateed Mr. Caesaro had just finished servin' eight years in Canon City for second-degree murder. Seems he took the business end of a shovel to a friend's head when he found the man in bed with his common-law wife. Now, I ain't judgin', mind you. The bottom line here is whether the *case* can pay. But murder trumps arson, any way you slice it." Closing the door, Ike found himself chuckling. "You gotta learn to mine for the diamonds in this business, CJ. They tend to come in rough-cut a lot of times, but that's what keeps the doors open."

When CJ flashed Ike a look that said, *I'm not certain I can,* Ike smiled knowingly. "No problem bein' a little uncertain at first. You'll learn." And for the next five days, with Ike showing him the ropes, that was exactly what CJ did.

Following more than a week of Ike's instruction, CJ sat relaxed in Nobby's, a Welton Street restaurant, bar, and pool hall in Denver's historically black Five Points community, nursing a beer and winding down from the week. Across the room he could see that Leander Moultry, longtime Five Points pool shark and hustler, was in what Ike would have described as a cesspool of trouble again.

This time Leander's troubles weren't money trouble, or woman trouble, or gambling trouble, or even trouble with the law. It was easy enough to see that. This time Leander had beaten flashy-dressing, slow-thinking Billy Larkin at five straight games of eight ball and taken him for a thousand dollars; then, gloatingly squeezing his testicles in typical 1971, in-your-face, baddest-brother-in-the-'hood fashion, he'd called Billy a jelly-headed, sissified, tit-sucking mamma's boy. Leander was in trouble, all right. Trouble enough to threaten the five-foot-six, bird-faced little pool hustler's life.

As Leander stuffed the final game's winnings, two crumpled, damp hundred-dollar bills, into his shirt pocket, Billy said, rumbling anger rising in his voice, "Don't cup your nuts at me, you slimy throwback. Loosen your grip on 'em or I'll give you a real reason to hug your jewels." Cocking his arm, Billy raised the fat end of his pool cue above his head as his girlfriend, Ray Lynn Suggs, and his half-sister, Coletta Newby, rushed across the stale-smelling barroom, pool hall, and greasy spoon toward him.

"Billy, no!" Ray Lynn shouted, grabbing Billy's arm too late to stop the cue's descent. When the hardwood stick slammed against the edge of the pool table and snapped, its lower half skittered across the floor toward a crowd of a dozen onlookers who were waiting to see Billy and Leander tangle.

Trapped between the pool table and a grease-stained cinder-block wall, Leander crouched, prepared to spring at the much larger Billy. Billy cocked the upper half of the cue, ready for a second swing, as Ray Lynn and Coletta both screamed. A split second later Billy's broken half of the pool cue came to a loud, abrupt halt when it slammed into the outstretched lower half that CJ had retrieved from the floor.

"You heard the lady, Billy. Drop the cue." CJ's eyes darted back and forth between Billy and Leander, men he'd known since kindergarten. Watching Billy cock his arm again, CJ shook his head in protest. "I wouldn't do it, Billy."

"Ain't your fight, CJ," Billy grumbled, contemplating whether or not to take on the six-foot-three, 225-pound CJ.

"Listen to CJ," Coletta yelled at Billy.

Billy thought for a moment, pondering his next move. He'd won eighteen thousand dollars three days earlier playing Policy, the lottery game that most black folks in Five Points simply called "the numbers." It was the most he'd ever won playing Policy, and in his view Leander had just stolen a thousand dollars of those winnings from him. War hero or not, to his way of thinking CJ Floyd had no damn right to interfere.

Ignoring CJ's plea, Billy took another powerful cut at Leander's head. In the time it took Leander to dodge the blow and Billy to take aim again, CJ tackled Billy at the knees, sending him crashing shoulder-first onto the floor. Seconds later CJ and Nobby Pittman, the bar and pool hall's owner, were on top of Billy, struggling to pin him to the floor.

"You ain't gonna get my liquor license lifted for tryin' to kill somebody in my place," barked Pittman, a onetime semipro football player with skin so dark it seemed to have a sheen. "Hell, no!"

"That little weasel was cheatin'," Billy shouted, continuing to thrash.

"You lost!" Pittman shouted. "Be glad you didn't lose your whole damn wad."

"I'll kill that little rodent," mumbled Billy, arching his neck and struggling to see exactly where Leander was.

"Leander's gone," said Ray Lynn, who was now down on one knee, stroking Billy's head. "As soon as you hit the floor, he ran out the door."

"Gone with my money," Billy wheezed, spent from grappling with Nobby and CJ.

"There's more where that came from, baby. You're still fat in the wallet," Ray Lynn said with a grin.

Ignoring Ray Lynn, Billy gasped for air. "I'll kill that MF."

"Let him up, mister, please!" Ray Lynn begged CJ.

"Yeah, you and Nobby get the hell off him!" Coletta chimed in.

"You gonna behave?" CJ asked, shifting most of his weight off Billy and onto one knee.

When Billy didn't answer, Nobby kneed him in the ribs.

"Yeah." Billy let out a painful grunt as both men stood.

For the next half minute, Billy lay motionless with Ray Lynn stroking his head and Coletta despondently shaking hers. Finally struggling to his knees, rubbing his ribs, and dusting himself off, Billy shot Nobby and CJ a defiant, spiteful look. "All that goes around comes around," he said, glancing toward the pool hall's exit. "I'll get even with that little rodent, Leander, sooner or later in spite of the two of you. Come on, Ray Lynn, let's get the hell outa here." Locking his arm in his girlfriend's and still unsteady on his feet, Billy wobbled across the room, through the front door, and out into the star-filled Denver night as Coletta, staring hatefully back at CJ and Nobby, brought up the rear.

The next morning, after having slept reasonably well for a change, CJ was in the kitchen of his small three-room apartment, which took up most of the second floor of the old Victorian he'd been raised in, sifting through a coffee can full of cat's-eye marbles and looking for his favorite eighty-year-old steelie shooter that he'd recently realized he might have mistakenly dropped into the can two years earlier, just before leaving for his first tour. Glancing toward his sparsely furnished living room, which minus the dozens of posters that had adorned the room's walls during his teenage years, was now decorated with only a few Indian pots, a Navajo rug, and a couple of license plates and furnished simply with a couch and a reading lamp, he extracted several marbles, stared at them, and found himself thinking about Wiley Ames.

During the week he'd spent trying to get a handle on the ins and outs of the bail bonding business, he'd barely thought of Ames; now, seemingly out of nowhere, the image of the murdered war veteran had drifted back up along the edges of his thoughts. He wasn't certain why, especially since Ike, after working his way through his endless list of contacts, hadn't been able to dig up much on what the Denver press had labeled the GI Joe's murders.

Most of what Ike had been able to find out had come from his longtime friend Vernon Lowe, a bug-eyed, flashy-dressing slip of a black man who for years had been the city morgue's chief morgue attendant. According to Vernon, Ames and Quan Lee Chin had each been killed by a single shot with a .44 Auto Magnum pistol.

Chin, per the record-sniffing Vernon, was a Princeton grad, class of 1968, and a concert cellist. By Vernon's account, Chin had bled to death quickly and Ames had died more slowly, ultimately succumbing to irreversible shock and multiple organ system failure. Vernon had been able to find out that Ames's only next of kin was a niece who lived in eastern Colorado on a small ranch outside the town of Sterling. But it was Ames's boss, Harry Steed, and not the niece who'd made the arrangements for his funeral. A service that CJ, acquiescing to advice from Ike, had not attended.

Chin had had no one to walk him up the stairs. No girlfriend, no brothers or sisters, no grieving parents, and as far as Ike had been able to tell, no friends in general. He'd left the world with a Princeton education, seven hundred dollars in his pocket, a return plane ticket to New Jersey, and, according to a *Denver Post* report, a cello. Sensing that the cops, the coroner, and the DA's office were keeping things concerning the GI Joe's murders a little close to the vest, Ike had called in a marker from a contact of his in the fencing and stolen-goods community who'd told him that Ames had been busted more than once for fencing stolen goods.

"Not very much to go on," Ike had said when he'd first shared the information he'd gathered with CJ. Realizing that it was a lot more info than any homicide cop assigned to the case would have given him, CJ had thanked Ike and, not until that very moment, moved on.

Digging a hand back into his can of marbles, he'd for the moment put all thoughts of Wiley Ames aside when the thud of footsteps on the grated metal fire-escape landing outside his kitchen door sent him, coffee can in hand, to his back door.

"You in there, CJ?" Ike called from the landing.

"Yeah, the door's unlocked."

Ike, who'd sealed off the inside stairway access to the business offices downstairs years earlier, stepped into the apartment, shaking his head. "Got some news for you. Ain't pleasant, but I thought you'd wanna know."

"Shoot," said CJ, taking in the painful look on his uncle's face.

"Couple'a hours ago the cops found Billy Larkin sprawled out dead as a dewdrop in the middle of an alley over in Five Points. His head was split open like a ripe summer melon. The cops told his mamma and that half-sister of his, Coletta, that it mighta been a meat cleaver that brought Billy to his end. Marguerite's downstairs cryin' her eyes out right this minute."

"Damn." CJ dropped the marbles in his hand back into the coffee can and draped an arm supportively over his uncle's shoulders, well aware that Billy Larkin's mother, Marguerite, and Ike had enjoyed an on-again, off-again romance that spanned nearly twenty years. "Anything I can do to help?"

"You can find out who killed Billy." Ike's words were direct and unrehearsed.

"What?"

"Find out who killed the boy, CJ. Think of it as sort of a trial by fire. I've gotten too damn slow to handle somethin' like this on my own, and Marguerite would never forgive me if I tried and failed."

CJ eyed his uncle with dismay. "I wouldn't know where to

start. Rounding up bond skippers, well, that's one thing. But a murderer? That's pretty far up the food chain for me at this stage, don't you think?"

Ike stared at CJ with an earnestness CJ hadn't seen in years. "You been all gung-ho to find out who killed that Wiley Ames. How's this any different? And you just spent two years trackin' down them Vietcongs, didn't you? And they were busy shootin' at you. Just think of runnin' down Billy's killer as pretty much the same kinda thing."

CJ returned Ike's stare. He'd never, to the best of his recollection, even once disappointed the man. Not even during his teenage years, when Ike's drinking had been at its zenith. Moreover, he'd never been able to say no to a man who against all odds had built a successful business and carved out a life for himself and his nephew on Denver's otherwise all-white Bail Bondsman's Row.

"I'll help you," said Ike, noting the confused, tentative look on CJ's face. "I may not be able to wrestle in the mud with your new-age kinda roughnecks, but when it comes to logistics, sortin' things through, and finessin' the cops, I can still hold my own."

CJ rolled his tongue nervously around his cheek, recalling how Ike had once chased bond skippers across most of the Rocky Mountain West, occasionally hogtying the worst offenders to the rails of his pickup for delivery to city and county jails. "Why not let the cops handle it, Unc?"

Ike glanced down toward the floor below, where he knew Marguerite Larkin was waiting, and shook his head. "First off, there's Marguerite. I got a duty to find out what happened to her only child. Second, in case you forgot, this here's still America. Ain't no white man with a badge or no status quo maintainin' DA clutchin' a briefcase really gonna care too much about findin' out who split some Five Points wannabe gangster's black-ass head half open. 'Case you missed it, CJ, this ain't Vietnam. You back home now, and back here things are pretty much the same way you left 'em."

Suddenly CJ found himself thinking about his friend Henry Bales and the buddies they'd left behind on the battlefields of Vietnam, from the country-assed white boys to slick-talking Harlem brothers. All of them were friends of his who would never have the chance to straighten out anything. Gritting his teeth, he walked over to a dusty tobacco tin that sat on the table in the kitchen. He opened the tin, glanced down at the cellophane-wrapped Purple Heart and Navy Cross inside, and stared at the medals for a good long while before he snapped the lid shut, looked up at Ike, and asked, "Where do I start?"

Chapter

6

Marguerite Larkin was an aging, fair-skinned, large-boned, one-time knockout of a black woman with thinning, too-often-dyed reddish-brown hair. Her face was puffy and her eyes were bloodshot from a night and morning of crying, and the cup of coffee she'd been nursing for over an hour in Ike's office had turned cold by the time she'd once again told Ike and the recently arrived CJ how the police had found her baby, Billy. How she'd thrown up when she'd been forced to identify his body, and how she'd wandered Five Points aimlessly for hours afterward until Coletta Newby had spotted her sitting at the bus stop across from Mae's Louisiana Kitchen, a Five Points soul-food eatery, and taken her home.

Setting her coffee cup aside and snorting back mucus, she looked up at Ike, her eyes laden with sorrow. "Leander Moultry's the one who killed my Billy. Coletta's certain of it." She thumped the top edge of her coffee cup with a middle finger for emphasis. "Leander and Billy had a fight over at Nobby's place last evening. Coletta told me the whole story. After that fight, Leander came after my Billy and killed him. That's what happened. I know it in my bones."

"Maybe not," CJ said, surprising not only Marguerite but Ike as well. "I was there at Nobby's when it all happened," he added, watching his uncle struggle to separate a stack of coffee filters from one another with uncooperative, arthritic fingers. "There really wasn't a fight. What happened was that Billy tried to bean Leander with a pool cue after he lost a thousand bucks to him at eight ball. Claimed Leander had been cheating."

"Then the little worm probably was," Marguerite shot back.

Winning his battle with the filters, Ike slipped a new, coffee-filled filter into the brew bin of his coffee maker. "A thousand dollars! Where the hell'd Billy get that kinda money?"

Marguerite looked surprised. "I thought you knew, Ike. Last week Billy got lucky at Policy. He hit the numbers for eighteen thousand. It's been all over Five Points this whole week."

"Did the cops find any of the money on Billy?" asked CJ, surprised at how quickly and cop-like he'd asked the question.

"No," Marguerite said, choking back tears. "His wallet was missing, and, according to Coletta, so were his watch and glasses. Nothing on him but his driver's license. Don't matter one way or the other, really. Leander killed him. He was out there looking for revenge."

"And Coletta was the first one the cops called after they ID'd Billy?" asked Ike.

"Yes. I told you that already."

"Why'd they call her?" CJ asked, looking puzzled.

"'Cause they couldn't get in touch with me, I guess. And she is kin. She and Lannie Watkins are the ones identified Billy's body."

"I see," said CJ, picturing Lannie Watkins, Coletta's itinerant, saxophone-playing boyfriend, in his head.

"What about that girlfriend of Billy's, Ray Lynn? Has she talked to the cops?" asked Ike.

"I don't know. But I do know this. She and Billy were planning on getting married or at least she said they were." Marguerite broke into a series of false starts, then began to cry. Choking back tears, she said, "Ray Lynn wouldn't have been my choice for Billy, but then you never know."

Ike shot CJ a look that said, *Check out the girlfriend,* just as the coffee began gurgling its way into the pot behind him. Stepping over to Marguerite, he squeezed her shoulder reassuringly. "How 'bout a refill to warm you up before I take you back home?"

"Okay," Marguerite said absentmindedly. "And you promise you'll find out who killed my Billy?" she asked, blotting back a new rush of tears with a tissue.

"We sure will," said Ike, eyeing CJ as if to say, *Won't we?* as several final orphaned gurgles erupted from the coffee maker.

Rosie's Garage, once a run-down eyesore of a gas station at the corner of Twenty-sixth and Welton Streets, was now a Five Points government-Enterprise-Zone business success story—and an automotive-repair-shop jewel complete with spotless concrete drives, three service islands sporting six late-1940s-vintage pumps, and a garage with three service bays. The tall, stately gas pumps with their crowning white enamel globes had in the space of only a few years become Denver landmarks, and whenever the city pols wanted to showcase black community business successes, they never failed to single out Rosie's, which was also a place where Five Points gossip often got its first legs.

Rosie Weeks was counting out change from a twenty to a customer at the garage's front-office cash register when CJ walked in. Finishing the transaction the way he always did, Rosie said, "Come see us again, now, hear?" When he looked up and saw CJ, he smiled. They'd long since patched up their differences, even had dinner at Mae's Louisiana Kitchen twice since their earlier argument. "CJ, my man, hear you've been busy playin' referee," Rosie said with a wink.

"Where'd you hear that?" CJ asked, giving Rosie a quick high five before pulling up a nearby stool.

"Coletta Newby. She stopped in 'bout an hour ago and filled up that little MG of hers. Said you kept Leander Moultry from gettin' brained by her half-brother, Billy, over at Nobby's last night."

"I did," said CJ, looking chagrined. "But Billy got himself killed a few hours later."

"Heard that, too. Terrible thing."

"Any rumors floating around about who out there might've punched Billy's ticket?" asked CJ with what seemed to Rosie to be a strangely deep-seated earnestness.

"Leander, of course. Only name I've heard. You know, CJ, if I didn't know better, I'd peg you as some inquisitive cop."

"And you'd be wrong. Unc just asked me to nose around a little, you know, on account of his connection to Billy's mamma, Marguerite."

"Oh." Rosie nodded understandingly. "Ain't really heard much, but I can pretty much tell you why Billy bought the farm."

CJ snapped a bag of corn nuts off a half-empty display rack, opened the bag, and popped a handful of the salty nuts into his mouth. "Go ahead," he mumbled, munching.

"The stupid blockhead has been flashin' the money he won at Policy around the Points left and right. Even gave me a little taste of it. Paid me fifty-five bucks the other day to wash, wax, and tune up that junker Plymouth of his."

"Sounds like Billy was itching for a visit from Bonnie and Clyde."

"Better than takin' another hit from that leech of a half-sister, Coletta. The girl was into him for ten grand, easy. I know for a fact Billy's the one who put up a good slice of the money it took to set her up in that bullshit dance studio of hers that went south while you were in 'Nam. The place stayed afloat for about a year. Folded four or five months before you come home. Billy was mad as shit about losin' his money. Lots of folks say he was thinkin' about takin' Coletta to court. Wouldn'ta made no difference if he did. No way in the world she coulda ever paid him back. Close to every dime she makes sales-clerkin' at the May D&F goes to keepin' that connivin', saxophone-playin' live-in of hers in whiskey and silks."

"Lannie Watkins?"

"Yeah." Rosie nodded and frowned.

"That's the second time this morning his name's come up."

"Here's a third. When Coletta stopped in here for gas, most of the front seat of her car was jam-packed fulla Billy's clothes. Recognized 'em right off. All iridescent and showy, you know how he was. She even had a couple of them Panama straw hats he was so fond of wearin'. I think she was takin' the stuff to Lannie. You ask me, it's sorta sick. The man ain't even cold yet and she's givin' away his clothes. How the hell'd she get Billy's clothes, anyway?"

Shrugging and storing the information away for later retrieval, CJ asked, "Anybody else who might've had it in for Billy?"

"Nobody I can think of 'sides Leander. Nobody's seen him around since he and Billy locked horns. Word on the street is the cops are dyin' to hear his story."

CJ stroked his chin and popped another handful of corn nuts into his mouth. "Leander's wired a little strange, I'll give you that, but I'm not sure about him being a killer."

Rosie flashed CJ an insightful look. "Things around here have changed a lot since you went to Vietnam, CJ. Ain't no way of tellin' what folks are capable of no more. People been at each other's throats over that war. Choosin' up sides and pointin' fingers, if you know what I mean. And not just white folks—black folks, too. There's a bucketful of tension over Vietnam, CJ. The kind that can turn somebody with a few loose wires into a killer."

"What's all that got to do with Leander?" CJ asked, eyeing the foot-long scar running down the back of his left forearm, a souvenir from mortar-shell shrapnel.

Surveying the room as if to make certain no one was listening and lowering his voice, Rosie said, "Leander's got connections downtown, CJ. The high-rankin' political kind. Word makin' the rounds is he's an informant for the cops and that his job is to finger everybody from war protesters to dope dealers down here on the Points."

CJ laughed. "There's no way in hell that little weasel would've been authorized by anybody to go after information worth killing for."

"Maybe not. But I know for certain that Leander's one of the reasons the cops have been able to pretty much wipe out the dope traffic around here. Maybe the cops and the politicians were through usin' Leander, so they set him up for killin' Billy to wipe the slate clean."

"Sounds to me like you've been watching too many spy movies, Rosie, but I'll be sure to ask Leander about his snitching ways when I see him."

"Good luck findin' him. He's gone underground, from what I hear."

"I'll find him," said CJ, surprising himself with his sudden bravado. "One last question, Red. What's with that girlfriend of Billy's, Ray Lynn? Never laid eyes on her before last night."

Rosie smiled. "Girl's just out slummin', my man. She lives in Cherry Hills with the well-to-do right whites. The only little black stone among 'em, I'm told. Her daddy's a judge, and I hear tell he don't appreciate her hangin' around with us unwashed types down here on the Points."

"Things *are* changing," said CJ with a start. "Black folks living in Cherry Hills!"

"Progress," Rosie said with a shrug. "Think Ray Lynn mighta had a reason to pull Billy's plug?"

"Who's to say? Perhaps—or maybe her father the judge did Billy in."

"Like I been sayin', nothin' would surprise me."

"Yeah," said CJ, rising from his stool. "Thanks for taking me to school on all the changes around here, Red. Knowledge is power, like they say. Right now I've gotta run."

"Speakin' of money, you owe me fifteen cents for the corn nuts."

CJ reached into his pocket and flipped Rosie a quarter.

"Where you headed?"

"To find somebody who's gone underground," said CJ, heading toward the door.

"Watch yourself, man."

Adjusting his Stetson and buttoning his vest, CJ said, "Plan to," and lit up a cheroot as he headed for his Bel Air. By the time he'd slipped behind the wheel, he'd mapped out a preliminary strategy for finding Billy Larkin's killer. First he'd find Leander Moultry; next he'd talk to Coletta and Ray Lynn. That evening he'd do a little snooping, maybe even slip inside Billy Larkin's Five Points apartment. All of a sudden he was glad Ike had asked him to help find Billy's killer. Running down the murderer just might turn out to be the jolt he needed to set his head straight— a primer lesson that could also serve as the investigative framework to help him find Wiley Ames's killer. As he nosed the Bel

Air down Speer Boulevard toward the hobo jungles of Denver's Platte River Valley, a place he knew Leander had frequented as a teenager, he knew one thing for certain. Whatever the risk, the world of private investigation, if that was what he'd somehow stumbled into, had to be a hell of a lot safer than Vietnam.

"The cops are sayin' the motive for Billy's murder was robbery, no question," said Ike. Looking up at CJ from the king-sized, half-finished, early-evening dinner basket of fried chicken wings on his desktop, he tossed a bone onto a paper plate. "Sure you don't want nothin' to eat? Got plenty." When CJ didn't answer, Ike shrugged and said, "Suit yourself. They only found forty cents in change in Billy's pockets, you know. And would you believe it? When I pressed one of them tin-badge-wearin' blowhards for more info, a white guy I thought I knew pretty well, and a guy Marguerite went to high school with, the SOB told me to keep my nose and crippled ass outa police business." Realizing finally that CJ, who'd been jotting notes on a legal pad, was only half listening, Ike tossed a chicken bone at CJ's head.

Dodging the bone, CJ pushed the legal pad aside and adjusted his weight in one of Ike's uncomfortable side chairs.

"Mind tellin' me what the hell you're doin'?" Ike demanded.

"Trying to figure out who killed Billy."

Ike frowned and shook his head. "You spent the whole damn afternoon, and you couldn't find Leander. Now you're sittin' here actin' like you're studyin' for the bar exam on the heels of tryin' to call the daughter of the only black district court judge in the state, expectin' her to incriminate herself in a murder. You got a hell of a lot to learn about investigation, boy."

CJ set his pen aside and eyed his uncle sheepishly.

Deciding he'd back off a bit, Ike said, "Don't take the criticism too hard; try and learn somethin' from it. Here's a couple of investigatin' tips for you to gnaw on before you spring yourself on Coletta or go breakin' into Billy's apartment like you been claimin' you're gonna. Whoever killed Billy killed him over money, just like the cops are sayin', to get revenge, or outa spite. Eighteen grand's a powerful incentive, but revenge and spite are equally powerful reasons to kill. So when you go talk to Coletta, keep her nervous and on the defensive. See if she sweats. People with nothin' to hide generally don't."

"Anything else I should do?"

"Take these with you," Ike said. Glancing out his office window toward the fading evening light, he took a .38 and a slim-jim door jimmy out of a desk drawer and slid them across the desktop toward CJ. "Gun's registered to me, so don't shoot nobody 'less you have to. The slim-jim ain't," he said with a grin, watching CJ eye the gun tentatively. "And remember, when you jimmy the door lock, wait for a click before you push the door open."

CJ nodded and slipped the slim-jim into his shirt pocket, still hesitant to pick up the .38. "What about the pistol? Think I'll need it?"

"Maybe, maybe not. But let me ask you this. When you was

in Vietnam, did that boat you was assigned to ever go out on patrol without that machine gun they had you tendin'?"

CJ thought for a second before slipping the .38 into the pocket of the jacket hanging from the back of the chair.

"Call me if you need me," said Ike, grabbing the TV remote on his desk and snapping on the small black-and-white television across the room. "I'll be watchin' the fights."

Wondering if he was indeed prepared for what he was about to do, CJ stood and headed for the front door, leaving Ike listening to a gravel-voiced TV announcer belt out the Friday-night fight ticket.

CJ didn't like spying on people; it was the kind of thing that made him feel guilty. But for five minutes, he'd been peering through the window of Coletta Newby's four-room Five Points bungalow into the first-floor living room, where Coletta and a bare-chested Lannie Watkins were kissy-face on a red velvet couch in front of a flickering color television. Running the list of questions he planned to ask Coletta through his head, he rose from behind a large, protective mugho pine, strolled up the steps to Coletta's front doorstep, and rang the doorbell.

Twenty seconds later, as he prepared to ring the doorbell again, Lannie Watkins swung the door open. In a tone as sour as it was dismissive, Watkins, a stubby, balding, forty-year-old black man with a noticeable paunch, who seemed to be enjoying the fact that he was for once standing a full six inches above the much taller CJ, asked, "Whatta you want?"

"I'm CJ Floyd, and I'd like to speak to Coletta."

"I know who the hell you are." Watkins turned and yelled back into the house, "Coletta, there's somebody here at the door wants to talk to you."

Puffing up her hair and adjusting her clothes, Coletta shouted, "Let 'em in."

Waving CJ in, Watkins led him toward the living room.

Looking more and more surprised as they approached, Coletta, still seated, reached up and shook CJ's hand. "CJ, what on earth brings you from Bail Bondsman's Row over to my neck of the woods?"

"I'm looking into what happened to Billy as a favor to my Uncle Ike and Marguerite," CJ said, aware that Coletta, who'd shared only a father with Billy, had a relationship with her stepmother, Marguerite, that had always been a whole lot colder than even lukewarm.

Coletta suppressed a frown. "And I'll bet that redbone of an old witch told you I had something to do with what happened to Billy."

"No."

Coletta glanced toward Lannie, who now stood next to the room's soot-stained fireplace with his right hand resting on the tarnished brass head of a cast-iron poker. "Well, if it's information you're after, chew on this. That eighteen thousand everybody's talking about that Billy claimed he won at Policy wasn't all his. I know for a fact he had a partner. Somebody that worthless half-brother of mine probably welshed on."

Uncertain why Coletta happened to know so much about

her half-brother's gambling habits, CJ asked, "Any idea who the partner might've been?"

"Not for sure, but I'd put my money on that new girlfriend of his, Ray Lynn Suggs. And Marguerite, of course."

"So you're thinking maybe one of them could have killed him over what should've been their share of the Policy winnings?" CJ eyed Watkins, who'd cupped his hand tightly over the head of the poker.

"Coulda and woulda. Shit, everybody knows Marguerite was once a madam. Anybody capable of sellin' their body is sure as hell capable of sellin' out and maybe even killin' their own son."

"Food for thought." CJ shot another sideways glance at Watkins. "What's the story on the girlfriend, Ray Lynn?"

"She'd been hugged up to Billy since the beginnin' of the summer. Latched on to him like a magnet. I'm willin' to bet she knew where he kept everything important, includin' his money. Rich girl, poor girl, everybody loves havin' a few extra Benjamins."

Remembering Ike's directive to keep Coletta on the defensive, CJ asked, "Any truth to the rumor that you owed Billy money or that he was planning to take you to court over the money he'd invested and lost in your dance school?"

"I didn't owe Billy nothin'!" Coletta's near bellow forced Lannie Watkins's hand. He slipped the poker he'd been fingering out of its stand.

CJ pulled Ike's .38 and aimed it squarely at Watkins's belly without so much as a blink. "Don't be stupid, friend. Raise that poker and trust me, you'll never see another day."

"Get out of here, CJ Floyd. Get out of here now!" Coletta screamed. "I'd heard that war in Vietnam turned you into an animal, but I didn't want to believe it. Guess what they're sayin' out there on the street about you's right."

Sorry that he'd pulled the gun, looking defeated and at a loss for words, CJ slipped the .38 back into his pocket and stepped backward toward the front door as Watkins, poker at his side, tracked him step for step. Unlatching the door and pushing it open with his butt, CJ stepped outside and slammed the door in Lannie Watkins's face. As he turned and headed down the sidewalk for the Bel Air, the ghosts of Vietnam seemed to move along with him. He expected that for the first time in two weeks, he'd get no sleep that night.

Chapter

7

Billy Larkin had lived for years in a government-rent-subsidized Five Points apartment building that looked as if it had intentionally been constructed to appear run-down. As CJ made his way up the building's clanking center-atrium metal staircase, trying to shake off war flashbacks and what was now a sour stomach, he kept asking himself what Coletta Newby might possibly be hiding. She hadn't seemed very upset about her half-brother's death, and the only thing that had set her off was his mention that she'd owed Billy money. He was pretty sure she wouldn't have had the nerve to kill Billy herself, but he wouldn't put it past the overly protective Lannie Watkins.

On the drive from Coletta's to Billy's, he'd had the sense that he was being followed, but after parking the Bel Air, scouting out a two-block perimeter, and looking for any signs of a tailer, he'd turned up nothing.

The apartment building's four-story atrium had echoed with the sounds of crying children and blaring TVs when he'd walked in. The noises had barely subsided by the time he'd reached Billy's fourth-floor apartment at the end of a long, dark hallway. A bit winded from taking the stairs, he slipped on a pair of gloves, approached the door to the apartment casually, looked around, slipped his slim-jim out of his pocket, and popped the door lock in a matter of seconds. Once inside, he flipped on a light to find himself in a tiny hallway that opened into a small living room that contained only a cedar chest, a rickety porch rocker, and, flanking the cedar chest, a couch marred with cigarette burns. Scraps of paper, a week's worth of *Denver Post* sports pages, and a pocket-sized calculator rested on top of the cedar chest.

When he thought he heard a noise from what he could see was the kitchen, he hit the floor spread-eagled. He fumbled briefly for his gun before realizing that the sound was the weighted end of a venetian blind banging against the frame of a half-open window. Relieved, he hopped up and quickly searched the kitchen. Finding nothing of interest there, he moved on to Billy's bedroom. Nothing seemed out of place there, and except for a few of Billy's flashy clothes that Coletta had evidently left behind and the .32 stashed in a top drawer of a dresser, the sparsely furnished bedroom could have been his own.

The neatness of the place told CJ that probably neither cops nor Billy's killer—unless his killer had been Coletta—had made it to Billy's yet. Feeling a little let down, he shook his head and surveyed the bedroom again. Billy Larkin had been dead for close to twenty-four hours, the victim of a violent street attack, and his death apparently wasn't important enough to have warranted a simple visit to his apartment from Denver's finest. Still shaking his head, he walked back to the living room, thinking as he did that when it came to serving and protecting the people of Five Points, some things just never changed.

Frustrated, he sat down on the lumpy couch, pushed the *Post*'s sports sections aside, and picked up a half sheet of paper from the top of the cedar chest. One side of the paper was filled with six columns of penciled numbers. The barely legible words *good bet, possible winner,* and *lucky set* had been printed near the bottom right-hand corner of the paper. *Lay down $50.00* had been printed with a noticeable back slant to the letters just beneath the other words, and the two zeros after *50* were boldly double-underlined. CJ picked up a second half sheet of paper with a different set of much more legible columns, numbers, and notes from one of the couch cushions. Pretty certain that the two half sheets listed the numbers Billy had used to come up with a winning combination for his eighteen-thousand-dollar Policy hit, CJ was about to stuff the two sheets in his pocket for Ike to look at later when he decided instead to examine the printing on both more closely. Concluding in the end that two different people had done the printing, he found himself staring at the more neatly printed of the two sheets. There was something about the boldness of the printing that he thought he recognized. He couldn't put his finger on it, but he had the feeling he'd seen the same printing style before.

Satisfied that he'd gleaned as much as he could from his search, he folded the two pieces of paper in half, slipped them into his pocket, and checked his watch. It was eleven-thirty. He hadn't eaten all day, and, suddenly lamenting not having shared in Ike's chicken-wing feast, he listened to his stomach growl.

At least he'd made a dent in things, he told himself. In the morning, he'd go over what he'd found out at Coletta's and at Billy's with Ike, try once again to track down Leander Moultry, and set up a face-to-face meeting with Billy's girlfriend, Ray Lynn. Luckily he still had an hour and a half before Nobby's place closed. With his stomach rumbling, he walked boldly out of Billy's apartment, down the hallway, back down the staircase, and out into the night.

Halfway into the eight-block drive to Nobby's, the driver of the car that had been tailing CJ ever since he'd left Coletta's turned on that car's headlights.

Nobby's was busy, jumping with the pulse of late-night black life in Denver. People were lined up two deep at the bar, ordering drinks as if the evening had just started, and the old Seeburg jukebox was blaring "Standing in the Shadows of Love," a Four Tops tune, the words of which CJ knew by heart.

Working his way across the crowded barroom, stopping briefly to shake hands and acknowledge friends, and past the pool-table area toward what Nobby called a restaurant, CJ felt unusually closed in. Nobby's seemed smaller and a bit grimmer than it had before Vietnam. An apartment-sized, closed-in kitchen, five tables, and twenty rickety chairs provided the total preparation and seating space for the restaurant. An order window poked through one of the kitchen's grease-stained walls. Behind it one of Nobby's part-time cooks was busy preparing food.

Lusting for one of Nobby's juicy, three-quarter-pound cheeseburgers and steaming-hot fries, stateside delicacies that he'd been deprived of for the better part of two years, CJ looked around for someone to take his order.

Sweating from nothing more than being trapped inside the cramped juke joint and wiping his brow, Nobby walked up, grabbed CJ's right hand, and began pumping his arm. "Must be a full moon. Been swamped all night."

"Money, money, money," said CJ, shouting to be heard above the noise.

Nobby smiled. "Too bad it ain't like this every night. Then maybe I'd be able to afford a set of new shocks for my ride. What can I get for ya, CJ?"

"Cheeseburger, medium rare, fries, and a Molson Golden."

"Got ya!" Nobby jotted down the order, turned, and walked over to the order window, where his skinny, long-faced, nylon-stocking-cap-wearing cook took the order ticket. "Ten minutes and you'll be singin' my praises," Nobby said, stepping back over to CJ. "Just like when you was a kid. Now, aside from my cookin', what brings you out tonight?"

"Been looking into what happened to Billy Larkin."

Nobby's eyes widened.

"As a favor to Unc and Marguerite," CJ said almost apologetically, aware that Nobby, a man who disliked PIs and hated cops and who'd been a bag man, petty thief, and serious drug user in an earlier life, remained suspicious of any activity designed to accommodate what he liked to call the white man's law.

"Guess that's a valid reason. For a second there, though, you were soundin' like some damn flatfoot."

"Not in this lifetime," said CJ, happy to have Nobby's blessing. "Got any ideas on who might've wanted Billy dead?"

"Have you talked to that girlfriend of his? The one who was in here screamin' her lungs out last night?"

"I tried to get her on the phone, but all I got was a hang-up in my ear."

"You ask me, she's the one who put it to Billy. Prissy-assed high-society bitch. Been down here on the Points stickin' her nose in where it don't belong for a good little bit now. Maybe you need to try and contact Ms. Suggs a little harder. Or maybe you just ask Ike to."

Bristling at the idea that Nobby thought he needed Ike's help, CJ said, "I can handle Suggs."

Aware that he'd touched a nerve, Nobby said, "Didn't mean no harm by the comment, CJ."

"No problem," CJ said with a shrug, thinking that given Coletta's and now Nobby's testimonials about Ray Lynn, she needed to be right up there at the top of his suspect list. He was about to ask Nobby exactly how long Billy had known the Suggses when the bartender walked up and interrupted.

"The high-rollers boat must've sailed in today, boss," the bartender said, sounding breathless. "Need change for a couple'a hundreds." He shoved two hundred-dollar bills at Nobby and nodded a greeting to CJ.

Patting down his pockets and realizing he didn't have that much change, Nobby said, "I'll have to go get it from the back."

"No rush," said the bartender. "The way the two fish who

gave me them hundreds are drinkin', I won't owe 'em nothin' more than a ten-spot by the time you get back."

Nobby looked at CJ and shrugged. "Gotta run," he said, winking insightfully. "Don't wolf down your food when it comes. You ain't a kid no more, CJ. Oh, and here's one last piece of advice. Check out that damn freeloader, Lannie Watkins. He didn't have no love in his heart for the man who derailed that dance studio of Coletta's. It was gonna be his gravy train."

CJ sat back in his chair and watched Nobby disappear into the next room, which was filled from floor to ceiling with a smoky haze. When his piping-hot burger and fries and ice-cold beer arrived a few moments later, courtesy of Nobby's harried-looking cook, he found himself once again thinking, *Home.*

The burger's salty sweetness was exactly the way he remembered. He purposely let the burger's flavorful juices run down from both corners of his mouth before he dabbed the grease away with a napkin. As he listened to the din of the crowd and the backbeat of the music from the jukebox, he had the sense that perhaps, after losing two years of his life to some lost-world Asian hellhole, he might in fact be able to reconnect with the world again. That if the emotional-stability gods saw fit, he might be able to make it through a full week without having nightmares—and then a month—and finally a year.

Relaxing back in his chair, cheeseburger in hand, he watched Nobby return from his back office with a wad of cash in his right hand. Telling himself that if a onetime heroin addict like Nobby Pittman, who'd done hard time for beating the owner of a house he'd burgled nearly to death, could find business success, he could certainly rise from the ashes of what with time would be just another forgotten war.

For the next thirty minutes, he simply sat back and enjoyed the food, the libations, and the music while absorbing the home-again Five Points atmosphere. Finally rising to leave, he stopped Nobby on his way out. "Just as great a burger as I remembered," he said, rubbing his belly.

"Could've told you that when you set foot inside the door," said Nobby, grinning broadly, knowing the difficulty CJ was having readjusting. "Sometimes what a man needs more than anything to get him back in the flow is what he's always known. Be sure and give Ike a shout-out for me when you get home."

"Sure will," said CJ, adjusting his Stetson before stepping out into the chilly October air. For the first time in a long time, he felt good about his chances of making it through the night without his war demons grabbing him by the throat.

Surprised at how cold it had turned, he raised the top on the Bel Air when he reached it, latched it down, and slipped behind the wheel. He fumbled in the dark along the front seat for a jacket he'd always kept there before leaving for Vietnam, then realized the jacket wasn't there. Muttering, "Damn," and thinking that no matter how well the night had turned out, nothing was ever exactly the same, he cranked the car's engine.

Easing away from the curb and heading for Bail Bondsman's Row and home, he leaned forward and turned on the radio. Dr. Daddy-O, Denver's premier black DJ, was talking his usual trash as a prelude to cuing up a tune. "And here for you boys and girls, ladies and gents, givers and takers, movers and shakers, is a heart-stopper, tree-topper, mood-builder, and love-filter to titillate your inner senses. Got ya Mr. Bill 'Smokey' Robinson caught in that reflective, lost-love kinda mood we all know too well, singing about what he no longer has in that sorrowful kinda way that only Smokey can." A split second later, Smokey Robinson broke into his classic Motown rendition of "Ooh Baby Baby." Swaying to the song's slow, mournful beat and listening to Smokey's lament, CJ nosed the Bel Air down Welton Street toward home.

The food, the music, and indeed Five Points itself had momentarily totally captured former first-class gunner's mate CJ Floyd. So much so that he failed to notice that he was being followed by a car that stayed with him most of the way home.

Chapter

~ 8

Looking slightly less puffy-eyed than on the previous day, Marguerite Larkin was busy in Ike's kitchen the next morning, answering CJ's questions and serving the two men she cared about most a breakfast of hash browns, buttermilk biscuits, pancakes, and scrambled eggs. Watching CJ pat his stomach and wave off a second stack of pancakes, she said, "Sorry I put off your call yesterday, CJ. You understand, don't you, honey? Sorrow does these kinda things to you. But I'm here to answer the bell this mornin', tell you everything I know about that Suggs girl. First off, I've got no clue why she's at Metro State." Marguerite walked around the kitchen table and refilled Ike's nearly empty cup with coffee. "I'd expect a card-carryin' silver-spoon-in-her-mouth black debutante like her to be going to Harvard or one of those high-falutin', snobby all-girls' schools back East. I never could understand why she was slummin' it here at home at some city college, rubbin' shoulders with the unwashed like my Billy." Marguerite's eyes welled with tears.

"Maybe she didn't have the grades for Harvard."

"Real likely. My take on her ever since the first day Billy introduced her to me is that she was sorta slow." Marguerite slapped her hand down on the table to punctuate her assessment. Eyeing CJ pensively, she said, "Since you're so intent on heading over to Metro State to check her out, give the little witch my regards, and while you're at it, ask her if she plans on showin' up at my baby's funeral. Could be she don't care to hang around with us common folk. The same way she maybe didn't want to hang around in that alley after she killed Billy."

"Calm down, Marguerite," said Ike, pulling the suddenly quivering Marguerite gently to him. "That girl didn't kill Billy."

"Don't be so sure, Isaac. She's pure, high-octane evil."

Ike shook his head, knowing that anytime Marguerite called him by his given name, there was no room for further discussion. Easing Marguerite down onto his lap, he said to CJ, "Why don't you make that trek on over to Metro State like you've been talkin' about and talk firsthand to Ray Lynn? I'll hold down the fort here."

Sensing that Ike and Marguerite could use some quiet time, CJ said, "Think I will. But first I'm gonna drop by Rosie's and see if any of the gossip-mongers that hang around there can tell me where I can find Leander. He's been putting the dodge on me pretty good."

"He'll turn up," said Ike. "Weasels like him always do."

"Hope so," said CJ, who'd moved to the kitchen doorway. "Especially since he threatened to kill Billy."

"Mouthin' off about doin' somethin' and doin' it are two different things, CJ."

"Yeah," said CJ, stepping back into the kitchen to grab a biscuit before bolting out the back door.

"That boy needs to learn to listen," Ike said to the now much calmer Marguerite. "It'll cost him in the end if he don't."

"He's bullheaded, Ike. Just like you."

"No. He's more like his poor gotta-do-it-her-way-or-else mamma than me, I expect." Ike kissed Marguerite softly on the cheek. "Just hope that trait don't end up costin' him his life one day like it did her."

CJ drew the same blank at Rosie's that he'd been drawing everywhere in his attempt to get a line on Leander Moultry's whereabouts. Not a single one of the gaggle of bullshitters and breeze-shooters who hung out at the garage could offer him any help. He hung around until he figured he'd worn out his welcome with his questions, then headed for Metro State. Once he was on campus, he had the feeling that his attempt to connect with Ray Lynn Suggs was going to be equally unproductive. But thanks to a friendly lady in the admissions office, a busty black woman who claimed to flat out love her some law-and-order Judge Suggs, CJ had Ray Lynn's fall academic schedule in hand less than twenty minutes after setting foot on campus. When he ran across a Metro State student he'd gone to high school with, a skinny little owl-eyed math wiz who'd helped him wade through geometry, and the whiz kid put Suggs squarely on campus that day, CJ had the sense that it just might turn out to be a red-letter day.

"Her BMW's parked in front of the Student Union, illegally,

with a ticket folded in half and tucked under a wiper blade. That's campus cop code to let her slide," his former classmate said. "It's noon, so she's probably in the Student Union cafeteria eating lunch alone, like always. Too good to hang with us commoners, you know."

CJ thanked his former schoolmate and headed for the Student Union, where for the next ten minutes he stood around twiddling his thumbs, trying his best to look inconspicuous. He was close to packing it in when Ray Lynn pushed her way through the cafeteria's chow line, looking as if the food in front of her couldn't possibly meet her expectations.

When CJ scooted in behind her, food tray and utensils in hand, announcing as the line moved slowly forward, "Terrible about Billy," Ray Lynn reacted with a start.

It took her a few seconds to realize after turning to face CJ that the person behind her was the pool-cue-shattering man who'd been at Nobby's the night Billy had been killed. Looking puzzled, she asked, "It's Floyd, isn't it? Why are you here?"

"I'm trying to find out who killed your boyfriend, Ms. Suggs."

"I'd suggest you let the police do that, Mr. Floyd."

"Aren't you interested in finding Billy's killer?" said CJ, watching as she selected a tomato-and-cucumber salad and a carton of orange juice and placed them on her tray.

"Of course I am. But we assuredly don't need your help."

Certain that the *we* in her high-pitched response included her father, CJ said, "Guess you don't need a leg up when your daddy's a judge."

"Sometimes you don't," Ray Lynn said coolly, jamming her tray into the person's in front of her without even the hint of an *excuse me.*

"Did Billy have any enemies you know of?"

"Leander Moultry, but you knew that already. By the way, have you told the police you were there at the center of the altercation Leander had with Billy? I understand they're out to interview every possible suspect." There was an irritating smugness in her tone.

"I sure have," CJ said, bending the truth. "What about you? Got a good alibi handy for them when they show up?"

Ray Lynn's eyes narrowed in anger as she shoved her left hand at CJ. "The ring on my finger is an engagement ring, in case you've never seen one. It's the kind of thing people exchange before they get married. Billy gave it to me a couple of weeks before he was killed."

"So two weeks ago you were looking to hold on to Billy forever. Like they say, things change. Especially when there's money on the table. You two lovebirds didn't by any chance happen to go in together on Billy's winning eighteen-thousand-dollar Policy ticket, did you?" CJ broke into a half smile. "A whole loaf's so much better than half, wouldn't you say?"

"You're scum," said Ray Lynn, nudging her food tray forward.

Ignoring the comment, CJ asked, "What did your father think about you and Billy tying the knot?"

Ray Lynn's anger boiled over. Pointing toward the cafeteria's west wall and talking loudly enough that people turned to listen, she said, "See the big guy over near the corner? He's an off-duty cop who moonlights as campus security. I can have him over here in no time if you'd like."

CJ eyed the burly off-duty cop and stepped out of line, suspecting he'd pressed his encounter with Ray Lynn as far as he dared. "Guess I'll just have to get your father's take on what he thought of having Billy as a son-in-law from him."

"You do that. Daddy so admires war veterans. And while you're at it, be sure to keep reminding yourself that he's a lawyer and you're a possible murder suspect." Fishing in her purse and flashing CJ a hateful smile, she took out a ten-dollar bill and handed it to the cashier. "Have a great day, Petty Officer Floyd." Watching puzzlement spread across CJ's face, she said, "I know more about you than you think," smiled, and walked away.

CJ glanced in the cop's direction one last time before heading the opposite way. Within minutes he was halfway across campus. When he reached the Bel Air, he was sweating in the bright one o'clock sun. He hadn't gotten very much new information out of Ray Lynn Suggs other than the fact that she'd been engaged to Billy. But he'd learned a few valuable peacetime lessons: Just as in war, never charge into enemy territory without checking for snipers, never underestimate your enemy's capabilities, and have the good sense to realize that your enemy might know a thing or two about you.

Easing behind the wheel of the Bel Air, he glanced around to make sure he hadn't been followed. It wasn't until he'd eased from his parking spot and out of the sun's glare that he realized there was a parking ticket tucked under his windshield wiper. Shaking his head and heading for Bail Bondsman's Row, he reminded himself that, as Ike was so fond of saying, "Boy, you got one hell of a lot to learn."

A gruff-looking man with a waxed handlebar mustache and muttonchop sideburns stood talking to Ike when CJ pulled into the driveway at home. The dark, oily-skinned man looked to CJ like he might be Italian or Spanish, or maybe even from the Middle East. He eyed CJ and the Bel Air briefly, shook Ike's hand, and quickly walked off down Delaware Street. He was two houses away by the time CJ reached the Victorian's front porch.

"New client?" CJ asked, nodding toward the rapidly disappearing man.

"Nope, just a man peddlin' information. I put the word out yesterday that you were lookin' for Leander Moultry. Finally got a bite. The guy who just left lives, or I should probably say used to live, in the same buildin' as Leander. Makes himself a little extra cash each month keepin' an eye on the tenants for the landlord. Lets the landlord know when somebody's about to skip. He claims that Leander moved a bunch of stuff outa his apartment early yesterday mornin'. Figurin' that Leander was plannin' on skippin' out on his rent, the guy followed Leander when he took off in a rented truck. Seems Leander's decided to take up residence in Commerce City. Even got the address of his new digs," Ike said with a wink, handing CJ a torn piece of grocery bag he'd scribbled the address on.

"Commerce City. That's one hell of a short trip, don't you think? Puts Leander less than twenty minutes from right here."

"Yeah, but it's the kind of place you can sure as hell get lost in. The town's got enough transient motels, migrant workers, illegals, and out-of-work roustabouts to qualify for disaster assistance. And with all its oil refineries, the place flat-out stinks." Frowning, pinching both nostrils closed, and sounding like someone with a bad cold, Ike asked, "So what did you get outa the Suggs woman over at Metro State?"

"Not much. When she threatened to sic some rent-a-cop on me, I split. But I did find out that she and Billy were engaged."

"Ouch! I'm sure her daddy didn't like the idea of becoming a father-in-law to the likes of Billy."

"My take, too. She did throw one curveball at me. Said the cops have me on their radar as a murder suspect."

Ike broke into a broad, knowing smile. "And she's right. The homicide cop handlin' the case is a sergeant named Hancock. He dropped by here a little after you headed off to Metro State. Known him for years. White, smart enough, and honest. He asked me a few questions about you, mostly havin' to do with how you were settlin' in after Vietnam. I told him you were doin' just fine and sent him packin'. But he'll be back. It's the way cops operate, half a step forward, two steps back. Just tell him the truth when he shows up next."

"Okay," said CJ, sounding less concerned than the look on his face seemed to signal.

"As for Judge Suggs, I'm thinkin' me and him need to have a friendly little chat."

"You know him?"

"Yeah," Ike said, frowning. "Served with him in Korea the winter of '51 and '52. He was an up-buckin' horse's ass back then, and I don't think he's changed much. Why don't you follow up on Leander?" Ike patted his belly and belched. "Right now I'm headed to meet Marguerite over at Mae's Kitchen for lunch. You're welcome to come along."

"Thanks, but I've got loose ends I need to tie up."

"Suit yourself."

CJ watched his increasingly arthritis-ravaged uncle wobble his way across the front porch and head toward the garage for his Jeep. He hadn't smelled alcohol on Ike's breath, but he knew Ike's recent sobriety couldn't last. He needed the numbing effect liquor gave him to take the edge off his pain. Alcohol had been his elixir ever since he'd come home from the Korean War with a Bronze Star, two legs full of shrapnel, and a severely injured back.

CJ watched Ike struggle to get into the Jeep before heading up the fire-escape stairs to his apartment. "Tough SOB," he muttered to himself.

Twenty minutes later, with a ham sandwich in one hand and his Wiley Ames file open in his lap, CJ was seated in his living room talking to a woman named Cheryl Goldsby's answering machine. Goldsby, Wiley Ames's niece and next of kin, lived on a small horse ranch on the Colorado eastern plains just outside the town of Sterling. He'd talked to her briefly on the phone a couple of days before Wiley's funeral and she'd sounded more aloof and standoffish than grief-stricken. Since she represented a possible thread to the murders and since in his one phone conversation with GI Joe's owner Harry Steed, Steed had recommended that CJ needed to talk to her no matter what, CJ figured he might as well pay her a visit. He had no idea as he hung up the phone after leaving his return-call request whether she was screening her messages or if she'd respond to the one he'd just left. All he could do was be hopeful and wait. Setting the phone aside and taking a bite of his sandwich, he decided he'd be a little less aggressive with Cheryl Goldsby than he'd been with Ray Lynn Suggs.

Ike Floyd wasn't used to sitting in the cherrywood-paneled barrooms of exclusive private clubs, so he found himself feeling slightly self-conscious as he shared a beer with Denver District Court Judge Otis Suggs at the city's exclusive Capitol Hill University Club. He and the judge had had occasion to bump into one another since their military service in Korea, but they'd rarely offered each other more than a passing nod, and the two men had uttered only a few forced pleasantries to each other since a subservient-looking waiter had delivered their beers.

Suggs, a large, brown-skinned black man with a thin, tubular, crane-like neck, hairy ears, and uneven teeth that seemed much too big for either of his jaws, eased back in the wingback leather chair he'd been sitting in when the club's concierge had walked Ike to his table a few minutes earlier, took a sip of his beer, eyed Ike's nearly empty mug, and asked, "Sure you don't want another beer, Isaac?"

"Nope. I ain't lookin' to get high, Otis. What I'm lookin'

for is information. How about givin' me the straight scoop on your daughter and Billy Larkin's relationship?"

"And just what is it you'd like to know?" asked Suggs. Every word dripped with condescension.

"Just wonderin' how a ne'er-do-well like Billy could find his way up to your neck of the woods."

"He didn't," Suggs said smugly. "Ray Lynn found him. At Metro State. Larkin was a grounds-crew maintenance worker there until they fired him. Marguerite would've surely mentioned him working there to you. The two of you are still an item, aren't you?"

"We sure are," Ike said proudly, wondering as he fiddled with his beer mug how many other things about him the judge had had some beleaguered law clerk dig up since he'd called to ask Suggs to meet with him a few hours earlier.

"Beautiful woman," said Suggs. "It's a shame about her past."

"No more than it is about yours," said Ike, biting back his anger. "I'm hopin' you've kicked that gamblin' problem you had during Korea. Wouldn't want to think you got crossways with your future son-in-law over eighteen thousand in gamblin' winnin's."

Suggs eased forward in his chair. Baring most of his oversized teeth, he said, "I don't need money, Isaac. Look around you."

Ike glanced at his beer mug instead. "I'm thinkin' Billy was killed over that Policy hit of his. News about it's been in all the papers," he said with a wink. "And from what my nephew's told me, it's a pretty safe bet he had a partner. Somebody who wanted more than his or her share of that eighteen thousand."

"Well, it certainly wasn't me." Suggs finished what was left of his beer in a single quick gulp. "So I'd suggest you troll for your killer somewhere else. But before you do, here's some advice. Send that nephew of yours to bother Ray Lynn again, and I can assure you he'll pay dearly. She told me all about him accosting her this afternoon."

"I didn't send CJ anywhere. He tends to go where he chooses on his own."

"Cute. Real cute." Suggs took a deep breath and leaned farther forward in his chair. "Don't screw with me, Ike. I can take that nephew of yours down, and you, too, if need be, in a fraction of a second. You're out of your element, Sergeant."

Ike erupted in laughter loud enough to turn a few heads at the bar. "All these years and you still can't sight your coordinates in right, can you, Lieutenant? You're the one who's outa his element. In case you missed it, Judge, we're dealin' with murder here, not one of your cronies cheatin' on his golf score at the country club. And like it or not, your daughter's got a connection to that murder. I'm thinkin' you shoulda hooked her up with one of those country-club types instead of a groundskeeper, Otis."

Suggs set his beer mug down with what was meant to be a discussion-ending clunk. "We're done here, Ike. You're free to leave, and on your way out, consider this. I can make your life miserable."

"No more miserable than you did twenty years ago, Lieutenant. Here's hopin' you haven't made too many similar stateside friendly-fire miscues along the way since then. But then again, how could you? You're not packin' around a howitzer."

Choking back his anger, Suggs said, "The door's waiting, Ike."

Ike rose slowly and continued to stare judgmentally at Suggs, thinking all the while about how Suggs's arrogance and battle-field incompetence had cost him a half-dozen friends. Hobbling toward the door, he mumbled, "Asshole," and simply shook his head.

"You're on my list, Ike," Suggs called after him when he'd nearly reached the exit, surprising everyone in the room.

"The same way Billy Larkin was?" Ike shouted back over his shoulder, thinking as he left that any army officer capable of whitewashing his role in the death of six of his men was certainly capable of committing murder.

Commerce City, a northern Denver suburb dotted with oil refineries and garbage landfills and filled with miles of swampy, mosquito-infested Platte River bottom, had always smelled to CJ like a mixture of motor oil and stagnant water.

He'd never understood why the city fathers had saddled their town with a name like Commerce City, but he knew from his war experiences that there were far worse choices to be made. His navy patrol boat, the *Cape Star,* had once been pinned down by mortar fire in an estuary rimming a Vietnam village whose English-translated name he later learned to be Bird Shit. Smiling to himself, he eased the Bel Air off Colorado Boulevard, the main thoroughfare that connected Denver and Commerce City, and cruised down Fifty-eighth Avenue past blocks of dilapidated clapboard houses, dozens of junker cars and trucks up on cinder blocks, and nearly palpable hanging-by-a-thread sadness.

When he spotted 6442 E. 58th, the address he was looking for, he shook his head. The rambling wooden three-story tenement with its peeling paint and boarded-up windows, sitting as it was in the middle of a lot without a single blade of grass, looked like something left over from the sweatshops that had blanketed the East Coast in early-nineteenth-century America.

Wondering why Leander would have picked such a derelict to hide out in, he eased past the house and parked two houses away in front of a vacant lot. An alley ran along the back side of that lot and Leander's building. He decided to approach the tenement from the rear, uncertain how many families the building housed or whether anyone was inside. Telling himself that he'd find out soon enough, he made his way across the lot full of beer cans, used diapers, old newspapers, and broken glass. The burned-oil smell of partially refined petroleum had him frowning and walking slowly until the distinct pop of a rifle shot sent him diving headfirst into the dirt. Kicking himself for being unarmed and swearing that he'd never in his life make that mistake again, he scrambled for a nearby trash can and cover. Thinking, *One more shot so I can see where the hell you are,* he rose, adjusted his weight onto one knee, and caught a glimpse of the sniper. It was a half-second glimpse of a man dressed head to toe in black who suddenly, carrying a rifle in his right hand, was on the run. *Cold feet,* CJ told himself, aware that when it came down to actually killing another human being, it could sometimes be hard to pull the trigger. Suspecting that he was more than likely dealing with a novice rather than a pro, CJ took off full-bore down the edge of the alley after the shooter. When he stumbled over a tricycle, overturning it in his sprint, a child began crying and, like dominoes falling, heads began popping out through the suddenly open windows of one of the three-deckers. Soon every window in the building seemed to be filled with people shouting in Spanish and pointing.

He was less than three yards behind the shooter when the man dropped his rifle. Bigger and faster than his assailant, CJ vaulted over the rifle and dove for the man. Tackled at the knees, Leander Moultry let out a grunt as CJ rode him to the ground. Quickly rolling the much smaller Leander over onto his back, CJ straddled him, clamped both hands around the terrified little pool hustler's throat, and squeezed.

Leander's face was a deep, anoxic shade of purple by the time a half-dozen migrant workers gathered around the two black men on the ground. When one of his fingernails dug into Leander's skin, drawing blood, the darkest of CJ's days in Vietnam began flickering news-reel-like through his head.

"You're gonna kill him, mister!" a young boy with a thick Spanish accent shouted as Leander's once frantically wiggling body went limp.

"*Sí!* Let him up!" screamed the woman holding the boy's hand.

Close to tears, the boy yelled, "Get off him! Get off him! Get off him!"

CJ wasn't sure whether it was the boy's rhythmic chant, his own adrenaline rush subsiding, or the fact that he suddenly realized that the fingers of his right hand were wet with blood that caused him to release his death grip on Leander Moultry. But whatever it was that stopped him from strangling the little pool hustler to death came just in time. Lifting the rifle and the barely breathing pool shark in his arms, CJ started walking toward the Bel Air.

"Don't let him die, mister!" the boy who'd been chanting yelled as the woman holding his hand tugged him in the opposite direction, shouting, "No involve, Pedro, no involve!"

Halfway to the Bel Air Leander began to gasp for air and wriggle in CJ's arms. "Cool it," CJ ordered, glancing back to the spot where a half-dozen witnesses had watched him nearly choke a man to death. Everyone had disappeared.

"I think you mighta ruptured my windpipe," Leander wheezed as CJ set him down hard in the Bel Air's front seat.

"If I had, you'd be dead. Now shut up." CJ sprinted to the rear of the car, popped the trunk, slipped the rifle inside, took out a coiled thirty-foot length of yellow tow rope, and headed back for Leander, who was regaining his senses by the second. "You're gonna ride home real safe and secure, Leander." Tying the tow rope to the Bel Air's front seat frame, he looped the rope around Leander's legs several times.

"I ain't gonna run," Leander protested, his words hoarse and barely audible, as CJ completed the hogtie.

"I know you aren't, unless you're the new Houdini," CJ said, checking the tension on the rope.

Walking around the front of the car, he slipped behind the wheel and cranked the engine.

"Where we goin'?" Leander asked, his words a sudden fearful whisper.

"To talk to Ike."

Leander looked relieved. "Fine by me. But I can tell you right now, I didn't kill nobody."

CJ nodded and swallowed hard without answering, aware as he pulled away from the curb, trembling, that he, on the other hand, very nearly had.

Chapter

9

It was six-thirty by the time Ike finally stopped peppering Leander with questions. Looking nearly as worn out as Leander, Ike eased back in his desk chair, glanced across his desktop at CJ and the handcuffed, glum-looking Leander, and announced, as if offering the final enlightening touch to a sermon, "Don't think Leander's the one that killed Billy, CJ."

"Well, he sure as hell tried to kill me," CJ protested, glancing around Ike's office as if he expected a Greek chorus to begin chanting on his behalf.

Vigorously shaking his head, as if that might erase the fact that he had indeed taken a shot at CJ, Leander said, "I told you. I was just tryin' to scare you off. I don't like being stalked and I don't appreciate nobody tryin' to pin some murder on me. Shit, I knew all along you were comin' my way, CJ. My landlord called and told me some big guy sportin' a Stetson and wearing a riverboat gambler's vest might be comin' after me." Leander smiled. "Described you to a T is what he did, and for no more than me promisin' to slide twenty bucks his way for keepin' an eye out for anyone askin' questions about me. Hell, if I'd'a wanted to kill you, I could've anytime I wanted to for sure."

"Well, your landlord pulled a double-switch on your ass because he's the one who told another tenant about you pulling up stakes, and that guy spilled his guts to Ike about where I could find you. Guess forty dollars in your pocket still beats twenty any day."

"Fuckin' Greek!"

"Would the two of you stop with the one-upmanship for a second?" said Ike. "Leander's landlord sure as hell didn't kill Billy and since Leander swears that he and Billy didn't go in together on that winnin' Policy ticket, I say we're pretty much back to square one with this killin'."

"I've been tellin' you that all along. 'Bout time the two of you listened. I wouldn't've shared nothin' with a blockhead like Billy. The dumbass fucker. Now, you done with me here?"

"No need for name-callin' the dead," said Ike, recognizing that Leander was feeling at least half his oats again. "Think we should let this little puke go?" he asked CJ.

"Might as well."

"Good." Leander rubbed at his sore neck with cuffed hands and stood. "Would you get these damn handcuffs off me?"

Staring Leander down as he moved to uncuff him, CJ said, "Don't ever shoot at me again, Leander. You hear me?"

Leander sheepishly eyed the floor, suspecting that if he ever took another shot at CJ, he'd have an eternity to regret it. Rubbing his wrists, he said, "Since the two of you are so hell-bent on findin' Billy's killer, here's a tidbit for you. Shouldn't give you shit after the way you've treated me, but I've already passed it on to the cops, so what the hell? Since you're so damn keen on Billy havin' a partner in with him on that winnin' Policy ticket of his, I'd be lookin' in the direction of that stuck-up girl-friend of his, Ray Lynn. She had dumbass Billy's nose open a mile wide. Word on the street is she's pregnant and that because of that, Billy was gonna ditch her. I don't think her daddy the judge woulda liked that one bit."

"Well, well, well. Here come the judge," said Ike. "Looks like I might need another private session with my old field-artillery lieutenant."

"Tonight?" CJ asked eagerly.

"Nope. Marguerite and me got eatin'-out plans for tonight."

"What about Marguerite bein' Billy's partner?" asked Leander. "After all, the woman was once a whore. Hell, for all we know she coulda offed him over that Policy money."

"Get the hell outa here, Leander!" Ike yelled, rising from his chair as Leander made a beeline for the open office door.

Grabbing Leander by the arm and shoving him though the doorway, CJ said, "Outa here, Leander, before I get to think-ing we're back in Commerce City."

"She coulda killed him, ya know," Ike said, looking up at CJ with a dour face.

"No way."

"Anybody's capable of killin', CJ. We both know that. Just takes the right kinda circumstance."

Ike slowly and thoughtfully rose from his seat, grabbed a jacket off the wall hook behind his desk, and stared pensively at CJ. "You don't look no worse for wear after being shot at," he said, changing the subject. "Next time you go after a little turd like Leander, think before you act. Like I said, anybody's capable of killin' given the right circumstances. See you later." He pivoted and headed for the front door.

"I'll do that," said CJ, who'd learned the truth in his uncle's statement during Vietnam. Looking guilty and a bit disoriented, he stared through the open office doorway for a solid two minutes before he rose and headed for his apartment upstairs.

Thirty minutes later, sitting at his kitchen table after polishing off a beer and a couple of cheroots, CJ found himself thinking about the myriad of reasons someone might have wanted to kill Billy Larkin. The reason topping his list remained money. Eighteen thousand dollars' worth of it that could have soothed Otis Suggs's fears of taking a step down the social ladder, mollified Ray Lynn's revenge over a potential dumping, and erased Coletta Newby's indebtedness. Strangely, however, everyone on his list of suspects seemed to have a straight-up motive for killing Billy except for Coletta's poker-wielding, gravy training boyfriend, Lannie Watkins.

Easing out of his chair, he walked over to his refrigerator and slipped the two half sheets of paper he'd taken from Billy Larkin's apartment from beneath a couple of Cheyenne Frontier Days refrigerator magnets. Studying the decidedly different printing styles on the two sheets, one rich with big, black, looping letters that slanted to the left and the other as close as you could come to a scribble, he shook his head and sighed. He was almost certain he'd seen the larger, neater printing before, but he couldn't place where. Convinced that the two pieces of paper were key to Billy Larkin's murder, he decided he'd run down Lannie Watkins and find out if one of the handwriting specimens belonged to him.

Folding the pages and stuffing them into his shirt pocket as his stomach gurgled loudly, he decided that a little music and a burger might not only help ease the tensions of the day but also stoke his energy level before he took off after Watkins. Slipping his Stetson off a hook near the kitchen door, he reluctantly lit up a third cheroot and headed for Nobby's to grab a bite to eat, telling himself as he bounded down the fire-escape stairs that as soon as he found Billy's killer, he was going to make a concerted effort to stop smoking.

Nobby's was subdued and pretty much weeknight-empty when CJ walked in. He shook hands with a couple of people he knew as he crossed the barroom, waved to a woman he'd gone out with in high school, and headed for the jukebox. Marvin Gaye was wrapping up "Stubborn Kind of Fellow," a tune CJ's former gunnery chief, who had been born and bred in Motown, had blasted over loudspeakers as a wake-up call every morning during CJ's first tour of duty in Vietnam. He slipped a quarter into the old Seeburg, punched in E7 and G5, and leaned against the jukebox, hoping the E7 selection, "My Girl," would be the next song. Unlike the night Billy had died, no one was playing pool, and the only activity on the juke joint's dance floor turned out to be a middle-aged couple scrunched together as if they were one.

"CJ, my man. How's it hangin'?" Nobby called out, approaching CJ with a wad of small bills crumpled in his right hand.

"About half," said CJ, giving Nobby a fist bump before taking a seat at a table next to the jukebox.

"You do look a little ragged around the edges," Nobby said, stuffing the bills into his pocket.

"Had a dog of a day."

"Hell, I can fix that in less time than a rattlesnake strike. How about a plate of fried chicken, beans, and 'slaw? You need to pass on them burgers and fries for a change?"

"Next time," said CJ. "I've been thinking burger and fries ever since I left the house. How about a medium-rare cheeseburger, coleslaw, an order of fries, and a Coke?"

"Suit yourself. And maybe when your order's up, you'll tell ol' Nobby about that dog jumped into your day."

"Yeah," said CJ, watching Nobby jot his food order on a ticket before whirling around to respond to his bartender, who was complaining about being nearly out of ice.

CJ's G5 selection, "What's So Good About Goodbye," was ending when ten minutes later the sweet, melodic sounds of "My Girl" finally erupted from the jukebox. CJ was relaxed back in his seat, humming along to the refrain, when Nobby's always harried Hispanic short-order cook delivered his food.

"Here ya go, CJ," the cook said, placing the order down and turning to head back to the kitchen.

CJ had pinched off a fry and eaten it before he realized that his coleslaw was missing. "I had an order of coleslaw, too, Hector," he called out to the retreating fry cook.

"Wasn't no 'slaw on your order ticket," Hector said, returning. "Have a look."

He slid the ticket across the table.

CJ glanced down at the grease-stained ticket. *Burger, medium rare $1.75, fries 50 cents, Coke 45 cents, total $2.70.* "Guess Nobby missed it."

"Guess so," said the cook, shrugging. "I'll have your 'slaw up for you in a second."

CJ was two bites into his cheeseburger and still eyeing the ticket when something odd and worrisome began to gnaw at him. At first he thought it was the fact that he'd just that moment realized that Nobby had raised his prices. Placing his burger back down on his plate, he picked up the ticket and examined his order more closely. It wasn't until his third reading that he realized that it was the printing on the ticket that had grabbed his attention. When his stomach started to quiver the same way it always had when the *Cape Star* had set out on a mission during Vietnam, he mumbled, "Shit."

Reaching into his shirt pocket, he slipped the two half sheets of paper he'd taken from Billy Larkin's apartment out and spread them out on the table. As he silently read off the numbers on his food-order ticket, he realized that the order's back-slanting 5's and 7's were dead ringers for those on one of the torn half sheets and that the hastily scribbled block-letter E's and undotted i's in *possible winner, lucky set,* and *good bet* were nearly identical to the E's and i's in the words *burger, fries,* and *medium rare.* The clincher, however—the thing that told him the same person had more than likely authored both items—turned out to be the identical sets of double underlines beneath the 70 on his $2.70 bill and beneath the zeros in the $50.00 that had been jotted at the bottom of one of the half sheets of paper he'd taken from Billy's.

There was little question in his mind now that Coletta Newby and Leander Moultry had both been right about Billy having a partner, and that partnership had probably cost Billy his life. Slipping the order ticket and the papers from Billy's apartment back into his shirt pocket, he got up from his chair. His entire insides felt queasy.

"You can pay at the bar, you need to, CJ," the cook called out through a haze of smoke, wondering where CJ, who hadn't finished his food, was headed. "Just show 'em your order ticket."

CJ didn't answer. He knew the drill, but instead of stopping at the bar, he walked past it and headed toward Nobby Pittman's office.

A two-inch-tall stack of five-dollar bills, a short stack of tens, and a fifth of Jack Daniel's sat in the center of Nobby's desk. Nobby, surprised by CJ's unannounced entry, shot a glance toward the top desk drawer to his right. "Shit, CJ, you scared the hell outa me," he said, sounding relieved. "Thought you might be a damn robber."

"No," said CJ, his tone noticeably somber.

"Drink?" asked Nobby, shoving the bottle of Jack Daniel's across the desktop.

"Nope."

"Suit yourself. Whatta ya need?"

"A few answers, Nobby. That's all."

"'Bout what?"

"About Billy Larkin's murder."

"Terrible thing. But I'm afraid I can't help you much more there."

"I think you can." CJ stepped up to the desk and laid his food-order ticket and one of the half sheets of paper he'd taken from Billy's on the desktop. "Recognize these?"

"The one on the left's the order I took for your dinner. Never seen the other one."

"I think you have."

"You callin' me a liar?" Nobby sat upright and defiant in his chair.

"No. Just hoping to jog your memory."

"I said I never seen it."

"Strange. The writing on that sheet matches the writing on my food ticket."

Nobby eyed the top drawer once again. "Damn, CJ. Bein' a war hero ain't enough? Now you're a handwritin' expert, too?"

"Don't claim to be either, Nobby. But I'm betting a real hand-writing expert will say that the same person wrote both things. Why'd you kill Billy, Nobby?" CJ asked, recalling Ike's advice about ratcheting up the pressure on a suspect.

Nobby scratched his head and smiled. "Let's say we keep what's on them papers 'tween me and you, CJ. You stand to make yourself a grand richer if we do."

"Can't."

"Two grand, then."

CJ shook his head.

Nobby shrugged. "Suit yourself." In one quick, sweeping motion he pulled the top desk drawer open, extracted a snub-nosed .38, and aimed it squarely at CJ's chest. "You just spent two years seein' what bullets can do to a man, CJ. Take the two thousand."

When CJ didn't respond, Nobby shook his head. "Billy tried to stiff me. Wanted to keep all that Policy money for hisself. Can you believe that? With me bein' the one who originally picked the winnin' numbers, and me layin' down half the hundred bucks for the ticket. Never should've okayed that numbers runner shellin' out all that money to Billy after we hit. But I was gonna be outa town for most of the week, and I trusted Billy the same way I've always trusted all you Five Points kids. See what you get for puttin' your trust in people? Guess havin' eighteen grand in his pocket was just too much of a burden for Billy to handle. Especially with that high-maintenance new woman of his advisin' him. When I come for my share of money, Billy said he wasn't givin' me squat. Said that woman of his told him possession was nine-tenths of the law. I pleaded with him to give me my share of the winnin's for three days, but he wouldn't budge. In the end, I had to get what was rightfully mine. You can understand that, can't you, CJ?"

"Afraid I really can't."

The pleading stare on Nobby's face turned slowly into a look of rage. Nodding toward a chair in a darkened corner of the room and with the .38 pointed squarely at CJ's chest, he said,

"I want you to walk over there and park your ass in that chair while I think this out."

"You think long, you think wrong," said CJ.

"Shut up, CJ, and sit!"

CJ eased down into the lumpy, overstuffed chair, his eyes locked on the .38, uncertain what the onetime semipro football player who just about everyone in Five Points claimed had taken too many hits to the head would do. After a half minute of silence, Nobby said, "Gonna have to kill you, CJ. Ain't no other way."

"You need to be smarter than that, Nobby. They tap you for one killing, and you might be able to plea-bargain yourself a life sentence, maybe even just twenty years. Two killings, and the state will dispense with your ass permanently for sure."

"If I get caught. Get up. We're headin' out the back." Nobby motioned CJ toward a doorway near the opposite corner of the room. "Go ahead. Move."

CJ headed for the doorway, aware that the door opened onto an alley. He found himself praying for the right moment to make some kind of defensive move as the sounds and then the smells of the Mekong River Delta suddenly filled his head. As he slipped through the doorway and out into the moonlit night, he could have sworn he heard the roar of F-100s overhead and the sound of machine-gun fire in the distance.

"We're gonna walk down two blocks and around the corner to where they found Billy. It's the same place they'll be findin' you. I'm figurin' that when the cops start scratchin' their heads and listenin' to the hubbub your murder's bound to generate, they'll think we got us a serial killer down here on the Points. One who likes finishin' off his victims in the very same spot. And don't think about runnin', CJ, 'cause if you do I'll just have to plug you in the back and cart you there."

Spotting a Dumpster jutting out into the alley several yards ahead, CJ felt a sudden rush of hope. Telling himself that when he reached the Dumpster, he'd leap behind it, scrounge up some kind of weapon, a stick, maybe a rock, perhaps even a bag of garbage, and fend Nobby off, he was less than five feet from the Dumpster when he heard a familiar voice behind him shout, "Hold your horses right there, Nobby!"

He and Nobby turned in near unison to see Ike Floyd standing twenty feet behind them, his hunched, arthritic figure awash in the glow of moonlight and a flickering overhead streetlight. The .45 Ike had carried during Korea was aimed directly at Nobby's midsection.

"Had my eyes on you ever since you stepped out your back door with CJ in tow, Nobby. I don't know what the hell's goin' on here or why you're holdin' that peashooter of yours on my nephew, but you better drop the fuckin' thing."

Nobby squeezed off an errant shot in Ike's direction as, with a painful grunt, Ike dropped to the ground on his belly. Steadying the .45 with both hands and aiming up at Nobby, Ike squeezed off two rounds. The first shot missed its mark. The second slammed into Nobby's right thigh, sending him sprawling face first onto the ground.

CJ was on top of him, full straddle with a knee to the back of his neck, in seconds. Moments later Ike stood over them both, shaking his head. Looking up at Ike, who had his .45 trained on a moaning Nobby's belly, CJ said, "Nobby killed Billy. It was all over that Policy money just like you thought."

"Figures," said Ike, looking back toward several heads that were now poking out of Nobby's back door. "Best get our story together for the law. Cops'll be checkin' in here real quick."

"When did you get to Nobby's?" CJ asked, applying palm pressure to the oozing wound in the shocked and totally defeated-looking Nobby Pittman's leg.

Ike smiled. "Been trailin' you off and on for a couple'a days. Checkin' on how well you were doin' with your assignment."

"What?" said CJ, looking embarrassed.

"You didn't really think me and Marguerite could be eatin' as much as I kept claimin', now, did ya?" Ike couldn't help but chuckle. "You may'a been a big dog in Vietnam, CJ, babysittin' that .50-caliber of yours, but when it comes to bail bondin', bounty huntin', and dealin' with the Five Points bottom feeders we got 'round here, you just another unschooled pup, son."

"So you decided to glue yourself to my tail?"

"Somethin' like that. Watched you make your phone calls, followed you to Coletta's, to Billy's apartment, even tailed you when you went to Metro State to talk to the Suggs girl. Finally ended up followin' you here to Nobby's tonight. You never saw me once and that means I ain't as washed up as some folks think. When you left your food unfinished and headed for Nobby's office like you'd just been stung by a bee, I knew somethin' was up. Only one way outa Nobby's place besides the front door, everybody in Five Points knows that," Ike said, glancing back toward Nobby's office door.

"Why?"

The look on Ike's face turned deadly serious. Watching Nobby grunt back his pain, Ike locked eyes with his nephew. "'Cause, CJ. You're the only kin I got in the whole damn world. Wouldn't want no harm comin' to you. Besides, when it comes to breakin' in new hires, it's a matter of policy."

Part 2

Settled In

AUTUMN 1976

Chapter

10

America's bicentennial year, a year filled with pomp and circumstance and self-congratulatory political posturing, was also the year of Nobby Pittman's first five-year parole hearing.

CJ had been way off the mark when, on the night he'd pegged Nobby as Billy Larkin's killer, with a .38 aimed at his chest, he'd told the slow-thinking former semipro lineman that he'd surely get either the death penalty or life for a second killing. In fact, murder and attempted murder had simply earned Nobby a twenty-four-year sentence in Colorado's maximum-security prison in Canon City and the chance of serving just five years before being granted parole.

CJ had never been able to square the fact that the legal system would allow such an early opportunity for parole, but Ike had said to him right after Nobby's trial, "Ain't no way to understand the American judicial system, no matter how hard you try, boy. Just gotta learn to go with the flow." CJ was learning to take Ike's advice to heart.

Sitting with Ike and Rosie Weeks at an oversized table at Mae's Louisiana Kitchen on the day of the hearing, nursing a postlunch frosted mug of beer, CJ looked frustrated. Mae's, an understated plain brown wrapper of a place squeezed between Rufus Benson's House of Musical Soul and Benny Prillerman's Trophy and Badge, sat squarely in the heart of Five Points. A neighborhood gathering place since 1937, Mae's had been run by the Sundee family for just short of forty years.

In true Louisiana tradition, the restaurant was nothing more than a long, narrow box, reminiscent of a New Orleans shotgun house. The entryway was tunnel-like, with barely enough room for three people to stand. At the back of the entry a hostess, often the late Mae Sundee's daughter, Mavis, greeted people at a mahogany pulpit that had belonged to Mavis's preacher grandfather but had long since been modified for more pedestrian use.

Fifteen tables covered with checkerboard oilcloth hugged both walls. Most tables seated only two, but a few jutted out to accommodate as many as six, so the main aisle down the middle of the restaurant undulated in and out, increasing and decreasing in size to produce an obstacle course that made it difficult for any waitress to work. The restaurant's only concession to extravagance were its Colorado-marble floors, ceilings of ornate stamped tin, and spotless stainless-steel kitchen.

The smell of high-cholesterol, mouthwatering, Southern-fried food hung in the air as Rosie, fiddling with the handle of his beer mug, eyed CJ and said instructively, "You still don't get it, CJ, and you being a bail bondsman and all. In the US of A, you kill somebody and you wanna get off, you take out a second mortgage on your house—or like Nobby, your business—

hire yourself the city's best white lawyer, one who's been lookin' for a long time to build a little black-community rep, have him convince a sympathetic jury and judge that you've been mentally slow all your life and you didn't really know what you were doin' when it came to killin' a welsher like Billy Larkin, and bingo, the gas chamber turns into a prison sentence of twenty-four years, and likely a lot less."

Ike nodded in agreement and took a sip of beer. "You need to soak up some things a lot better, CJ. You've been out there on the streets five years now, and you've damn sure written enough bonds, chased down enough bond skippers, and talked with enough double-talkin' lawyers and jackbooted cops to know that more often than not, the system's rigged."

"Doesn't make me have to accept it."

Looking disgusted, Ike said, "Better grab yourself a chunk of reality, boy. Idealism's for fools."

Feeling ganged up on and with no real rebuttal to offer, CJ stared into his beer. In the five years that he'd been back home, he'd largely shaken off his war demons, and most nights now he was able to sleep in peace. He'd found a line of work that suited him, and along the way he'd learned to make use of investigative talents he never would have guessed he had. Since Billy Larkin's murder, he'd rekindled friendships and made new friends, gotten back into collecting Western memorabilia and antiques, and even started attending swap meets and flea markets again when he could find the time. A few months earlier, he'd shelled out all of four dollars to become a member of the Rocky Mountain region's Automobile License

Plate Collectors Association, and recently he'd overheard Ike tell a friend, "You know I think the boy's pretty much settled back in."

Some things, however, remained both unsettled and unsettling. Interacting with women was uncomfortable, precipitated perhaps by the fact that during his time in Vietnam he'd seen so many women either killed or turned into whores in order to survive. No matter how hard he tried, he still often found it difficult to control his temper, and at least once a week, he caught himself slamming his hand down on a table and feeling guilty about not convincing a potential client to use his and Ike's service, or about getting stiffed on a bond. What still churned his anger the most, however, as much as anything, was that he'd made so little headway in finding out who'd killed Wiley Ames.

He'd filled four two-inch-thick Pendaflex hanging folders with newspaper accounts and police reports about the murders, not to mention the snippets of gossip and pages of interview notes he had. He'd talked to everyone from GI Joe's owner, Harry Steed, to the cop who'd directed him away from the murder scene the morning of the killings, and he still had almost nothing to show for his persistence other than the fact that over the years he'd struck up a friendship with Harry Steed and managed to make an enemy of Wiley Ames's niece, Cheryl Goldsby. Over time, Steed had grudgingly admitted that, like the cops, he suspected that Ames had been killed as a result of his involvement in the fencing of stolen goods. Ames's supposedly loving niece, Cheryl, didn't seem to care.

Watching CJ stare intently into his beer, Ike asked, "You see any fish swimmin' in there?"

"Not today." CJ relaxed back into his seat and smiled.

"You ain't really thinkin' about Nobby at all," Ike said insightfully. "I know where your head is, boy. You're thinkin' about them GI Joe's killin's again. Sooner or later you're gonna have to drop that suitcase."

Ike slapped his hand face down on the table to punctuate the point just as Mavis Sundee, the eighteen-year-old daughter of the restaurant's owner, waitressing her last few weeks before going back to college in Boston, walked up.

"Need any refills here?" Mavis asked, clearing away Ike's and Rosie's plates.

"None for me," said Ike.

"Me, either," Rosie chimed in.

"CJ?" Mavis asked, smiling.

"No, but I'll have a slice of sweet-potato pie to go," CJ said, ordering his favorite dessert.

"Keep orderin' pie at noon and you're gonna earn yourself a paunch," Ike said before turning to address Mavis. "When you headed back East?" he asked the exotic-looking, dark-olive-skinned woman who more than a few of the restaurant's white patrons seemed to think was Spanish rather than black.

"In a couple of weeks," said Mavis, eyeing CJ, on whom, although seven years her senior, she'd had a crush for years.

"You still studyin' business accountin' so Willis will have a reason to rope you into comin' back here to the Points and runnin' his businesses?"

"I sure am. But we'll have to see about me running those businesses of his. Who knows, I may head off to California to find my fortune after college," she said, looking directly at CJ.

"Hope not," CJ said, sounding flustered. "Wouldn't want to lose any of the Queen City's beauty to the Left Coast."

Looking surprised by the uncharacteristically forthcoming comment, Mavis said, "I'll have your pie up front for you along with your check. Oh, and CJ, before you leave, my dad needs to talk to you about something. He's standing out front."

"I'll catch him on my way out," said CJ, admiring the sensual fullness of Mavis's lips, the slender grace of her athletic body. "Have a good year back in Beantown."

"I will." She flashed everyone at the table a smile before walking away.

"Looks just like her mamma," said Rosie, watching CJ's eyes follow her up the center aisle until she disappeared through the kitchen's swinging doors.

Realizing that both of his companions were staring at him and feeling self-conscious, CJ scooted his chair back and stood. "Better see what Willis wants," he said, heading for the front of the restaurant to find Willis Sundee and evade the teasing that was certain to follow if he remained.

As CJ made his way to the entryway, Ike, nudging Rosie with an elbow, said, "Girl's always thought CJ was Superman, and up 'til recently I don't think CJ's as much as glanced her way twice."

"He's glancin' now."

"Yeah. Hard enough to give most folks a headache," Ike said, trying his best not to snicker.

CJ reached the restaurant's entryway as Willis Sundee was saying his good-byes outside to a couple of longtime patrons. With a full head of wavy silver hair, smooth, nutmeg-brown skin, and green eyes, Willis, the son of Louisiana Creole parents who'd moved to Colorado in the early 1900s, looked every bit the ethnic gumbo mix he was.

He greeted CJ with a firm handshake as he stepped back into the restaurant, then looked around as if to make certain no one was watching them. "Let's step back outside for a second," he said. "Don't want anyone to hear this." Quickly he and CJ were standing outside in the bright noonday sun.

Looking around apprehensively, Willis said, "Got a problem, CJ. One I'm hoping you'll help me handle."

"You couldn't possibly need a bail bond, Willis," CJ said with a grin.

"No, no, nothing like that." He looked up and down the busy noonday Welton Street. "What I've got is a problem with my produce and meat supplier. He thinks I should pay him quite a bit more than invoice in order to keep the quality up on the stuff he delivers. Otherwise, according to him, I could start to receive *second-rate goods.*"

"Sounds like a shakedown."

"It is," Willis said indignantly. "And it's pretty common in the restaurant business. For most of my years in the business, I've been able to steer clear of it."

"Why don't you just call the cops?"

"Because I've got no proof he's trying to shake me down other than a few insinuating conversations. Besides, I'm too small in the grand scheme of things for it to matter to the cops or the larger judicial system. They know what goes on in the restaurant business, and to them it's just part of the cost of being in the game."

"I'm not sure how I can help you, Willis. Maybe you should spell it out."

"I was hoping you could help me the same way you helped Lody Gissman with those two thugs who threatened him last year, the ones who wanted him to start paying parking-lot protection money so his furniture-store customers would find their cars intact when they left his store."

"That was a little different, Willis. I caught them in the act."

"And you whaled on 'em like nobody's business," Willis said, beaming.

Thinking back to the events that had led to his nearly serving jail time for assault, CJ said, "That was a different situation, Willis."

"So what did the law want Lody to do? Wait for those hoodlums to bash in a dozen windshields? I've got pretty much the same situation here."

"Maybe not. Your problem could be bigger. Produce means trucking, and trucking more often than not means the Teamsters, and the Teamsters means the mob."

"Not with this deal," Willis said, shaking his head. "The guy wanting to squeeze me is an independent. No union folks involved. He's only got four or five trucks, and he mostly supplies small establishments, minority businesses like mine."

"I don't know, Willis. Maybe you should run the problem past Ike."

"He can't do what you can do. Least, not anymore, and here's another kicker. The guy putting the squeeze to me supplies other businesses here in Five Points. Watt's Grocery, Kapri Fried Chicken, Elwood's Burger Den, just to name a few. None of us can afford to have the union folks who supply Safeway or the other big supermarket chains and restaurants stock us. For what we'd have to pay 'em to deliver, we'd go broke. We have to go independent to cut our costs."

CJ shook his head and sighed. "So who is this guy?"

"Name's Walt Reasoner," Willis said eagerly. "His company is Epic Produce & Meats. He operates out of North Denver, west of Globeville. Just talk to him, CJ. That might be enough."

"I'll see what I can do. But I still think you should go to the cops."

Ignoring CJ's recommendation and with a huge smile on his face, Willis said, "Great. What are you charging for investigating things these days, anyway?"

Until that moment, CJ hadn't thought much about what he charged for anything but bail bonds. In fact, he hadn't charged Lody Gissman anything to solve his problem. He'd taken on Lody's problem because Ike and Lody were lifelong friends, and Ike had asked him to. It had been the same thing when he'd dealt with Winifred Hickman's abusive husband. Ike had asked him to do that, too. And with Sammy Newcomb's thieving, bond-skipping nephew, whom he'd pretty much hogtied to the back of a rented pickup and dropped at the police station in Clovis, New Mexico, as part of a bounty hunting job Ike had passed his way. Realizing that over the past couple of years he'd done much more pro bono private investigating and bounty hunting than he'd imagined, CJ said, "Sixty bucks a day and expenses."

Willis nodded his quick consent. "You're on the clock right now, as far as I'm concerned. I'll call you with info on where you can find Reasoner."

Willis reached out to shake CJ's hand and seal the deal just as Mavis stepped outside. With the wind blowing and sunlight beaming through her coal-black hair, she held up CJ's boxed slice of sweet-potato pie. "Here's your pie, CJ." Eyeing CJ sheepishly, she added, "Are you going to help Daddy with our problem?"

"The best I can."

Looking relieved, she flashed Willis a look that said, *Told you so.* "Sure hope you settle things before I head back off to Boston."

Uncertain why he said what he did, other than the fact that he had a sudden unshakable urge to please Mavis, CJ said, "I will."

CJ spent most of the rest of the afternoon writing a bond for a small-time Five Points car booster who'd gotten high on cocaine and a stolen Denver Regional Transportation District bus. Following a fifteen-mile police chase north on I-25, he'd flipped the bus onto its side and down into an irrigation ditch, suffering, as luck would have it, not a single scratch. After being apprehended and asked why he'd stolen the bus, the thoroughly stoned, blasé-sounding car thief, a pint-sized black man with a voice an octave higher than Mickey Mouse's, said, "'Cause I never boosted no bus before, officer."

A little before 5 p.m., after getting a call from Willis Sundee with the business address and telephone number for Walt Reasoner's Epic Produce & Meats, CJ gave up on watching traffic gear up for its rush down Thirteenth Avenue and west past Bail Bondsman's Row for the Denver suburbs. Instead he plopped down in his office overlooking Delaware Street and stuck his nose back into the thickest of his Wiley Ames folders.

Each time he sat down to restart his investigation, usually after having been away from it for months, he felt as though he should simply pack it in. It seemed that no one, except perhaps Harry Steed, really cared what had happened to the one-armed former alcoholic. Ames's stick-figure niece, Cheryl Goldsby, a sour-faced woman of about thirty-five, had pretty much told him so when he'd visited her on her isolated Colorado eastern plains ranch outside Sterling some five years earlier. Goldsby's significant other, Ramona Lepsos, a squat, muscular, overly suntanned woman with a bulbous nose and crooked teeth, had ultimately butted into his and Cheryl's conversation to punctuate the point, angrily pointing out to CJ that Ames hadn't liked her and Cheryl's kind and telling him with a finger wagging in his face that she hoped he didn't have the same views.

CJ had left that meeting feeling as unwelcome as an interloping voyeur with nothing more to show for his efforts than the feeling that he somehow needed to prove he wasn't antigay or homophobic.

Except for a cache of collectibles that the niece freely admitted Ames had left her, and which she refused to let CJ see, and the five hundred dollars each he'd left the Denver Rescue Mission and a local VFW post, as far as CJ could see, Wiley Ames hadn't left behind much of an estate.

CJ had grudgingly accepted the official police position that Quan Lee Chin and Wiley Ames had been victims of a professional hit. It was clear that the motive for the GI Joe's murders hadn't been robbery, since Harry Steed had acknowledged that nothing in the pawnshop had been taken and, after a close inspection, the cops had concluded that all of Ames's personal possessions were intact. The .44 Mag murder weapon, leaked to the press early in the investigation and corroborated by Ike's longtime friend Vernon Lowe, had never been found.

CJ had no idea what Ames and Chin might have been fencing, but Harry Steed's take, in the face of considerable pressure from the cops, who for months had him near the top of their suspects list, had always been that they'd been fencing stolen Indian artifacts.

Drumming his fingers on the desktop and idly flipping through the contents of a folder, CJ wondered why he was struggling again with the Ames case and, more pointedly, why he continued to dig into the five-year-old killings that no one else seemed to care about. It certainly wasn't because he'd once promised himself he'd find Ames's killer. He was long past the stage of honoring promises he'd made during a period in his life when he'd felt guilty about being alive and remained haunted by war-induced night terrors.

The real reason was simple: investigating things had become a part of him. The night he'd almost been killed by Nobby Pittman, an investigative novice, as it were, stumbling into a world he barely understood, had sent him spiraling headlong and forever in that direction. And, much like his RTD bus-stealing client, he found that each new case, even each new trek after a bond skipper, gave him a special rush.

Setting the first folder aside, he picked up the second folder, shook his head, and started poring through the information he'd gathered on Quan Lee Chin. No one connected to the GI Joe's murders seemed to know much about Chin, including the cops, Cheryl Goldsby, and Harry Steed.

Chin's life had apparently started in New Jersey when he had enrolled at Princeton as a twenty-year-old immigrant studying music. He seemed to have had no childhood, at least nothing CJ could dig up; the only concrete information he had on Chin was that he was from Taiwan and, according to scrounged-up Princeton records, had been a gifted student and a stellar cellist. CJ had been able to glean one other piece of information about Chin during a phone call two years earlier with one of Chin's former professors. According to the professor, Chin had had a great love of the ocean and a passion for fishing, and he'd been friends with a Denver Symphony cellist, a woman named Molly Burgess.

Bored with looking through papers that he knew pretty much word for word and aware that he had a more immediate problem to address, CJ decided that in the name of thoroughness, he'd drop by GI Joe's in the next few days and ask Harry Steed if he had any new information about the case. Slipping the piece of paper on which he had jotted Walt Reasoner's business name and phone number from his pocket, he checked his watch, picked up the phone, and called Epic Produce & Meats. After giving his name to the woman who answered, he was quickly put through to Reasoner.

Sounding heavily stuffed up as if from a cold, but pleasant, Reasoner asked, "What can I do for you, Mr. Floyd?"

CJ was blunt. "Willis Sundee asked me to look into a problem he's having with your produce delivery service. I'd like to meet with you and talk about it if I can."

"I see. Good man, Willis. Surprised he didn't want to handle our negotiations himself, but that's his business. We can meet whenever you'd like."

"The sooner the better."

"How about here in my office in about an hour?" Reasoner said, pausing to cough. "I'll give you the address."

"I've got it. I'll be there in an hour."

"Good. Very good. See you then." Reasoner suppressed a sneeze and cradled the receiver.

CJ sat in momentary silence, staring out toward the rush-hour traffic before placing his GI Joe's folders back in a nearby file cabinet. Looking around the room and for some reason feeling suddenly closed in, he told himself that perhaps if he painted the walls white instead of beige, the space would open up. It was something to think about, he thought as he headed for his apartment to get his jacket and snub-nosed .38, taking the Victorian's rarely used inside stairway that he'd recently reopened because as Ike loved to remind him, "Every rabbit needs more than one hole."

Chapter

🦎 11

CJ decided to drive Ike's 1947 Willys Jeep to Epic Produce & Meats instead of the Bel Air. The restored World War II–vintage four-by-four was in close to mint condition save for its transmission and windshield. The original windshield had been shot out twelve years earlier as a more youthful Ike had chased a drunken, bond-skipping Apache Indian on a Harley down an arroyo south of Santa Fe, New Mexico, dodging scatter from a sawed-off shotgun.

Ike had eventually shot the Apache in the leg, turning him into a lifelong cripple. He had never forgiven himself for that shot, often reminding the sometimes overzealous CJ, "Ain't no need to kill or maim a man in order to do your job."

Turning off I-70, CJ took a road that looped behind Denver's National Western Stock Show complex. With Ike's advice at the forefront of his mind, he patted the .38 in his jacket pocket and reminded himself that no matter what transpired at Epic Produce & Meats, his job was to stay calm.

He spotted the produce company's building with its high-pitched corrugated-metal roof just before reaching Sixtieth

Avenue. The roof gave the building the look of a Western barn. As he drove onto the company's recently resurfaced parking lot, he realized that more than half of the parking spaces had reserved signs. Thinking that Reasoner employed an awful lot of important people, he parked in a nonreserved space, hopped out of the Jeep, and headed for the front door.

The building's sprawling lobby was dimly lit and hot. Following a sign with a finger stenciled below the word "Offices," he walked down a short hallway into an austere waiting room that contained only two chairs and an unmanned reception desk. He was about to ring a bell on the desk when a door just to his left opened and a man a shade taller than CJ stepped into the reception area.

"Help you?" the man asked, in a nasally tone that CJ now recognized as being straight from east Texas.

"I'm looking for Walt Reasoner. I'm supposed to meet with him. I'm CJ Floyd."

"You've found him." Reasoner walked up to CJ, clasped his hand firmly, and pumped it once.

"Glad I was able to catch you so late."

"You tend to stick around a little longer when you run your own shop," Reasoner said, motioning for CJ to follow him into his office, where a massive rolltop desk flanked by three folding metal chairs dominated the bare-walled room. Nodding for CJ to take one of the chairs, Reasoner seated himself behind the desk and asked with a bluntness that surprised CJ, "Now, what kind of business are you in that would have you running interference for Willis Sundee, Mr. Floyd?"

"I'm a bail bondsman."

"I see." Reasoner looked reassured, as if he'd put the final piece of a puzzle in place, as CJ slid the metal chair a little closer to the desk, took off his Stetson, and held it in his lap.

"I'm a smoker; hope you don't mind." Reasoner took a pack of Luckys out of his shirt pocket, tapped out a cigarette, lit up, and took a long, satisfying drag. "Will and I have been doing business for quite a while. I'm sorta surprised, to tell you the truth, that he'd balk at a little price increase. That is why you're here, isn't it, Mr. Floyd?"

"Yes," said CJ, thinking Reasoner hadn't known Willis Sundee long enough if he called him by a nickname he abhorred. "Willis says it's more than a little price increase you're hitting him with. He says you want to stick him with a 40 percent increase on everything you supply across the board."

"It's the cost of doing business in these heady times, Mr. Floyd. There're lots of other suppliers around. Ol' Will's always free to do business with them."

"He tells me most of them are giants. Willis is too small a fish to swim in that sea. But I'm guessing you already know that."

Reasoner smiled slyly. "Didn't realize you could see that far inside my head. Let me tell you a story, sir. Just to set things straight." Reasoner's tone was filled with condescension. "I started this business in my early twenties, straight out of Texarkana. A little over a month ago I turned forty-four. During my time in this business, I've fought off greedy suppliers, bad employees, economic downturns, unaccommodating banks, and even the mob. And fortunately, at the ripe old age of forty-four, I've carved out a niche for myself. A niche that lets me charge whatever the market will bear for my services, to put it bluntly. If the big suppliers out there scare ol' Will, maybe he should try somebody smaller."

"There aren't any such beasts around here, he tells me. Seems like once upon a time there were, but they've all been squeezed out by the big boys. Squeezed to the point that the mom-and-pop outfits out there, like Willis's, have been forced to depend on you." CJ stroked his chin thoughtfully. "I'm wondering if perhaps those other smaller suppliers who've all disappeared might not have had a little help from you with deciding to close down shop. Guess I'll just have to do a little digging and find out."

Reasoner leaned forward and gave CJ a long, hard stare before stubbing out his cigarette in the oversized clamshell ashtray on his desk. "You seem real good at thinking for other people, Floyd. So you can take this thought with you and leave. I can charge whatever I like for my goods and services, and if for whatever reason there's no other competition around, that's in my best interest. It's American free enterprise, friend. You and ol' Will should take notice of that."

"No question there, but the system doesn't allow you to strong-arm people along the way or threaten them if they don't step in line."

CJ didn't so much as flinch when Reasoner jumped to his feet and took a step around the desk toward him.

"Outa here, jerk! Now!"

Rising slowly, CJ slipped on his Stetson. "Lay off Willis Sundee," he said, squaring up his hat.

His face flushed with anger, Reasoner said, "Here's a message for you to take back to Sundee, mind reader. He pays the freight or he gets no goods."

"I'll pass along the message."

"Good. Now, here's a second message for you both to chew on. In business, you either set an example or you're made an example of."

CJ, who'd started to leave, pivoted in his tracks. "Hope that's not a threat."

"Take it however you like, Floyd. Now get the shit outa my office."

Reasoner clicked a switch on his desktop, and the lights in the room suddenly dimmed. CJ shot a parting glance back at the darkened, hulking figure sitting behind the rolltop, smoke rising from a newly lit cigarette, and repeated, "Lay off Willis," before gently closing the office door.

CJ was back home at his kitchen table, sipping a Coke and talking on the phone to Willis Sundee, by seven-thirty. Smoke from a cheroot rose from the ashtray next to him. "I talked to your boy Reasoner. Sounds like a take-no-prisoners kinda guy."

"He can afford to be," Willis said. "I've talked to a dozen other small restaurant owners across the city today about switching suppliers. No way any of us can. He's the only game for the small guy in town. Over the years he's tied up just about every mom-and-pop in the city. Got us all sucking from his sugar tit. Giannelli's in North Denver, La Cueva, a Mexican place up on Colfax, Huc Tran's Sweet Asian Flavors on Capitol Hill, you name it. The SOB's had a game plan all along."

CJ took a long, surprisingly unsatisfying swallow of Coke. "Can't you all pool your efforts and get Reasoner to cut you a deal?"

"Afraid it's too late. We should've spit out the Epic Produce & Meats bit and thrown in with the big suppliers years ago. They don't want us now. Not enough money to be made on the deal. Reasoner's already outright threatened Tran. In addition to delivering his produce and meats late, lower-shelf stuff at that, he's been telling Tran how wonderful his recent remodel looks and how he'd hate to see any kind of damage come to it."

"Hell, Willis. It sounds to me like Reasoner's straight out of some '30s gangster movie. Why don't you just call the cops?"

Willis sounded defeated. "I told you, I have no proof. Anyway, Tran called them and nothing happened. He thinks, and I tend to agree, that somewhere along the line some politician and more than likely a few cops are getting paid off. We're addicts strung out on Reasoner's drug, CJ, and we can't get off. So what do I do?"

"For the moment, you pay Reasoner's freight until I get a better handle on things."

"Okay. But don't leave me hanging too long. The bastard could run me outa business."

"I won't let him do that." Looking frustrated, CJ shoved his half-finished Coke aside. "I'll talk to you tomorrow," he said, hanging up and taking a final drag on his cheroot as he tried to gauge just how determined and ruthless a businessman Walt Reasoner actually was.

At seven forty-five the next morning, CJ was back at his kitchen table, unshaven and dressed only in sweatpants, with papers from his GI Joe's Ames files spread out everywhere. It had come to him during the night, largely because of Willis Sundee's inference about how Walt Reasoner had been so methodical in the way he'd carried out his small-business squeeze, that he needed to be equally methodical in his investigation of the GI Joe's murders and try one more time to hook up with the one person he still wanted to get back in touch with: Molly Burgess, who'd been the Denver Symphony Orchestra's second-seat cellist at the time of the murders.

Burgess, CJ had learned, had had a second time around audition session with Chin the day before the murders. He felt a little guilty about the fact that Willis's comments about Reasoner had him digging back into the Ames case instead of dealing with Willis's problem, but he'd get back to Reasoner. There was plenty of time.

He had no idea whether Burgess was still with the symphony, or for that matter still even in Denver. But as he scanned the piece of paper on which he'd jotted notes about her two years earlier, the single asterisk at the top of the page told him that he'd indeed only talked to her once. Shaking his head, mumbling to himself, "Details, damn it, details," and aware that it was too early to call the symphony offices, he told himself he'd call at midmorning. Deciding to pass on another cheroot, he got up and headed off to take a shower. He'd almost reached his bathroom when the sound of someone knocking on his kitchen door turned him around. Walking quickly back to the door, he opened it to see Petey Greene, a friend of his since grade school, standing on the fire-escape landing with a cardboard box tucked under his right arm. Looking apprehensive and shivering in the chill of the early-morning September breeze, Petey said, "Sorry to come by so early, CJ, but I wanted you to look through this box of mine and tell me if there's anything in here worth taking up to the Mile High Flea Market on Eighty-eighth Avenue this afternoon. I'm sure hopin' there is."

CJ smiled, aware that his skinny, brown-skinned visitor, a man with a pencil-thin mustache, half-inch-thick prescription lenses in his glasses, and a permanently furrowed forehead, made his living as an antique scrounger and book scout, combing Denver's streets for anything he could sell for a profit. That included the snitch-type information he would peddle to bail bondsmen, PIs, and cops. He also knew Petey wouldn't be on his doorstep that early unless he knew CJ could throw him a bone that would mean a little money.

"Come on in," CJ said, looking past Petey toward the cloudy fall day.

"Didn't know better, I'd swear we're in for snow," said Petey, shuffling into the kitchen and placing his cardboard box on the kitchen table on top of the GI Joe's papers.

"It'll come soon enough," said CJ, eyeing the box.

Noting CJ's interest, Petey said, "Go ahead, have a look inside. That's why I'm here."

CJ nodded and began sorting through a cache of old Christmas ornaments, some of them broken, soiled oil-company road maps from the 1940s and '50s, electrical switch plates, bottle caps, key rings, school-desk inkwells, and, near the bottom of the box, a three-inch-thick, rubber-banded stack of old postcards. Wedged between the postcards and the road maps was a single, pristine-looking Canon City, Colorado, prison spur, a Western collectible gem that CJ knew had been crafted fifty to sixty years earlier as a rehab-mandated project by some Colorado State Penitentiary inmate.

CJ took the spur out of the box, certain it was the item that had instigated Petey's visit. "Got the mate to this?" he asked, examining the spur carefully.

Petey shook his head. "Got some other ones at home, but no mate for that one."

"Well, if I were you, I'd get to looking for it because if you find it and it's as mint as this one, you'll have yourself a seven-hundred-and-fifty-dollar set."

"Sorta figured that," Petey said with a grin.

CJ went back to sorting through the box, quickly examining several of the postcards, pushing the stack aside, and moving on to several vintage Rocky Mountain National Park souvenir key rings, half-a-dozen or so old soda-bottle caps, and two dog-eared Louis L'Amour paperback books. "The postcards might bring you a few bucks," he said. "But nothing else here hits the mark, Petey."

"Thanks, CJ. Thanks," said Petey, busy reexamining the spur. "I knew you'd be on top of what this baby was worth.

By the way, I ain't seen you at a single auction, swap meet, farm sale, or even up at the flea market in months. What's up?"

"Been busy."

"Well, you're missin' out. I've seen lots of license plates and tobacco tins and more than a few bits and spurs around. Your kinda stuff. Even ran across an old cattle-brand book at the flea market last week."

CJ's eyes lit up. Thinking of his prized 1906 Colorado brand book, he asked, "What state and what year?"

"Didn't get the year, too many other people were pawing at it, but it was an old one all right, Wyoming, I think. Leather-bound and no bigger than an appointment book you might stick in your shirt pocket."

"Damn. That size and leather-bound. The book would've had to be turn-of-the-century or earlier."

"Like I said, you been missin' out."

"Yeah," said CJ, clearly disappointed.

"Well, you better get back at it, man. The flea market's up and runnin' Wednesday through Sunday 'til the end of October. With a find like that brand book I mentioned showin' up there, seems to me you owe it to yourself to drop in."

With visions of some rare turn-of-the-century thousand-dollar cattle-brand book dancing in his head, CJ said, "I'll make it a point to. Maybe even today."

"Great. Maybe I'll see you there." Petey slipped the spur back into the cardboard box, asking as he tucked it safely away, "You ain't in need of no info on anybody's comin's and goin's, deeds, doin's, or whereabouts, are you?" It was Petey's way of offering CJ a little payback for the Canon City spur appraisal.

"Nope. Nothing on the docket for today."

"Well, let me know when you are. Ike, too."

"I'll do that."

Petey secured the cardboard box under his left arm and headed for the door, pushing the kitchen door open to a sky that was far cloudier than when he'd arrived.

"No question about it now. It's gonna snow," he said, stepping out onto the fire-escape landing.

"You might be right," CJ said, eyeing the sky and realizing that since Petey's arrival the temperature outside had dropped a good ten degrees.

"You can buy me a beer next time I see you if I am," said Petey, heading down the stairs.

"I'll do that." CJ scanned the darkening sky, thinking the odds were pretty high that he'd soon owe Petey Greene a beer.

By the time CJ had showered and gone downstairs to learn from Ike that he'd be the one sticking around the office to "cover the floor," a task that amounted to sitting around and twiddling his thumbs waiting for business, he'd already had his daily dose of head-banging with Nordeen Mapson, the inefficient, next-to-worthless part-time secretary whom Ike had kept on the payroll for years because her long-deceased father had been Ike's best friend. When Nordeen got up to leave at eleven thirty, thirty minutes early, claiming that she needed to meet a man about a roofing problem at her house, CJ complained bitterly to Ike.

Ike answered, "You find somebody better, bring 'em the hell in for me to look at. Just remember, though, I ain't payin' anybody no more than what I pay Nordeen right now."

"And we're getting next to nothing for that, Unc. Nordeen's worthless."

"She knows how things around here work. Counts for somethin'," Ike said from the seat behind his desk.

"And she loses things, never shows up on time, leaves early, and always has a spit-in-your-face attitude. Yesterday I asked her for a file I needed on the spot, and it took her thirty minutes to find it."

"Like I said, find me someone better and bring 'em on in."

"I will," CJ said sharply. "And maybe then we can update a few other things around here." The instant the words left his mouth, he knew he'd said the wrong thing.

"What the hell's that supposed to mean?"

Thinking, *In for a penny—in for a pound,* CJ said, "We could use a filing system that works, Unc, and maybe even a dictating and transcription system, and it would be nice to get one of those IBM Selectric typewriters like Herman Currothers has."

Ike detested Herman Currothers, a chubby, bug-eyed weasel of a man who owned Triple A Bonding Services three doors up Delaware Street. Currothers was a disagreeable tightwad who openly disliked just about everyone, and who made no bones about his distrust of minorities, gays, and educated snobs, so saying they needed the same kind of office equipment as Herman Currothers was tantamount to throwing gasoline on a fire.

"I wouldn't use nothin' that redneck asshole has," Ike said, fuming. "You listen here, Calvin Floyd. The name on the sign above the front door of this buildin' reads, 'Floyds Bail Bonds.' Means I own the joint, lock, stock, and barrel, and that I get to run it my way. I ain't so arthritic or so old I can't think. The buildin' you live in is mine, the clients you service are mine, and most important, this business here belongs to me. You get to wantin' it any other way, I'm afraid you'll have to strike out on your own, son."

"I didn't mean ... "

"Don't matter what you meant. I been feelin' your uneasiness about the way I run things around here for a good long while. The air needed clearin', and now it is."

The room fell silent until the only noticeable sound was the ticking of the mantel clock that sat on the hundred-year-old barrister's bookcase to the right of Ike's desk. That silence would surely have lingered if Marguerite Larkin hadn't stepped through Ike's partially open office door to ask, "Ike, sugar, you ready to go to lunch?" When Ike cocked an irritated eyebrow, she said, "Excuse me," and stepped back out into the hallway.

"I'll be back around one-thirty," Ike said, rising out of his chair and grimacing from the ever-present arthritic pain. Suppressing one of his increasingly frequent gear-grinding coughs, he headed for the door.

With his chest feeling tight, suddenly tongue-tied, CJ simply nodded. He'd seen his uncle's bitter stubbornness surface before, but Ike usually reserved such flashes, which could sometimes escalate into flat-out anger, for the handful of dirty cops, corrupt judges, and mindless repeat offenders he couldn't stomach.

Feeling guilty as he watched Ike and Marguerite walk away, CJ had the sense that he'd be mending fences for at least the rest of the week.

Chapter

12

Marguerite Larkin's voice was filled with determination. "You need to let loose of your old-timey ways, Ike Floyd, before they kill you. Everybody from Five Points to Shreveport knows Nordeen Mapson's next to worthless. You're the only one on the planet who'd let her keep hangin' around collectin' a check. Sure, her daddy was one of your best friends, but he's dead and gone now, baby. You can't carry his lazy offspring forever." Marguerite dusted off her hands, a sign that let Ike know she wasn't finished, and glanced around at the lunch crowd packing Mae's Louisiana Kitchen, nodding at several people she knew. Lowering her voice, she said, "CJ's right. You need to upgrade at the office, and that upgrade means sayin' goodbye to Nordeen."

Ike, who'd barely looked up from his food since Mavis Sundee had brought him the luncheon special, a fried catfish plate with two sides of coleslaw, butter beans, sourdough biscuits and honey, and lemonade, picked up a napkin and wiped his hands. "I don't particularly like change, Marguerite."

"You're tellin' me?" Marguerite forced a smile. She'd stuck with Ike through his days of heavy, lost-world drinking, then guided him through years of jumping on and off the wagon. She'd suffered with him as arthritis had gradually tightened its grip on him, slowing his gait, sometimes breaking his spirit, and finally bending him over. She'd spent more than twenty-five years loving the man who'd convinced her when she'd been selling herself to men for fifteen dollars a pop that she had a brain that was the clear equal of her statuesque beauty and that she couldn't forever wallow in self-pity over the fact that she'd been abused and sexually molested as a child.

Ike had been the one who'd urged her to go to school. The one who'd been there on his feet, yelling and clapping, when she'd received her Denver Business College associate degree, and the one who'd years earlier given her the money to start a bookkeeping business that now employed four people and did the lion's share of the books for nearly every business in Five Points. Ike had been there to encourage her when she had been afraid to expand, and he'd been with her every step of the heartbreaking way when her only child, Billy, had been murdered. There weren't many people in the world who could tell Ike Floyd, as she liked to put it, that his shit was raggedy. Marguerite Larkin was one of them.

Setting aside his napkin, Ike suppressed a sigh. "CJ ain't no businessman, Marguerite. What the hell's he know about upgradin'? If I wasn't around, the boy'd end up givin' half his services away. Besides, why should I spend money upgradin' when any minute CJ could be out the door? If he had it his way, he'd be operatin' one of them antique stores down on South Broadway peddlin' license plates, tobacco tins, and spurs."

"But he's not. He's there coverin' your sorry, close-to-broken-down behind every day." She followed this remark with a smile and a quick wink. "Just like me."

Her smile seemed to soften Ike. Stabbing a final silver-dollar-sized piece of catfish with his fork, he asked, "You willin' to help teach CJ the business side of things? The money side, I mean?"

"Sure. But first you gotta promise me you'll buy some new equipment and part ways with Nordeen."

"The girl's got nowhere to go."

"Neither did I when you met me, in case you don't remember. She'll find work. And Ike, you're gonna have to let CJ help with hirin' a replacement and stop bein' a one-man show."

Ike took a lengthy drink of lemonade, eyed the consummate love of his life, and muttered, "Change. I hate it."

Extending her right arm circus-barker style and sweeping it around in a 180-degree arc, Marguerite said, "Everybody in here knows that. But change is somethin' can't nobody stop. Not even you, Ike Floyd."

Deciding he'd hung around the office long enough without the slightest whiff of any business, CJ walked outside to wash the Bel Air. The day's earlier clouds had given way to a partly sunny, crisp, sixty-degree afternoon. His clash with Ike still had him upset, and he hoped washing the car would help ease the tension he was feeling.

When Ike pulled into the driveway in the '71 Olds 442 Cutlass Supreme he always tooled Marguerite around in, CJ wasn't certain whether to greet them, continue getting out the hose, or head back inside.

"Any business come around while I was gone?" Ike called out, pulling the Cutlass to a stop and swinging the door open.

"Nope," said CJ. He watched Ike struggle to get out of the Olds, delighted that Ike was at least speaking to him again.

Ike's shrapnel-filled arthritic right knee gave way just as he reached the front of the Cutlass, and he reached out and grabbed the hood ornament for support as Marguerite and CJ came running. "Fuckin' Korea," Ike muttered as CJ looped an arm under his shoulder and steadied him. "Never shoulda been there," he grumbled. His war protest over, he waved off CJ and Marguerite and limped toward the garage.

"Whatta you need from the garage, Unc? I can get it," said CJ, taking in the look of determination on Ike's face.

"No, you can't. You don't know where the hell to look."

CJ glanced at Marguerite for some kind of explanation, but she shrugged and followed Ike through the open double doors of the garage.

Ike flipped on the garage's single hanging, bug-splattered, hundred-watt bulb, grunted as if to say *I'm all right now,* and hobbled toward a cabinet on the back wall. Gritting back his pain, he swung the cabinet door open and began rummaging around inside. "Know it's here somewhere," he said, digging through shelves of clutter. "Yeah, yeah. Here it is. It's a picture of me and your mom when we were kids." He teased a dust-covered eight-by-ten, sepia-toned photo in a cheap wooden frame from between the old *Reader's Digest* condensed-book compilations and handed it to CJ.

CJ swallowed hard and held the photo up to the light. He'd seen only a couple of photos of his mother in his life, and never one of her as a child. Wearing shorts and a T-shirt that read, "Reds," Ike looked to CJ to be about ten, so he suspected his mother couldn't have been much more than five. She was wearing a sundress and straddling a tricycle, and both children sported high-top shoes. CJ felt strangely queasy as Ike took the photo back and dusted off the glass with his shirtsleeve.

"I'm thinkin' that picture was taken back home in Cincinnati in the early '30s, before the war." Ike was eye to eye now with CJ. "Need you to get it reframed. A family picture like that deserves a better frame." Ike shot a quick glance at Marguerite before handing the photograph to CJ. "Gonna be makin' some changes in the office here pretty soon. Figured I'd hang a picture or two of family around the office when I did. That one you're holdin' and maybe one'a you in your navy uniform gettin' that Navy Cross of yours pinned on. Think you can round up one'a them medal-ceremony photos of yours for me?"

"Yeah," said CJ, his throat nearly gone dry.

"Good." Ike closed the cabinet door, did an about-face, and headed for the door. "Marguerite's gonna help us find some secretarial help." His words seemed to echo off the walls.

Halfway to the open garage doors, Ike's knees buckled again. When CJ moved to help him, Ike defiantly waved him off, and as CJ and Marguerite watched the stubborn Korean

War veteran struggle to walk back to the house, they knew better than to lend a hand. Ike had disappeared inside when CJ turned and asked Marguerite, "What happened at lunch?"

Hooking her arm in CJ's, she smiled and said, "Simple. Me and your uncle had one of our productive kinda conversations."

Two hours later, feeling as euphoric as he had in months, and with Petey Greene's advice to get out more circling in his head, CJ pulled into the Mile High Flea Market's quarter-mile-square asphalt parking lot just north of Denver. He had B.B. King blaring on the radio and the top down on the Bel Air. Thanks to Marguerite, he and Ike were not only speaking, but for once they seemed to be completely on the same page. To add to his sense of contentment, an hour earlier, with a little sleight-of-hand, he'd been able to get an inside track on Molly Burgess. After going back through his notes on her, he'd called the Denver Symphony office and told the naive-sounding person who'd answered that he was a college friend of Burgess's, a fellow cellist who several years earlier had played with her in the Des Moines Symphony, and that he'd been trying unsuccessfully to get in touch with her. After a little more pleading and prodding on his part, the clerk had suggested that he might even be able to catch Burgess at the orchestra's 2 p.m. rehearsal the next day, when the musicians would be preparing for a Friday-night tribute to Beethoven. CJ had thanked the accommodating man and hung up, suspecting as he did that confronting Burgess at a rehearsal with sixty or seventy fellow musicians around might not be the best way to extract information from her about Quan

Lee Chin. What he needed to do, he reasoned, was talk to Burgess alone, especially since she'd been so evasive over the years. It took him a while to decide on a tactic that made sense. He finally settled on one that involved some degree of risk but was at least a plan, and since he had no phone number or home address for Burgess, he figured he'd go with it.

Friday evening he'd take Mavis to the symphony and enjoy a little Beethoven, figuring that his chances of hooking up with Burgess immediately after that performance were equal to his odds of catching up with her during a rehearsal. There'd be fewer of her orchestra-mates around as they scurried away from the performance and headed for home. He could pose as an autograph-seeking fan, and in order to appear less intimidating, he'd have a date on his arm. Whether or not his plan would work, he didn't know. But at least he had one.

Nosing the Bel Air past a group of screaming teenagers spraying one another with water pistols, he found a parking space near the flea-market entrance and no more than twenty yards from the kettle-corn concession stand. The rich, buttery caramel smell wafted his way as he slipped out of the Bel Air.

He was through the flea market's front gate and in line at the concession a half minute later, scanning the huge complex with its hundreds of booths where vendors hawked everything from Indian trinkets to race-car tires. Hoping to spot Petey Greene but knowing he'd probably have to walk the entire grounds to find the little hustler, if Petey were there at all, CJ paid for his kettle corn and took off to the north, leisurely walking one of the flea market's quarter-mile-long aisles.

Before he'd left for Vietnam, vendors had as often as not sold their wares from their vans or the beds of pickups. In the years since, things had changed, and for the most part vendor spaces had become more permanent.

Popping a handful of kettle corn into his mouth, he strolled up to a leather-maker's booth to examine a row of wallets laid out on a weather-worn metal display table. He was admiring a wallet with expandable pockets when Petey Greene's unmistakable squeaky voice erupted behind him: "CJ, my man! You're here, and did you pick the day!"

With his Coke-bottle-thick glasses slightly cockeyed on his face, Petey grabbed CJ by the arm and tugged him away from the table. "Been hopin' you'd show. They got your kind of flavors here today. Just about all of 'em."

"Brand books?" CJ asked excitedly.

"Nope, but damn near as good. License plates by the bushel. Come on, I'll show ya."

Petey broke into a fast-paced walk down the aisle, deftly weaving his way between people as only someone who was accustomed to navigating the flea market two to three times a week possibly could. "Down here, down here," he said, waving for CJ to keep up.

He stopped his surge at a small booth with a candy-striped canvas front awning. The hand-carved wooden sign sitting on a table in front of the two-sided canvas booth read, "Gaylord's Antiques." Half-a-dozen rusted, abused-looking license plates, an equal number of Swiss army knives in various sizes and shapes, a couple of miniature mantel clocks, and two decent-looking 1920s-vintage inkwells sat on the table. A white Chevy Suburban, with its rear hatch raised and badly in need of a wash, was parked behind the booth. A line of wooden boxes filled with merchandise sat on the ground a few feet from the Suburban's front bumper.

"Brought you some business," Petey said to the stoic-looking man sporting a Panama hat who was seated behind the table. Petey grabbed CJ, who'd finally caught up, by the arm and pulled him toward the table. "My friend CJ Floyd here is in the antique-collectin' business. The man hidin' behind the Panama is Gaylord Marquee," Petey said to CJ. Shoving the cache of old license plates aside, to the surprised vendor's dismay, he said to Marquee, "Show him your good stuff, Gaylord."

"You collect plates?" Marquee asked CJ, looking him up and down, his accent unmistakably British.

"Of sorts," said CJ, staring at the man's badly yellowed teeth and ruddy spider-veined complexion before eyeing several wooden boxes filled with license plates that sat behind the table on the ground in front of the Suburban. He couldn't help but think from the chagrined look on his face that Marquee was somehow sorry he and Petey had shown up.

"Come on," said Petey, feigning a punch to CJ's arm. "There's no *of sorts* to it. CJ here's got a collection of license plates that would make your head spin, Gaylord. Come on, man, let him have a look at your good shit. You're in a buyin' mood, right, CJ?"

"Sure am," said CJ, wondering why Marquee seemed hesitant to show him his wares.

Noticing that CJ's eyes remained locked on the boxes behind him, Marquee said, "My stuff's pretty high end."

"Just what I'm looking for," CJ said, suspecting that perhaps Marquee's goods were stolen.

Nodding and eyeing CJ suspiciously, Marquee reached behind him, pulled a box forward, pushed aside everything else on the table, hefted the box, and plopped it down. "Have a look, but be careful."

CJ flipped quickly through a half-dozen porcelain plates, most in good condition and most quite common. Fifty- to one-hundred-dollar plates, nothing special, he thought, continuing his perusal. When a rare 1915 black-on-white Vermont porcelain tag caught his eye, he started to lift it out of the box.

Marquee grabbed his hand. "Leave it in its place. I'll take anything you're interested in back out once you've worked your way through the whole box—that is, if you are serious."

CJ was close to telling the haughty beak-nosed man to shove his license plates up his ass when the 1933 Ohio plate behind the Vermont plate tipped forward, revealing an early Colorado municipal tag—a plastic-wrapped Monte Vista town plate with telltale cracks along its top edge and a perfectly centered number 87, flanked by a small M over a V. Looking dumbfounded and certain that the plate was the same one Wiley Ames had shown him five years earlier, CJ said, "This one looks interesting," and ran a finger along the top edge of the plastic. "Want to take it out? I'm done with this box."

"It's a Colorado town tag," Marquee said, teasing the Monte Vista plate up and away from its neighbors. "Nineteen nine or ten. Rare but not so rare if you know what I mean. Two twenty-five's what I'm asking."

"It's got a few chips."

"They all do from that vintage. Any serious collector would know that."

"Okay if I have a closer look?"

"Go ahead. Just don't take it out of the plastic."

CJ held the license plate up to the hazy sunlight. "Don't have many early townies like this in my collection. Where'd you find it?"

"Scrounging around."

"Up in the mountains?"

"Don't remember." Marquee cocked a suspicious eyebrow.

"It's a beauty. How long have you had it?"

"You buying or not?" Looking peeved, Marquee reached for the plate.

Inching the plate out of the Englishman's grasp, CJ laid it down on the table and reached for his wallet. "Yeah, I'm buying."

"Two twenty-five plus tax. Cash or check. I don't take credit cards."

"Looks like you've picked a winner there, CJ," said Petey, who'd been noticeably silent.

"Sure hope so." CJ teased five fifty-dollar bills out of his wallet. Knowing he'd be eating lean for the rest of the month, he handed Marquee the cash.

Seeming no more pleased than if the sale hadn't been made, Marquee fished change out of a cigar box on the table and, without counting it out, handed it to CJ. "You can keep the baggie," he said, smiling smugly.

Holding the license plate protectively against his hip, CJ asked, "Any idea if this baby came out of a larger collection? I'd sure like to know if it has any sisters or brothers."

"Got no idea," Marquee said brusquely.

Thinking, *Sure, you don't,* CJ asked, "Mind if I have a look at the rest of your stuff?"

Marquee hesitated before answering. Then he reluctantly reached back and lifted the box closest to him up onto the table.

With Petey Greene hovering, breathing garlic breath over his shoulder, CJ sifted through that box and several more over the next ten minutes. The only special plate he ran across among the hundred or more he looked at was a state-shaped single-digit 1927 Tennessee plate. "Uncommon," said CJ, eyeing Marquee. "Where'd you get it?"

"You're ghastly full of questions, chap," said Marquee. "Are you writing a reference book on license plates or something?"

"No," CJ said, noting the irritation in Marquee's voice and realizing that he'd tweaked the Englishman enough to have pushed him into British idiom. "Just like to add a little history to my finds."

"Well, that bird there doesn't have one."

Thinking, *More slang,* CJ tucked the Monte Vista plate under his arm, telling himself that Gaylord Marquee deserved a lot more scrutiny. Turning to Petey, he said, "I'm down to my last twenty, Petey. Think it's time to go."

Petey handed CJ the kettle corn he'd been holding on to for him, most of which he'd eaten, and said, "I'm thinkin' you scored pretty good," as they walked away.

Feeling Marquee's eyes glued to them all the way to the Bel Air, CJ said, "Marquee sounded real British."

"He is. He's from Bristol."

"How long's he been in Denver?"

"Ten, eleven years I know of. Maybe longer. Why?"

CJ slipped the Monte Vista plate from under his arm, eased it out of its baggie, and held it up to the light. Studying the plate intently, he said, "Got a job for you, Petey. One of those ear-to-the-ground kind of gigs you're so good at."

"Shoot," said Petey, beaming with pride as CJ lowered the unsleeved plate.

"I want you to dig up everything you can for me on Marquee. Where he lives, who he hangs out with, where he sells his wares besides the flea market here, where he gets his goods from, and exactly how long he's been in Denver. And while you're at it, I need you to dig up something else. Run down what you can for me on a guy named Walt Reasoner. He owns the Epic Produce & Meats Company up in North Denver. Same deal as Marquee—where he lives, who his acquaintances are, and any kind of lowdown you can get on his business dealings."

"Easy money," said Petey.

"Same charge as usual?"

Petey shook his head. "My prices have gone up. Inflation. It's fifty bucks nowadays for a lead that's solid. A hundred for the kinda info you're askin' for."

CJ thought about his nearly empty wallet, before he reluctantly said, "Okay."

"I'll have the skinny for you on Marquee pretty quick. Might take a little longer for Reasoner. Why you want 'em scoped out, anyway?"

"Because they're interesting people," CJ said, breaking into a smile.

"You're thinkin' that plate Gaylord sold you might've been stolen, aren't you?"

"Maybe. And Petey, the info can wait 'til Saturday. Tomorrow evening I'm headed to the symphony."

"Damn. You buckin' to suddenly get cultured?"

"Absolutely." CJ winked at his longtime friend, slipped the Monte Vista license plate back into the baggie, and lit up a cheroot, thinking as he took his first satisfying drag about how to approach Molly Burgess the next evening.

Chapter

🦎 13

On his way home from the flea market to Bail Bondsman's Row, CJ kept thinking he'd missed something important in sizing up Gaylord Marquee. No question Marquee was glib, circumspect, maybe even a little down-home slick. But there was something else about him that was unsettling. Something beneath-the-radar sinister. He couldn't put his finger on what he might have overlooked, but he'd missed something about the man that was important, he was certain of that.

With a little luck, Petey Greene might square things up for him—shed a little daylight, in essence, on Marquee—but for the moment, the Monte Vista plate sitting on the seat beside him had moved him closer to a solution to the GI Joe's murders than he'd ever been.

When he pulled into his driveway, Ike was standing on the front porch staring out onto Delaware Street and shaking his head. It was ten degrees colder than it had been at the flea market, and as CJ stepped out into a stiff twenty-miles-per-hour breeze, gripping the Monte Vista plate tightly, he knew for sure that Denver was headed for snow.

"What's shakin', Unc?" he called out, tucking the plate under one arm, cupping his hands together, and blowing into them.

Looking as if his world had collapsed, Ike said, "Nordeen quit. Skedaddled outa here a few minutes before you pulled in. Told me there wasn't no way in hell she was gonna have me workin' her like no dog."

"So we hire somebody else."

"I've got that covered, least for now. Marguerite's gonna help out two days a week 'til we get a replacement." He glanced up, then down, Delaware Street, eyeing each of the other six Victorians that made up Bail Bondsman's Row. "But the competition don't care whether we got a secretary or not, and we both know things been a little lean around here lately, so I'm hopin' we get somebody soon."

"We'll make out okay."

"Expect we will." Ike glanced at the license plate tucked under CJ's arm. "Where you been, anyway?"

"The Mile High Flea Market. Bought myself something. Have a look. It's a Monte Vista town plate from around 1909 or 1910." He handed the plate to Ike. "It was part of Wiley Ames's collection, I'm sure of it."

Ike studied the plate briefly, then shook his head. "You ain't gettin' ready to reconstitute the GI Joe's murder shit, are you?"

"I'm looking into some things."

Ike frowned and tugged on his earlobe, something he had a habit of doing before offering advice. "You need to let that mess go, boy. The cops never found nothin', and I'm thinkin' that no matter how long you dig around, neither will you. We got other issues to handle around here right now."

"Don't worry, it's a back-burner issue for now. Besides, I'm busy working on something for Willis."

"Willis payin' you?"

"Yes."

"Good." Looking relieved that CJ had had the good sense to charge for his services instead of working for free, as he far too often did for friends, Ike said, "Marguerite's comin' by in a little bit to finish typin' up some things that Nordeen left hangin'. Got an aggravated-assault case to post up, and on Artie Wilson, no less. The dumbass popped some white boy in the head with a beer bottle down at El Chaparral last night. I'm guessin' we made the mortgage money for today."

Thinking suddenly about his own nearly empty wallet, CJ asked, "Can you lend me fifty bucks, Unc? The license plate just about cleaned me out."

Looking at CJ as if he were a teenager who'd overspent his allowance, Ike shrugged. "Where the hell you headed you need fifty bucks?"

"To the symphony."

Ike slipped out his wallet, took out a fifty-dollar bill, and handed it to CJ. "I know there's more to my fifty disappearin' and that symphony trip than what you're tellin' me, CJ. Spit it out."

"There is. And I'll tell you about it when I get back from listening to a night of Beethoven tomorrow evening," CJ said with a wink.

"Fine. Just don't forget about returnin' my fifty when you do."

"I'll have it back to you tomorrow," CJ said, knowing that by then Willis Sundee would have paid him in advance for an initial week's work.

"You headed to the symphony by yourself?"

Walking backward toward the Victorian's fire escape, CJ said, "Nope. I'm planning on taking Mavis."

Ike broke into an ear-to-ear grin. "Good choice. And it's about time."

"Yeah," said CJ, feeling guilty that the reason for his symphony outing had far more to do with Molly Burgess and the GI Joe's killings than it had to do with Mavis.

An hour and a half later, CJ walked into GI Joe's with the Monte Vista plate in his hand, looking for Harry Steed. He hadn't been inside the pawnshop in two years, but it hadn't changed much save for the fact that Wiley Ames's Wall of the West had been replaced by floor-to-ceiling shelves stocked mostly with Indian pottery, and the whole store seemed more dim, dusty, and cluttered than ever.

Harry Steed looked up from a mini–boom box he'd been fiddling with, caught a glimpse of CJ, smiled, shoved the boom box aside, and scurried from behind the counter. Draping an arm over CJ's shoulders and pumping CJ's right hand, the gregarious, balding, owl-eyed, deeply tanned Steed said, "You just caught me. Another ten minutes and I would've been closed. What in the hell's up, Mr. Bail Bondsman extraordinaire?"

CJ patted the slightly slump-shouldered World War II vet on

the back. "Glad you stayed. Sorta late for you to be open, though, isn't it?"

"Just trying to earn a poor man's dollar. We can't all be media darlings, getting our picture plastered on the front page of the *Denver Post* with a Colorado Bureau of Investigation top-ten fugitive strapped to the back seat of our Jeep."

"Lighten up, Harry. I've heard enough about bringing in Juarez over the past three months from Rosie Weeks and that crowd that hangs out at his garage to last me a lifetime."

"I know that crowd. Perceptive folks," said Harry, who several years earlier, at CJ's urging, had begun taking his own vintage '49 Buick Roadmaster to Rosie's for service, but only after making certain that Rosie's charges were 10 percent lower than those of the shop where he'd been taking the car for years. Rosie, who simply called Harry cheap, had never bought into CJ's argument that the portly pawnshop owner was simply frugal. "What did they pay you for bringing in Juarez, anyway?"

Having learned years earlier that it was money and gamesmanship more than anything that made Harry Steed tick, CJ said, "Fifteen hundred."

A high-pitched whistle filled the air. "Not bad." Stroking his chin and looking deeply reflective, as if that kind of money might make him take a stab at bounty hunting, Steed shook his head. "Too much risk and not enough reward." If the reward had been double the fifteen hundred dollars, CJ expected Harry might have reconsidered. When Steed asked, "What brings you down to my neck of the woods?" the dollar signs in his eyes had slowly started to disappear.

"What else?"

"Not Wiley." Steed shook his head. "Let it go, CJ."

"I've heard that already today, from Ike."

"Then I'd listen." Steed leaned back against the counter. "Old ghosts are the most dangerous kind, they say."

"Maybe. But I've got a new lead. It came my way unexpectedly today. You know that license-plate collection of Wiley's? The one he left to his niece?"

"Of course. I'm the one who appraised it for her. Middle-of-the-road stuff, but decent."

"Well, I'm thinking she didn't get all of her inheritance. One of the plates, a Monte Vista municipal tag from about 1909 or 1910 that Wiley showed me the day after we first met, turned up at the Mile High Flea Market today. An antique dealer named Marquee was packing it around. You ever heard of him?"

"Nope, not a name I recognize. What's the big deal, anyway? Maybe Wiley's niece sold the plate to him."

"That was my first take, too, but when I asked Marquee where he got the plate, he tap-danced around the issue like he was Fred Astaire."

"Sometimes it's best not to reveal your sources when you're in the resale business. You know that as well as I do, CJ."

"Yeah, yeah, I know. But Marquee's hiding something. No question about it."

"So sue him."

"Come on, Harry. I'm here for help, not stand-up comedy. You ever hear from that niece of Wiley's, Cheryl Goldsby?"

Steed shook his head. "Haven't seen or heard from her since

she had me appraise Wiley's things five years ago. She packed up what was in his condo and here at the store a few days after I sent her a written appraisal and took off. Had another woman with her both times." Harry scratched his head thoughtfully. "I'm sure I told you that a long time ago."

"You might have," said CJ, knowing that his initial un-schooled investigation of the GI Joe's killings had been nothing more than a fragmented guilt-driven rush to nowhere. "What was his collection of stuff worth back then?"

Looking even more puzzled, Steed said, "I told you that, too. Four to five grand, tops. He had some World War II memora-bilia—German guns, flags, helmets, and some old sepia-toned photos that had some value. Some license plates worth something and a nice collection of inkwells. That's about it."

"And you're sure Goldsby took it all?" CJ asked, his memory of events from five years earlier clouded by post-traumatic stress.

"Every tin can and bottle cap. She and the woman with her loaded up a pickup here and then at Wiley's condo and took off outa Denver like nobody's business. You ask me, I think they were dykes. Anyway, the one with Cheryl was a nosy sort. Wide-bottomed and thick and with sticky hands. Picked up damn near everything in here and had a look at it while Goldsby loaded the truck up mostly by herself. I had the feeling she knew a whole lot more about the antiques and collectibles business than she let on."

"Hm, you know what, Harry? I'm thinking it's time for a road trip. One I should've probably taken a while back."

"Where to?"

"To visit Cheryl Goldsby and that special friend of hers. When I visited her a month or so after Wiley's funeral, she shooed me off pretty fast."

"You thinking maybe she or the girlfriend might've killed Wiley?"

"Stranger things have happened."

"I don't know, CJ. That's stretching it, if you ask me. And for what? Cheryl inherited everything Wiley had."

"Could be he had more. We know for sure that he and Chin were in the fencing business. Maybe they had other stashes. Stashes that only Cheryl and the girlfriend knew about."

"Maybe. But I'm here to tell you that Wiley kept just about everything that was valuable right here, where he had the use of a free alarm system. So if he had a stash, where the hell was it?"

Looking stumped, CJ shrugged. "You got me. But I intend to find out if he had one."

"I'd be careful if I were you. Remember what I said about ghosts."

"I'll do that. In the meantime, I need you to do me a favor. Can you do a little asking around about that guy I mentioned, Marquee? He works your side of the street, Harry. Antiques, Indian pawn, Western collectibles, stuff like that, and he's British."

"I'll do what I can."

"You're the man," CJ said, giving the pudgy, balding pawnbroker a high five. "Don't take any wooden nickels," he said, turning to head for the front door and the short drive over to

Rosie Weeks's garage. As he walked by one dusty display case after another filled with valuable antiques and pawn, he suspected that a man as frugal and as into the game as Harry Steed had probably never had a single wooden nickel foisted on him in his life.

More than a few Five Points locals claimed that Rosie Weeks's now successful business had flourished on the strength of his wife Etta Lee's brains and Roosevelt's back. In truth, they'd contributed equally to that success. Like CJ, Rosie had been a car lover all his life. But while CJ had always simply admired automotive beauty, engineering, and style, Rosie did him one better: he understood what made cars run.

Only CJ, Ike, and Willis Sundee were allowed to call Rosie "Red," a nickname he'd earned in high school because he liked his hamburgers on the raw side of rare.

Like Mac's Louisiana Kitchen, Rosie's Garage, a well-established Five Points gathering place, had become much more. The gigantic garage's back storage room, known locally as "the den," was a place where you could gamble, play the numbers, buy liquor on Sundays, or if you had a mind to, just hang around all day and shoot the breeze. Rosie didn't mind folks loitering, especially since those same folks and their cars accounted for a significant portion of his business, but if he caught people cursing in front of a female customer, or if a back-room poker game turned sour and ended up in a fight, he sent everyone packing. No one, including Denver's black politicians or the cops, ever made mention of what everyone knew went on in Rosie's back room, especially since both groups were being paid a hefty monthly sum to look the other way.

Rosie was busy hand-sprinkling the concrete floor of one of the garage's service bays with an oil absorbent compound from a five-gallon pail when CJ walked in. When Rosie glanced up from what he was doing, a genuine smile of long-term friendship spread across his face. "Ain't seen you all week, CJ. Where the hell you been?"

"Working," said CJ, walking over and giving Rosie a fist bump.

"Sure hope you got a thick wad of green to show for it."

"Not yet, but I'm working on it. Problem is, I may need a little help."

Rosie set his pail down. "Don't like the way you said that word, *help*, CJ. Like the word somehow needed me to prop it up."

"It's light work, Red," CJ said, his tone reassuring. "If it even comes to that."

Rosie shook his head, slowly at first, then a little faster. "You know Etta Lee don't like me helpin' you with your jobs, CJ. Every time I do, a bucket of trouble always seems to come my way."

Recalling the time Rosie had helped him bring down a car chop ring only to end up with a broken nose and a couple less teeth, CJ said, "No chop shops involved here, Red. I'm just trying to keep somebody from putting the squeeze on Willis Sundee. Having you as backup would sure be nice."

"Which means you need muscle. Which means you've more than likely already pissed somebody off."

"Let's just say that a certain somebody and I don't see eye to eye. I talked to Willis on the phone about that fact a few minutes before I headed over here. The man squeezing Willis's nuts has Willis pretty upset. He's a local restaurant produce and meat supplier who doesn't like the fact that I paid him a visit on Willis's behalf."

"Sounds sorta angry."

"No more angry than Willis is paying me to be. Bottom line's this, Red. I really don't need you to do much of anything but keep an eye on Mae's for me for the next couple of nights."

"How come you can't keep an eye out?"

"Because I've gotta help Ike with office paperwork tonight, and tomorrow night I'm taking Mavis to the symphony."

"Etta Lee'll have my head, she finds out."

"It's important, Red. Wouldn't ask you if it wasn't."

Rosie frowned, and kicked a dollop of oil-soaked compound off the toe of a work boot. "Don't like the idea of anyone puttin' the squeeze on Willis, but maybe you should just call the cops."

"And wait for Lady Justice to show up? Rosie, come on. We'll all be old and gray by then. Besides, the guy threatening Willis is more than likely in bed with the cops. Willis says he's threatened a half-dozen other restaurant owners, as well, telling them to get in line with his new fee schedule or else. And you know what? There hasn't been so much as a peep or finger-lift out of the cops to help. Come on, Red. It's only for two nights."

"And all you want me to do is keep an eye on Mae's?"

"That's all. A little surveillance from when they close until they open back up at six. Hell, you'll be right here at the den and just up the street for most of that time. I need you to keep an eye out for anything suspicious. Strange cars, people moving in and out of the area who look like they don't belong, any activity in the alley behind Mae's, that kind of stuff. Like I said, light work. You in?"

Rosie offered a reluctant "Yes."

"Good. I'll be wearing a pager. I'll call you later with the number. Just page me if something looks troublesome."

Looking surprised, Rosie said, "First you're off to the symphony and next you're wearin' one of them doctor's pagers. What's up with you, man? You lookin' to switch from bein' a bail bondsman to an MD?"

"Nope. I'm looking at taking Mavis to the symphony, that's all. Nailed the date with her down a little after I talked with Willis."

"I'll be damned. Sure hope you know what you're doin'. You know how protective Willis is of his little girl."

"She's a woman now, Rosie. Besides, it's just two friends out enjoying a little music for the evening," CJ said, feeling a sudden twinge of guilt.

"Hope you got somethin' appropriate to wear, Mr. Highbrow. Somehow I'm thinkin' your Stetson and riverboat gambler's vest won't fit in."

"I'm covered, bought a new sport coat just today."

"Roll over, Beethoven," Rosie said, smiling.

Meeting Rosie's smile with one of his own, CJ winked and said, "Absolutely."

Chapter

14

Without the least bit of hesitation, Mavis had said yes to CJ's invitation to go to the symphony a few hours earlier. Now, as she and longtime friend and sounding board Odetta Jefferson, lead waitress at Mae's, closed up the restaurant for the night, Mavis was having second thoughts. Headed toward the rear of the restaurant with a dozen salt and pepper shakers on a serving tray, Mavis brushed past Odetta and sighed.

"Awfully heavy-soundin' bit of air you're gettin' rid of, girl. If I didn't know better, I'd think you just found out you'd put on ten extra pounds," the perpetually dieting head waitress said.

"Just wondering if I did the right thing, Odetta. That's all."

"Hell's britches, girl. You've been waitin' for CJ to ask you out officially like this since you were in your teens. Now he goes and asks you—and out on one of them classy kinda dates, no less—and you get the willies. I'd think you'd be feelin' like you just struck gold. I know I would."

"I'm just a little apprehensive, I guess."

"About what? Not knowin' when to clap?"

"No. What I'm worried about is the six years of difference in our ages, and the all-too-often opposite way we view the world, and whether our uneven serrated edges actually match up."

"You're bein' real kind to CJ and extra hard on yourself. Everybody knows you ain't got an unpolished edge to you. Now, CJ, he's another matter. But then again, he wasn't raised as comfortable as you, and you never did no two tours of duty in Vietnam. Don't matter, really. The two of you've got real good reasons for bein' who you are. What matters is the man's good-lookin', steady workin', loyal to his friends and family, and most of all, he ain't got no jealous girlfriends out there wantin' to scratch your eyes out. What else could you want?"

"I don't know, Odetta. Anyway, it's just a date."

"Don't be anywayin' it with me, Mavis Sundee. Spit your problem on out."

Mavis took a deep, reflective breath. "Do you know what they said about CJ right after he came back from Vietnam?"

Odetta rolled her eyes. "No, what did *they* say?"

"That CJ was different from when he left. That he has a hard time concentrating now, and an even harder time controlling his temper. I've seen the temper problem firsthand—saw it one day this past summer when he caught a couple of Five Points hoodlums stealing parts from Rosie's Garage. I had the feeling from the look on CJ's face when he all but slammed them both through a wall that he might have killed them both if Rosie and I hadn't intervened. And I know for certain that for a couple of years after he came home from Vietnam, he walked the streets alone all hours of the night."

"You might've, too, if you just came back from two years of killin' people. But that ain't what's got you all hot and bothered, either. Quit your half-steppin' and unload your problem."

"Okay, okay. I'm wondering why all of a sudden CJ's so hot to take me out, and to the symphony, no less. A blues concert, jazz at El Chapultepec, a movie even. Those I could understand, but the symphony? Classical music has never been his cup of tea. You know that."

"Maybe he's just branchin' out."

"I don't think so. I've got the strangest feeling that I'm headed to the symphony to be nothing more than an ornament on his arm. That he's really going there for some other reason."

"And I'm thinkin' you've been takin' too many of them college psychology classes."

"Maybe. But I can't shake the feeling."

"Then let me go in your place, girl." Odetta strutted down the restaurant's center aisle, one arm locked in an imaginary CJ's.

"No, I'm going, if for no other reason than to shake this feeling."

"Now you're talkin'. Best to take things the way they come in life. Ain't no other way."

"I guess so," said Mavis, setting the tray of salt and pepper shakers on a nearby table.

"Ain't no guessin' to it—you ain't about to change CJ, and he ain't changin' you. And like you said, it ain't nothin' but a date, remember?"

Mavis nodded, just once and very slowly. "Yeah, that's all it is, a date," she said, aware that deep down she was afraid of coming face to face with her dreams only to find out they weren't at all what she'd expected.

Walt Reasoner sat alone at the bar in Eddy Cox's Place, a neighborhood watering hole in the mostly Italian section of North Denver, sliding an empty beer mug back and forth across the bar from his right hand to his left. He was about to ask the bartender, the bar's only other occupant besides two people sitting at a table near the back, for a new frosted mug of Coors on tap when a pasty-faced man wearing an out-of-place summer straw hat sidled across the room and plopped down on the bar stool next to him. "You called? I came," the man said, cocking his hat to one side before slapping Reasoner on the back. "What's your problem, Wally-boy?" he asked, addressing Reasoner by a nickname he hated.

Looking startled and clearly offended, Reasoner waved for another beer and said, "Got a problem with a shine over in Five Points who doesn't want to step in line with my program. And drop the Wally-boy, okay?"

"They like to be called blacks nowadays, Wally-boy. You need to listen to the nightly news more often."

Reasoner shot the man an angry look as the bartender set an icy mug of beer down in front of him. "You here to give a fucking civil rights lecture or help?"

Flashing the bartender a set of perfectly aligned white teeth, save for a noticeable gap between his two top incisors, the man in the straw hat waved off service. "I'm here for whatever you need, Wally."

"Good. What I need is for you to get that shine with the problem to queue up with the rest of the flock I've spent the better part of two years corralling. Two expensive, business-building years of keeping my competition out of the picture, flatfoots from sniffing around, and do-good bureaucrats off my ass."

Straw hat laughed. "Don't flatter yourself, Wally-boy. Those competitors you're talkin' about don't want the business. It's too fuckin' small and way too fragmented. I work for them, remember? As for those politicos you're payin' to look the other way so you can keep your share of the produce market—hell, they'd turn on your ass in a second if they figured it would benefit 'em." The man sucked a stream of air through the gap between his front teeth. "And the cops—come on, now, Wally. You don't think they really give a shit. It's a shine you're havin' problems with, remember?" The man smiled and slapped Reasoner on the back. "So how hard do you want me push?" He reached up and adjusted his hat back off his forehead.

"Hard enough that he gets the message."

"What's his name, and where's he located?"

"Willis Sundee, and he owns a greasy spoon called Mae's Louisiana Kitchen over in Five Points."

"There you go again, Wally-boy, being outa touch." The man shook his head. "Mae's Kitchen's gotta be the top soul-food restaurant in the state. Best ham hocks and butter beans I've ever eaten." He rubbed his belly a couple of times before the look on his face turned deadly serious. "Whatta ya want? A little intimidation, water damage, fire?"

"Whatever it takes, Louie."

Louie Jordan's face lit up. "Fire's been workin' good lately."

"It's your call. Just make sure it's enough of a push to make Mr. Sundee get back in line, and enough to make everybody else I'm servicing sit up and take notice."

"I'll handle it. No problem."

"Good. We'll settle up when you're done."

"Times are tight, Wally-boy. This time I'm gonna need a little somethin' down."

"How much?"

"Half. Let's say fifteen hundred."

Reasoner sat back, reached into his pants pocket, and after making sure the bartender wasn't looking extracted a wad of cash. Leafing off eight hundred-dollar bills, he handed them under the bar to Jordan. "You're fifty ahead, Louie."

"I'll take that as a show of confidence."

"Take it however you like. Just leave my message with Sundee, and don't screw up."

Jordan smiled. "Wouldn't stay in business very long if I was a screw-up, Wally. I'll let you know when the message has been delivered." Jordan stuffed the cash into his pocket, brushed his straw hat forward with two fingers, and headed for the now empty parking lot, with Walt Reasoner a couple of steps behind.

A year earlier, on a lark and because of the street's name, Gaylord Marquee had visited a recently renovated old home on Denver's south Gaylord Street. An enterprising East Coast–transplant architect swimming in construction-loan funds from a New

Jersey bank and wanting to get a foothold in Denver had turned the house into a tastefully done Tudor. Marquee had been so impressed with the quality of the workmanship that he'd bought the home on the spot. He'd furnished the 2,400-square-foot, six-room two-story with schoolhouse antiques, Navajo rugs, and 1930s craftsman-style furnishings that included a rare blackboard, school clock, and a couple of pupils' desks from the 1920s.

Exhausted from a busy day, Marquee was talking on the phone in the home's great room, squeezed into one of the under-sized right-armed school desks, complete with its original inkwell and the initials *PG* carved into the desktop, and twiddling a pencil as the person on the other end of the line berated him.

"I know you think that charming little accent of yours causes most people to think you're brilliant, Gaylord. But not me. I should've never gotten in bed with you or Chin. I'm getting phone calls and questions from people that I don't want to answer."

"So lie low and keep your mouth shut. Who's asking questions, anyway?"

"Cops, after all this time no less, and other people I'm tired of either dodging or holding at bay. I think it's because it's the five-year anniversary of the killings."

"I see," said Marquee.

"You don't sound surprised."

When Marquee didn't answer, his caller said, "Well, get them off my back."

"I'll do what I can."

"Do better, Gaylord. After that, you can go back to putting on airs." The caller erupted in a high pitched half grunt and slammed down the phone.

Biting back his anger, Marquee hung up as well. Rising from his chair, he walked across the room to the blackboard, picked up a piece of chalk, and printed the word *Jackass* in two-inch-high letters near the bottom of the board.

Petey Greene had had one hell of a good week. He'd sold two first-edition copies of Jack Kerouac's *On the Road* that he'd stumbled across at a Goodwill store in suburban Wheat Ridge to an eager book dealer on Denver's antiques row for a hundred and fifty dollars each. He'd found the jug wine he loved on sale for $4.99 a half gallon at Argonaut Liquors on East Colfax Avenue and bought a case of it. And best of all, he'd wrangled two snooping assignments out of his friend CJ Floyd.

Thinking that he'd be in the grapes and flush for a couple of months, Petey peeked his head above the front wheel of his moped, raised the five-hundred-dollar Bausch & Lomb binoculars he'd scored a few years earlier for thirteen dollars at a garage sale to his eyes, and sighted in on the guest-room window of Walt Reasoner's home.

Reasoner's place hadn't been all that hard to find. Petey had simply made a call to a 250-pound Denver DMV supervisor, a Latina he'd been servicing for years, and asked her to punch up Reasoner's home address and phone number for him. After a brief detour for a beer at the Satire Lounge on East Colfax, he'd dropped by Epic Produce & Meats, scoped it out, and followed Reasoner from his office to Eddy Cox's Place and then to his home. He'd jotted a few notes about the man in the straw hat that Reasoner had walked out of Eddy's Place with and had noted the license-plate numbers of both men.

Snickering softly and lowering his binoculars, he couldn't help but think how much he enjoyed playing snoop. Like collecting antiques, snooping not only took him away from the mundane, it always carried an air of excitement with it.

He'd once run down a bookmaker and loan shark for CJ, a man who'd threatened to blow up Rosie Weeks's back-room gambling establishment, the den, because it was cutting heavily into his business. Things had ultimately come to a head one snowy January afternoon when CJ had confronted the bookmaker in the parking lot of the man's bank with Petey standing scared as hell only a few feet away. With heavy wet flakes of snow falling on them all, CJ had reminded the bookmaker that he'd be wise to stop making threats. When the bookmaker had reached into his coat pocket for his .38, CJ had dropped him with a right cross so quick and violent it broke the bookmaker's upper jaw and lower denture. The fractured denture's sharp plastic edge severed an artery in the man's mouth, sending blood from the agape bookie's mouth down onto the new-fallen snow.

The thing Petey remembered most about that confrontation was the lost look on CJ's face immediately afterward. A guilty, forlorn look that as much as said, *Forgive me.*

There wouldn't be that kind of excitement tonight, Petey lamented as the lights in Reasoner's living room went out and the house turned dark. Nothing even close to it. But every job couldn't be as adrenaline-popping. Snooping, after all, was a lot like scrounging for antiques, he told himself as he slipped onto his moped. In both worlds, things tended to run hot and cold.

Chapter

🦎 15

CJ's two-hour early-morning drive from Denver to the northeastern Colorado farming and ranching community of Sterling started out calmly enough, but by the time he'd reached the South Platte River bottom town's outskirts, he found himself nervously drumming his fingers on the steering wheel of Ike's Jeep.

His upset had nothing to do with any potential confrontation he might have with Goldsby or her lover, Ramona Lepsos, or with not yet having wrapped up Willis Sundee's problem, or with the fact that he'd been pulled over for speeding and fined seventy-five dollars just ten minutes earlier. It had everything to do with his impending trip to the symphony with Mavis that evening.

The genesis of CJ's nervousness was concern that Mavis might somehow realize she was mainly a prop to add a degree of authenticity to his still incompletely thought-out plan to ambush Molly Burgess.

During his five years as a bail bondsman and frequent bounty hunter, he'd caught unsuspecting clients, cops, and even attorneys off guard—more often than not with either Rosie or Ike at his side. Most of those confrontations, however, had taken place in back alleys, bars, and seedy apartments, never at a Denver Symphony Orchestra performance, and never with a woman like Mavis in the mix.

Still drumming his fingers, he took a deep breath and turned onto the county road that led to Cheryl Goldsby's ranch. He was two miles down the gravel washboard stretch of road that dead-ended at Goldsby's when the reason for his upset finally registered completely: deep down he suspected that he was afraid of making a fool of himself at the symphony. Suddenly he had the feeling that he'd made a huge mistake. He'd picked the wrong time and place to ask Mavis to ride shotgun with him. Disgusted with himself, he slammed an open palm down onto the steering wheel and mumbled, "Damn!" just as the arched entryway to the forty-six acres that Cheryl Goldsby called Box Elder Ranch came into view.

Goldsby had been reluctant to agree to his visit when he'd talked to her on the phone the previous day, and he had the feeling she never would have consented if Ramona Lepsos hadn't bellowed in the background, clearly enough for him to hear, "Let him come, Cherie. You need to get this shit with your uncle settled once and for all."

He could only imagine that Cheryl's response, "Shut up," had sent Ramona packing since he heard no rebuttal.

As he eased the Jeep beneath the tempered-oak, sixteen-foot-high archway with the weathered "Box Elder Ranch" sign that hung from the crossbeam swinging back and forth in the wind,

CJ found himself thinking more about how he would have to put his best foot forward with Mavis that evening than about what he would ask Cheryl Goldsby.

After parking the Jeep and nearly losing his Stetson to the wind, he headed for Goldsby's modest frame ranch house, where she greeted him on the front porch with a faint "Hello."

A sandy-haired woman in her late thirties, Goldsby walked with an upright propriety that as much as said, *I'm better than you*. Her plump, cherubic face and almost triangular deep-set eyes gave her an odd jack-o'-lantern look and her thin, bony frame helped to create an eerie appearance of a pumpkin on a stick.

Taking a deep breath and wheezing asthmatically, she forced a smile and said as if she were in a rush to send CJ on his way as quickly as she could, "Let's go down to the pond and talk, Mr. Floyd."

"Lead the way," said CJ. They had never shaken hands.

"You remember Ramona, of course," she said, waving for the stocky woman with a crew cut who stood just inside the house to join them on the porch.

"Yes," said CJ as Ramona Lepsos, who looked as if she didn't really want to be there, appeared and politely shook his hand.

They walked down a hill toward a cattail-encircled pond fifty yards west of the house, with CJ clutching the Monte Vista plate in an envelope in his hand.

"As I suspect you know, Mr. Floyd, I only agreed to talk to you again because Ramona insisted." Cheryl flashed Ramona a look that was a clear reprimand. "You intruded on my grief five years ago, and now, for whatever reason, you're back. Can you tell me what gives, Mr. Floyd?"

"I'm still trying to find out who murdered your uncle."

"Sometimes it's best to let sleeping dogs lie." She stopped, flashed Lepsos a look that as much as said, *Isn't that right, Ramona?* zipped her jacket up a notch, and eyed the slate-gray sky. "We're in for a long, hard winter. Gray clouds this early in the fall always spell the way," she said, frowning. "So what's up with that new lead you mentioned on the phone, Mr. Floyd?"

CJ glanced skyward before slipping the Monte Vista plate out of its envelope. "I stumbled onto a license plate that I'm sure belonged to your uncle at a flea market yesterday. The man who sold it to me is an antique dealer. He wouldn't tell me how he got the plate."

"And what makes you so sure the license plate belonged to my Uncle Wiley?" Cheryl asked, stopping abruptly, barely looking at the plate.

"Because Wiley showed the plate to me the week he was murdered. At least, I'm pretty sure it's the same plate."

"'Pretty' is an imperfect word, Mr. Floyd. One that I suspect was dreamed up by lecherous old men. Anything more specific you can tell me about the man you bought the license plate from?"

Ramona punctuated Cheryl's response with a supportive nod.

"Not really." Deciding that it might be wise to withhold information about Gaylord Marquee for the moment, CJ slipped the Monte Vista plate back into its envelope, and tucked it under his left arm.

"How well did you know my uncle, Mr. Floyd?" Cheryl asked, walking toward the pond once again.

"Not real well. I'd only known him a couple of days or so when he was murdered."

"Good for you. Unfortunately, I knew the man all my life. Sadly, I had to live with him for the four years I was in college at the University of Denver. Economics left me no choice. My Uncle Wiley was a bitter, devious, selfish man, Mr. Floyd. You'd have learned that about him if you'd known him longer."

"He didn't seem that way to me."

"That's because you met him post-AA. I knew him before that."

Reflecting on his own uncle's alcoholism, CJ said, "A drinking problem doesn't necessarily make you a bad human being. Harry Steed says Wiley had pushed that drinking problem behind him years ago."

"Of course Steed would say that. Wiley was Steed's poster child. His gold-star reclamation. The two of them fed off one another," said Cheryl, stopping at a weather-worn wooden bench at the edge of a three-acre pond and taking a seat.

Looking up at Ramona and CJ, who remained standing, she said, "You look disappointed, Mr. Floyd. Sorry to disenchant you, but here's another tidbit for you. Those four years I lived with my uncle while I was in college were sheer hell. A swinging pendulum of erratic days, sometimes weeks, that were filled with nothing but yelling and shouting and nights that all too often ended up with me cleaning up my uncle's urine and vomit. And to top it off, he was nowhere as upstanding as you and most people believe."

"Wanna spell out how?"

Erupting into a broad smile, as if she'd been waiting for years to give her answer, Cheryl said, "He and that Chinese man who was killed with him were dealing in stolen goods. They were big-time fences, Mr. Floyd."

Puzzled as to why she hadn't mentioned that issue five years earlier and wondering whether she'd told the same story to the cops, CJ said, "It's a little late for a confessional, don't you think? Besides, I'm well aware of the hearsay. Just never seen the proof."

Cheryl sounded disgusted. "Could be the reason you're still drawing a blank all these years later is because you don't want to open your eyes to reality."

Her pensive stare had CJ suddenly second-guessing himself and the thoroughness of his initial hit-and-miss, less-than-methodical investigation of the GI Joe's murders. "Could be I missed a few things," he said ruefully.

"Real likely. So, for one reason and one reason only, I'm going to help you with what you might have overlooked. That reason being that I don't want you coming back out here to my ranch ever again." Pointing toward a dilapidated shed fifteen yards away and up a slight incline, she rose, eyed Ramona as if for some reason she needed her approval to proceed, and said, "There's something I want you to see." She flashed Ramona a look that said, *You're the one who wanted closure here,* and headed for the shed as CJ and Ramona trailed after her.

A few steps from the shed, she pulled a key ring out of her pocket and fumbled with a half-dozen keys before finding the one she needed and slipping it into the door's lock.

A wave of dust and mildew wafted up to greet them as she pushed the door open and flipped on a nearby light switch. The uneven earthen floor was moist, with just enough pond seepage to make it slippery. "Watch your step; it's easy to slip and fall in here," she warned CJ as she waved for him and Ramona to follow her in.

The shed's only window sat cockeyed in a west-facing wall, covered with plastic that let in a fuzzy square of light. The light seemed to settle on a drab green chest that CJ recognized immediately as Wiley Ames's army footlocker.

With her key ring dangling from a pinkie, Cheryl walked over to the footlocker, brushed away a curtain of cobwebs, unlocked it, and flipped the top back. Slipping aside the army blanket covering the contents, she said, "Have a look, Mr. Floyd. Go ahead, pick one up and examine it."

CJ stooped down and with a puzzled expression picked up the largest seashell in three rows that ran parallel along the length of the footlocker.

"You picked a good one. A Cooper's nutmeg." Taking in the look of puzzlement on CJ's face, she continued, "Exceptionally clean and exquisitely ornamental. You're looking at the exoskeleton of a mollusk, Mr. Floyd. There was once a living, breathing animal inside that shell—a snail. They're quite adaptive creatures. The one that lived in that particular shell was capable of burrowing beneath resting angel sharks and sucking their blood. Kind of ghoulish, isn't it?" she said, laughing. She gingerly moved aside the first layer of shells, which rested on a blanket, to reveal a second layer resting on another blanket. "There are lots more shells here to have a look at. Shells with nobs and ribs and teeth. Shells that scientists once thought could only be found in the belly of a bottom-feeding fish. Shells that are worth a considerable amount of money, in fact."

"Quite an impressive amount of seashell knowledge," said CJ, placing the Cooper's nutmeg shell back among the others. "Where'd it all bubble up from?"

"From a lifetime of study. I grew up on the California coast. Lots of shells to play among. And along the way, I picked up a PhD in marine biology."

"So I'm guessing you think these seashells are somehow connected to your uncle's death?"

"In one way or another, yes. Ramona finished up her PhD at UC Santa Barbara the same year I did. My parents died in a car wreck my final semester of high school, and my Uncle Wiley paid for my schooling afterward. I think that in one way or another, he expected to be repaid. And he was. Ramona and I repaid him with our knowledge of seashells. Shells that he bought and sold on what you'd describe as the black market. Shells that his associate Quan Lee Chin, in his travels with various symphonies here and abroad, pilfered from dealers, shops, museums in Thailand, and collectors." Noting the look of

amazement on CJ's face, she boastfully said, "As with most collectibles, Mr. Floyd, you have to know what you're looking at.
Ramona and I did.

"The most valuable shells were the ones they stole from
museums. A single seashell can easily be worth a thousand dollars." She picked up the nutmeg. "Gather yourself fifty of these
little puppies and you've got yourself fifty thousand dollars'
worth of inventory. There're close to fifty shells in this footlocker, Mr. Floyd. You do the math."

"Real money, as they say. And of course you've never told
the cops about your uncle's criminal dealings?"

"Why would I? And where's the proof they were acquired
in any way that was criminal? The inventory has always been
stored out here on the ranch with me. Wiley only took shells
with him—and never more than three or four at a time—if he
had a sale pending in Denver."

"Telling the cops what you're telling me might have helped
them find his killer."

The look on Cheryl's face hardened. "Perhaps. But somehow, you still seem to be missing the point. Let me spell it out
a little more clearly for you. I didn't much care for my uncle.
He reminded me without fail, each and every time I saw him
after I moved out here, that he paid for my schooling so I could
become somebody respectable, and instead I turned out to be an
overeducated dyke. I hated him, Mr. Floyd, with a passion you
can't possibly understand."

"Maybe not, but it seems that the man you have so much
disdain for left you one hell of a bequest."

"Who else could he have possibly left anything to? I was his only family."

"The shells' real owners, perhaps?"

"No more cat-and-mouse, Mr. Floyd, okay? The footlocker's contents are mine. Passed on to me by virtue of the fact that they've always been here on this property and in my possession, not my uncle's. The contents are mine to do with as I please. I've only shown them to you because you're not a cop, we're five years down the road from my uncle's murder, which hasn't tainted me in any fashion, no one can possibly prove the shells aren't mine, and Ramona asked me to wipe the slate clean."

CJ shook his head. Based on their long-past initial meeting, he never would have expected that the then despondent look-ing Cheryl Goldsby had cared so little for her uncle. Thinking, *Missed by a mile,* he asked, "Anything else in the footlocker besides seashells?"

"Just about everything that was there in that footlocker when my uncle died, aside from the shells, which I placed inside myself, is still there. I haven't removed very much. You might call it my retirement plan. This and the boxes of less valuable stuff Ramona and I hauled out here from GI Joe's and my uncle's condo."

"Mind if I have a closer look?" CJ asked, setting his Monte Vista plate aside on a footstool.

"After I take out the shells. I wouldn't want any damage coming to my inheritance." Cheryl knelt and carefully removed forty-eight seashells, aligning them in rows of eight on a blan-ket on the floor. She then took two tobacco tins and a porcelain license plate from the footlocker and handed them to CJ. "Not quite my taste," she said, dusting off her hands. "But I know that all three things are reasonably valuable." She continued sorting through the contents.

CJ held the low-numbered, mint-condition 1920 Nevada plate up to the muted light. "The plate's worth a hundred and fifty to a hundred and seventy-five bucks. The tobacco tins maybe a hundred each."

Seemingly unconcerned with the value, Cheryl was almost to the bottom of the footlocker when CJ asked, "Did Wiley or Chin have any special buyers or sellers they dealt with?"

"I never knew." She handed CJ a license plate wrapped in tissue paper.

"Ever hear him mention an Englishman named Gaylord Marquee?"

Cheryl stopped what she was doing and stared thoughtfully at CJ as he unwrapped the plate. A look of recognition crossed her face. "I never knew him or what his name was, but Wiley did do business with a man who could have been English. He used to come by Wiley's condo when I was in college. An odd-looking man with badly yellowed teeth. I'm almost sure his accent was British."

"That would have been Marquee." CJ glanced toward the footstool. "He's the one who sold me that license plate."

"Then maybe he's the one who killed my uncle."

"Perhaps," said CJ, peeling back a final layer of tissue paper and realizing that he was holding a 1913, nearly mint-condition first-of-state South Dakota license plate in his hands. Trying to peg the rare plate's value, he said, "Good value here. Is that about it?"

"Yes." Cheryl ran a hand along the bottom of the chest to make certain. Watching CJ continue to examine the license plate, she asked, "So that one's pretty special, you think?"

"It's pretty rare."

"What's it worth?"

"I'm not sure. Seven, maybe eight hundred bucks," said CJ, suspecting by the smug look on Cheryl's face that she likely already knew the plate's value.

Looking pleased, Cheryl winked at Ramona.

"What did you do with the rest of Wiley's stuff?"

"Sold it. Gave it away to Goodwill. Most of it was junk."

"Hope you were right in your assessment," said CJ, laying the South Dakota plate back down in the footlocker after wrapping it in tissue paper. "How long's it been since you saw Marquee?"

"Fifteen years, at least, if in fact we're talking about the same man." She took a step back from the chest and locked eyes with CJ. "Do you really think he might've killed my uncle and that Chinese man?"

"Like I said before, perhaps," CJ said, retrieving the envelope with the Monte Vista plate.

Carefully placing the footlocker's contents back in place, she asked, "Can you find him?"

"I hope so," said CJ, still uncertain as to why Cheryl Goldsby had let him in on her secrets and puzzled even more as to why Ramona, the person who'd urged her to do so, had been so quiet. "It's real likely that you could lose what's in that foot-locker if I find your uncle's killer and the contents turn out to have been stolen."

"If and when you do that, what's in this trunk will have been sold, Mr. Floyd. And if not, holding on to what's mine is really my problem, not yours, isn't it?"

Placing the last of the seashells back in the footlocker and closing it, she said, "We're done here. I've eased my conscience, complied with Ramona's wishes, and let you feast your eyes on a few rare treasures. I don't expect we'll be seeing each other again, sir."

"Unless it's at a murder trial. Hope we're both on the same side of the table then."

Ignoring the inference, Cheryl snapped the lock on the foot-locker closed. "Ramona and I will walk you back to your vehi-cle, and just so you're aware, in case you get any ideas about coming back for an unannounced visit, we're armed to the teeth out here, Mr. Floyd."

"So you'd shoot me and think nothing of it?"

"Absolutely," said Cheryl, her eyes fixed coldly on CJ's. "Absolutely," she reiterated, glancing at Ramona, who was nodding in agreement like a puppet whose every string was being pulled by her puppeteer.

Chapter

16

CJ's trip back to Denver took a full three hours and had him knifing the Jeep into forty-five-mile-per-hour crosswinds strong enough to have overturned a semi loaded with sugar beets on a desolate stretch of I-76 between Sterling and the town of Brush.

Inching past a flagman and three state patrol cars before finally reaching the sprawled-out tractor-trailer with its eighteen wheels poking up like stubby rubber feet, CJ found himself trying to size up Cheryl Goldsby. She clearly wasn't the sad, dutiful, grief-stricken niece. Nor was she the loving, grateful recipient of her uncle's generous bequest. What she was was a calculating, bitter woman who, by virtue of a little luck and her bloodline, had squirreled away a nice little windfall. She'd played cat-and-mouse with him the whole time he'd been at her ranch, no question about that, inferring one moment that she wanted her uncle's killer caught and suggesting the next that she couldn't care less and might in fact be the killer herself.

She certainly wasn't an antique collector in the truest sense, and he still couldn't figure out why she'd agreed to his visit other than apparently to appease her lover. No matter. He intended to check both Goldsby and Lepsos out from stem to stern and determine whether Cheryl's little footlocker of treasures had been incentive enough for either woman to kill Ames and Chin.

Moving past the wreckage, CJ found himself wondering whether Ames had left behind other footlockers full of valuables, and whether he might have been not merely his niece's benefactor but also her fencing partner.

What he needed to do was dig a little deeper into what Ames had left behind, and if there was anyone who might know the true value of Wiley Ames's estate, it would be Harry Steed. Although Steed had always been pretty closemouthed about Ames, seemingly wanting to be loyal to his friend's sympathetic image, CJ suspected that if pressed, Steed would be more forthcoming.

Picking up speed and watching snow clouds gather to the west, he settled on a game plan. He'd talk to Harry about Cheryl Goldsby and Ramona Lepsos the next morning, get Harry's take on just how big a fencing operation Ames and Chin might have been spearheading, determine whether Ames might have left behind a larger estate in the way of additional footlockers, and then, with Petey Greene's help, move on to Gaylord Marquee.

As he sped past Brush, he decided that the rest of the day belonged to Willis and Mavis Sundee. He'd bought a new Stetson, vest, and sport coat for his symphony outing that evening, which he needed to pick up on the way home, and he had Petey Greene and a less-than-eager Rosie Weeks staking out Mae's

Louisiana Kitchen for any sign of Walt Reasoner. With the feeling that he'd covered his bases, he accelerated into the stiff southeasterly wind and turned up the Jeep's radio, not to the sounds of Motown but to eastern plains Colorado country western.

For Petey Greene, everything was coming up roses. He had the lowdown on both Walt Reasoner and the water buffalo Reasoner used to do his persuading, and now he had a potential lead on a connection between Gaylord Marquee and Quan Lee Chin. The information had cost him every cent of the money CJ had paid him up front, and that was the reason he was sitting in Ike Floyd's office, slouched down in one of Ike's sawed-off chairs, asking for money while Ike stared down at him from behind his desk.

"Hell, Ike. Everybody knows you and CJ work hand in hand. I ain't askin' for nothin' but a C-note."

"You're workin' for CJ, Petey, not me." Ike erupted in a series of violent coughs that prompted Petey to cover his mouth and nose with a hand.

"Shit, man. You got the flu?"

"No. Just somethin' in my chest."

"Well, if I was you I'd get myself checked out." Petey tentatively lowered his hand. "Especially with what looks like an early winter movin' in. Weatherman says tonight it's gonna snow."

Reaching across his desk for a half-full glass of water and taking a long, slow swallow, Ike said, "I'll do that, Petey."

"I ain't shittin' you about seein' a doctor, man. You sound like an engine that's thrown a piston. I had a cousin who put off about seein'—"

CJ poked his head in the door, a garment bag slung over his right shoulder, and interrupted. "Didn't know you were talking to a client, Unc. Sorry."

Ike suppressed a cough. "No client, just Petey. He's lookin' to get paid for some surveillance you got him doin'. What's up?"

"He's helping me with that problem I told you Willis was having."

"And the Ames case," Petey added eagerly.

"Yeah, that, too."

Eyeing CJ's garment bag and smiling, Ike said, "Well, before you head out to the symphony with Mavis, you best square up with Petey. I already told him I ain't the one payin'."

Petey let out a wolf whistle and rolled his eyes. "Mavis Sundee, shit, CJ, you're minin' gold."

"And if he don't watch out, some of the slag's gonna come crashin' down on his head. You got too many balls in the air, CJ," Ike said, erupting in a new series of coughs.

Adjusting his garment bag, CJ said, "We've got it handled, don't we, Petey?"

"Sure do," Petey shot back. "I got the lowdown on both of them bohunks you've had me trailin', Reasoner and Marquee." Sounding as if he were reciting a long-remembered poem, Petey said, "Reasoner's pretty much all show and no go. Likes to intimidate people when he can but hires out his dirty work.

Mostly to a North Denver strong-arm wannabe mobster named Louie Jordan. Now get this: Jordan likes to go by the name Detroit Whitey." Petey erupted in laughter.

"I wouldn't be so quick to laugh, Petey," said Ike. "I've heard of Jordan. He's a thickhead out of Croatia. Word is, he'll kill you for sport."

"Go on, Petey," said CJ, irritated by Ike's unsolicited counsel.

"Okay. Word I got, and I did some serious diggin' here, is that Whitey or Jordan or whatever the hell he calls himself has knocked a few heads and even burned down several buildings for Reasoner. Got a heads-up on where both Reasoner and Whitey live from a woman I know down at DMV, and I called Rosie like you told me for backup this evenin'."

"You've got Rosie in on this, too?" Ike said, shaking his head. "If Etta Lee finds out, she'll brain the both of you."

"She won't. The job's just short term. We'll have Reasoner in his place by tomorrow, or the next day at the latest."

Erupting out of his chair, Ike said, "Goddamn it, CJ, you're screwin' with Teamsters and longshoreman types here. The kind that don't mind bustin' a few kneecaps or puttin' a hole in your head."

"Reasoner's got no mob connections I could find," CJ protested.

"If Jordan's involved, it's the closest thing to it. After five years in this business, I'd'a thought you might've learned some things." Gasping for air, Ike wheezed and shook his head. "Let me make some phone calls and see if I can't get this fuckin' freight train you've got rollin' from jumpin' the tracks."

"I can handle things."

"My ass you can!"

"Who are you calling?" CJ asked with a hint of acquiescence in his tone.

"Some people who might be able to get your twenty-five-year-old, know-it-all ass out of a sling. Now, you and Petey get your butts outa here, okay?"

When Ike reached for the phone and broke into a new series of violent coughs, CJ realized that his uncle's brow was peppered with sweat. "Did you go to the doctor like I told you to?"

"Goin' tomorrow," Ike choked out. "Now get the shit outa here before I brain ya both."

Adjusting his grip on the garment bag, CJ nodded for Petey to follow him.

When they reached the small front office where Marguerite Larkin had spent the morning interviewing secretarial prospects to replace Nordeen Mapson, Marguerite looked up and adjusted a stack of papers on the desk. "I heard the temperature rising back in Ike's office, CJ. What gives?"

CJ shrugged. "Nothing. Just a little disagreement about the way I'm handling a case. Sometimes I believe Ike thinks I'm still a kid."

"In some ways you still are," Marguerite said boldly. "Did you ask him if he went to the doctor?"

"He said he's going tomorrow."

"Two pigheads," Marguerite muttered softly.

"What?"

"Nothing." Marguerite rose purposefully from her chair and

headed for Ike's office. "I'm takin' your uncle to the doctor right this second, whether he likes it or not. Lock up for me, okay?"

When the door to Ike's office slammed and CJ heard Marguerite yell, "Ike Floyd!" he knew his uncle was in for a battle he wasn't going to win.

Fifteen minutes later, Petey Greene sat across from CJ at CJ's kitchen table, nursing a beer and watching the first wet snowflakes of fall land on the fire-escape railing outside. "That Marguerite don't take no prisoners. She had Ike bundled up and outa here for the doctor's in less time than it takes for me to satisfy one of my women," Petey said with a wink, admiring CJ's new Stetson, which hung on a wall hook nearby.

CJ eyed the five-foot-seven-inch wisp of a would-be ladies' man and smiled. "She can be a force."

"Tell me about it. Hear tell she's fightin' with the parole board about them wantin' to reevaluate Nobby Pittman's sentence. On her own, without no lawyer."

"You wouldn't want to cross her," CJ said, nudging his barely touched beer aside. Suddenly all business, he asked, "So what's the lowdown on Gaylord Marquee, Petey?"

"Hell, I got more on him than on Reasoner," Petey said, beaming. "'Course I've known the man a while longer. Here's the dope. He's been here in the States for about eighteen years, accordin' to the old guy who owns Ploughshares Antiques over on South Broadway. I've known him for about half that time. Never had any dealin's with him that weren't on the up and up, but Thirsty, the guy from Ploughshares, claims that Marquee's been in on some transactions he knows about that teetered on the edge of bein' legal."

"Like what?"

"Thirsty told me Marquee tried to sell him some Indian artifacts a few years back that he was positive were stolen from Mesa Verde—you know, those Indian ruins down in the southwest part of the state where Colorado, New Mexico, Arizona, and Utah all meet up."

"Yeah. Near Four Corners." CJ slipped a box of cheroots out of his shirt pocket, tapped out one of the miniature cigars, and lit it.

"How can you smoke them things, man? They smell like burnin' cowshit."

CJ shrugged. "Just a habit I brought back from a place where some folks were trying their best to blow my head off." He took a long, slow drag on the cheroot and blew a smoke ring. "Bad habits can be hard to break, Petey."

"Guess they can be." Petey scrunched up his nose. "Anyway, ol' Thirsty didn't bite on that Indian stuff Marquee was sellin', and when a guy down in Colorado Springs finally did, he ended up gettin' busted. Cost him ten thousand bucks and a suspended sixty days in jail. And you know what? He never ratted out Marquee. Thirsty thinks it was because Marquee either shelled out the money for his fine or they had themselves a bunch of other bigger transactions waitin' in the hopper. You still thinkin' that license plate you bought off Marquee was hot?"

"More than likely."

"So what's your plan? You gonna bust Marquee?"

"I'm not sure yet," said CJ, mulling over his options. "What else have you got on Marquee?"

"Not much. He likes dogs. Used to breed, in fact. I'm surprised he didn't have one of 'em with him at the flea market the other day. Pit bulls. Mean, snarly sons of bitches."

"Anything else?"

Petey took a sip of beer. "He likes classical music. Usually has it blarin' when he's at the flea market. Now, that's a second strange thing. Wasn't no music neither the other day."

CJ's eyes lit up. "Well, well, well. A classical music lover. Hell of a good thing to know."

"You onto somethin' with the music, CJ?"

"Maybe, maybe not. I'll just have to see."

"You gonna bust in on Marquee later at his house?"

"Nope. Just going to the symphony."

"Oh, yeah. Just you and Mavis. How the hell'd a junkyard dog like you pull that off?"

"I wowed her with my charm," CJ said, winking.

"Well, if you did, you need to package it up and sell it, my man."

CJ laughed. "I'll work on that. In the meantime, I need a few other things from you, Petey."

"Shoot."

"I'll need Marquee's home phone number, his address, and the phone number of that antiques dealer friend of yours, Thirsty."

"No problem." Petey slipped a grease-stained slip of paper

out of his pocket and began writing. After jotting down Marquee's address and phone number and the phone number of Ploughshares Antiques, he looked up. "I'm needin' somethin', too, CJ."

"Yeah, I know." CJ fished his wallet out of his back pocket.

"You read my mind."

"What do I owe you?"

"Two hundred even."

"Damn, Petey. You're gonna break me."

"Maybe. But just think of what a broke-assed man like you's gonna have waitin' for him after the symphony this evenin'. That is, if you play your cards right. Shit, I'd give up the two hundred on the spot for a chance at somethin' like that." Noticing the frown on CJ's face, Petey added, "Damn, CJ. I didn't mean no offense to Mavis."

"None taken."

"Well, you're sure as hell eyein' me like Mavis has pretty much snatched your mind."

CJ counted four fifties out onto the table, most of the up-front money Willis Sundee had paid him for the Reasoner assignment. "Thanks for the info."

"No problem." Petey scooped up the bills, folded them in half, and shoved them into a pants pocket. He was up out of his chair and moving toward the door the next instant. "One last thing. I'd watch out for them dogs of Marquee's if you go after him. They're pretty damn vicious."

"I'll keep an eye out."

"I'd do more than that. I'd have me some heat around if I was you to slow 'em down." Petey swung the kitchen door open to a blast of cold air and snow. "Hope you score big this evenin', man."

"I intend to," said CJ, thinking more about the information he hoped to coax out of Molly Burgess than scoring with Mavis.

"Now, that's the lady-killer I know," Petey said, closing the door.

"Yeah," CJ said, glancing across the room toward his new Stetson and sport coat and hoping that his plan to mix business with pleasure didn't turn out to be one big mistake.

Chapter

🦎 17

Back from the doctor and the pharmacy with a ten-ounce bottle of cough suppressant and an appointment for chest X-rays the next morning, Ike answered the phone in his office, where he, CJ, and Marguerite had just finished looking over the only three applications they'd received for the secretarial position. "Hell, I might as well'a kept Nordeen," Ike grumbled, eyes rolling. "Can't read half the chicken scratch on these apps." He slammed the applications down on the table, eyed Marguerite while shaking his head, and barked into the receiver, "Floyds Bail Bonds."

When Ramona Lepsos said, "I'd like to speak to CJ Floyd," Ike mumbled, "It's for you," handed CJ the phone, and went back to pouting.

Adjusting the receiver against his ear, CJ said, "CJ here."

"This is Ramona Lepsos, Mr. Floyd. I wasn't sure if you'd gotten back to Denver. Glad I caught you. When you were here earlier today, I ..." Lepsos's voice trailed off to a whisper.

"I can barely hear you," CJ said, crossing his lips with an index finger and nodding for Ike and Marguerite to remain silent.

"What I want you to know," Lepsos continued, almost as softly as before, "is that those seashells Cheryl showed you would never have ended up in her uncle's possession without her help."

"Stolen?"

"You bet. She has the kind of connections you need to move that kind of stuff."

"Why tell me about it now?"

"Because I couldn't very well tell you with Cheryl standing right there. Besides, she only showed you what was in that footlocker in order to get me to stop riding her about something that could very well tie her to a double murder. It's always made me nervous having the footlocker around."

"Strange tactic on her part. Seems to me anybody seeing the contents of that footlocker would move her to the top of their list of suspects. Me included."

"It's a little odd, the way she looks at things, Mr. Floyd. And what she didn't tell you is that she inherited a lot more from Wiley Ames than what you saw at the ranch this morning. She's been selling the stuff off for years. And that man you mentioned, Gaylord Marquee? She lied about him, too. She knows Marquee, all right. Over the years he's helped her peddle tons of her uncle's stuff. I'd be willing to bet she's up a good seventy or eighty thousand dollars from selling off Wiley's shit."

"Sorta puts a new slant on things. Why so confessional all of a sudden, Ramona? You barely said a word when I was there at the ranch."

"Because Cheryl and I are through. Things pretty much ended for us an hour or so after you left. Answer enough for you?"

"It's an answer."

"And it's my final one on the issue. We're dealing with a lying, vicious, vindictive woman here, and one hell of an actress to boot." Ramona's voice cracked as she continued, "I thought she loved me. Boy, was I the fool. You know who she really loves? Herself. Cheryl Goldsby and nobody else. I'd watch my back if I were you, if you're planning to continue looking into those GI Joe's killings."

"Do you think . . . ?" Suddenly CJ was listening to a dial tone. "Damn," he grumbled, cradling the receiver and looking confused.

"What's up?" asked Ike, taking in CJ's puzzled look.

"Looks like my trip to Sterling today is already paying dividends. That was a woman I talked to this morning calling with a lead on the GI Joe's murders."

"Who is she?"

"A woman scorned, and like they say, hell hath no fury." Thoughtfully rubbing the barely visible cleft in his chin, CJ said, "Guess maybe I should fill you in."

"Guess you should," said Ike, suppressing a cough before rising and walking Marguerite to the door. "Skim off your pick of the litter from our slush pile and call her," he said, handing Marguerite the applications.

"Okay, but . . ."

"Just do it, Marguerite, okay?"

Shaking her head, Marguerite walked away without a response.

"Think we'll find a replacement for Nordeen?" CJ asked, watching Marguerite head down the hallway toward what had been Nordeen's desk.

"Let's save the issue for later." Ike rolled his eyes. "Now, tell me what happened up in Sterling."

CJ spent the next fifteen minutes bringing Ike up to speed on what had happened in Sterling and where he was with the Wiley Ames murder case, finally filling him in on what he suspected was the real murder motive and sharing his list of suspects. Ike coughed on and off the whole time.

Watching Ike run the information he'd given him through his head, his eyes dancing constantly as if they were connected to some number-crunching computer, CJ finished his summary and asked, "Anything you think I might've missed?"

"It's not what you missed. It's what you glossed over. Let's start out with the Goldsby woman. Why the hell would she agree after all this time to talk to you?"

"To get me to close the book on her uncle's murder and get me to thinking that her trunkful of supposedly legitimately inherited goodies, appreciating by the day, more than likely takes her off the hook for killing Ames."

"I don't think so. Besides, who's to say she didn't kill Ames and Chin for the stuff in that trunk in the first place? And suppose you hadn't bought into her little setup? Suppose you'd flat-out called her a manipulating liar from the start, like that girlfriend she just dumped did?"

"I'm thinking she would've run me off the place in nothing flat."

"Yep. And sent you scurryin' back to Denver with the idea planted firm in your head that she had somethin' to hide."

"Which I still believe," said CJ, slightly taken aback.

"So she miscalculated. Could be she's coverin' for somebody else."

"Who?"

"Her girlfriend, Ramona, or ex-girlfriend, it sounds like now. Who's to say she's bein' straight with you anyway? Did they look like a couple of lovers who were in the midst of a spat when you were there?"

"Not really."

"So maybe the Lepsos woman killed Ames and that Chinese fellow at Goldsby's directive?"

"Damn, Unc. You're stirring the hell out of the pot here."

"And if you ask me, it needs a bunch more stirrin'."

"So what should I do?"

"Dig deeper than the surface, like you've been doin'. Find out more about anyone within an eyelash of a connection to those killin's, and dog the shit outa them. Goldsby, Lepsos, your friend the pawnshop owner, Steed, and the English guy, Marquee, who sold you that license plate yesterday."

"Marquee's not a problem. I've got Petey Greene latched on to him, and Steed I'll talk to myself. But there is one person I haven't been able to connect with. A woman named Molly Burgess. She's a concert cellist who's given me the runaround for years."

"Then maybe you should let somebody else do the chasin'. Sounds to me like she's got your scent. Make her have to sniff out another one."

"Are you up for running her down?"

"Nope," Ike said, rising and wheezing like an asthmatic as he got out of his chair. "But I'm bettin' that for a couple of old General Grants, Petey Greene would give it a whirl."

Happy that Ike had offered him an alternative to confronting Molly Burgess that evening, CJ smiled and said, "I'm betting he would, too."

Looking concerned, Ike said, "Just make sure Petey don't turn himself into a batterin' ram when it's just a crowbar that's needed. Gotta watch Petey, CJ. He's got a healthy taste of little man's syndrome."

"I'll tell him to tread lightly when it comes to Burgess."

"Do me one better," Ike said with a wink, walking to the doorway in response to Marguerite's call from the other room. "Tell him to flat-out back off on any confrontation with the women if the setup ain't right. He needs to remember he's a man."

CJ offered an acquiescent nod and watched Ike hobble out of the room, suspecting that Marguerite's call of frustration couldn't possibly bode well for their secretarial search and realizing that when it came to the art of investigation, he had one hell of a lot to learn.

Twenty minutes later, he was on the phone making sure that Rosie was set to stake out Mae's Louisiana Kitchen and keep his eye out for any Walt Reasoner sightings. After giving Rosie instructions to page him on the pager he'd rented for the evening if anything unexpected happened, he checked in with Petey Greene to find out if all was quiet on the Walt Reasoner front and offer Petey the assignment of running down the elusive Molly Burgess.

Petey agreed happily. An hour later, all Petey could think about after scoping out the Epic Produce & Meats offices, which had looked to him to be dead for the weekend, was heading over to stake out Gaylord Marquee's. He thought that at the rate CJ was passing out money, he'd be set with whores for a month.

When he called CJ to tell him that he'd spotted a woman in a pickup parked in front of Marquee's house, slumped down behind her steering wheel and looking nervous, CJ sounded pleased. When Petey added that the woman was a melon head with sandy hair and funny shaped eyes, an elated CJ yelled, "Jackpot!"

Twenty minutes later, when he called CJ back from a pay phone outside a 7-Eleven to tell him that Marquee had come home, greeted the woman affectionately, and hustled her into his house, Petey could hear cash registers ringing. When he finally asked, "Who was she?" and CJ laughingly told him, "A woman who owns a ranch and a bunch of seashells," Petey simply said, "Oh."

A few minutes after Petey's second call, CJ came downstairs to Ike's office from his apartment, using the inside stairs. He was wearing his new blue blazer, gray slacks, and spit-shined boots and nervously twirling his Stetson in his right hand. He'd wrapped up his final business for the day but remained disappointed that he hadn't been able to set up a meeting with Harry Steed for the next morning. After four failed attempts to reach

Steed by phone, he decided to scrub the meeting that he'd hoped would give him additional insight into Cheryl Goldsby and what besides a footlocker full of treasures she might have garnered as the sole beneficiary of Wiley Ames's estate. He almost failed to notice Ike, who appeared out of nowhere from the darkened dining room, humming, "Dum da dum dum."

CJ broke into a broad smile.

"You know it's snowin' outside, don't ya?"

"Yeah."

"Where the hell's your coat?"

"In the Bel Air."

"Guess maybe you don't really need no coat when you've got somebody as fine as Mavis Sundee hangin' on your arm. Word'll be all over Five Points by mornin' that the two of you were out at the symphony."

"Like they say, gossip and bad news always travel fast."

"It's the way of the world," Ike said with a shrug and a parting cough. "Have a good time, and give Mr. Beethoven my best."

"I'll do that," said CJ, opening the front door and heading out into the snow, leaving behind footprints nearly as deep as the grin on Ike Floyd's face.

That wet, heavy, first-of-the-season snow had intensified by the time CJ reached Mavis's house, and when they arrived at Denver's Auditorium Theater a little past seven, three inches of snow had fallen. All the way to the concert hall, CJ tried his best to remember what he'd learned in high school about

Beethoven, but all he could dredge up was that the famous composer had been a long-haired deaf musical genius.

The fact that the programs he and Mavis were handed on their way to their seats summarized Beethoven's life and career in a single page made him feel even more inept. Mavis, who, except for a single strand of pearls, was dressed elegantly in black from head to toe, seemed as comfortable as if she went to the symphony every week.

Once seated, CJ thumbed through the program and felt a strange sense of relief. When he scanned the orchestra's musicians for Molly Burgess, spotting the second-seat cellist who with one leg shorter than the other limped to her seat, he couldn't help but think that the small-boned, red-haired musician looked almost childlike. He could have sworn when she glanced briefly up toward his section and her eyes moved past him that there was a hint of recognition on her face, but he couldn't be certain.

When Mavis leaned over and said, "The cellist seems to have caught your eye," a lump formed in his throat.

Trying his best to look neither embarrassed or guilty, he said, "Just watching her get adjusted."

"The secondary strings are pretty insignificant in the music they've chosen for tonight, anyway. The primary strings and the percussionist are the musicians to watch."

"I'll keep my eyes peeled," CJ said, turning his attention from Burgess to the orchestra's semicircle of kettle drums.

Nervously drumming his fingers on the cover of his program, CJ found himself staring at Mavis as she searched through her clutch for lip gloss and wondering what on earth had possessed him to bring her along on what was essentially no more than a stakeout. Drinking in the glow of her flawless dark-olive skin and the graceful arch of her neck, he all but blurted out, "Mistake."

"Something the matter?" Mavis asked, catching him in midstare.

"Nope. It's just that for a second there, I had this fleeting image of beauty being forced to spend a night trapped with the beast."

"If you are referring to us, CJ Floyd, I'm not trapped anywhere. I'm here because I want to be, and hopefully so are you."

Before he could respond, applause interrupted as the first-chair violinist walked across the stage toward his chair. "I absolutely am," CJ said, loudly enough that the man seated next to him favored him with a reprimanding stare.

He and Mavis didn't say anything more to one another until the conductor, greeted with thunderous applause, stepped up onto the podium and raised his baton.

"Watch the violins and the drums," said Mavis, winking at CJ as the baton fell.

All CJ could think of as he and Mavis wove their way through the exiting shoulder-to-shoulder crowd after the concert was how much energy had been on display during the hour-and-a-half performance. Mavis had been right. Beethoven's Eighth Symphony in particular, the evening's featured piece, had kettle drums, strings, and tuba playing galore. Ike, it turned out, had been right on all counts, too. Any plan to ambush Molly Burgess, with or without Mavis in tow, would have been a bad idea. Watching Mavis shiver and at the same time look excitingly vampish with her coat collar turned all the way up, he locked a supportive arm in hers as they stepped outside in twenty-degree temperature and six inches of fresh snow. Thinking, *Molly Burgess be damned,* he admired how beautiful Mavis looked against the backdrop of snow.

"Goodness," Mavis gasped as a blast of frigid air greeted them at the corner of Fourteenth and Curtis Streets.

By the time they'd reached the Bel Air, Mavis's teeth were chattering. As CJ cranked the engine, she said, "You looked preoccupied all night, CJ. Were you looking for someone?"

Surprised by Mavis's astuteness and uncertain what to say, he said, "Remember that cellist I was staring at before the concert started?"

"Yes."

"I think she's linked to a friend of mine's murder."

Mavis's simple, matter-of-fact "Why so?" caught CJ by surprise. He dusted the snow off the brim of his Stetson and placed it on the back seat. "Because she knew a second guy who was killed along with my friend, and she's been dodging me for a long time." The Bel Air fishtailed briefly as they reached the icy northern edge of the Fourteenth Street parking lot.

"If your problem's that she keeps dodging you, why not try to catch her before she comes to work? That would be better than trying to intercept her after a performance, don't you think?"

Feeling embarrassed and suspecting that Mavis recognized that she'd been at least partially a prop for the evening, he said, "Yeah," followed quickly by, "Did you enjoy yourself?"

"Absolutely."

"Then we'll do it again," said CJ, inhaling the scent of her perfume in the chilly air as the twenty-year-old classic Chevy struggled to heat up.

"I hope so."

He'd eased into the slow-moving postsymphony traffic on Fourteenth Street when his pager went off. He slipped it off his belt, punched the pager's backlight, and recognized the incoming phone number on the tiny screen as that of Rosie's Garage. Having left Rosie with instructions not to page him unless it was an emergency, CJ swallowed hard.

"Pretty late page," said Mavis.

"Yeah. It's Rosie. He's calling me from the garage. I'd better get to a phone and call him."

"Emergency?"

"Let's hope not."

The look of concern on CJ's face told Mavis that he wasn't being totally truthful. "Why don't we just head straight there? It's only a few blocks over to Welton, and from there it's a straight shot to the garage."

Heeding Mavis's advice, CJ made a quick left and headed for Welton Street without responding, thinking as he accelerated, *Educated, beautiful, and insightful to boot—damn, am I out of my league.*

In the six-and-a-half minutes it took to get to Rosie's Garage, the snow never let up. When the Bel Air finally slid to a stop in front of one of Rosie's service bays and CJ partially rolled down his window, Mavis let out a silent sigh. Their fishtailing trip from the symphony had been alarming, but it was the determined, slightly fearful, wide-eyed look on CJ's face—a look she hadn't seen there since the early months of his return from Vietnam—that had her worried.

Within seconds, Rosie came rushing out of the garage with his Colorado State University hooded sweatshirt tugging at his belly and a watch cap in hand. "We need to haul ass over to Mae's this second," he yelled. "Some SOB's been nosin' around in the alley back'a the place for a good fifteen minutes. I left Petey standin' watch while I came and paged you. Hope to hell I didn't make a mistake, leavin' him there on his own."

Realizing only as he peered through the Bel Air's fogged-up windows that Mavis was in the front seat with CJ, Rosie said, "Mavis, didn't know you were there."

Her voice rising, Mavis asked, "What the heck's going on at Mae's, CJ?"

"Something that could turn ugly. You need to stay here."

"The hell I will."

"CJ, we need to move it!" Rosie hollered.

In one quick, fluid motion, Mavis, a former high school gymnast, was over the front seat and into the back seat. "Rosie, get in!" With her face just inches from CJ's, she shouted, "Let's go!"

Feeling Mavis's warm breath on his neck, CJ muttered, "Damn," and took off with Rosie still trying to adjust his girth in the front seat. Two minutes later, the Bel Air's headlights and engine off, CJ coasted to within twenty yards of the west entrance of the block-long alley behind Mae's.

"Hope Petey's still holdin' down the fort," Rosie whispered.

"You and me both," said CJ, looking up at the streetlight that stood a little to the east of Mae's back entry, then glancing beyond the light toward the hazy three-quarter moon and falling snow.

"There he is!" Rosie leaned forward in his seat and pointed through the fogged-up windshield toward a partially stooped figure outfitted in black who stood just a few yards beyond the streetlight.

"What the hell's he doing?" CJ whispered.

"Beats me," said Rosie.

"He's fiddling with something next to our back-door stoop," said Mavis. "Can't see what it is."

"We don't wanna spook him and get him running Petey's way," said CJ, spotting Petey's head as it bobbed up from behind a trash can. "He looks big enough to flatten Petey on his way out and keep going. I'm gonna circle around the front of Mae's and plug up the other end of the alley," he said, slowly getting out of the Bel Air.

"Try not to scare Petey shitless," said Rosie.

"Don't you think we should call the police?" Mavis asked.

"There's no time," CJ said, stooped and duck-walking away from the car.

"Be careful, CJ," Mavis whispered.

CJ didn't hear her warning as he worked his way around the corner of the building that housed Prillerman's Trophy and Badge and onto the Welton Street sidewalk. When he slipped and fell in a pool of icy slush before beginning a sprint down Welton, he mumbled, "Shit," brushed the slush off his new sport coat, and took off.

He'd reached the alley's east entry when he slammed chest-first into the fleeing Petey Greene. Petey screamed, "CJ!" just as a loud pop that sounded like an exploding firecracker erupted in the alley. Within seconds, CJ spotted smoke rising from what looked like the kind of incendiary flare he'd used to expose enemy machine-gun nests during Vietnam.

"What the hell's going on?" he asked, helping Petey to his feet.

"There's a guy down the alley who's trying to torch Mae's," Petey said, loudly enough to cause the man in black he was pointing at to look their way.

Realizing he'd been spotted, the man turned to run in the other direction. When he caught sight of a hulking, snow-covered Rosie Weeks and the Bel Air blocking his exit, he turned and ran back the other way. The glow from what was now a porch fire illuminated the man as he raced toward Petey, knocking him aside as if he were a rag doll before slamming a shoulder and all his weight into CJ's ribs.

Grunting in pain, CJ reached for the man's hood, grabbing one of the drawstrings, as they went down in a heap.

Back on his feet now, Petey wrapped both arms around the man's legs as CJ, cutting off his airway with the drawstring, tried to gain control of the solidly built arsonist.

Howling and swinging wildly as they groveled in the snow, the man slammed a fist and pinkie ring into CJ's forehead, opening a two-inch-long gash.

With blood streaming down his forehead, CJ screamed, "You fuckin'—" and did his best to knee the man in the groin as he slammed his right palm into the sweet spot just above the man's nose. The loud crack that followed, akin to the sound of a tree limb snapping, sent the man writhing in pain and rolling in the snow until he eventually stopped moving.

When Petey screamed, "You finished him, CJ. The fucker's out cold," CJ said, "Yeah," concerned suddenly that he might have killed the man. Scooting over on his knees to the arsonist, CJ passed a hand in front of the man's mouth. When he was certain their firebug was still breathing, he let out a sigh of relief. Shivering in a post–adrenaline rush, he looked back toward Mae's to see Mavis and Rosie using two fire extinguishers they'd retrieved from inside the restaurant. The restaurant's back porch, overhead fascia, and steps were charred and smoldering, but the fire looked to be under control.

"Petey, run inside Mae's and call the cops."

"You sure?"

"Yeah."

"They'll be askin' questions."

"So we'll answer them. Hurry up."

As Petey raced for the restaurant, CJ slipped the hood off the man whose septum he'd broken. One of the man's nostrils was streaming blood. Checking again to make certain that the man was breathing, CJ watched his head flop back and forth in the wet snow. As the semiconscious man's eyes opened wider and his lower lip quivered in obvious pain, CJ realized that the blanket of snow the man was lying in and the man's thick head of hair were nearly an identical white match.

Chapter

18

Rosie Weeks had a knee planted firmly on Detroit Whitey's chest when two Denver cops, guns drawn, responded not to Petey Greene's 911 call but to a burglary-in-progress call that had come in less than a minute earlier.

With his nose bleeding and gasping for air, Whitey moaned, "Get him off me," at the younger of the two confused-looking cops who stood less than three feet away.

"Get off him," the young cop ordered, the barrel of his revolver aimed squarely at Rosie's chest. "Hands in the air."

"Son of a bitch tried to burn down Mae's," Rosie yelled up at the cop, pointing toward Mae's charred back porch, where CJ, Petey, and Mavis stood next to the two spent fire extinguishers.

"Get the fire department out here," CJ shouted at the older cop, who, pointing his finger like a weapon at CJ, yelled, "They're on the way. Meantime, the three of you stay the hell put."

When Mavis took two steps in Rosie's direction, the young cop, his gun still drawn, ran toward her, shoved her backward, and knocked her off balance into CJ. "Can't you hear, lady? Stay put."

When CJ reached out to grab the cop's arm, Mavis wrapped her arms around him in a bear hug. "CJ, no!" Only the sounds of sirens in the distance served to defuse the situation.

"Stay the shit here with your girlfriend, buddy, and don't move! You, too, shorty," the cop said to Petey, holstering his gun.

As the young patrolman walked back toward Rosie, who was standing, arms in the air, with rivulets of melted snow and beads of sweat streaming down his cheeks, CJ wanted to scream, "You dumbass! The guy on the ground's who you want!" But with Mavis still hugging him protectively, he did as he was told.

"Hey, I ain't your torcher," protested Rosie to the older cop, who was busy cuffing him. "The guy on the ground's your man."

"What have you got, sarge?" the young cop asked, eyeing Rosie, then Whitey, as wailing fire-engine sirens closed in.

"The big fellow here says the guy on the ground tried to torch the building behind us.

"What's your name?" the sergeant asked Rosie, ignoring Detroit Whitey's moans.

"Rosie Weeks."

"You workin' with the three down there?" he asked, pointing toward CJ and Mavis and Petey.

"Yes."

"Doing what?"

"Helpin' out."

"Sure," the cop said sarcastically, deciding that with things under at least some semblance of control, he could take a look at the man on the ground. As he knelt next to the partially hooded man, he smiled and a sudden hint of recognition crossed his face. "My, my, my, Louie Jordan. What the hell's an old-time torcher like you doing out on a snowy night like this?"

When Whitey didn't respond, the wily old sergeant answered for him. "Setting fires to try to stay warm, I'd bet." Eyeing Rosie, and to the clear disappointment of his young partner, he said to the other cop, "You can uncuff Weeks. After that, why don't you go take the other three people's statements? And call for an ambulance while you're at it."

"Okay," said the younger cop, heading to where CJ, Mavis, and Petey stood in the headlight glare of an approaching pumper truck. The sergeant watched the younger man trot eagerly into the headlights, then turned back to Rosie. "Why don't you start from the beginning for me, Weeks?" he said, staring down at Whitey, who, fully conscious now, said, "I need medical attention, damn it!"

"You'll get it," the sergeant said. "In the meantime, Louie, my boy, I'd get busy polishing up my story."

CJ had barely slept thirty minutes all night after his arrival home from the District 2 police substation just after 1:30 a.m. Over nearly three hours, he, Rosie, Mavis, and Petey had given more statements to not just cops but more sleepy-eyed arson investigators than he would ever have imagined the city and county of Denver employed. Fifteen minutes into the lead investigator's unrelenting questioning, CJ had the sense that Fire Lieutenant Archie Simms was the kind of ambitious, take-no-prisoners man who likely had his eye on someday becoming the city's fire chief.

They'd all finally left the substation in Willis Sundee's vintage '58 Buick Roadmaster under sleet-spitting skies after promising Lieutenant Simms, who seemed eager to work through the night, that they would do everything they could to assist him in his investigation.

Willis, who'd dropped CJ off at home first, seemed puzzled by CJ's parting comment: "Sorry I let you down, Willis. Never should've let anybody get that close to Mae's, but I'll make it up to you in the morning—count on it."

"No need for that. We're over the hump now," Willis had said, hoping to assuage CJ's feelings of guilt.

"Yeah," CJ had said as he'd gotten out of the car. "But I'm gonna make certain we don't get shoved back down the hill."

Now, as CJ sat slouched behind the steering wheel of Ike's Jeep, hoping to intercept Walt Reasoner as Reasoner arrived for work, his parting words to Willis Sundee the previous night echoed in his head.

All his life he'd hated to fail at anything, and the fact that he'd left the door open for someone to burn down Mae's, whether they'd succeeded or not, represented a failure.

He had no reason to doubt that in the end the cops, eager-beaver Lieutenant Simms, and the legal system would coalesce to mete out justice to Detroit Whitey. But he had the uneasy feeling that they might not be so efficient when it came to Reasoner.

Rest-broken, guilt-ridden, and determined to do something about the possibility that Reasoner might skate, he found himself smoking a cheroot and pinched behind the wheel of the

Jeep, intent on making certain that Reasoner, who he was sure had sent Detroit Whitey on his arson mission, would pay.

When his pager went off and the numbers 888 popped up on the screen, he knew that Petey Greene, who'd staked out Reasoner's house since early that morning, had just seen Reasoner leave, presumably headed for work.

Pegging the odds of Reasoner heading straight for work as pretty high, especially since Reasoner likely hadn't heard from the incarcerated Detroit Whitey, CJ thought back on what Ike had once told him about hiring out a job instead of doing it yourself: *Roll out a throng and it'll get done wrong.* Feeling more guilty, he took a final drag on his cheroot and stubbed it out in the Jeep's ashtray.

Ike's words were still swirling around in his head when Walt Reasoner's Mercedes-Benz pulled into the Epic Produce & Meats parking lot. When the late-model diesel eased into Reasoner's assigned parking space in the totally empty lot, and Reasoner stepped out and shut his door, looking as if he owned the world, CJ yelled, exiting the Jeep, "Hey, Reasoner, wanna hold up?"

Startled, Reasoner looked up to see CJ only two strides away. "What do you want, Floyd?" He squared up to face CJ.

"Not much. Just want to bring you up to date. Your firebug got squashed last night, my man."

"Got no idea what you're talking about."

"Then I guess I should lay things out for you. You sent someone to burn down Mae's Louisiana Kitchen last night. A torcher out of Detroit. Goes by the name of Detroit Whitey."

"Sorry, but I don't know the man."

"Well, he sure as hell knows you."

Reasoner took a step forward. "Get the hell off my property, Floyd. Now!"

The stale aroma of garlic and alcohol curled up into CJ's face as he grabbed Reasoner by the collar of his jacket, and slammed him back into his car door. Pressing a knee firmly into Reasoner's belly, he said, "The cops will get around to you eventually, asshole. Then, unfortunately, the system will pussyfoot around with you while your lawyer wastes your money and the taxpayers' time. So I figured in order not to waste such precious commodities, I'd drop by and discuss things with you in a quick-solution kind of way."

With Reasoner struggling to get free, CJ grabbed him by a hank of hair and slammed his head into the door frame of the Mercedes. Woozy and barely able to stand, Reasoner listed from side to side. "And just to tie things up all nice and neat, the way I promised Willis Sundee I would when I took this job, I want you to think about this. If at any time in the future a single hair on Willis's head looks like it's out of place to me, or if for some reason on a day when things aren't going particularly well for him he begins looking stressed out, I'll figure you're back trying to put the squeeze on him, and we'll go a round or two like this again." CJ had pulled his knee out of Reasoner's gut and taken a step back when a Jeep Wagoneer sporting Denver Fire Department emblems on the front doors pulled into the parking lot and sped toward them. Archie Simms was behind the wheel.

"He assaulted me," Reasoner wheezed, dropping to his knees and pointing at CJ. "Arrest his black ass."

Waving off the cop who shared the front seat with him, Simms ignored Reasoner's plea and asked, "Are you Walt Reasoner?"

"Yes. Now, cuff the fucking SOB!"

"I'll have Sergeant Tully here do that just as soon as you answer a few questions. And just so you know," Simms said, smiling, "the sergeant and I have worked lots of arson cases together. He's very seasoned." Reasoner's jaw dropped as the burly sergeant stepped out of the Wagoneer, grabbed CJ by the arm, and muscled him aside but never cuffed him.

"I think we can talk freely now that Mr. Floyd here is under control," said Simms.

Surprised that a veteran police sergeant would allow Simms to dictate procedure, especially since the two of them had arrived on the scene of an apparent assault, CJ had the feeling that someone higher up than either man had cleared the way for them to operate outside the procedural rule book.

Sounding solicitous, Simms said, "I'd like to ask you a few questions about a fire that someone tried to start over in Five Points last night, if that's okay, Mr. Reasoner."

"I've got nothing to say to you without my lawyer," Reasoner said, gingerly patting his throbbing head.

"Of course," said Simms. "Why don't we go into your office? You can call him from there."

Simms started off boldly for the front door of the Epic Produce & Meats offices, as if to show he was clearly in charge, then paused to whisper to CJ, "If you want to get out of this gracefully, Floyd, I'd play things my way." The look on Simms's face spoke volumes. CJ had seen the look on the faces of apple-polishing naval officers bucking for promotion and on the faces of South Vietnamese soldiers who'd publicly defended the American war effort but secretly supported the Vietcong. He'd seen the look on the faces of the slick-as-shit lawyers Ike always claimed would sell their mothers down the river for a nickel and on the faces of Vietnamese whores shilling for the pimps they knew would cut their throats if they ever stopped. He knew the look all right. It was the look of someone for whom the end always justified the means.

Smiling as if he enjoyed hearing the sound of his own voice, Simms asked, "Are you on board?"

"Yeah," said CJ as Sergeant Tully relaxed his grip on CJ's arm.

"Good" was Simms's only response.

An hour and forty minutes later, Reasoner left his offices in hand-cuffs with his lawyer at his side. Not the cuffs of Sergeant Tully but those of a Denver police commander with an up-bucking personality that matched that of Lieutenant Simms.

As CJ and Simms stood just outside the building's front door watching Reasoner being carted away, Simms said, "Sometimes bad things actually happen to bad people. Detroit Whitey's a two-time loser. The third time around earns him serious time, and I'm sure Whitey doesn't want things to get that serious. He'll cooperate. Sorta like you, I expect," Simms said pointedly. "Reasoner's the fish we want, Floyd. Remember that."

"I've committed it to memory."

"Good. The DA, Commander Theisman, and I appreciate it."

"Just thinking, though, that sometimes those bad things you mentioned happen to good people."

Simms flashed CJ an insightful smile. "It's the way of the world, Floyd. The way of our not-so-gentle world."

Part 3

The Hidden Linkages

SPRING 1977

Chapter

19

It didn't take much for Detroit Whitey to roll on Walt Reasoner and cut a deal with the Denver DA's office that would end up buying him significantly reduced prison time. Extortion and contracting with someone to commit arson, Reasoner learned, could turn out to be a lot more serious than mere attempted arson. The day that the final Whitey-Reasoner plea-bargain deal came down, six months after CJ's parking-lot encounter with Lieutenant Simms, turned out to be a surprisingly balmy fifty-degree college spring break weekend the following March.

CJ and Rosie were seated at one of Mae's back tables having lunch when Petey Greene rushed in, sprinted the length of the restaurant, and plopped down in a chair next to CJ. "Reasoner's gettin' seven years. As for our boy Whitey—and you can take this to the bank—even though it ain't come down official yet, he won't do much more than a year."

Amazed at Petey's ability to extract information out of the criminal justice system before it was official and before it appeared in the newspapers or TV, Rosie, who tended to discount Petey's prognostications, said, "How the hell you have such an inside track on everything that goes down in the Queen City beats the hell outa me, Petey."

Petey broke into a broad, toothy grin. "I keep my eyes on the prize and my ears to the ground, that's how. If you did the same, you'd know they're plannin' on puttin' up a Sinclair discount station over in Curtis Park. A place like that, no more than four blocks away from you to boot, could end up puttin' a knot in your business, don't you think?"

"I know what folks are plannin', Petey, and I've got my own plans for them, in case you're wonderin'."

"Yeah, and—"

"Got any other news hot off the wire?" CJ asked, hoping to forestall one of Petey and Rosie's all-too-frequent arguments.

"Sure do," said Petey, chagrined that CJ was trying to stop his gossip-mongering. "Been keepin' my eye on Gaylord Marquee off and on ever since last fall, just like you asked me to, CJ. Never too close for him to suspect I'm doggin' him, though."

"And you ain't come up with shit," said Rosie, well aware of CJ's endless attempts to bring closure to the GI Joe's murders.

"Wrong, as usual, Red. Didn't really have much of anything 'til today, though." He winked at CJ. "You know that woman, the one you told me owns the ranch up by Sterling and the one I saw at Marquee's place last fall?"

"Cheryl Goldsby?" CJ asked excitedly, having made no progress in solving the GI Joe's murders in months.

"Yeah. Well, she was back last evenin'. Tight-fittin' jeans, boots, big head, and all. Right on Marquee's front doorstep. All mousy-lookin', with her hair in a bun and sportin' wire-rimmed glasses this time. She was drivin' a pickup and pullin' a horse trailer."

"Sure sounds like Goldsby," said CJ.

"Yeah," said Petey. "And she had another woman with her."

Before Petey could describe the other woman, CJ said, "A dark-skinned woman with a crew cut? Built like a fireplug?" thinking that perhaps Goldsby and Ramona Lepsos had patched up their differences.

"Nope," said Petey. "A little redhead."

CJ's eyes widened. "Did she walk with a limp?"

Scratching his head and looking befuddled, Petey said, "Sure the hell did. I was gonna mention that next."

"I'll be damned," said CJ.

"Who is she?" asked Petey.

"A fiddler of sorts. She's that cellist with the Denver Symphony I've had you trying to ferret out—Molly Burgess. I've been trying to get a line on her for months, ever since the night Detroit Whitey tried to torch this place. Haven't had much luck. The party line I've been getting from the symphony's PR people is that she's been on sabbatical with an orchestra back East. Strange that she'd head off on a sabbatical so soon after Mavis and I caught her performance at a Beethoven concert last fall."

"Sounds to me like she mighta spotted you at that concert and decided to haul ass," said Petey.

"Question is, how'd she know I was there? The place was packed."

Petey laughed. "How many black folks were at that concert, man?"

"A sprinkling."

"Well, there ya go."

"Come on, Petey," said Rosie. "Your paranoia's showin' again."

"Come on nothin'," protested Petey. "There CJ is, all six-foot-three of him sittin' at the symphony peerin' down on this cello-pluckin' woman, and with somebody as fine as Mavis Sundee snuggled up next to him. Hell, the two of ya probably stuck out like ink blots on a white lace curtain."

"We weren't snuggled up, Petey."

"So maybe you weren't," Petey said, with a grin. "Least not like the two of you been all this week."

"Didn't know you were lookin' to replace Dear Abby, Petey," said Rosie.

"I ain't. But like I said earlier, ears to the ground, eyes on the prize."

"One day your nosiness is gonna buy you more trouble than you figured on purchasin', my man."

Thinking, *It never ends,* CJ said, "Would you two stop? Got anything else for me on what went down at Marquee's, Petey?"

"Nothin' I could see. The two women went inside, stayed in the house for forty-five minutes or so, came back out, and left. Ten minutes later Marquee split, too."

"Did they deliver anything to Marquee?"

"They went into the house with a couple of cardboard boxes the size of a microwave. Didn't come back out with anything."

"Strange," said CJ. "The three of them being so blatant."

"Hell, they didn't know I was there. Folks tend to be open

like that when they don't know they're bein' watched." Petey looked over at Rosie. "Ya gotta be on your toes in my business, Red."

Refusing to take the bait, Rosie remained silent.

"So whatta ya want me to do next?" asked Petey. "I'm gonna be at a swap meet this weekend. A biggie. I'm thinkin' Marquee will likely be there for a change, too. He ain't been around much at meets for awhile. He does some international travelin', you know. I can keep an eye on him for you, no charge."

"Okay," said CJ, aware that in the end, Petey would find a way to not only collect for his recent Molly Burgess sighting, but put himself on the clock for additional pay. Checking his watch, CJ said, "Uh-oh. I've gotta go catch up with Mavis before she heads over to Damon Foods with Willis to put in their meat and produce order for the week."

"How's it workin' out with Willis gettin' his stuff from the big boys instead of Reasoner?" asked Rosie.

"Not bad, and a whole lot better than being extorted or having your business torched." Watching Rosie and Petey nod approvingly, he was happy to see that for at least once that day they could all agree on something.

For fifty-two years, Willis Sundee had lived in the same Five Points 1920s-vintage home he'd been born in. The sand-dollar-tan, craftsman-style house with white trim at the corner of California and Twenty-seventh Streets was surrounded by an immaculately groomed yard.

The house was as much a part of Mavis Sundee's life as it

was of her father's. Robbed of her mother, Mae, who'd suffered a heart attack when Mavis was barely six, Mavis had spent her formative years roaming the home's seven spacious rooms. She'd been encouraged by Willis to excel in academics and athletics, as had her older brother, Carl, a former Denver Prep basketball star who was now an electrical engineer in Dallas. Equally athletically gifted, Mavis had turned down a gymnastics scholarship to the University of Denver, choosing instead to attend Boston University, where she was majoring in business.

Although it was rarely discussed between her and Willis, Mavis was expected to one day take over her father's businesses—enterprises that included the ownership not simply of Mae's Louisiana Kitchen but also of an insurance agency, a Welton Street Laundromat, and nearly a dozen rental properties sprinkled throughout Five Points and Curtis Park. Although she'd once dreamed of becoming a veterinarian, business was as much a part of her blood as it was of her father's, and although she sometimes had visions of forever standing at the entrance to Mae's greeting diners, she'd long ago realized that the burden of keeping the wheels of her father's businesses turning, as the powerful and necessary engine that had driven him past depression following her mother's death, was one she would likely bear for a lifetime.

Mavis was busy in an upstairs hallway adjusting the lock on a suitcase that had jammed on her recent flight home from Boston when CJ rang the front doorbell. Dressed in faded Denver East High School basketball shorts and an oversized T-shirt, she dropped what she was doing and bounded down the stairs. When she slipped on the bottom step and went cascading onto the Spanish-tiled entryway floor, CJ, startled by the loud thud, yelled, "What the hell?"

Rising and brushing herself off, Mavis swung open the front door. "Tripped," she said, looking embarrassed.

"Damn! I thought a herd of cattle might be headed my way."

"Bad choice of words when you're in any way describing a woman, Mr. Floyd."

"Sorry."

"No harm, no foul," she said with a wink, clasping CJ's right hand affectionately in hers as he stepped into the house. Leading him toward the kitchen, Mavis asked, "Can I get you something to drink?"

"No. I just had lunch at Mae's with Rosie and Petey Greene."

"Were the three of you talking your usual secret-society kind of stuff, whispering about what dark alleys to head down next?" She took a can of Coke out of the refrigerator, pulled the tab, and, along with CJ, scooted a stool up to the kitchen's center island.

"Nope. No alleys today." There was a clear hint of frustration in CJ's tone. "But I do what I do, Mavis."

"I know. But I don't necessarily have to like what you do," she said, kissing him softly on the cheek.

"All of us can't go to expensive private colleges back East." Wishing he could take back his words the second he'd uttered them and worried that he and Mavis were about to head down the same bumpy dead-end road they'd been traveling since their night at the symphony months earlier, he searched for something neutral to say.

Hoping to sound supportive rather than judgmental, Mavis asked, "So what are you investigating next?"

"I'm back looking into the GI Joe's killings," CJ said with a shrug.

"Please be careful."

"Always am."

"You up for the movies tonight?"

"Yeah, and by the way, how's that new meat and produce supplier of his treating your dad?"

"So far, so good. I haven't heard any complaints, anyway." Looking slightly chagrined she spun her Coke can slowly around on the countertop. "It doesn't seem like I've been home for almost a week. Can you believe it? Tomorrow it's back to Boston."

CJ leaned over, ran a hand through her hair, and twisted one of her thick black curls onto his fingers before softly planting a kiss on her lips.

"Where do you think we're headed, CJ?" Mavis asked, sounding troubled.

"To somewhere special, I hope."

"Me, too." She pulled CJ toward her until their lips met again. The kiss they shared was neither soft nor brief but one of lunging tongues and hungry anticipation, a preamble to forty-five minutes of intimate lovemaking that followed.

Two hours later, adrift on a sea of postcoital bliss, CJ walked into Ike's office to find Ike, with a handkerchief pressed to his mouth, in the midst of a violent coughing spell.

Ike matter-of-factly jammed the handkerchief into a pants pocket the instant he caught sight of CJ. "So, what's up, Sherlock?"

Determined not to once again let Ike sweep the issue of his increasingly violent coughing spells under the rug, CJ asked, "What did Doc Haskins say about your cough?"

"He said I'm fit enough to go mountain climbin'." The look of concern on CJ's face short-circuited Ike's con. "What the old geezer said is that I shoulda quit smokin' and drinkin' years ago. Charged me fifty bucks to tell me what the shit I already knew." Ike gnawed his lower lip with the edge of his two top front teeth, a sure sign to CJ that he was having trouble dealing with his health issue. "Well, he did throw in a chest X-ray and some half-assed examination. The skinflint." Ike nudged his handkerchief a little farther down in his pocket and gave CJ a look that said, *Case closed.* "Where you comin' from?"

"Mavis's."

"You're headed down the right road there."

"I'm not so sure," said CJ, leaning sideways against the edge of Ike's desk. "I always feel like we're from two totally different worlds."

"You are. But what the hell does that matter? Sometimes I wonder about you, boy. You got yourself a woman as fine as wine and as classy as they come, who's wantin' to be with you pretty much every second, and you're busy psychoanalyzin' the damn situation. You better grab that brass ring while it's there for the grabbin', son." With one hand to his mouth, Ike suppressed a cough. "Second-guessin' the sweetest dollop'a honey you're ever gonna have dropped your way is plain stupidity. Got any more gripes you wanna share?"

"No."

"Good, 'cause things around here are lookin' up. We got us a new secretary headed our way. She's second cousin to a girl Etta Lee went to school with back in Detroit. Dropped by Etta Lee and Rosie's yesterday to let 'em know she was in town. They got to talkin', Etta Lee told her I was lookin' for a secretary, and the next thing you know, she's here interviewin' with me and Marguerite. Marguerite's as happy as a pig in slop after helpin' out all these months."

Beaming, Ike continued, "Marguerite's out walkin' her down Bail Bondsman's Row and showin' her the lay of the land right this second. They should be back any minute."

"That's one problem solved, at least."

"And a big one. Now, since you been bent on numberin' the problems around here from one to a hundred lately, got any others I can solve?"

"Nope. Just happy to know that having somebody around here full-time to help out should free us both up a little."

Ike shook his head knowingly. "I know where you're headed, CJ, and I don't like it. That GI Joe's murder case you keep wantin' to bump your head up against ain't earnin' us one penny."

"I never expected it would," CJ said defensively. "It's just a problem I promised myself way back that I'd solve. And since you brought the issue up, how about I run something about the case by you? I've spent a good six months trying to get a line on that cellist, Molly Burgess, I mentioned to you a good while back. Petey's been running most of my interference. She's the one I was hoping to hook up with the night Walt Reasoner tried to torch Mae's. Supposedly she was friends with the Chinese guy who was killed at GI Joe's."

"Yeah, Chin. I've pretty much heard the whole story before, CJ."

"Well, here's a new chapter. Last night my mysterious cellist—her name's Molly Burgess, in case you forgot," CJ said with a grin, "showed up at a house here in Denver with Cheryl Goldsby, Wiley Ames's niece. Goldsby's the one with the ranch out by Sterling, remember?"

"Yeah, yeah. So, what's your point? Ain't no law against showin' up in Denver, or knowin' Wiley Ames's niece, or for that matter bein' gay, neither."

"The point's this. I'm thinking that the Burgess woman is a replacement for Goldsby's old girlfriend. And here's another wrinkle. The house they showed up at is home to a guy who sold me one of Ames's rare license plates a few months back. The both of them were in on the GI Joe's murders, Unc, I know it."

"Okay. Now give me a reason they killed two men."

"They were after rare seashells, the best I can figure. Ames was fencing the shells for Chin, who'd stolen them from museums in Thailand. Goldsby pretty much admitted it to me."

"Strange that she'd admit to anything that could link her to a couple of murders. What were the shells worth?"

"Ten, maybe twenty grand, according to a couple of marine-biology-professor types I've talked to at the University of San Diego. I can go get my notes."

Ike shook his head. "No need. That's an awful slow-runnin' money spigot, you ask me. Goldsby, Chin, Ames, and maybe the cellist dividin' up that kinda money—hell, they'd barely each come out with five grand. Nope, my guess is that if somebody was fencin' something, it woulda had to've been worth a lot more than twenty grand to end up buyin' both Chin and Ames plots in the cemetery."

"Maybe they weren't all in it together," said CJ. "No reason why one of them couldn't have struck out on their own."

"More likely than your threesome or your foursome. Even so, your lone wolf still wouldn't'a ended up with much of a haul."

"People have been killed for a whole lot less."

"And for a whole lot more," Ike said, his tone insistent. "You got any other suspects?"

CJ shrugged. "An ex-girlfriend of Goldsby's named Ramona Lepsos, and there's GI Joe's owner, Harry Steed."

"Any chance either of them coulda been in on the seashell-fencing scam?"

"I checked Steed out stem to stern, and so did the cops right after the murders. I even had an ex-navy buddy of mine who's now a Denver cop do some checking. Steed came up clean as a whistle. He's a skinflint and a hoarder of all kinds of things, from what I've been able to gather over the years, but fencing stolen goods would be way off the mark for him."

"Then I'd get to checkin' on Goldsby's ex-girlfriend."

"I'll do that," CJ said, reacting to the sound of the front door slamming.

"Ike, you in the back?" Marguerite Larkin called out from the front entry.

"Yeah. In my office with CJ," Ike said, unable this time to suppress a series of lengthy dry coughs.

"Great. I'll bring DeeAnn back to meet him."

The short, buxom, clear-eyed woman who walked into Ike's office just ahead of Marguerite looked to CJ to be about his age. Her hair was done up in an exquisitely coiffed Afro, and her clothes looked expensive. In the back of his mind, CJ had half expected a Nordeen Mapson clone. DeeAnn Slater was anything but that.

The black miniskirt she was wearing did wonders for her shapely, slightly knock-kneed legs, and her white form-fitting mock turtleneck pullover was equally flattering in a different way.

Walking from behind his desk and straight up to her, Ike said, "DeeAnn, like you to meet my nephew, CJ Floyd."

"DeeAnn Slater," she announced proudly.

"Pleasure," said CJ.

"CJ's my wingman," Ike said, trying not to cough.

"Your uncle's been singing your praises," said DeeAnn, her response deep, throaty, and sensual.

"I pay him to do that," CJ said with a smile.

"Better keep him on your payroll, then," DeeAnn said, turning to face Ike. "Marguerite's toured me up and down your block. Interesting. Seems a little strange that every bail bondsman in Denver would be camped out here on Delaware Street. Lots of competition concentrated in one place."

"It's just the way things have worked out over the years," said Ike, impressed by DeeAnn's quick assessment of things. "No matter. We get our share of the pie. You still ready to start tomorrow?"

"Absolutely."

"Good. You can begin with tryin' to make some sense outa my last secretary's filin' system."

"Sure thing." Eyeing CJ, who was trying his best not to stare at what he was certain DeeAnn Slater enjoyed showing off, she asked, "Have you got anything special you want me to take care of, CJ?"

"Nope."

"Then we'll see you tomorrow morning at eight," said Ike. "And Marguerite, on your way out why don't you show DeeAnn where we rustle up our morning fog lifter?"

"Okay," said Marguerite, escorting DeeAnn out of Ike's office and down the hall toward the coffee alcove.

They were barely out of earshot when Ike, excitedly rubbing his hands together, said, "Nice little surprise, Ms. Slater, don't you think? And willin' to come in on a Saturday mornin' to get started. Can't beat that."

"Sure can't," said CJ, sounding like someone who'd stumbled across something both tantalizing and treacherous. "Can't beat it with a stick."

The lights inside Gaylord Marquee's house had been out for twenty minutes when, kneeling with a phone receiver in one hand and peering over a bedroom windowsill, Marquee announced to the person on the other end of the line, "The little sawed-off runt's been casing my house on and off for a good week now, maybe even longer."

"And you're sure it's the same person?"

"Of course. His name's Petey Greene. Calls himself an antique dealer. A street hustler is what he is."

"Does he know anything about our dealings?"

"I don't think so. But then again, I can't be sure. He's a slick little SOB. He's got a camera with him again tonight, taking pictures. He's probably got shots of me from every spot in the damn county."

"Not good. Not good at all. You'll have to take care of him. He might be smart enough to put two and two together."

Marquee shook his head in protest. "I'm not taking care of anybody."

"You sound like a man with a sudden case of cold feet, Marquee. Strange, considering all that stiff-upper-lip British army background of yours."

"Screw you."

There was a truncated snicker. "No need to use filthy language, Marquee. But one way or another, I'll expect you to handle Mr. Greene."

"How?"

"You'll think of something. Just make sure no fecal matter ends up being slung my way."

"Wouldn't dream of slinging any shit your way," said Marquee, gritting his teeth to control his anger as he hung up and peered down on Petey Greene and the moped he'd only partially hidden in a clump of shrubs.

Chapter
🦎 20

Petey Greene had on his engaging, boy-next-door, only-the-straight-poop, honest-to-Betsy, reel-in-the-sucker look. He'd perfected that face over years in order to capture those uninformed, unseasoned, just-gotta-have-it buyers who showed up at swap meets, flea markets, antique auctions, and garage sales with fat wallets and no brains, hoping to score big because they'd heard from some loquacious friend, distant relative, or office coworker that a friend of a friend had stumbled across a Remington, Russell, Picasso, or some other priceless art object at a similar gathering for no more than the price of a pair of tennis shoes.

License-plate swap meets, however, weren't among his favorites for two reasons. They tended to attract too many knowledgeable people and not enough suckers, and the attendance was usually too small to garner a really big score. The Rocky Mountain Automobile License Plate Collectors Association meet he was headed for that morning wouldn't draw more than a hundred and fifty people, most of whom knew quite well how to play the trade-and-barter game. There'd be a buck or two to be made, no question, but coming home with a serious profit wasn't generally in the cards.

He'd show up nonetheless because what counted at the end of the day in the business he was in was to have your name and, even better, your face out there for potential buyers to see.

Walking with a half-finished cup of black coffee in one hand from the cluttered bedroom into the living room of the Five Points apartment he'd rented month to month for nearly five years, he reminded himself to think positive. It could, after all, turn out to be a red-letter day.

Whistling "Sittin' on the Dock of the Bay" off key, he pulled back the once white lace window curtains his doting mother had given him as a housewarming present when he'd first moved into the apartment. A smile crossed his face as he took a look outside. The now dingy curtains seemed to perfectly frame the cloudless blue sky. It was the kind of swap-meet day that just might lend itself to his successfully pulling off his salted-mine scam, he told himself, checking to make sure his moped was locked down securely in the slip tent he rented for thirty-five dollars a month.

Unlike his friend CJ Floyd, or Gaylord Marquee, he didn't have much of a license-plate collection, and certainly no license plate among those he owned would bring top dollar. He owned a few vintage porcelains, none that were very rare and none that were mint, that he'd been trying to peddle for over a year. Most people who'd looked them over were well schooled enough to spot their lightly chipped and faintly crazed porcelain or to notice the extra postproduction holes, flaws that considerably diminished their value. Nonetheless, the plates could look inviting to a novice, and until they were examined closely, they could appear, as Petey loved to boast, *absolutely golden.*

He reminded himself that all he needed for the day was one good sucker, that one unsuspecting collector who, after realizing he couldn't afford the pristine, eight-hundred-dollar, mint-condition 1914 porcelain plate he'd just drooled over down the aisle, strolled disappointedly up to Petey's table to find a sympathetic face and pretty much the identical plate at half the price. Once the hook was set, Petey knew only too well how to finesse his fish, judiciously using words like *overpriced* and *East Coast specialist* to describe the price-gouging vendor his mark had just left.

One glassy-eyed sucker was all he needed for his day to come up roses. That, and Gaylord Marquee's presence at the swap meet. A morning of shadowing Marquee would earn him a few extra of CJ Floyd's dollars, and when all was said and done, he just might end the day four or five hundred dollars richer.

Setting aside his coffee cup, he pulled the curtains fully open and stared out into the bright morning sunshine, thinking that it just might turn out to be a special kind of day.

CJ bounded down the fire-escape stairs from his apartment for the swap meet a little before eight-thirty, determined to scope out the grounds for any sign of Gaylord Marquee before the meet's scheduled 9 a.m. start. Thanks to Petey Greene's snooping, he knew that Marquee, Cheryl Goldsby, and Molly Burgess had some kind of connection. What he really needed to find out was whether or not, five-and-a-half years earlier, that connection had sparked a couple of murders. He'd tried to catch Petey by phone before leaving home without any luck, and he hoped the two of them could share notes on Marquee before the swap meet opened. All he'd gotten was a busy signal, and he suspected that the lecherous little con artist had unplugged his phone in order to ensure himself a night of uninterrupted pleasure with a couple of hookers.

What he needed most from Petey were the photos of Marquee, Goldsby, and Burgess that Petey had bragged about taking. The photos would certainly help in any flat-out confrontation he might have with Marquee, and since Petey had promised to bring them to the swap meet, where he also expected to collect payment for his services, there was no reason to expect Petey wouldn't be there.

CJ was halfway across the driveway and almost to the ungaraged Bel Air when DeeAnn Slater poked her head out the front door to the office and yelled, "Sounded like a wrecking ball slamming into the side of the building. Figured I'd better come have a look."

"No, just me heading out," said CJ, his eyes locked on the miniskirted DeeAnn. "Guess I should've told you about using the fire escape."

"So now I know." She walked toward CJ, stopped a couple of feet away from him, and rested a hand seductively above her slightly cocked left hip.

"Ike up yet?" CJ asked as the words *God, what a body* worked their way through his head.

"Yes, and he's been coughing up a storm. Sorta worries me, to tell you the truth."

"That makes two of us," said CJ, looking concerned. "Keep an eye on him and call Marguerite to come by and help if you run into a problem organizing things. I should be back in a couple of hours."

DeeAnn nodded and shifted her weight from one hip to the other. "Ike tells me you were in Vietnam."

"Yeah."

"I had a brother who was killed over there."

A lump formed in CJ's throat. "I'm sorry."

"Thanks," DeeAnn said, reaching out and clasping CJ's right hand in hers.

The warmth of her touch froze him in his tracks momentarily. Slowly easing his hand out of hers and heading for the Bel Air, he said, "If you ever need to talk to me about your brother, I'm here."

DeeAnn nodded without answering.

As he backed down the driveway with his eyes locked on the retreating figure of the new hire, he simply shook his head and whispered, "Damn."

Petey Greene's moped had been giving him headaches for weeks, stopping for no good reason, flooding when he tried to start it, sputtering and coughing its way up hills. As he headed for the swap meet, helmetless and with his fingers crossed, he hoped the temperamental scooter would be cooperative that day.

Traffic on the westbound Sixth Avenue freeway was Saturday-morning light as he nosed the moped into a surprisingly stiff breeze on his way to the Jefferson County Fairgrounds just west of Denver.

A foam-lined, toaster-oven-sized box filled to capacity with license plates was strapped to the moped's rear luggage carrier. He'd chosen his fare for the swap meet the previous evening, placing each license plate in a Ziploc freezer bag for protection and capping off the assemblage with the 1914 Pennsylvania porcelain plate he planned to use as sucker bait.

Sputtering along the freeway, underpowered and ten miles an hour below the speed limit, he was decked out in his trademark bone-white painters bib overalls. He hadn't been able to shake the feeling that it was going to be his day since leaving his apartment. Humming "American Pie" to himself and tapping his foot to the beat of the Don McLean song, he swerved to miss a pothole. He'd barely straightened the moped back out when the driver of a Chevy Suburban that had been closing in on him gunned the big-block V-8's engine.

Hearing the engine roar and suspecting that the driver was irritated by his dawdling and swerving, Petey moved toward the median, glancing back over his shoulder to make certain he was out of the impatient driver's way. He barely had time to let out a terrified scream as the Suburban sped to over ninety miles an hour, plowed into the moped, and slammed driver and scooter into the guardrail that lined the concrete median. The crunch of the moped and the grinding of the fishtailing Suburban's bumper against the guardrail blended into one as license plates, scooter fenders, and engine parts flew everywhere. Petey's unprotected head bounced from pavement to guardrail as he rocketed headfirst down the freeway, landing ninety feet beyond the point of initial impact.

By the time the Suburban's driver gunned the damaged vehicle west, the driver of a trailing vehicle had his car stopped on the shoulder. Three other vehicles had pulled over and stopped by the time the first driver reached Petey. Seconds later, the Suburban that had slammed into Petey dropped over a rise and disappeared into the Rocky Mountain foothills.

As four terrified witnesses to the hit-and-run stood over Petey Greene's contorted, rag-doll-like body, the driver who'd seen the whole thing unfold felt along Petey's wrist for a pulse.

"Do something!" screamed one of the newcomers.

"There's nothing to be done," the kneeling man said softly.

"How the hell do you know that?" a third man yelled.

"He's got no vitals," came the reply.

"You sure?"

Looking surprisingly calm and clearly less upset than the other witnesses, one of whom had turned his back and walked away to keep from throwing up, the man nodded and said, "I'm a trauma doc at Saint Anthony's Central. Believe me, this man's dead."

CJ had been at the fairgrounds for almost an hour without spotting either Gaylord Marquee or Petey Greene when word began to circulate through the crowd that a license-plate collector from Denver had been killed in an accident on his way to the event.

Thinking at first that the victim might have been Marquee, CJ stopped at a booth in the midst of the buzz to ask the vendor, a bearded man wearing a top hat and sporting 1870s-style muttonchop sideburns, if he knew who the victim was.

"Sure," the man said. "A little colored fellow name'a Petey Greene. Talked too much, but not a bad sort. Too bad—yep, really too bad."

"Shit!" CJ slammed a fist into his open palm.

"Take it you knew him," the man said in response.

"Since grade school." CJ pivoted and broke into an all-out sprint for his car as the man in the top hat stared in amazement at how quickly a six-foot-three, 230-pound man could move.

Rosie Weeks, Etta Lee, Marguerite, Petey Greene's mother, and DeeAnn were all standing in Ike's office by the time CJ got home. On the way, he'd stopped for nearly an hour at the site of the hit-and-run, where a bevy of cops was still on scene, and had even driven what he believed to be the killer's escape route on the access road that paralleled the freeway a couple of times before a cop from whom he'd tried to get information had told him in no uncertain terms to move on.

Syrathia Greene, who'd just come from identifying Petey's body at the Denver General Hospital city morgue, was standing stupefied in front of Ike's desk, one arm locked in Rosie's, when CJ walked in.

Ignoring CJ as he stood looking helpless in the office doorway, Rosie said, "Don't think Mrs. Greene's gonna take no for an answer, Ike."

"You all know I don't do that kind of investigatin' no more," Ike shot back.

"You ran down Nobby Pittman for killin' Marguerite's boy, Billy," Rosie countered.

Ike stared at CJ but aimed his response at Rosie. "That was five-and-a-half years ago, and CJ's the one did all the legwork on that case, not me." He broke into a series of coughs.

"Then maybe CJ should handle looking into Petey's killing," said DeeAnn, surprising everyone with the straightforward comment.

"Hey, hey, hold on a second." CJ stepped into the office and tossed his Stetson onto a wall hook. He was eye to eye with Syrathia when she slipped her arm out of Rosie's, pulled a wad of bills out of her purse, and stuffed them into his left hand. "That's five hundred dollars, Calvin. Find out who killed my Petey."

As CJ stood dumbfounded, he had the odd sense that he was headed somewhere he'd been before. The authoritative look on Ike's face all but dared him to offer a refusal.

"Oh, thank you, Calvin, baby!" Syrathia stepped over and smothered CJ in a hug. "It's a cinch the cops won't do much of anything. Petey was just another street hustler who finally got what was coming to him, as far as they're concerned."

Caught in Syrathia's bear hug and Ike's continued stare, CJ eyed DeeAnn as he labored to breathe. Thinking, *Welcome to my world*, all he could do was flash DeeAnn an acquiescent smile.

Chapter

21

It was midafternoon and the skies had clouded over when CJ, looking for any inside dope he could get on the Petey Greene hit-and-run case, met his lifelong friend and the city's chief morgue attendant, Vernon Lowe, at Dozens, the Lower Downtown breakfast and lunch eatery where Vernon ate at least three times a week. Their waitress, a Latina half Vernon's age whom the womanizing morgue attendant had once dated, seemed eager to rush them out the door before the restaurant's 3 p.m. closing time.

"You guys want anything else?" she asked, sailing their check onto the table, where it lodged under CJ's plate.

"Nah," said Vernon. "Full to the gills. Just gonna finish up my coffee." He flashed the waitress a wink.

Ignoring the wink, she said, "That's because, as usual, you're eating too late." Her tone reflected the fact that she knew Vernon intimately. "You, too, CJ," she said, clearing the table.

"Could be," said Vernon, eyeing the dark-haired waitress from head to toe as she walked away. "Should've stuck with that woman," he lamented.

Having suffered through Vernon's laments about his love life before, CJ simply said, "Yeah, Vernon. Sure."

"I ain't shittin' you, CJ. Me and Molita clicked. Just wasn't the right time for either of us."

"Too many fish in the sea?" asked CJ, tossing one of the slightly built, flashy-dressing morgue attendant's favorite sayings his way.

Vernon smiled. "Yeah, I need to remember that, especially when I see that tush on Molita." He took a sip of coffee and drummed his fingers on the table.

Hoping that their discussion of the hit-and-run accident that had cost Petey Greene his life might yield a few more nuggets of information, CJ asked, "So the cops are saying whoever plowed Petey into that median did it on purpose?"

"Not the cops, CJ. Only one cop's even been around to sort out things. Ol' Doc Woodley's the one sayin' Petey's death wasn't no accident. Him and that pathology-resident friend of yours, Henry Bales, who came by. He's on a two month hematopathology rotation here at DG. They're both singin' the same song."

Woodley, the keen-eyed, Cuban-cigar-smoking Denver City and County coroner and an old poker-playing buddy of Ike's, was a man CJ had known since childhood. CJ had absolutely no reason to doubt him, and Henry Bales, who was in the second year of a four-year pathology residency, of course, he trusted with his life. "What are they basing their suspicions on?" asked CJ.

"Mostly on the fact that we found just about every bone in

poor old Petey's body fractured when we did the post. And I mean compound-type fractures with bones pokin' outa the skin."

"Thought you said earlier Petey died from a fractured skull."

"He did. But that ain't the point. The point is that for Petey to have all them push-through bone fractures like he did, the vehicle that slammed into him, at least accordin' to Doc Woodley, would've had to'a been gainin' speed when it hit him. On top of that, the one cop who dropped by the morgue just after we finished postin' Petey was a homicide type. After thumbin' through all of Woodley's postmortem notes, he told us both that there wasn't a single tire mark anywhere on the pavement within fifty yards of where Petey was hit. Means the person drivin' the vehicle wasn't thinkin' about brakin'."

"Did he mention the make or model of the vehicle to you?"

"Nope. He was sorta close-mouthed about that. But I heard later from one of the pathology department's medical transcriptionists who gets her jollies outa stickin' her nose into anything that even smells like a homicide that one of the eyewitnesses claimed the vehicle that creamed Petey was a Chevy Suburban. A white one."

Reacting with a sense of recognition rather than surprise, CJ stroked his chin and whispered, "Damn."

"You know the vehicle?"

"Not for sure, but I've got my suspicions."

"How about a heads-up, then?"

"I'm thinking that the hit-and-run vehicle might've belonged to an antique peddler named Gaylord Marquee."

"Don't know him."

"No loss on your part. He's a haughty, nose-in-the-air, former-British-army-officer type. I had Petey tailing him—trying to help me close the door on those GI Joe's killings from a few years back."

"Damn, CJ. I thought you'd let loose of that GI Joe's case a long time ago. The cops never pinned them two killings on nobody, best I can remember. And I'm here to tell you for a fact, wasn't nothin' surprisin' that turned up in the posts on them two dead men that even that nosy medical transcriptionist of ours woulda been interested in."

"There was one thing."

Looking surprised and trying to jog his memory, Vernon asked, "What? I know for certain it wasn't the murder weapon."

"You're right. That would've been a .44 Mag. Pretty common gun when you come right down to it. What was unusual was the pinpoint accuracy of the shots. The *Rocky* and the *Post* both did stories on it. Just two shots, Vernon, and both of them dead-on. Shots that were fired from an archway a good fifty feet away from the victims. You have to be a damn good marksman to pull that off. Good enough, in fact, to have earned yourself a sniper classification in the British army."

"I'm startin' to get your drift," said Vernon.

CJ nodded, took a sip of tepid coffee, and frowned. "I had Ike check out Marquee. Even had him talk to an old British army buddy he served with in Korea. A sergeant who was a member of the famous Scottish Argylls regiment. Marquee was a sniper all right, and a damn good one."

"Then I'd say you need to talk to the man."

"Top of my agenda," CJ said with a smile.

"So you're thinkin' when it's all netted out, Petey's death is tied to those GI Joe's killin's?"

"Absolutely."

"Awful long, windin' stretch of river from here back to there," said Vernon, rising from his chair and brushing himself off.

Looking reflective, CJ said, "Sorta like the Mekong."

It took a couple of seconds for CJ's Vietnam river reference to register. When it did, Vernon said, "There is a difference, though. Nobody's shootin' at you."

"Give 'em time, Vernon. Just give 'em a little time," CJ said, standing and following Vernon out of the restaurant.

After swinging by Marquee's house and finding no one there, CJ went back to his office and made two quick phone calls. The first was to Ramona Lepsos, but instead of her, he got a gruff-sounding woman who told him Ramona wasn't in. He left his phone number and asked the woman to have Ramona call him back. Then he immediately called Rosie Weeks.

Rosie, who was in the midst of dropping the transmission out of a one-ton pickup when the call came in, sounded perturbed. Wiping transmission fluid and blood from a scraped knuckle off his hands with a shop rag, Rosie hesitated when CJ asked if he could give a vehicle the once-over and tell him whether it might have been involved in a hit-and-run accident. He answered, "Probably," then swallowed the word whole when CJ told him that the damage assessment might involve breaking and entering.

An hour later the lifelong friends stood in Gaylord Marquee's backyard, a few feet from the side entry to his garage. "How do you know he ain't here?" Rosie asked, looking around and sweating.

"Because I came by here and checked things out after meeting Vernon Lowe for lunch."

"Hell. He coulda come back home since then."

"He's not here, Rosie. Trust me," said CJ, who ten minutes earlier had again checked out the house, the grounds, and the garage for any sign of Marquee before waving for Rosie to join him from his hiding spot behind a massive old oak tree.

"Etta Lee finds out I'm into helpin' you with this kinda shit again, she'll brain me."

Jimmying the side door to the garage open, CJ said, "She won't find out. And watch out for dogs."

The mixed smell of mildew and machine oil greeted them as they entered the three-car garage. "There ain't but one vehicle in here," said Rosie, quickly surveying the garage. "And a bunch of boxes," he added, eyeing the cardboard boxes that lined every wall.

"Let's have a look at it." CJ headed for the vehicle, his footsteps echoing off the painted and polished concrete floor.

"It's a Suburban, and it's white," said Rosie, looking around for any sign of dogs.

"And the front end's smashed," said CJ, examining the Suburban's badly damaged front bumper and left front quarter panel. "How's that for coincidence?"

"So what did you need me for?" Rosie asked, reacting with

a start to the sound of the wind rattling against the garage's only window.

"To offer an expert opinion on what might've caused the damage and to help me take some paint-chip samples that I'm hoping Vernon can match up to the paint they found on Petey's body at the autopsy."

"Shit, man. Maybe you shoulda been a cop."

CJ flashed Rosie a look of disbelief. "Are you crazy?"

"Well, you're sure as hell actin' and soundin' like one."

"Would you just get over here and take a good look at the damage?"

Rosie approached the front of the car carefully, examining every angle and curve. Skilled not simply at repairing automobiles, he'd restored more than a dozen over the years. Stepping back, he eyed the Suburban's damaged front end as if he were looking through the viewfinder of a camera. Squatting, he ran his hand beneath the bumper, shook his head, and duck walked to its point of maximum structural damage, where the bumper was badly crimped and the fender sunk to within inches of the left front tire. Glancing back and noting that the nose of the vehicle was barely puckered and that the grill was only slightly bent, Rosie felt along the floor and began sniffing.

CJ, who'd watched close-mouthed until then, asked, "What are you doing?"

Rosie answered, "Checkin' for antifreeze."

"See any?"

"Nope." Rosie stood with a grunt. He chipped a couple of metal flecks away from creases in the damaged fender, mumbled,

"Paint chips," and handed them to CJ, who slipped them into a sandwich bag he had taken out of his pocket.

"So what do you think?" asked CJ, his curiosity having gotten the best of him.

"I don't think this chariot hit nobody."

"What?"

"I said, I don't think this vehicle's been in an accident. Especially not a hit-and-run."

"Why?"

"'Cause the body damage ain't there to support it. You ever seen a car that's run into a deer?"

"Yeah."

"Well, hittin' a deer would pretty much be the equivalent of hittin' a hundred-and-fifty-pound man. And if you were doing seventy, maybe even eighty miles an hour, like you told me Vernon said the vehicle that hit Petey was doin', you'd'a blasted the hell outa your front end. Done a damn sight more damage than what I'm seein' here."

"You're sure?"

"Damn it, CJ! Have I ever asked you whether or not you were sure you could handle that damn .50-caliber machine gun you were strapped to during Vietnam? Yeah, I'm sure. I ain't certain what caused the damage here," he said, eyeing the Suburban's front end once again. "Coulda been somebody swingin' a ball-peen hammer and a crowbar, for all I know, but this baby didn't hit anyone."

"Then either somebody's trying to set Marquee up or Marquee's leaving one hell of a false trail for the cops."

"Why would anybody do that?"

"Beats me."

Rosie jerked his head around to the sound of the garage's metal roof rattling in the wind. "You ask me, I'd vote for somebody tryin' to set Marquee up. Now, can we get the hell outa here?"

Glancing at the boxes lining the garage's north wall, CJ said, "I was thinking maybe we should have a look inside some of these boxes of Marquee's and then maybe have a look inside the house."

"Well, I sure as hell ain't stickin' around if you do."

The sound of a vehicle outside sent Rosie sprinting for the door and CJ dashing to the window. An Emery Air Express truck was pulled into Marquee's driveway. The driver got out, jogged briskly to the front door, and rang the doorbell. When no one came to greet him after several additional rings, he left a delivery tag on the door handle, dashed back to his truck, and sped off.

CJ watched the truck round the corner and disappear before whispering, "Let's split." Once outside, he walked causally from the garage to the front door, retrieved the delivery notice, and, close on the retreating Rosie's heels, headed back the two blocks to where he'd parked the Bel Air.

"Damn it, CJ. You're stealin'," Rosie said, eyeing the delivery tag as they slipped into the car.

"Nope. I'm borrowing temporarily," CJ countered, examining the delivery notice.

"What's it say?"

"That they'll be back for redelivery tomorrow. And so might we," said CJ, watching Rosie turn ever more nervous by the second as they drove away.

Rosie complained all the way home about the risk they'd be taking if they broke into Marquee's garage a second time, so intently that by the time CJ dropped him off at home, he was happy for some peace and quiet. He plopped in a Muddy Waters tape and, tapping his foot to one of the famous bluesman's Mississippi Delta laments about his best friend stealing his dog and his wife, lit up a cheroot, rolled down his front window to let in the crisp early-spring air, and headed home.

DeeAnn met him as he pulled into the driveway, ashen-faced and looking terrified. The Bel Air was still rolling when she raced up to it, grabbed CJ's arm, and said breathlessly, "Ike passed out a little bit ago while he was making a pot of coffee. The paramedics came and rushed him to Denver General. They think he might've had a heart attack. Marguerite went with them."

Biting through what was left of his cheroot, CJ gripped the steering wheel with both hands and stared straight ahead.

"You okay?" DeeAnn asked, taking in the blank stare on CJ's face.

"Yes." CJ's answer was barely a whisper.

"Think we better head for Denver General," said DeeAnn, scurrying around the front of the Bel Air and slipping in.

CJ simply nodded. The bone-numbing chill that had started in the soles of his feet had worked its way into the depths of his chest. When he backed the car out of the driveway and onto the busy street without so much as a backward glance in the rearview mirror, DeeAnn screamed, "Watch out!" Before she could say anything else, they were doing seventy miles an hour down the middle of Delaware Street.

Marguerite Larkin was pacing the floor of a dimly lit anteroom just outside the emergency room when CJ and DeeAnn arrived. The nauseating institutional smell of disinfectant mixed with floor wax had her on edge, dredging up memories of her days as an often-beaten prostitute.

Rushing to embrace her, CJ asked, "How's he doing?"

"I don't know." Marguerite's eyes welled with tears. "They won't tell me anything."

CJ groaned in exasperation and walked across the room to where a woman in a dingy white uniform sat behind a desk. "I'd like to get some information on my uncle's status. Ike Floyd's the name," CJ said, doing his best to control his temper.

"I'm sorry, you'll have to talk to the doctor who's treating him." The woman's tone was slightly condescending and absolutely firm.

"Who's that?"

Consulting a single canary-colored sheet of paper on the desk, she said, "Dr. Brimley's attending cardiac cases this evening."

"So you can't tell me anything about my uncle's condition?"

"You'll have to talk to Dr. Brimley, sir."

CJ wanted to scream at the woman, force her to do something, curse at her if necessary, but with visions of a navy corpsman racing through waist-high Mekong River estuary grass and muck to attend to his wounded arm, he instead mumbled, "Henry," and asked, "Is there a phone here I can use?"

"Right over there." The woman pointed to a courtesy phone on a nearby table. "You'll need to keep your call to two minutes, sir."

"Do you have a number for the pathology residents' room?"

Looking puzzled, she slipped a sheet of paper from beneath the blotter on her desk, ran a finger down a column, and said, "Extension 57551."

"Thanks." CJ hastily walked over to the courtesy phone, picked up the receiver, and started punching in the extension. As he dialed, he whispered, "Henry, please be there." When the man who answered announced, "Residents' room," CJ blurted, "Is Henry Bales there? It's urgent."

"Henry around?" the resident who'd answered yelled.

"He's over in the microscope room signing out a case," came the reply.

"Well, get him. He's got a phone call hanging." The resident turned his attention back to CJ. "He'll be here in a sec."

"Thanks."

Thirty seconds later, Henry Bales was on the line. "Dr. Bales here."

"Henry, it's CJ. I'm down in the ER. They just brought my Uncle Ike in, and they think he's had a heart attack. Nobody'll tell me a damn thing. I sure could use somebody running a little interference for me right now."

"I'm on my way," said Henry, surprising the resident who'd answered the phone with his quickness as he knocked a half-full Styrofoam cup of rancid, day-old coffee onto the floor and raced out the door.

A broad, been-through-hell-together kind of grin spread across Henry's face as he greeted his former shipmate with a fist pump and a hug less than two minutes after talking to CJ on the phone. "Aft gunner," he said with a wink, barely taking notice of DeeAnn and Marguerite, who stood across the room.

"Corpsman," came CJ's rote reply.

"Let's take a nibble at your problem," said Henry.

"Okay, but like I said on the phone, I can't seem to get past Nurse Ratched over there." CJ nodded in the direction of the receptionist.

"First off, tell me what happened."

"Ike passed out while he was making coffee." CJ glanced toward Marguerite and DeeAnn, who stood together looking nervous and holding hands. "What I need is a heads-up, Henry. Good, bad, it doesn't really matter, okay?"

"I'll see what I can do," said Henry, pivoting to head for the doors to the ER.

"Appreciate it."

"No problem," said Henry, leaving DeeAnn to wonder exactly who the tall, high-cheek-boned, American Indian–looking man in the coffee-stained white lab coat was.

Chapter

22

Henry Bales was sitting in the pathology department's case sign-out room breaking the rules again. But this time the rules were quite different from those he and CJ had broken to earn them both Navy Crosses. On that evening, against orders, they'd left the estuary-anchored *Cape Star* just before twilight on a mission to rescue a couple of marines, the only survivors from a platoon that had been surprised a couple of hours earlier by a river's-edge Vietcong machine-gun ambush. They'd left the *Cape Star* with CJ toting two M-16s and enough ammo for a firefight and Henry, thumbing his nose directly in the face of Geneva Convention noncombatant rules, packing a .45. The *Cape Star* had been ordered to stay put because an assault helicopter air strike had been called in to take out the enemy machine gunner, and no one wanted to risk having some overeager assault-chopper jockey take out a navy patrol boat by mistake. Knowing the lay of the land and aware that they could approach the enemy gunner from his blind side and eliminate him within minutes instead of wasting the time it would take to wait for the air strike, CJ and Henry had disobeyed orders.

In the space of just four minutes after leaving the *Cape Star*, CJ had killed the Vietcong machine gunner and Henry had treated the two injured marines. The marines were back at the *Cape Star* and in sick bay before the assault helicopter even took off.

Their actions initially garnered them both captain's masts and a reduction in rank. But as word of their heroics made it both up and down the chain of command, led by the cheerleading of a grizzled marine brigadier general who'd started out as an enlisted man in World War II, the captain's-mast findings mysteriously disappeared. When that same Wyoming born and bred general said that CJ and Henry were the kind of cowboys he wanted under his direct command, Navy Crosses suddenly appeared. Henry still wore a miniature replica of his Navy Cross pinned to his undershirt for good luck.

Adjusting the height of the chair he'd dragged up to one of the sign-out room's microscopes, Henry looked across the table at CJ, then down through the scope's eyepiece at a "quick prep" of Ike's sputum. "Just like old times," he said, glad that, for the moment at least, the ER doctors had ruled out the possibility that Ike had had a heart attack.

"If they find out I'm in here looking at this sputum sample with someone who's not authorized—and on top of that before I even show it to my attending—there'll be hell to pay," said Henry.

"Then we better not let whoever the hell *they* are find out," said CJ.

Henry flashed his nervously fidgeting friend a quick smile.

"Hope that lab coat of mine you're trying your best to split the seams on holds the nosies at bay, Dr. Floyd." Adjusting the slide on the microscope's stage, he hunched forward and said, "The news could be bad."

"Well?" CJ asked after Henry had scanned the slide for a good half minute.

Henry sat back in his chair, glum-faced. "Doesn't look good. Just about every cell in the prep is atypical. Nuclei twice their normal size, cells with no cytoplasm—I'm afraid it's probably cancer, CJ. Can't tell you for sure without seeing a lung biopsy, but I'm pretty sure."

CJ felt the back of his throat begin to tingle, then tighten. He'd known people who had cancer. A high school classmate of his had died from leukemia their senior year. But he'd never had so ominous a diagnosis hit so close to home. "What are his chances?"

"I don't know. I'd have to know a lot before I could give you any kind of prognosis."

CJ shook his head and bit back what he realized was not sadness but anger. "Ike won't let them treat it. I can tell you that right now."

"Let's get a definitive diagnosis before we get into that," Henry said, rising from his chair, walking over to CJ, and patting him reassuringly on the shoulder. "And let's get the hell out of here before somebody starts to get nosy."

When CJ didn't respond, Henry started for the door. He was almost through it before CJ followed. As they walked through the adjoining tissue preparation lab and he struggled out of

Henry's ill-fitting lab coat, CJ resisted the urge to scream, *"No!"* at the top of his lungs.

Molly Burgess was pacing the Idaho Springs, Colorado, motel room where she and Cheryl Goldsby had stayed for the past two nights and staring down at wax buildup on the badly warped linoleum floor.

"Would you sit down?" Cheryl implored from where she sat uncomfortably on a lumpy, calico-covered sofa.

"How the hell can you be so calm after this morning?" Burgess shot back.

"It's something I've learned to do over the years."

"Well, would you please pass your prescription on to me? I feel like throwing up."

Cheryl rose from her seat, walked over to Molly, and hugged her. "You're not at Carnegie Hall preparing for a concert, Molly. Marquee will cough up the money. Things will smooth out."

Looking disappointed, Molly said, "And this was supposed to be such a special weekend for us. Camping and hiking in the mountains, less than forty-five minutes from downtown Denver, and enjoying the seclusion. It's been more like a bad acid trip, if you ask me. Why did you have to get tangled up with Marquee?"

Cheryl laughed. "Money, Molly. Money. Something artists like you often have a hard time understanding." Cheryl ran a finger affectionately across her lover's cheek.

"I understand money, Cheryl. What I don't understand is the need for anyone to kill for it." Slipping away from Cheryl,

Molly returned to pacing the floor, head down, her eyes focused on the linoleum, unwilling to turn the discussion into what she knew would only escalate into another argument.

CJ had been sitting alone in the darkness in Ike's office, in Ike's chair, for close to an hour, suffering as he recalled all the things his uncle had done to try to turn him into a decent human being. No matter how hard he tried, he couldn't remember Ike ever letting him down, even during the heaviest days of his drinking. Ike had never passed judgment on CJ, never told him that he needed to do this or that, or insisted that he be more like someone else and less like who he was. Ike had simply always been there for him—occasionally inebriated but always and absolutely there.

Over the past couple of hours, the words *lung cancer* had worked their way so deeply into his subconscious that CJ swore those two words alone were responsible for his headache and the ringing in his ears.

It had taken CJ, Henry, and Marguerite the better part of a half hour to get Ike to agree that he needed to be admitted to the hospital. CJ, Marguerite, and DeeAnn had left Denver General knowing that the doctors wouldn't have a definitive diagnosis on Ike's condition until late the next day after a lung biopsy.

He would very likely have sat all night in Ike's chair, staring into the darkness and wishing away his anguish, if Ike's phone hadn't rung. He let it ring five ear-piercing times before he slipped a cheroot out of the soft pack in his shirt pocket, toyed with it briefly, and finally picked up the receiver. "Floyds Bail Bonds."

"CJ Floyd, please."

"Speaking." CJ tapped one end of the cheroot on the desk-top.

"Mr. Floyd, glad I caught you. This is Ramona Lepsos. I got your message."

Still less than focused, CJ said, "Thanks for calling back. I'm hoping you can help me with a little more info about that Englishman, Gaylord Marquee, the guy Cheryl Goldsby was playing stolen-goods-fencing footsies with."

"How can I help?"

Deciding he might as well be blunt, CJ asked, "Think Marquee's the kind of person who could kill someone?"

"What?"

"Do you think Marquee's capable of murder?"

"Not really. My impression was always that Marquee and Cheryl's uncle Wiley were just a couple of bumbling old farts."

"What about Molly Burgess?"

"She'd be capable of anything, in my book. Why all the questions about murder, anyway?"

"Because a friend of mine who was staking out Marquee's house for me was killed in a hit-and-run accident this morning. It's possible Marquee was behind the wheel of the vehicle that killed him."

"What on earth did your friend find out about Marquee that could've possibly driven Marquee to commit murder?"

"Not much, as far as I can see, other than the fact that he'd spotted your old girlfriend, Cheryl, and Molly Burgess outside Marquee's house recently."

"Maybe the three of them were exchanging seashells," Lepsos said with a chuckle.

"Yeah. And then again, maybe they'd spotted my friend and they were busy planning how to get rid of him. No way you would've had an inkling of what they were up to, is there?"

"No. I'm just a fifth wheel, remember?"

"So you've told me."

"Well, it's the truth!"

"That's always the best tack in my book. Here's another question for you. Did you ever meet Quan Lee Chin, that Chinese guy who was killed along with Ames? He was a concert cellist just like Molly Burgess, you know."

"Never met him."

"I see," said CJ, trying to gauge whether Ramona was lying. "Any idea where Burgess and Cheryl might be now? I tried calling them at the ranch, but no one answered."

"Haven't the foggiest. I'm trying to forget the past and live in the present, Mr. Floyd."

"Good idea. By the way, any chance Cheryl owns a Suburban?"

"Nope. Just a couple of pickups."

"And you drive a . . . ?"

"A Dodge Ram Charger, midnight black. I didn't run down your friend, Mr. Floyd."

"Of course you didn't."

"Hope you find his killer."

"Or killers," said CJ. "Appreciate the call back."

"Sure," said Ramona, hanging up and leaving CJ staring once again into the darkness.

Within moments of cradling the phone, Ramona was out of her chair in the living room and back in the bedroom of the Denver apartment she'd recently leased. Retrieving the four absolutely pristine early-1900s porcelain license plates and half-dozen rare seashells she'd stolen from Cheryl Goldsby the day Cheryl had left her from a small box beneath her bed, she took a seat on the edge of the bed and examined each item. "Steal from me, and I'll steal from you," she whispered as she slipped the pistol her father, an Albuquerque former cop, had carried most of his career out of the box. Checking the gun's fully loaded clip, she muttered, "Payback's a bitch, Cheryl. Sooner or later we all find that out."

CJ was still sitting in the chair when DeeAnn stepped into Ike's office and turned on the lights. Startled to see CJ there, she said, "In my rush to get Marguerite home, I forgot I left the keys to my apartment here. I spent the last couple of hours consoling her. Are you okay?"

"Yeah."

"Good."

"Did you know Marguerite was once a prostitute?"

CJ nodded.

"She had to have been as tough as nails to dig herself outa that hole."

"She still is."

Sensing that nothing she said would draw CJ out of his shell, she said, "You can't sit here all night," walked over, and clasped CJ's right hand in both of hers.

"I know. I was just thinking about when I was a kid and how Ike, half drunk at the time, taught me how to ride a bicycle." CJ shook his head and smiled. "And on a hill, no less. Said I'd pick up speed going downhill, and that would help me keep my balance."

"Did it?"

"Sure did. I went flying down that hill like a bat outa hell. Never felt even once like I was going to fall. I also had no idea how the shit I was going to stop. A cottonwood tree at the bottom of the hill solved that problem. When I looked back up the hill, with one knee bleeding and a busted lip, all I could see was Ike looking horrified as he raced toward me screaming, 'Are you okay?' He picked me up and squeezed me so hard I could barely breathe. It was probably the first time I realized how much he cared."

DeeAnn took a seat on the edge of Ike's desk and nodded understandingly. "I'm guessing the two of you are a lot alike."

"In a lot of ways we are, and in some ways we aren't."

"He'll make it through this, CJ. So will you."

"Yeah," CJ said with a sigh. "You ever lose anybody that close to you?"

"My brother, but you already knew that, and of course my dad. He was a jazz musician. I never really saw a lot of him when I was growing up. He was on the road a lot. Even so, we were close. He was killed in a car wreck just before I turned fourteen. I hurt real bad after that for a long, long time."

"Guess I'll be luckier. At least I'll be prepared," CJ said, rising from his chair.

"What you need to prepare for is doing what you've always done. Ike's being sick won't change the need for that." Realizing that CJ was staring directly into her eyes and feeling suddenly self-conscious, DeeAnn asked, "Is my hair out of place?"

"Nope. Just wondering where you get all your insight."

"From living life, Mr. Floyd. Where else?" she said, easing off the edge of the desk.

CJ slipped his arm around her waist and started walking her to the door. When they reached the doorway, bumping hips as they squeezed through, DeeAnn said, "Tomorrow's gonna be rough."

"Yeah," said CJ, feeling the softness of her body press against his. Suddenly remembering, as if the devil were sitting there on his shoulder to remind him, that he was scheduled to take Mavis to the airport at eleven the next morning, he repeated, this time more softly and with a bit of uncertainty in his tone, "Yeah."

With his lip curled upward into a snarl, Gaylord Marquee, just awakened by Molly Burgess's phone call, said, "In case you don't have access to a clock, Ms. Burgess, it's midnight." He glanced at the three-chime antique alarm clock on the nightstand next to his bed and frowned.

"I know what time it is, Marquee. I'm calling to find out if you've heard about what happened to that man you mentioned had been casing your house."

"I understand he had a minor accident."

"Minor! He's dead."

"A major accident, then."

"I hope you or Cheryl didn't have anything to do with that."

"I certainly didn't," said Marquee. "As for your girlfriend, I really can't say."

"You're a lying manipulator, Marquee."

"And you're a bloodsucking opportunist, my dear. Who's to say you didn't run that snooper down?"

"Screw you, twerp."

"Afraid you'll never have the pleasure. But then again, that's something someone with your sexual preference couldn't possibly appreciate."

Marquee's lips curved into a sly, judgmental smile as he heard Molly Burgess slam the receiver down.

Chapter

23

Deciding that office busywork wasn't going to help take his mind off Ike's plight and knowing Henry wouldn't have a solid diagnosis of Ike's condition until late the next day, CJ decided to drop by GI Joe's and see whether Harry Steed might have some insight into the whereabouts of Gaylord Marquee. The last time he had mentioned Marquee to Harry had been months before on the telephone, when they'd discussed Marquee being a possible suspect in the murders.

Except for a fresh coat of paint on the front door and different merchandise in the windows, GI Joe's hadn't changed much since that day in 1971 when he'd walked in looking for the license plate he'd hidden there.

Harry was busy waiting on a customer when CJ arrived a little after nine. Steed waved and went back to what he was best at: dickering, selling, and wrangling a deal.

In all his years of digging into the lives and habits of people with connections to the GI Joe's killings, CJ had learned more about Harry Steed than perhaps anyone else. Even so, he'd never truly interacted much with Steed. Anyone who'd ever offered an insightful comment about Steed, from the close-to-the-vest homicide detective who'd initially worked the GI Joe's murders case to Cheryl Goldsby, had made no bones about the fact that Steed admitted that Ames and Chin had been fencing stolen goods. No one, however, could link any fencing activities directly to the pawnshop itself, and certainly not to Steed, whose cooperative attitude, meticulous sales records, and sterling reputation had him pretty much off the list of suspects early in the investigation.

CJ had never had the sense that Steed had killed Ames or Chin, especially over a mere twenty to twenty-five thousand dollars' worth of stolen seashells. But knowing firsthand that Nobby Pittman had killed for less was enough to remind him to never eliminate anyone.

As he strolled down the aisles of the pawnshop looking at things that hadn't been moved from their dust-ringed spots in display cases for years, he had the sense that places like GI Joe's weren't long for this world. When he spotted a vintage American Library Association poster featuring a soldier and sailor posing for a World War I war-zone reading campaign, he stopped. The poster hung cockeyed on the wall above a display case less than fifteen feet from where Wiley Ames's Wall of the West had been. He was still admiring the remarkably pristine 1918 poster when the customer whom Steed had been helping brushed past him, muttering, "Hope he offers you a better deal on that poster. Fuckin' skinflint!" The man rushed out the front door in a huff.

With the bell above the door still jingling, Harry appeared as if out of nowhere and positioned himself behind the glass-topped case in front of CJ. Squaring his shoulders defiantly, he said, "Unreasonable—wanting a hundred and fifty for some beat-to-crap, scarred-up old bootjack. Sent him packing is what I did." He grabbed CJ's right hand and began pumping it. "Good to see you, CJ."

CJ slipped his hand out of Harry's weak, clammy grip and said, "Less than a satisfied customer, I take it."

"SOB wanted something for nothing. I'm not selling any of that today." Eyeing the poster, ever the salesman, he said, "See you've got your eye on a real gem. Vintage World War I. I'll let you take it off my hands for two hundred even."

"Steep."

"Aren't many more around like that one, trust me."

"I'll have to think about it."

"Suit yourself," said Harry, deciding to save his hard sell for later. "Now, what else are you here to do me out of today?"

"A little info if you've got it."

"Not murder-case information, I hope. Damn it, man. It's been five-and-a-half years."

"And counting. What I'm after is anything you have on Gaylord Marquee. Something that could have slipped your mind. Something you might've forgotten to tell me in the past."

"You planning some kind of assault on Marquee?"

"Maybe. Yesterday a friend of mine who was tailing Marquee for me was killed in a hit-and-run accident. Haven't been able to locate Marquee since."

"Damn. And you're thinking maybe Marquee was behind the wheel?"

"I don't know. What I do know is that a Suburban parked in Marquee's garage has serious front-end damage and that he's recently been in contact with Cheryl Goldsby, that niece of Wiley's, and a special friend of hers named Molly Burgess. Any chance you can connect the dots between those three?"

"Don't know Burgess. But like I've told you before, Cheryl and Marquee are plain and simple a couple of money grubbers."

Unwilling to tell Harry that more than a few people he'd talked to over the years had said the same thing about him, CJ said, "I think Marquee and Goldsby were dealing in rare stolen seashells. Cheryl even let me see her stash once. I don't think she would've done that if she'd killed Wiley, or if she thought you could prove the goods were stolen. She's smart. Real smart. I've been trying to wrap my arms around why anyone would kill what looks like three people now for a few stolen seashells. And to tell you the truth, Harry, I'm stumped."

Harry laughed. It was an insightful sound that as much as said to CJ, *And you never will.* "That's because you're not in the business of moving the merchandise, CJ. You're purely and simply a collector. There's a difference. When you deal with selling things, whether or not it's mindless little trinkets, stolen seashells, or that vintage World War I poster up there on the wall, the bottom line is moving the goods, end of story. But if you're a collector, it's the demand for the thing you've got that sets the money bar."

"So what you're saying is that I shouldn't necessarily be looking at simply the value of something to establish a murder motive."

"Pretty much. Somebody out there might need that one mundane-looking seashell you've got to complete their collection. And if you've got the goods, you're the car's driver."

"Hate to ask, Harry, but you weren't in on Wiley and Chin's seashell-fencing scam, were you?" CJ asked.

Harry cackled. "Here's my straight-up answer for you: no way I'd involve myself in some dumbass fencing scam. And here's a little more smoke for your investigative pipe. I'll use that poster you're looking at as a hopefully instructive example, even thought it could cost me. There's not much flow of those kinds of posters around the pawnshop circuit anymore, so you might think, given its rarity, that the poster would fetch a quick top dollar. Problem is, the demand's not there. Selling something like that requires zeroing in on a specialist. A buyer like you, for instance, who's heavy into Western memorabilia. It wouldn't matter if I had a thousand posters like that, mint condition to the hilt, if I couldn't find myself a specialist. I'd be dead in the water."

CJ stroked his chin thoughtfully. "So maybe when it comes to the killings, in addition to not appreciating the killer's need for the mundane, in order to complete a collection, for example, I've also been looking at things from the perspective of a specialist for too long."

"It's what I'm saying," Steed said with a grin. "Maybe you should start looking for a high-volume seller like Marquee and forget about your specialists and hoarders."

"But what if Cheryl and Marquee teamed up and took over handling the sale of her uncle's stolen seashells? Then they would've scored a double whammy: high-volume seller meets specialist supplier. Frankenstein meets the Werewolf, more or less."

"It's an idea. Especially since, as a rule, buyers don't generally care who the hell they buy from. Cheryl steps in to take the place of her uncle, Marquee steps in to replace Chin, and bingo, even with Wiley gone, you've maintained yourself a nice little profit center. One that's run by a couple of new faces but that can keep on running for as long as the supply of goods lasts."

"Tidy little cottage industry. But why kill my guy Petey?"

"Beats me," said Steed. "Maybe your guy got closer to them than he should've."

"Yeah, maybe," said CJ, clearly not convinced. "Looks like now all I've got to do is find Marquee."

"Better you than me," said Harry, glancing up at the World War I poster. "Special for the day, 15 percent off the two hundred."

CJ couldn't help but smile at Harry's persistence. "Like I said earlier, I'll have to think about it."

"Okay. But tomorrow the price goes back up to two hundred."

"Not even your original 10 percent discount?"

"Not even," Harry said with a smile. "I'm a seller, not a hoarder, my friend."

"So what you're counting on is that there's another specialist hoarder type like me out there somewhere," CJ said, turning to leave.

"You've got it," Harry said with a wink.

CJ found himself chuckling as he left, thinking that skinflint or not, Harry Steed was definitely one of a kind.

CJ stopped by Denver General Hospital a little before 10 a.m. to check on Ike. Feisty, looking fully recovered from his ordeal the previous evening, and sounding like an inmate planning a prison break, Ike bombarded him with a single question the instant CJ walked in: "When the hell do I get outa here?" His weak attempt to mask his shortness of breath with a thoughtful, deep-inhaling pause couldn't hide the fact that the onetime Golden Gloves champion was facing a formidable foe.

"You get out after they do your biopsy and run some tests," said CJ, trying not to think about the diagnostic preview he'd had the previous evening.

"Fuckin' medical bureaucracy gone amuck, if you ask me. I'm feelin' fine." His grayish skin cast and hollow cheeks spoke otherwise. "One good thing, though—I know there's at least one good doctor on the staff. Henry Bales has been in here to check on me twice already this morning."

Relieved, CJ said, "Good."

Wheezing and looking as if he desperately needed to cough but couldn't, Ike sat farther up in bed. "Where you headed from here?"

"To take Mavis to the airport."

"She's headed back to Boston already? Shit. She wasn't here no time."

"Just a week."

"The two of you still hittin' it off okay?"

"Yes."

"That's one hell of an unenthusiastic yes, boy."

"We're doing fine, Unc."

"So was Custer 'til he saw all them Indians headed his way. You wanna tell me the truth?"

CJ took a deep breath and exhaled slowly. "I'm not sure Mavis and me are cut out for the long run."

"What the shit are you talkin' about? The girl's been stuck on you, and Lord, don't ask me why, since she was a kid. You oughta be dancin' a jig and thankin' your lucky stars over the fact."

"Maybe that's the problem. You yearn for something long enough and in the end you find out it's not at all what you imagined. Or maybe you fantasize about hooking up with someone beautiful and cultured and classy only to realize that when all's said and done, you're reading through the same old princess-and-toad story."

"You been drinkin', CJ?"

"Come on, Unc."

"Well, you sure as hell sound like it." Ike coughed up a bloody string of phlegm into a tissue before gulping a couple of mouthfuls of air. "Let me clue you in on somethin'. Somethin' it looks like you damn sure ain't come to realize yet. There're things that don't come around but once in life. Things you need to grab ahold of for dear life before they pass you by as quick as a goddamn missile." There was sad insightfulness in Ike's tone. "I've been there. I know. I shoulda latched on to Marguerite, gave her babies, and strutted her around town like she was a goddess a long time ago. But I didn't, and damn it, she wouldn't let me. Said I'd be a laughin' stock if I married a former prostitute, and fool that I was, I listened to her. Now I'm here in this hospital bed sufferin' from somethin' that more than likely'll take me out, starin' at a shitpot full'a wouldas and shouldas. Don't make the same mistake as me, CJ. Nail down your future while you got the chance. You hear me?"

CJ nodded but said nothing.

"Good." Ike leaned forward in bed and took a deep, preparatory breath, but before he could say anything else, Marguerite walked into the room with a vase full of spring flowers in her hands.

Noting the intensely instructive look on Ike's face, she eyed CJ, who was looking at his watch, and asked, "Is he layin' it on thick again?"

"As thick as I can," Ike responded as, shaking her head, Marguerite set the flowers on a bedside table and kissed him on the cheek.

When she turned to give CJ a hug, he embraced her briefly and said, "I've got to run. I need to get Mavis to the airport by eleven-thirty."

"Then you better get going. I'll handle Dear Abby here," she said, playfully rubbing the blossoming bald spot on Ike's head.

"You take my words to heart," Ike said, exchanging a high five with CJ as he headed for the exit.

"I will." He was out of the room and halfway down the hall when Marguerite, who'd seated herself on the bed next to Ike and clasped his hands tightly in hers, said, "What were you pontificating about to CJ this time, Isaac?"

Looking at the woman he'd been in love with for twenty-five years squarely in the eye, Ike took a truncated breath and wheezed, "I was tellin' the boy about love and how when he finds it he needs to grab ahold of it for dear life. Just hopin' he listened."

For most of the short ride from Mavis's house to Denver's Stapleton Airport, CJ and Mavis remained silent. Mavis, who was fidgeting with the latch on her purse for most of the way, finally spoke up when CJ turned off Thirty-second Avenue onto airport property. "Holding things in won't help, CJ. And neither will shutting people out. You and Ike are going to need the support of every one of your friends to get through this. Please know that you can count on me and Daddy."

CJ nodded, aware that although Willis Sundee would be there for Ike to lean on, as would Rosie and Etta Lee, Henry Bales, and Vernon Lowe, Mavis would be back in Boston in a different world. A distant all-white world, for the most part, whose inhabitants would eventually become doctors and lawyers, politicians and intellectuals.

He pulled the Bel Air to a stop in front of the United Airlines departure gates, and as Mavis, dressed in calf-high leather boots and an elegant pleated Western skirt, got out, he couldn't help but revel in her distinctly refreshing, sophisticated beauty. She was the kind of woman who could be comfortable anywhere—unflappable, affable, and worldly. It wasn't until she reached up to pat her curly, windblown hair into place that she realized CJ was standing next to her staring.

Planting a soft, lingering kiss on his lips, she said, "I'm hoping you're liking what you're seeing, Mr. Floyd."

"That I am."

"Think about me while I'm gone, okay?"

"Okay. Sure you don't want me to walk you to the gate? I can still go back and park the car."

"Yes, I'm sure. You need to be with Ike."

"Try not to forget about us common folks back here in Denver."

"I never forget about home, CJ. Or where I've come from," she added, snapping the handle of her carry-on into place.

Wishing he could eat his words, CJ gave her a final kiss on the cheek. "Call me when you get there, okay?"

"Yes," she said, returning the kiss and heading for the terminal.

As he watched Mavis walk toward a set of revolving doors, her hair blowing casually in the wind, CJ found himself thinking about the haunting lyrics to a *West Side Story* song. The words *Stick with your own kind* threaded their way through his head as he slipped back behind the wheel of the Bel Air and headed for the office, knowing that DeeAnn would certainly be there by now.

Chapter

🦎 24

All the way home from the airport CJ found himself comparing DeeAnn and Mavis, confused as to exactly why the strange game of comparison had started, suspecting that maybe it was simply a protective mechanism to help him keep his mind off Ike.

Telling himself there was no way he could possibly compare someone he'd known all his life with someone he'd known so briefly, he slipped up the fire escape to his apartment and took the phone off the hook, hoping DeeAnn wouldn't realize he was back. But he'd been home less than five minutes when DeeAnn knocked on his kitchen door. Looking guilty as CJ swung the door open, she said apologetically, "I know you don't like people surprising you, but your phone's been busy. And you've got a phone call downstairs that sounds pretty urgent."

"From who?"

"The mother of that friend of yours who was killed, Petey Greene."

"Oh," he said, realizing that with all the other things on his mind, he'd forgotten about Petey.

"She's holding on the line."

CJ adjusted his vest and hitched up his pants as if such adjustments to his apparel were mandatory before he could talk to his former third grade teacher, Syrathia Greene. "I better go talk to her, then."

As DeeAnn pivoted to head back down the fire-escape stairs, he couldn't help comparing her with Mavis again. He'd watched Mavis walk down stairs before as well, and no matter the circumstances, she always moved with a fluid grace. In stark contrast, DeeAnn's descent was purely and absolutely meant to be sensual. The way she took each step, rotating her hips ever so suggestively before she planted her foot on the next step down, screamed, *I'm here for the taking.*

When she reached the bottom and glanced back up to see CJ standing halfway down the stairs, looking reflective, she said, "Hurry up, CJ! The lady sounded terribly distraught."

"Yeah, I'm coming," said CJ, surprising himself with how quickly he finished taking the stairs before a new set of comparisons could began tracking their way through his head.

Syrathia Greene's voice was hoarse from the mouth breathing that accompanies hours of crying. Unaware that Petey had been doing surveillance work for CJ or that the assignment might have cost her son his life, she responded to CJ's half-guilty "Hello" with a series of sobs. "Oh, CJ, why couldn't Petey have been more like you or Rosie? I feel so bad. I'm the one who made him the way he was. Overmothering him like I did, turning him into nothing more than a common hustler."

"Petey was a good person and a grown man, Mrs. G. No need to beat yourself up. I'm sorry you're the one calling me.

I should've called you, but I've been busy with Ike. He's been pretty sick."

"I'm so sorry. How's he doing?"

"He's at Denver General, and they're running some tests," said CJ, minimizing the seriousness of the situation.

"My goodness. Please give him my best," she said before returning to her dead son's failings. "Petey looked up to you, CJ. You being a war hero and all. Maybe a stint in the navy would've helped straighten him out." She burst briefly into tears. Composing herself but still sniffling, she said, "Anyway, the real reason I'm calling is because Petey left something here for you at the house. A legal-sized envelope with your name printed on the outside. The printing runs downhill. I never could get that boy to print in a straight line. He told me the evening before he was killed that the envelope contains photos of a bunch of antiques you wanted. I figured I should let you know it's here."

CJ thought, *What antiques?* then quickly realized that what Petey had more than likely left with his mother were actually his surveillance photos of Gaylord Marquee. "Oh, yes," he said, hoping he sounded earnest.

"I can drop them by your office if you'd like."

"No, no. I'll come by and pick them up. It'll give us a chance to talk."

"That'll be great. I've had a string of people in here all morning, but most of them have been my friends, not Petey's. It would be wonderful if you could bring Roosevelt along, too. I can still see you, Petey, and Roosevelt sitting less than attentively in my third grade class throwing spitballs at one another." She broke down again.

"I'll be there in thirty minutes, Mrs. G., and I'll have Rosie with me."

"Thank you, baby. It'll give me so much comfort to see you two boys." Syrathia Greene's voice trailed off as, muttering through her tears, she said, "If only Petey could've been more like the two of you," and hung up.

CJ caught up with Rosie Weeks ten minutes later after checking to make certain that Mavis's flight had left on time. In the midst of changing the oil on a high-performance Dodge dually, Rosie had three more oil changes waiting. When CJ told him that Syrathia Greene had asked to see him, Rosie, aware that any differences he'd ever had with Petey were forever behind them now, quickly agreed to go.

A few minutes later they were in Syrathia Greene's house, seated in her living room, exchanging small talk, laughing occasionally but more frequently fighting back tears. It was only when Syrathia handed CJ the envelope that Petey had left with her that the look on her face turned quizzical. "I'm not sure why Petey left those photos with me. It's almost as if he knew he wasn't going to be able to deliver them personally. Sort of strange, don't you think, CJ?"

"Just a coincidence." CJ glanced at Rosie, looking for backup that didn't come.

"Petey was all I had," Syrathia said, choking back tears. "Now I have nothing."

"Yes, you do, Mrs. G.," said CJ. "You've got the whole

Five Points community to lean on, and you've still got me and Rosie."

Smiling at CJ's attempt to comfort her, the gray-haired, spindly-legged woman who'd taught the two grown men seated across from her their multiplication tables, looked up and said, "I do at that, don't I?"

The room fell silent long enough for CJ to appreciate the sound of Rosie's heavy breathing. Suspecting that he and Rosie would likely remain there with the grieving schoolteacher for quite some time, he was busy contemplating what to say next when the doorbell rang.

"More company?" Syrathia rose and walked unsteadily across the room to the front door to find Willis Sundee standing in the doorway holding a cake tin. Her voice rose a full, delighted octave as she swung the door open and said, "Willis, please come in."

Willis stepped inside to see CJ and Rosie walking toward him. "Rosie, CJ," he said before giving Syrathia a sympathetic peck on the cheek and squeezing both her hands affectionately in his. "I'm so sorry about Petey, Syrathia. So terribly sorry."

Syrathia's eyes welled up with tears as CJ and Rosie greeted Willis with a couple of pats each on opposite shoulders. "Did you get Mavis off all right?" Willis asked, placing the cake on a nearby table.

"On the button," said CJ, "and I checked to make sure her flight left on time when I got back to the office."

"Great. I'm sure she's missing both you and the Mile High City already."

CJ smiled and said nothing. Thinking suddenly about comparisons, he felt rescued when, as he and Rosie gave Syrathia parting hugs, Rosie said, "Etta Lee said she'll be comin' by to see you this afternoon."

"She's an angel," said Syrathia, waving Willis toward the living room as CJ and Rosie stepped outside. As she watched her two former students walk away down the sidewalk, quietly discussing what might be in the envelope, she couldn't help but think once again that Petey should've been more like them.

CJ and Rosie didn't say much to one another on the short ride back to Rosie's place. It was almost as if Petey's death demanded one long lingering moment of silence.

When CJ pulled the Bel Air to a stop in front of one of the garage's service bays, the envelope Syrathia had given him slipped off the dashboard and onto his lap. "Might as well take a look at what's inside right now," he said, tearing an edge of the well-sealed envelope open.

"You think Petey had enough on Marquee to link him to them GI Joe's murders you've been lookin' into all these years?"

"I'm hoping so," said CJ, counting out the envelope's contents, eleven Polaroid photographs, and placing them in a neat stack on the front seat between him and Rosie.

"Some of 'em look pretty damn dark," Rosie complained.

"Yeah," said CJ, certain that it had been late evening when Petey had taken the photographs.

CJ placed the three top overexposed, almost totally black photos, in which Marquee's house was barely recognizable, on the dashboard and eyed the next photo in the stack. "Here's a photo of Marquee, Cheryl Goldsby, and that cellist, Molly Burgess, I've told you about."

"They don't look much like dykes in the photo," said Rosie, pointing at the two women. "The redhead's actually pretty good-lookin'."

"That's Burgess."

"Nice little tush on her."

CJ shook his head, thought, *Hard to change a brawler into a ballerina,* and flipped past three more photos in which Goldsby, Burgess, and Marquee were standing by the tailgate of Goldsby's pickup. "What's this?" CJ asked, bringing the next photograph closer to his eyes.

"Looks like a photo of a Quonset hut, and a pretty big one at that," said Rosie.

"Yeah, and here's another photograph of it," said CJ, examining a second close-up photograph of what was for certain a post–World War II galvanized-metal Quonset hut. Judging from the size of the pickup parked next to it, the half-moon-shaped building was at least a hundred feet long and maybe forty feet wide.

"Some kind of storage facility?" Rosie asked.

"Probably."

"Maybe it's where Marquee and them two dykes stashed all the stolen goods your buddy Ames planned on fencin'."

"Awfully big for that," said CJ, eyeing a third, badly out-of-focus Polaroid photo of the Quonset hut and tossing it on the dashboard. His eyes widened slowly as he examined the next photograph closely. "Take a look at this," he said, handing the Polaroid to Rosie.

"The Quonset hut again."

"Yeah, but look in the background toward the little patch of sky in the right-hand corner behind it."

"I'll be damned. A neon sign."

"I know that sign," said CJ. He grabbed the photo back from Rosie and held it up to the light. "Yep, I can make out the head and most of the right wing. No question it's the peace dove."

"I'll be damned, you're right," said Rosie, leaning forward, both eyes glued to the Polaroid. "It's that damn war-protest peace sign those crazy-ass hippies erected before you left on your first tour in 'Nam. Damn bird's wingspan has to be a good twenty feet."

"Maybe more," said CJ, who knew all about the dove but had only once driven past the gigantic homage to peace that sat on a pole five stories high in unincorporated Jefferson County southwest of Denver. "Didn't they put that thing up on what was once part of some famous Colorado ranch?"

"I'm not sure," said Rosie, "but Etta Lee'll know. She's got a folder full of photos and newspaper clippings of that damn neon monstrosity. You know how she hated that war, CJ."

"Yeah," said CJ, who sometimes still had the feeling that Etta Lee would never totally forgive him for serving in Vietnam.

Looking as if he could see the gears inside CJ's head churning, Rosie said, "So now that you've got yourself a good idea of where that Quonset hut is, you gonna bust into it? 'Cause if you are, count me out. I promised Etta Lee after that arson fiasco at Mae's that I wouldn't get involved in any more of your messes. Never shoulda gone with you when you broke into Marquee's garage."

"I understand, and you're right—I am going to bust in."

His point made, Rosie asked, "Whatta ya think Marquee, or whoever's using the place, is storing inside?"

"A slow boat to China, for all I know. But whatever it is, or was, Petey thought enough about the connection to follow Marquee there and photograph it. And you know what, Rosie? I'm thinking that Quonset hut just might represent the GI Joe's murder connection I've been looking for all these years."

"You ask me, I think Marquee and the two dykes were in on those killin's together."

"Could be," said CJ as Rosie moved to get out of the Bel Air.

"Sorry I can't go with you." Rosie stretched up and out of the car.

"No problem," said CJ, aware that if he really ended up needing help, he knew where he could find it. "I'll catch you later," he said, cranking the Bel Air's engine, backing away from the service bay, and turning to head home with Henry Bales, rather than Mavis or DeeAnn, on his mind.

Chapter

25

CJ pulled into his driveway to see DeeAnn sprinting across the grass toward him. Leaning down through the car's open window until they were almost nose to nose and sounding out of breath, she said, "CJ, you need to get to Denver General right now. Ike's doctor called about ten minutes ago. There's been a problem with his biopsy. He's in cardiac ICU."

Slamming the Bel Air into reverse and peeling back out of the driveway, he never heard DeeAnn yell, "Call me when you know something, okay?"

Like CJ, the three other occupants of the Lysol-scented waiting room outside the cardiac ICU looked as if the weight of the world could any second finally crush them. Glum-faced, with his heart racing and a strange, sour taste filling his mouth, CJ adjusted his weight in the uncomfortable chair where he'd been sitting for almost fifteen minutes waiting for word about Ike. He'd given the nurse sitting in a partially enclosed cubicle at the far end of the room his name and asked to speak with Ike's doctor as soon as he arrived. Looking put upon, she'd told him after eyeing a sheet of paper on her desk that Ike's doctor would be out to speak to him in a moment.

When, ten minutes later, the doctor had failed to appear, CJ called Henry Bales from a courtesy phone, catching Henry, who'd been the first-call hematopathology resident since midnight, in the pathology residents' room moments before Henry headed out for a long-overdue lunch break.

Thinking, *Please let him be all right,* and staring at the dingy gray wall in front of him, CJ bolted out of his chair when Henry arrived, unshaven and disheveled. "Been up all night. Just rotated off hemepath—man, what a nightmare. Any word on Ike?" Henry asked.

"Nothing."

Henry shook his head and fumbled with a button on his lab coat. "Can't pull any strings here." He squeezed CJ's shoulder supportively just as Ike's doctor, a balding, emaciated man with Dumbo-like ears and a bulbous nose, walked through the double doors of the ICU and into the waiting room. The look on the doctor's face as he walked over to the nurse who'd earlier spoken to CJ and said something to her before following the arc of her arm as she pointed toward CJ and Henry was a sad, duty-bound expression that both war veterans had seen before.

Walking up to CJ and greeting him with a firm handshake, the doctor said, "Mr. Floyd, I'm Dr. Lessman. Why don't we step into one of our conference rooms?" He glanced at Henry as he pointed to a doorway near the back of the room, noticing the hospital ID badge that was clamped cockeyed to the lapel of Henry's lab coat. "Dr. Bales, any special reason you're here?"

"I'm a family friend. Mr. Floyd and I were in the navy together."

"Come along, then," the doctor said softly as CJ and Henry followed him toward the conference room.

When they reached the door, CJ had the sense that he was somehow back in Vietnam on the pitching, yawing deck of the *Cape Star,* taking on river's-edge machine-gun fire.

CJ could think of only two things after learning from Dr. Lessman that Ike had died twenty minutes earlier, more than likely from a lung embolism he'd sustained during a routine diagnostic biopsy of his right lung. He realized first and foremost that he'd lost the most important person in his life, and second, as Ike had been fond of saying, that nothing in life is ever routine.

CJ couldn't help but think that the look on Ike's face was one of pure surprise as he and Henry stood quietly viewing Ike's remains. It was as if the death angel had tiptoed up to Ike and whisked him away without the required notice. When an orderly appeared to wheel Ike's body to the morgue for autopsy—mandatory protocol in the case of an unexplained inpatient death—CJ had Henry run down to the morgue to inform Vernon Lowe what had happened.

CJ spent the better part of the next hour talking to several of the doctors who'd attended Ike, and also to the hospital chaplain. It was only as he signed papers arranging for the post-mortem release of Ike's body to the Pipkin Mortuary that it finally hit him with the force of a hammer slamming into his skull that the man who had shepherded him through life, and for the most part molded him into a man, was indeed dead.

Now, as he and Henry sat outside the hospital on a bench reserved for smokers, with cigarette butts and candy wrappers blowing past their feet in the gusty wind, CJ wanted to scream, *No!* but even that word wouldn't come. Henry, who understood very well in medical terms what had happened, was reassuring, explaining that Ike's death had more than likely been quick and painless. But neither Henry's support nor his explanation mattered. What mattered to CJ was that Ike was gone.

The two Vietnam War comrades sat in silence, watching patients and hospital workers shuttle past them for several more minutes, until Henry finally asked, "Sure you don't want to talk to one of our hospital grief counselors?"

"No."

"It might help."

"What's helping is that you're here, man."

"For as long as you need me to be," said Henry, watching a terrified-looking boy no more than ten years old run by, crying, as he cupped what looked like a broken right arm in his left hand. "The medical beast that owns me is going to come sniffing after my ass pretty soon," Henry said as the boy sailed through the revolving doors to the hospital.

After sharing one of their been-through-hell-together looks, neither man said anything for another minute. Eyeing his solidly built, dark-haired former shipmate, a man he'd always thought resembled a Hollywood casting director's version of a brooding Indian in a B-movie Western instead of the three-quarters French Canadian with a dash of Oklahoma Cherokee thrown in that he was, CJ said, "Guess it's tragedy that generally brings folks together. We need to hook up more often, Bull Tamer." The nickname had been given to the onetime Colorado high school bull-riding champion by his shipmates in Vietnam.

"Let's make it a point to for sure," said Henry. "Call me later today, okay?" He rose and gave CJ's shoulder a comforting pat.

"Sure."

"And CJ, don't try handling this on your own."

"Read you loud and clear," said CJ, watching Henry head back toward the hospital entrance and disappear inside. Wondering how someone who'd grown up knowing the freedom of a ten-thousand-acre cattle ranch could cope with the city, CJ reminded himself that there were ways to cope with anything. As he walked away from Denver General, he took a deep breath, exhaled slowly, and considered the uncharted waters facing him.

Twenty minutes later, he was standing on the east bank of a section of the South Platte River a few miles south of what had once been the mud-flat confluence of the South Platte and Cherry Creek, and the place where the city of Denver had started. The spot where he stood overlooked a fifty-yard stretch of river that tumbled down a string of jagged rocks before spilling into a placid forty-foot-wide, boulder-lined pool. The section of river was as deserted as it had been the day Ike had taught him to fly fish there on a chilly early-April day seventeen years earlier. He could still hear Ike, his breath laced with alcohol, repeating after twenty minutes of instruction and dozens of bad casts on CJ's part, "Patience, CJ. You gotta learn to think about what you're doin', boy. Now, watch me one more time." Ike took back his fly rod and once again demonstrated the delicate art of fly casting to his nephew. "You gotta load up your line, boy," he said, reeling in his line. "Let gravity, the laws of physics, and the weight of your line do all the work for you," he said, preparing to cast again. "Keep it simple and think of it as one, two, three. Now watch: *one,* load up your line with your back cast; *two,* cast your line forward; and *three,* let your fly land as gently on the water as you possibly can. It's simple grade school arithmetic," Ike added as his fly landed delicately on the water.

Ike's words continued to reverberate as CJ now watched a seam of water thread its way through a cut bank and thought, *One, two, three.* All those years earlier it had taken him dozens more tries, more of Ike's demanding coaching, and even a little cursing on Ike's part before he'd laid down what Ike judged to be an acceptable fly cast. But he'd learned, and by his early teens CJ's fly-fishing skills were those of an expert.

As he watched the water near the edge of the pool gurgle around boulders, he knew that in six weeks' time, with snowmelt from the mountains in high gear, the stretch of water he was looking at would be unfishable. But the best summer fly fishing always arose out of patience, a virtue he'd have to learn to draw on even more in Ike's absence. He wasn't sure if he had what it took to continue to operate the bail bonding business Ike had nurtured from nothing. Maybe he'd have to move on and do something else.

Watching several fish rise near the edge of the tree-lined pool and knowing that in Ike's absence he couldn't just stroll along writing low-earning nickel-and-dime bonds while Ike did all the heavy lifting, he realized he'd have to do some heavy lifting of his own if he planned to stay in the game.

In the time he'd been watching the river, a stiff breeze had kicked up out of the west and the temperature had dropped several degrees. Buttoning his vest and wishing he had a jacket, he turned and headed back for the Bel Air. On his way up the rocky trail that led down to the river, he met a young boy who looked about eight years old, carrying a fly rod in one hand and a fishing vest that looked a couple of sizes too large for him in the other. The boy smiled and said, "Hi."

CJ said, "I saw a bunch of fish rising in an undercut near those cottonwoods." He pointed toward a stand of sixty-year-old trees.

"Thanks." The boy turned and yelled back up the path, "Dad, hurry up! Fish rising!"

When a man who'd been urinating in a clump of willows came rushing down the path, CJ chuckled and said, "Knock 'em dead."

Looking slightly embarrassed, the man smiled and said, "Think I'll leave that to my kid" as he sprinted down the path.

By eight that night, with his mental and physical exhaustion approaching levels he'd known during Vietnam, CJ was running on fumes. He'd made final arrangements with the funeral home and set a date for Ike's funeral, searched through Ike's files and found his handwritten will, and talked with Etta Lee Weeks three times by phone. With Etta Lee's and DeeAnn's assistance, he had called just about everyone on the list of more than eighty people they'd jointly compiled to be notified of Ike's death.

Talking to a Korean War buddy of Ike's who'd grown up with Ike in Cincinnati, where Ike's folks had settled after the West Virginia coal mines where Ike's father had worked had closed down permanently following a strike, CJ learned something about his uncle that he'd never known. According to the war buddy, Ike had refused a battlefield officer's commission and a transfer that would have taken him out of harm's way in order to remain with the men in his artillery unit. The reason, as Ike had supposedly told army brass, was so *the dumbasses don't end up gettin' themselves killed.*

CJ had informed every other bondsman on Bondsman's Row about Ike's death and asked Vernon Lowe, Rosie Weeks, and Willis Sundee to be three of Ike's pallbearers. His attempt at writing an obituary ended in failure, and when he phoned Mavis to tell her the news, struggling through a conversation that was mostly on-again, off-again silence, he had the sense that his pain would last forever.

When DeeAnn came into Ike's office, where CJ had isolated himself after coming home from the river, and timidly handed him Ike's arraignment appearance schedule for the next day, CJ flashed her a deer-in-the-headlights look and shook his head.

Hoping to take the edge off CJ's sorrow, she asked, "You want me to get you anything to eat before I head home?"

CJ's barely audible "No, thanks" had the doleful ring of someone who was struggling desperately to keep from being defeated.

"You need to get up and out of here, CJ. I know you're hurt-ing, but planting yourself here in Ike's office won't do you an ounce of good." She walked around behind him and began gen-tly massaging his shoulders.

"I didn't plant myself."

"You know good and well what I mean, CJ Floyd."

Her touch, soothing, lingering, and pleasingly soft, nearly brought him to tears. As she continued the massage with her breasts firmly pressed against the small of his back and the warm sweetness of her breath seeming to chase away his pain, he suddenly found himself wanting her in the most physical of ways.

When finally he turned and kissed her passionately, there was no resistance on her part, and later, as they made love, exploring every inch of one another on the threadbare Navajo rug in front of Ike's desk, CJ's pain temporarily disappeared.

It was only in the wake of their lovemaking, as he buttoned his shirt and DeeAnn struggled to find one of her shoes, that sorrow again intervened.

Kissing two of her fingers and touching them to CJ's lips, DeeAnn said, "Wonderful."

"Pretty much my word choice, too."

"Even so, you still need to get out of this office, if only for a little bit."

"I will."

"I can call more people if you need me to."

CJ shook his head. "No, go on home, DeeAnn. You've been here since before eight this morning."

"And leave you here by yourself?"

"I'll be fine."

"You enjoy being the loner, don't you, CJ?"

"No one enjoys being alone."

"There's a difference between being a loner and being alone, you know. One implies a certain self-imposed isolation. The other suggests a path that a person hasn't necessarily chosen. Being a loner's okay, I guess, but you never ever want to end up alone." She squeezed CJ's hand briefly, kissed him on the cheek, and walked slowly toward the door. "I'll see you tomorrow."

"Yeah," said CJ, still contemplating DeeAnn's insightful deconstruction of two similar yet very different words. He thought for a moment about offering a rebuttal, but she was already down the hallway and out the front door of the old Victorian.

Chapter
ꙮ 26

After more than five years, CJ's lost-to-the-world, post-Vietnam feeling of depression was back, gnawing at him from the inside out, causing his ears to ring, and saddling him with a stomach- and headache that made it difficult to breathe.

He'd given up on trying to sleep and found himself lying wide awake, counting off all the triggers that had sent him trotting back out onto the all-too-familiar playing field of post-traumatic stress. Rising from bed, he walked down the hall to his bathroom to get a drink of water. Reasoning that the major cause for his backward slippage was guilt, he turned on the cold water, cupped his hand under the tap, and took a calming drink. He was guilt-ridden over not being able to prevent Ike's death. He also felt guilty about being unfaithful to Mavis, even though the two of them had never made any forever-faithful vows, and about the fact that for more than five years he'd failed to solve a murder he'd promised himself he would. That double murder was now more than likely the reason Petey Greene was dead. It had taken a perfect storm of circumstances to trigger the kind of guilt he was feeling and to send his mind back to the killing fields of Vietnam.

He took another drink of water and stared into his medicine-cabinet mirror. Suspecting that if Ike were there, he'd likely say, "Quit feeling sorry for yourself, boy," CJ suddenly found himself frowning and thinking, *One, two, three.*

He tried to organize his thoughts. Dealing with Ike's death would take time. Time that would involve a progression to acceptance and closure that would probably take years. Effectively sorting out his relationship with Mavis and dealing with what might develop between him and DeeAnn would be time-dependent as well. But finding out who had killed Wiley Ames, Quan Lee Chin, and now very likely Petey Greene was a problem he could sink his teeth into right away.

Splashing a couple of additional handfuls of cold water onto his face, he turned to walk back to the kitchen and silently counted off, *One, two, three.*

Minutes later he was at his kitchen table, drinking a Coke and sorting through the packet of surveillance photos that Petey Greene had taken outside Gaylord Marquee's house, hoping to find something in the overexposed Polaroids that would mesh with the fact that the damage to Marquee's Suburban, at least according to Rosie, didn't fit for a vehicle that had been involved in a serious hit-and-run accident. He stared at the photos one by one and over and over until on one of his passes through, something struck him as strangely repetitive. In every one of the photographs, Marquee seemed to be looking back over his shoulder toward what CJ could clearly see in one photograph was his garage.

Studying that photo and wondering if he'd missed something important during his first sweep of Marquee's garage, CJ decided that a second look was in order—and, late as it was right then, Marquee might actually be home to provide him with a guided tour.

The antique kitchen clock on the wall above his stove read 12:35 when, dressed head to toe in black, CJ picked up the phone in his kitchen and called Henry Bales, hoping against hope that Henry would be home.

When the groggy-sounding, sleep-deprived pathology resident answered, "Hello," CJ said, "Bull Tamer, it's CJ. Need my ass covered on a mission."

Instead of saying, *What are you thinking? Goddamn it, CJ, this isn't the jungles of Vietnam and we're not fucking nineteen,* Henry dutifully asked, "How soon?"

"Meet me at my place as quick as you can. I'll fill you in then."

"It'll take me twenty minutes or so."

"I'll be here. And Henry, just so you know, this could get pretty sticky."

"No more sticky than directly disobeying an order from your superior during a time of war."

"Guess not. Twenty minutes, okay? See you then."

As he cradled the phone, for the first time in a long while Henry Bales thought about the fact that the bonds born of war were clearly the equal of those determined by blood.

Breaking and entering had never been CJ's forte, although he'd had high school friends, including Petey Greene, who'd been experts. But on the windy, forty-five-degree moonlit night that he and Henry Bales jimmied their way into Gaylord Marquee's garage, after making certain there were no nosy neighbors and no Marquee dogs around and discovering once again that Marquee wasn't home, things went smoothly.

"What are we looking for?" Henry asked after turning on the single overhead light in a garage that now reeked of a pungent, decomposing-flesh smell that they suspected came from a dead rodent.

"I'm not sure," said CJ, who on the drive over had brought Henry up to speed on the Petey Greene killing, the GI Joe's murders, and his five-year-plus attempt to solve the latter crime. He'd also laid out a division of labor: Henry would be responsible for going through the boxes on one side of the garage; he'd be responsible for inspecting the contents of the boxes on the other sides. "But there's a clue to those murders in this garage somewhere. I'm sure of it."

"So that's the Suburban you told me about," said Henry, glancing at the damaged Suburban before he stooped and started poking his way through the contents of a cardboard box.

"That's it, and it's registered in Marquee's name. I checked."

"Damn, I think I just found out why it smells like the bottom of a sewer in here," said Henry, turning over the box next to the one he'd been rummaging through and dumping out a bloated pit bull.

CJ tried not to gag as, seemingly out of nowhere, images of the bloated bodies of dead GIs bobbing up and down in the Mekong River shallows flashed through his head.

For the next several minutes, the two friends worked their respective sides of the garage in silence, digging through cardboard boxes, plastic storage containers, wire-mesh bins, and even several U.S. Mail cartons filled with everything from empty paint cans to water-damaged *Reader's Digest* condensed books.

"Hey, I think I've found something up your alley," Henry said finally.

CJ, who'd moved to sorting through an unlocked toolbox, the kind designed to straddle the bed of a pickup, turned away from what he was doing and walked over to Henry, who'd slipped a twenty-inch-square, eight-inch-deep cardboard box out of the larger box at his feet. "Your kind of stuff," he said, extracting three miniature Indian pots and several old license plates from the smaller box.

"Nice little stash," said a suddenly wide-eyed CJ, watching as Henry spread the contents of the smaller box out on the floor.

As Henry turned the license plates face up one by one, CJ whispered, "You've hit a damn mother lode, Bull Tamer!"

"Valuable?"

"Damn straight." CJ picked up one of the license plates and held it up to the light. "This baby I'm holding is a 1910 Connecticut porcelain passenger plate." He lined the eighteen-inch-long plate up with a slightly larger neighbor, then paired those two plates up with two others Henry had laid out until he had an almost perfectly rectangular grouping a bit larger than the size of an opened tabloid newspaper.

As CJ admired his assemblage of four exceedingly rare 1910 through 1913 porcelain gems, Henry asked, "How do you know they're from Connecticut? There's no state ID on any of them." Henry continued to stare at the largest of the four license plates—a plate stamped with a single letter C and bearing number 17249.

CJ broke into a broad, toothy grin. "The same way you know the name and location of every damn artery running down the back of my leg and where each one splits off before it heads from my big toe, Doctor." Tapping the largest plate with an index finger, CJ continued, "Color's nearly the only way you can date these puppies. White on red, the big boy here is a 1910; the blue on white is a 1911; white on green I'm pretty sure was the '12; and that leaves the white on blue as the '13. That block letter C just in front of each license-plate number tells me they're from Connecticut. We're talking money here, Henry. Hell, these four plates in the shape they're in, looking like they just came off the production line and with all their odd individual color and size variations, are probably worth three, maybe even four grand. Should've looked a little more thoroughly the first time I was here."

He moved excitedly from the Connecticut plates to another plate on the floor and whistled loudly. He picked the plate up, scrutinized it carefully, and said, "A fucking New Mexico preemie," before digging a hand into a box two down from the one the Connecticut plates had come from. "And here's a Colorado prestate, shit! And one from Texas!" Setting the plate on the floor and with a glazed look in his eyes, he said, "Do you know what the hell these are, Henry? Got any idea?"

"Beats me."

"They're what we call in the business 'prestates.' License plates that predate state-government-authorized, first-issue plates. In most instances, the prestates aren't as rare or as collectible as the actual first-of-state issues, but they're pretty damn rare." CJ quickly sorted through the remaining plates in the box, shaking his head as he did. "Prestates up the wazoo, and in mint condition—ten, maybe even twelve of them. Shit, I don't believe it."

"So what're they worth?"

CJ thought for a moment before answering. His response came with a certain degree of breathless awe. "The whole kit and caboodle? All the prestates and the Connecticut porcelains spread out on the floor? Ten, fifteen grand, easy." Looking as if he'd just realized his fly was open, he shook his head. "Boy, have I been trucking down the wrong damn road."

"How's that?" Henry asked, jerking his head around to the sound of a tree limb scratching against the garage's metal roof. "I'm gonna take a quick look outside. Make sure nobody's nosing around." He trotted over to the door they'd come in, opened it, took a quick look outside to see a symphony of tree limbs shifting in the heavy breeze, closed the door, and jogged back to CJ. "We've got no problem unless trees can talk," he said, sounding relieved.

CJ, who was busy wrapping the Connecticut plates in an old newspaper, muttered, "Been looking for love in all the wrong places, Bull Tamer. I always thought it was sorta strange that the GI Joe's killings would be linked to fencing stolen seashells. The money just wouldn't be there. But, truth be told, seashells are what I thought I'd find stashed here in Marquee's garage. I should've known the stakes had to be higher, especially if there're more plates around like these." He patted the now wrapped Connecticut plates almost affectionately and slipped the bundle under one arm. "One, two, three," CJ said, smiling.

"What?" asked Henry.

"Nothing. Just my Uncle Ike's shorthand for working through a problem the right way." Suddenly looking perplexed, he said, "You know what, though, Henry? Something's not quite right here. Things are just a tad off the track. Marquee's got something close to the mother lode sitting out here virtually in the open for anybody with a little larceny in their heart and a handy crowbar to take off with. No protection, no alarm system, and no deterrent. Now, if I owned plates this valuable, they'd be stashed away in a lockbox in some bank vault. That tells me something real important."

"Which is?"

"That either the mine here's been salted with these plates and the Suburban to get me or the cops looking Marquee's way or Marquee's got a shitload more of these babies squirreled away somewhere else."

"So you think Marquee killed your friend Petey, Ames, and the Chinese guy over a bunch of rare license plates?"

"Rare *stolen* license plates. That's the lynchpin. I'd set the odds at 80:20 that Marquee's the killer. And I'd take the same odds on him having killed poor Petey."

"Why lay off the 20 percent?"

"Gets back to my mine-salting theory, I'm afraid." CJ turned and glanced at the front end of the damaged Suburban. "I can't for the life of me figure out why Marquee would stash a vehicle that was involved in a hit-and-run killing in his own garage, why he'd leave all these plates lying around for just about anybody to find, even if he has lots of more valuable plates stashed away, and finally, and most importantly, why I can't seem to lay my hands on the man."

"Good enough reasons. So who have you got jockeying for the other 20 percent?"

"Believe it or not, three lovely ladies. Wiley Ames's niece, Cheryl Goldsby, her onetime lover who she tossed overboard recently, a lady named Ramona Lepsos, and Lepsos's replacement, a concert cellist named Molly Burgess."

"Girls just being girls." Henry lowered his voice and uttered in as dramatic a fashion as he could muster, "'When shall we three meet again? In thunder, lightning, or in rain?'"

"What?"

"Nothing. Just something Shakespeare had three witches say at the opening of *Macbeth*."

"Well, since Marquee's a Brit, I guess Shakespeare sorta fits."

"So what's next?"

"We'll leave here with the Connecticut plates. I'll find out what they're actually worth, and I'll try my hand at flushing out the witches."

"Makes sense. Who'll peg their value?"

"Harry Steed, the guy who owns GI Joe's. Trouble is, I don't think he'll enjoy ratting out Wiley, who I've got to guess was up to his elbows in fencing stolen license plates with Marquee."

"But Ames has been dead more than five years," said Henry. "The truth surely can't hurt him now."

"Yeah, but Steed and Ames had serious World War II history, sorta like you and me."

Henry nodded understandingly, looked around the garage, frowned at the lingering smell of death, and pinched his nostrils together. "Let's get the hell out of here. It stinks."

Shifting the Connecticut plates to his left arm, CJ headed for the door, cracked it open, peeked outside briefly, and, with Henry on his heels, stepped into Marquee's backyard. As they made their way toward the Bel Air, CJ whispered, "I can't for the life of me figure out where Marquee's hiding."

"Maybe he's not. Could be he's dead."

"Food for thought," said CJ as they slipped into the Bel Air, unaware that they were being watched from an upstairs-bedroom window of the stately English Tudor next door to Marquee's.

Gaylord Marquee stood naked, peering down on the departing Bel Air through the barely cracked plantation shutters.

"What are you looking at, Gaylord?" asked the woman lying in bed a few feet away. The woman, clearly pouting, wore only red fishnet stockings that stopped halfway up her thighs.

"Nothing, just a car."

"And that car's more interesting than me?" The woman frowned and poked out her lower lip.

"No, no," said Marquee, heading back for the bed. "I just thought it might be stopping at my house."

"Well, did it?" The woman toyed with one of her stockings.

"No, it kept on going."

"And that's exactly what I am going to need you to do for me the rest of tonight. Keep it going, Gaylord. You've been out of town most of the month, remember?"

"I can do that," Marquee said, smiling slyly.

"You'd better," she said as Marquee slipped into bed beside her and ran his hand up the inside of her right leg until it found pay dirt. He began toying with the tiny knot that would soon swell to the size of a BB. A knot that, when stimulated, gave the woman so much pleasure.

"We've got all night," she said, laying her head back on a couple of fluffed-up pillows.

"All night," said Marquee, concerned less with any offering or receiving of pleasure than with the fact that he'd seen two men leaving the vicinity of his home. Two men who'd gotten into a classic '57 drop-top Chevy he'd seen before. A car and driver he intended to check on thoroughly the next day.

Chapter

⚝ 27

CJ slept until ten the next morning, chalking up the surprisingly restful sleep to pure mental exhaustion. After a breakfast of buttermilk biscuits and ham, he arranged for Cicero Vickers, the bondsman next door, to handle one of his early arraignments and headed for GI Joe's. He arrived at the pawnshop just before eleven to find Harry Steed standing outside on the sidewalk examining a broken plate-glass front window. Two spider cracks ran diagonally down the middle of the eight-foot square window, crossing in a nearly perfect X near the middle.

CJ, who'd parked the Bel Air a block north on Larimer, felt uneasy about intruding on Harry's ill fortune. He felt even worse when Harry greeted him with a scowl that was obviously meant for the window-breaker and groaned, "How ya doin', CJ? Had a break-in last night. Can you believe it? A frickin' break-in!

"The son of a bitch got around my alarm system," Harry complained. "How the hell he did that beats the shit outa me. Three thousand dollars for a set of useless frickin' wires. Bad money after bad money, shit. Rewiring'll cost me. The window'll cost me, and sparring with the insurance company's gonna cost me. They'll increase my rates for sure."

"Did they get away with anything or do any more serious damage?" CJ asked, aware that as tight and as set in his ways as Harry Steed was, anything that either cost him money or knocked him out of his routine was a monumental setback.

"Doesn't look like it," said Steed, sounding slightly calmer. "But I haven't had a chance to check on everything yet. The cops just left. Why don't you come on in? I've got some coffee brewing in the back. Maybe a cup'll steady my nerves." Steed waved CJ ahead of him through the front door and continued to mumble obscenities all the way to the back of the pawnshop.

Harry's coffee, bitter and overbrewed, matched his disposition. CJ took three sips and set his cup aside. Harry, however, had finished a full cup of the burned-smelling, syrup-thick brew before he readdressed the break-in. "At least they didn't get any of my prize pieces or any money. I had a couple of grand in the safe."

Thinking that his license-plate discovery of the previous evening and the break-in might be connected, CJ asked, "Has Gaylord Marquee been in recently?"

"Yeah," said Harry, surprised at the apparent change in subject.

"Was he buying or selling?"

"Selling, as a matter of fact."

"License plates?"

"They are, after all, the man's game, CJ."

"I've been checking up on Marquee," said CJ, recalling something Ike had once told him: *Never give more than ya get when you're questionin' somebody, even if it's your mother.* "What are the chances that back when Wiley and Chin were killed, Marquee was supplying them with stolen license plates and not stolen seashells?"

"Equal to the odds that he was supplying 'em with the seashells, I'd guess."

"The plates would have been a lot more valuable, though, don't you think?" asked CJ, knowing that if anyone would have a line on the comparative values of the two items, it would be Steed.

"Depends on the year, the state, and the condition," said Steed. "Hell, CJ, you know that. License plates, seashells, or buggy whips, Wiley and that Chinaman were fencing stolen goods, and that's what got 'em killed. Doesn't matter much what they were fencing."

"Maybe," CJ said, thoughtfully stroking his chin. "What did Marquee try to sell you, by the way?"

"A 1912 New York porcelain. A piece of shit, really. Cracked and crazed all over. And a 1917 dealer's plate. I passed on the New Yorker. The dealer's plate was clean enough, so I bought it. Paid him nine hundred cash. Wanna have a look at it?"

"Sure." CJ followed Harry out of his office toward the back of the pawnshop. Midway down the wide center aisle, Harry stopped in front of a lazy Susan and spun it around. When he realized the top shelf was empty, he yelled, "Shit! I put that plate here on the top shelf along with a couple of eighty-year-old bootjacks. Those bootjacks were worth three hundred apiece. Goddamn it! Marquee saw me do it. That fucking son of a bitch! He came back in and robbed me."

Fuming, Harry took a giant step to his right, pulled out a drawer that contained a vintage Colt revolver, and waved the barrel in the direction of the cracked window. "I'll shoot the bastard with this gun or another one if I ever see him again, don't matter!"

"Calm down, Harry. There's no proof that Marquee's the one who broke in."

"The hell there ain't!" Harry continued erratically waving the gun. "You know what I'm thinking? That goddamn Limey's the one who killed Wiley and Chin."

"Eighty:20, and the odds are inching up," CJ said.

"How's that?" said the puzzled Steed.

"Nothing. Just thinking about an odds ratio I've been considering."

"Well, whether the odds favor Marquee breaking in here or not, I'm calling the cops back as soon as I have another look around the store to see what else might be missing. You can bet I'll give them my opinion about him."

"Reasonable enough," said CJ, puzzled over why Marquee would break in to GI Joe's and steal a single license plate and a couple of antique bootjacks. "Can you square up a couple of things for me before you call the cops back?"

"Why not?" Harry said bitterly.

"What do you think four mint-condition porcelain Connecticut plates, 1910 through 1913, might be worth?"

Thoughtfully eyeing the ceiling before responding, Harry said, "Five, maybe five and a half grand."

"Pretty much my guess, too."

"You seen anything like that around?"

"I've seen them advertised," CJ said, bending the truth.

"Well, buy 'em if you can. Anything under five grand and you've got yourself a bargain. You wanna stick around for the cops?"

"No," said CJ, suddenly depressed. "I've got to deal with a death in the family."

"Sorry to hear that. Somebody close?"

"My uncle."

Steed patted CJ supportively on the shoulder. "Then you better go handle that. I'll deal with the cops, and sooner or later, believe me, I'll deal with Marquee."

Turning to leave, CJ took a long, hard look at what had once been Wiley Ames's Wall of the West, thinking, as he looked at what was now shelf after shelf of what could only be described in the kindest terms as clutter, that in some odd sense, the GI Joe's murder case had come full circle. "I might give you a call later," he said.

"With more questions about Marquee?"

"Maybe. And maybe a few about Wiley's niece, Cheryl."

The mention of Cheryl Goldsby's name seemed to send Steed into a rage. "She's a lying, thieving, ungrateful dyke. You ask me, she and Marquee are birds of a feather. Never thought for one minute either of 'em would've killed poor Wiley, though. I guess sometimes you just end up being wrong about things." Steed lifted the receiver on a nearby rotary-dial phone to his ear. "You take care, now." By the time CJ reached the front door, Steed was on the line giving the unfortunate cop who'd answered a full piece of his mind.

The partly cloudy day had turned sunny, and as CJ walked up Larimer Street, all he could think of as he glanced skyward was that making final funeral arrangements for Ike couldn't totally dim the light.

It was becoming increasingly difficult for Korean War veterans to get approval to be buried at Fort Logan National Cemetery west of Denver. Bureaucrats liked to claim that declining space and the ever-increasing number of burial applications were the problem, whereas the real problem, kept pretty much under wraps for years, was that politicians, well-heeled bankers, lawyers, industrialists, high-profile local yokels, and fast-talking movers and shakers, many of whom had had only a whiff of service to their country, had been laid to rest in a place that should have been reserved for men like Ike Floyd.

The okay for Ike to be buried at Fort Logan, nonetheless, came quickly after a couple of strategically placed phone calls by Willis Sundee, and by the time CJ got back to the office, DeeAnn and Etta Lee Weeks had Ike's funeral arrangements pretty much nailed down.

DeeAnn was at lunch when he arrived, and Etta Lee gave CJ time to settle into his office and finish off a cup of coffee and a day-old donut before she walked in to fill him in on the particulars.

"We've got just about everything settled, funeral-wise," she said, sounding like her usual take-charge self. "Services will be the day after tomorrow. A mockup of the program should be ready by early this afternoon. I'll run it past you by three o'clock, okay? But I've gotta go check on Marguerite first. She's a nervous wreck. She loved Ike as much as life itself, you know. The two of them shoulda gotten married a long time ago. Tragedy they didn't."

"Yeah," said CJ, thinking about Mavis as he considered what he knew had been his uncle's greatest regret.

"Pallbearers are gonna be Rosie, Willis, Vernon Lowe, the Hopson boys, and a man named Charlie Thomas who served in Ike's field artillery unit during Korea. He called a little while ago. Said he'd be flying in from LA tonight. That okay with you?"

"Yes."

Etta Lee added, "Syrathia Greene stopped by earlier and brought the prettiest flowers. I put them in Ike's office on his desk. Must've set her back two hundred dollars, and in the midst of her own grief. Come on and have a look."

CJ followed Etta Lee to Ike's office, where the brightest and maybe the largest arrangement of spring flowers he'd ever seen sat in the middle of Ike's desk. Daisies, buttercups, tulips, streamers of emerald-green ivy, and a bunch of flowers he couldn't begin to name lit up the room. "Nice," he said, swallowing hard.

"Thought you'd like them," Etta Lee said, smiling. "Oh, and there was one other thing. You had a call that DeeAnn took. She said to tell you it was important. The message slip's on her desk."

"Thanks," said CJ, leaning down and kissing his best friend's petite, plump-cheeked wife on the forehead. "You know, if Rosie hadn't gotten to you first..."

"But he did," Etta Lee said, chuckling, as CJ headed for DeeAnn's tiny secretarial alcove.

"What you need to do, CJ Floyd," Etta Lee called after him, "so you don't end up forever on the outside of love looking in, is to quit your stumbling and hook up permanently with Mavis before some college boy swoops in and steals her away."

Instead of offering Etta Lee his standard "I'm on the case," CJ said nothing, which caused the normally opinionated woman to walk quietly away.

A neatly printed phone message from Ramona Lepsos sat near the left-hand corner of DeeAnn's desk. DeeAnn had checked the sheet's "urgent" box, jotted down Ramona's name and phone number and the time she'd called, and handwritten in bold red ink, "Important!!!"

CJ scooped the message up, walked briskly back to his office, plopped down at his desk, and dialed the number on the canary-yellow message sheet.

Ramona Lepsos answered on the third ring, sounding out of breath.

"It's CJ Floyd returning your call."

"Wait a sec. Let me set some things down. I'm busy moving furniture into my new apartment." Thirty seconds later, still sounding breathless, she was back on the line. "How's your murder investigation going?"

"It's going."

"How about I speed it up? I know where Cheryl and that bitch in heat of hers are holding hands. They're up in Idaho

Springs on some kind of lovers' retreat, staying at the Clear Creek Motel."

"So where'd your new info come from?" CJ asked, thinking that a thirty- to forty-minute drive from Denver to the mountain town of Idaho Springs might be in order.

"From a little birdie."

"No time to be coy, Ramona."

"Okay, I heard it from that antique hustler they're hooked up with, Gaylord Marquee. I went by his house a couple of nights ago and paid him a hundred bucks, and he ratted them out. The way I hear it, they're meeting some buyer in Idaho Springs who wants to relieve them of a bunch of their stolen goods. Seashells that Cheryl's Uncle Wiley latched on to for next to nothing that were stolen from Thailand's Phuket museum. Seashells Cheryl never showed you."

"Any chance they might be peddling license plates, too?"

"I don't know anything about that." There was hesitation in her voice that made CJ suspect she was either lying or holding back something important.

"Strange," he said. "I've had the feeling recently that the GI Joe's murders are linked more to stolen license plates than to seashells."

"Sounds sorta crazy to me. The only license plates I know of that Cheryl owned are the ones you saw at the ranch that day you were there."

"Could be I'm wrong. So what else have you got on Marquee?"

"Not much, only that he showed up out of nowhere at the ranch off and on over the years; he and Cheryl would conduct their business, and he'd leave. The fucking letch. Him and that filthy-minded guy who owns GI Joe's. Years ago, before either of them knew I was a lesbian, they each tried to hit on me. I was young and just brushed it off. Today I'd shoot their nuts off."

Ramona's tone of voice told CJ she meant every word. "Anything else about Marquee or Harry Steed I should know?"

"Not really, other than the fact that according to Cheryl, in addition to his seashell collection, Marquee collects old cars. So are you gonna head up to Idaho Springs and drop in on Cheryl and her little sweetie pie?"

"Probably," said CJ, thinking suddenly that perhaps the reason Marquee had left a Suburban that matched the description of a hit-and-run vehicle in his garage was because, as Rosie Weeks had suggested, he didn't realize the Suburban was there— or that Suburban wasn't *the* Suburban.

"Better do it fast. They're outa there tomorrow."

"You sure seem to know a lot about their comings and goings."

"Have you ever been in love or truly hurt, Mr. Floyd?"

"Can't say I have."

"Then you wouldn't understand. Why don't you just head on up to Idaho Springs? You just might find your killers there."

"You hate them that much?"

"More than you can ever know."

"Don't let it eat you up."

"Wouldn't dare. I'm just hoping my anger helps me destroy them. We'll talk again, Mr. Floyd. 'Bye."

CJ listened to a dial tone for several seconds before hanging up the phone, standing up, and walking across the room to get the extra pack of cheroots he typically left in a rotary-style telephone wall niche that was no longer used. He wasn't sure whether Ramona Lepsos was capable of murder, but he had no question that she was carrying enough pent-up anger to at least light the fuse.

There was always the chance that she'd killed Ames simply because he'd once made an ill-advised sexual advance, or a second one she'd failed to mention. Why she would have wanted to kill Chin, however, he couldn't answer.

Tapping out a cheroot, he lit up, took a long drag, blew a couple of smoke rings in the air, and watched them float toward the ceiling, aware that instead of distilling issues surrounding the GI Joe's killings, Lepsos's phone call had only muddied the waters. Muddied them so much that he couldn't decide whether to take off on a trip to Idaho Springs and drop in on Cheryl Goldsby and Molly Burgess or, come evening, continue with his plan to check out the Quonset hut he'd seen in Petey Greene's photos.

He had an additional day to catch up with Goldsby and Burgess before they left Idaho Springs, according to Ramona's information, so he decided to put off heading to the mountains and concentrate on making a visit to a peace sign and Quonset hut that evening, knowing very well that the sensible thing would have been to forget about the GI Joe's murders, concentrate on dealing with his grief, and get Ike buried. But, like Ike, he'd never been good at doing the conventional.

As she prepared to leave work for the day, after watching CJ fumble and stumble his way around the office for the rest of that afternoon jotting notes to himself, mumbling, and drinking coffee, DeeAnn felt the need to at least say something. Standing in the doorway of Ike's office and staring across the room to where CJ was writing on a notepad at Ike's desk, she said, "Trying to solve some dusty old murder case won't help bury your sorrow, CJ, no matter how much effort you put into it." CJ's failure to answer her brought a more focused, louder attempt. "Proving a point to yourself won't bring Ike back or answer any of the should'ves or would'ves you've got swirling around up there in your head. And it sure won't cancel out the two arraignments you need to have bonds ready for tomorrow morning, either. Go on upstairs, get yourself some rest, and clear your head. If you don't want to be here alone, you're welcome to come home with me."

"Thanks. I'll call it quits here pretty soon."

"Suit yourself," she said, walking seductively away. "See you tomorrow."

"First thing," said CJ, wondering how on earth Mavis could possibly compete with the pheromones one Ms. DeeAnn Slater seemed to leave everywhere. Licking one corner of his mouth as if he half expected the flavor from some decadent dessert to be there, he went back to poring over the several pages of notes he'd written.

He hadn't come up with any new suspects in the GI Joe's murders. Cheryl Goldsby, Molly Burgess, and Gaylord Marquee's names remained where they'd been all along, at the top of his list of suspects. But Ramona Lepsos continued to hold down a spot as well, and of course he couldn't leave out Harry Steed.

Tapping the head of his pencil on a notepad, he asked himself who of the people on his list stood to gain the most financially from the deaths of Ames and Chin. Any way he sized it up, Gaylord Marquee ended up with top billing. However, Marquee was missing in action, perhaps even dead, which to his way of thinking left Cheryl Goldsby as the next batter up. She was cold and calculating, no question about that, and if rare license plates had been the driving force behind the murders, she had some stashed away. The question he kept asking himself, however, was whether or not Goldsby had what it took to kill two people, and perhaps a third.

Molly Burgess, it seemed to him, had to be considered the odd woman out. He couldn't put his finger on what she had to gain from killing Ames, Chin, or Petey Greene. He'd never even seen her except at a distance one snowy night at the symphony. But he'd known for a long time that she'd had some kind of connection to Chin, and that made her acceptable fodder for the list. Besides, like Marquee, she was doggedly elusive. Elusive enough, as far as he was concerned, to have a tie-in to a couple of murders.

When he thought about who among his list of suspects could handle a .44 Mag, former British army officer Gaylord Marquee again rose to the top. But Goldsby and Lepsos, both outdoor types, and certainly Harry Steed, would know how to handle a weapon like that as well. As for the Petey Greene killing, anyone on his list could have been the killer.

He had laid down his pencil and moved back to trying to figure out why any of the people on his list, aside from Marquee, might have wanted to break into GI Joe's when the phone rang. "CJ here," he answered in a tone that was surprisingly combative.

"CJ, it's Henry. I'm wondering if you still need help tonight casing that Quonset hut you mentioned."

"No. I think I can handle it myself."

"You sure?"

"Yeah."

"Hell of a combination," said Henry. "A five-story-tall peace sign and a Quonset hut. Tall and stately, squat and fat. Still thinking that Quonset is stocked to the gills with boxes full of rare license plates?"

"Still am."

"You need me, you call me, okay?" Henry urged, concerned that CJ's response had been so clipped.

"You got it. Talk to you later." CJ cradled the phone and, deep in thought, decided to call Alfred Claymore, president of the Rocky Mountain Automobile License Plate Collectors Association, and have a talk with him about what else but the rare and the not so rare.

Chapter

⚜ 28

All CJ could think about after talking on the phone to Alfred Claymore, longtime president of the Colorado chapter of the Rocky Mountain Automobile License Plate Collectors Association, a man he'd known since his teens, was that if somehow license plates were at the heart of the GI Joe's killings, then Quan Lee Chin had been no more than someone in the wrong place at the wrong time on the morning of the murders. Claymore, who knew just about every license plate collector from New York to LA, said he'd never heard of Chin.

Guessing that Chin had more than likely been dropped on the spot along with the killer's real target, Ames, because he'd seen something the killer didn't want him to or because the killer wanted the cops traipsing off in the wrong direction, CJ whispered to himself, "Smart move."

As he nosed Ike's Jeep down Santa Fe Drive and accelerated toward Littleton, a southwest Denver suburb, feeling a little guilty and telling himself that he should've contacted Claymore as soon as he'd run across that first Monte Vista license plate at the Mile High Flea Market, he found himself wondering what kind of surprises he might find stashed away in an old Quonset hut.

Littleton, which sat just thirteen miles from downtown Denver, was a sleepy city that originally adjoined and now included Colorado's once famous Grant Ranch. As far as CJ had been able to tell from Ike's old topo maps, the Quonset hut and maybe even the peace dove sign he was headed to check out occupied what had at one time been Grant Ranch property.

In 1879 thousands of people had rushed to the Rocky Mountains in search of silver, and savvy prospector James B. Grant, a man who would eventually become Colorado's third governor, had been no different. Grant snapped up 1,280 acres of scrub oak, prickly pear, and elm, along with the acreage's water rights, which he had the foresight to realize were the lifeblood of the burgeoning cattle industry, and gave up his dream of panning for gold. A few years after first setting foot on land that included several water-rich lakes, Grant found himself overseeing a thriving, profitable cattle business.

Grant Ranch survived drought, flood, and cattle-trade ups and downs for over a century, but it couldn't survive the encroachment of civilization, and recently the property had been sold to real estate developers who'd promised to turn the ranch, with its unparalleled views of the Rockies, into a community of ecofriendly homes, lakes, ponds, and neighbors.

Whether that promise would ever come to fruition was anybody's guess, but as CJ eased the Jeep onto former Grant Ranch property, past barbed-wire fences that sported one "No Trespassing" sign after another, he stared out at the fading blaze-orange-and-magenta Rocky Mountain sunset and couldn't help thinking that no developer's promise could possibly match what he was looking at right then.

The best he'd been able to determine was that the peace dove sign and Quonset hut were on or near the southwest corner of the ranch, and the only access to that piece of land was via the old main headquarters road.

Bumping past the exquisitely restored log cabin that had once been Grant Ranch headquarters and driving into the approaching twilight, he slowed to take a good look at what was no longer a onetime cattle baron's home but a real estate sales office. The sign in the front yard, which shared three fenced-off acres of once irrigated pasture with a dozen or more majestic Colorado blue spruces, read, "Grant Ranch Homes, from the low $80s. Pick your homestead."

Shaking his head and thinking, *Progress,* CJ continued past the sales office and a small graveled parking lot. The lot was empty, and at seven o'clock on a Monday night, he felt pretty certain there were no sales agents around. The only sign of office life was the ribbon of light peeking out from beneath a half-lowered upstairs window blind. Suspecting that some forgetful sales agent had forgotten to turn off a light, he drove on.

Seventy-five yards past the sales office, the headquarters road turned into what was barely a cow path. As the Jeep dipped, bumped, and jiggled its way toward the southwest corner of the ranch, he was happy that he hadn't driven the Bel Air. A quarter of a mile later, he dropped over a rise, bottoming out the Jeep in a sandy rut. Briefly thinking, *What the hell am I doing here?* he spotted his objective, a Quonset hut rising like some silver-domed Indian mound in the distance, and behind it the peace dove sign.

Twilight was descending into darkness when he pulled the Jeep to a stop at a barbed-wire fence about forty yards from the Quonset hut. Looking up at the five-story-tall peace dove on a pole, which he could now see clearly was less than a hundred yards east of the Quonset hut, he found himself thinking, *Bigger than I guessed.*

Taking in the lay of the land and carefully assessing the position of the peace dove in relation to the Quonset hut, he could see that they were both sitting on a small, fenced-off plot with "No Trespassing" signs that were a different color than those for Grant Ranch. Gazing back south in the direction of Bowles Avenue, the road that ran east and west past the Grant Ranch property as it rose toward the foothills, he realized for the first time why the peace sign was such a visible landmark. Set on a rise that paralleled Bowles Avenue, the sign was visible whether you were approaching it from the mountains to the west, from downtown Denver to the north, or from the south as you came up Santa Fe Drive from Colorado Springs. He took a final look around before getting out of the Jeep, reached into the glove compartment, extracted his snub-nosed .38, and slipped it into the right-hand pocket of the lightweight jacket he'd traded his vest in for. Walking to the rear of the Jeep, he raised the back hatch and took out a pair of bolt cutters, a flashlight, and a pair of gloves before heading for the fence.

He snipped his way through the barbed wire in no time and,

with his jeans swishing loudly in the tall, dry grass, closed in on his objective. When he reached the Quonset hut's two fourteen-foot-high, south-facing sliding doors, he slipped the bolt cutters off his shoulder and went quickly after the lock securing the doors. It took a little longer to cut through the lock than the barbed wire, and it was only when a few rivulets of sweat worked their way down his neck that he considered the fact that a building with such a formidable lock probably also had an alarm system.

Mouthing, *Shit,* he stepped away from the door and walked along the east side of the 120-foot-long metal building. Having no idea where alarm wires might be buried in the soft clay soil or whether they might not be threading their way inside the conduit he could see running along the building's concrete apron, he stopped his search. Stumped, he stared up at the building's corrugated metal curvature and realized that the building had no windows. Thinking that there had to be some way to let outside light in, he headed for the west side of the building. Halfway down the west side he spotted a skylight covered by a heavy-gauge clear plastic that was snapping and clicking in the wind. The skylight was inset into the Quonset hut's metal shell several feet below the highest part of the arc.

He had no idea whether the skylight was wired with an alarm, but he intended to find out. Sprinting back to the Jeep, he slipped in, gunned the engine, and rammed the vehicle through the undermatched barbed-wire fence, purposely dragging two entangled six-foot-long steel fence posts and a broken twenty-foot length of fence along with him.

Glancing around into what was now early-evening darkness to make certain no one came rushing out of the quarter-moon darkness after him, he pulled the Jeep to a stop and took a deep breath. The only thing he could hear besides his own nervous breathing was the ever-increasing howl of the wind.

Nosing the Jeep forward, he positioned it directly below the skylight, killed the engine, and, with a pair of pliers he'd taken from the glove box, quickly wiggled and snipped the two steel posts he'd dragged along with him away from their four strands of barbed wire. He placed the steel posts on top of the Jeep's cab and stair-stepped his way from the front bumper onto the hood and up onto the top of the cab.

All he had to do now, he told himself as he stared up at the skylight, was to wiggle the plastic covering away from what he could see was a two-by-six-foot wooden frame using one of the steel posts, hope the skylight wasn't wired, and drop headfirst twenty feet down to the floor inside without breaking his neck.

Hoping that whoever owned the Quonset hut had never figured on someone inquisitive or foolish enough to risk a twenty-foot nosedive wanting to break in, he took a deep breath, jimmied the spear-shaped business end of one of the steel posts under the skylight's cover, and started teasing the plastic away from its moorings.

Hearing no alarm, he worked earnestly for a good two minutes, flashlight in one hand and steel post in the other, until he'd almost pried the skylight's cover away from its frame. When a stiff breeze finally sent the sheet of plastic sailing toward the peace dove, he found himself trying to maintain his balance in the wind.

Quickly back on task, he tossed the steel post to the ground and made a couple of unsuccessful attempts to jump up the two feet he needed to grab the bottom lip of the skylight's wooden frame. Momentarily out of breath, he wondered if his two hard landings on the top of the cab had done any serious damage.

A third attempt bought success, and as he hung, clutching the wooden frame with both hands, his body arched against the curvature of the Quonset hut, he had the feeling that he might be making one hell of a mistake.

Grunting and sweating, he pulled himself up and wriggled his body a third of the way through the skylight opening. He paused to tease his flashlight out of his jacket pocket, forced an arm back through the exceedingly tight opening, and snapped on the beam. He let out a gasp the instant he saw two rows of vintage automobiles lined up on the concrete floor beneath him. Counting off each car, he whispered, "Eight," and aimed the flashlight's beam down onto the black convertible directly below him. The car's hood ornament, graceful lines, and distinctive rear lights screamed, *Packard.* Guessing the model year to be either 1936 or 1938, he scanned the remaining cars quickly with the flashlight, thought, *What a haul,* and looked for someplace he could land safely.

When he spotted a pile of what looked to be either car covers or blankets several feet from the rear of the Packard, he muttered, "Now or never," wriggled the rest of his body through the skylight, briefly locked his knees for stability, zeroed in his landing site, and dove.

With both arms extended and his head tucked into his chest,

the landing was anything but soft. His hyperextended left arm took the brunt of the shock as he crashed into a pile of fluffed-up car covers that didn't provide much cushion.

Yelling, "Shit!" he heard his shoulder pop. Suspecting he'd dislocated the joint and grimacing in pain, he stood, eyed the broken flashlight bulb at his feet, awkwardly brushed himself off with his right hand, and tried to pop his shoulder back into place. After several unsuccessful attempts, he swallowed his pain and decided the best thing he could do right then was to make sure he still had his .38 and then find a light switch.

Patting his jacket pocket and finding that the .38 was still there, he walked along one side of the darkened Quonset hut toward the doors whose lock he'd snapped. Halfway there, he found a light switch and flipped it on. The light, barely enough to brighten the darkened Quonset hut, at least allowed him to get a better look at the cars. His eyes widened as he soaked in the elegant lines of the antique cars, but it was the absolutely pristine license plates attached to the front or rear bumpers or trunks that held his attention. Quickly realizing that each plate or set of plates came from a different Western state, he counted off the states aloud, as if he were some excited second grader called up to recite the names of the states in front of his class. "Colorado, Wyoming, Utah, Nevada, Arizona, Idaho, Montana, New Mexico." Every Western state of importance in the rare and collectible license-plate game was represented, and every license plate on every car was a first-of-state issue. As the words *Worth killing for* threaded their way slowly through his head, he finally understood what the GI Joe's killings had truly been about.

Chapter

29

His shoulder throbbing, CJ moved from car to car, basking in each automobile's unique classic beauty. What he now recognized as a 1939 Packard V-12 sedan, the lead car in the line of four closest to him, was an automobile he'd only seen pictures of. There didn't seem to be one thing that wasn't absolutely mint about the car, which had a mirror-like black-lacquer finish. When he spotted a ninth vehicle, a white Chevy Suburban with front-end damage that looked identical to the one in Gaylord Marquee's garage, sitting by itself in semidarkness near the doors of the Quonset hut, he knew immediately that it was that Suburban and not the one in Marquee's garage that had run down Petey.

Turning his attention back to the cars, he tried the Packard's driver's-side door. The door was locked. *Reasonable thing to do,* he thought, walking from the front of the car to the rear, where an undated, mint-condition, red-and-white first-of-state Wyoming license plate, complete with the Wyoming state seal and identical in every way to its mate on the car's front bumper, capped off the car's aerodynamic beauty. The undated plate's low issue number, 2, could just as easily have read, *"Ten grand."*

Moving slowly down the aisle between the two lines of cars, he could only shake his head in amazement. A set of 1915 Utah first-of-state plates adorned the front and back bumpers of a 1947 Plymouth four-door sedan with the infamous suicide doors.

A first-of-state set of 1914 Arizona plates was the crowning glory of a 1948 Chrysler Town and Country convertible, and a single-issue Colorado first-of-state plate from 1913 sat recessed in the center of the trunk lid of a 1937 Hudson Terraplane straight-eight that was its original olive green. A '55 Chevy hard-top, identical in color to his own cream-on-red Bel Air, sported a single-issue 1913 Idaho first-of-state plate. Montana 1915 first of states rode like jewels on the front and back bumpers of a 1946 DeSoto coupe with a sleek-looking sun visor, and when he spotted Nevada first of states on a 1952 Nash Rambler, he simply whispered, "Shit."

There, as if to cap off the Rose Bowl parade of vintage automobiles, peeking above the front bumper of a 1936 Auburn Boattail Speedster was a New Mexico first of state that, like its Colorado cousin, had been a single-issue license plate. Most collectors he'd talked to over the years felt that fewer than two dozen New Mexico first-of-state plates in mint condition like the one he was looking at even existed. But there, staring at him in the muted light in all its mint-condition glory, was a green-on-white, undated New Mexico first-of-state plate with the low issue number 8 sitting smack in its center. Guessing that the plate was worth at least fifteen thousand dollars, CJ let out a lengthy whistle.

He was interrupted by a voice rising from near the partially open front doors of the dimly lit Quonset hut. "Impressive enough to whistle at, indeed, Mr. Floyd. You're quite obviously a man who knows what he's looking at. I can only say that I wholeheartedly agree with your assessment."

When CJ jerked his head to the left and craned to see exactly where the response had come from, a current of pain shot through his injured left shoulder. Immediately recognizing the strange apparition standing in unflattering light twenty feet from him, CJ said, "Marquee." Marquee, who stood a couple of feet inside the Quonset hut's massive doors, which he'd opened just enough to squeeze through, smiled and said, "Hard to hear anybody approaching when you're so totally captivated, and here's a word of advice. You shouldn't drive your classic automobile to garage break-ins, Mr. Floyd. It's far too easy to spot."

"Yours?" CJ asked, pointing toward the cars, realizing that Marquee had probably been on his tail for awhile.

"No, I'm sorry to say his." Marquee stepped back and pushed one of the Quonset hut doors open wider to reveal a very perturbed-looking Harry Steed.

"Well, well, well," said CJ, wondering whether the two men could see the bulge of the .38 in his jacket pocket. "I pretty much figured Marquee was in on the kill, but you know what, Harry? You were way down on my list."

"I didn't kill anybody," Marquee protested.

"Put a damper on it, Gaylord," Steed ordered.

Squinting into the light as he tried to determine whether either man was armed, CJ said, "Quite a car collection you've got here, Harry. Not to mention the first-of-state license plates."

"You're trespassing, CJ," Steed said angrily.

CJ glanced up toward the single hanging overhead pool-table-style light he'd turned on earlier, thinking he might be in a better negotiating position if the Quonset hut were dark. He said, "Just something I had to do in order to find a killer. Mind telling me how you got all those first of states? Oh, wait a second. Guess you really don't have to do that. I'm betting they belonged to Wiley Ames."

"How I got them doesn't matter. What matters is you're an intruder." Steed slipped a holstered .45 from beneath his jacket, aimed it point-blank at CJ, and squeezed the trigger as CJ dove for safety beneath the Chrysler. He fired three quick additional shots before CJ pulled his .38 and with three shots of his own took out the overhead light.

"Get some more light in here, damn it!" Harry screamed at Marquee.

As Marquee raced for a second light switch, the former machine gunner, as expert at firing a weapon at what he could hear as at what he could see, squeezed off two rounds in the direction of Marquee's footfalls. The second shot slammed into Marquee's thigh. Screaming and writhing in pain, Marquee fell to the floor.

"Like we used to say in 'Nam, 'Even Steven in the dark.' You wouldn't want to shoot up one of your cars," CJ called out. "Or maybe even one of your precious plates, would you,

Harry?" Crawling toward where he had heard Marquee fall, CJ yelled, "Bad idea putting so few lights in this place," seconds before reaching the wounded Englishman.

In response to CJ's fire-drawing taunt, Steed squeezed off three more shots that pinged off the concrete in front of CJ. "Seven rounds down," CJ whispered, propping Marquee up and using him as a shield. When Marquee shrieked, "No!" CJ grabbed the terrified Englishman by his shirt collar and, half choking him, said, "I'll call the goddamn fire in on your head, Marquee, or maybe just shoot you myself if you don't cooperate."

"No! No, please!"

"How the hell did Harry get all those license plates?"

"Like you said, he stole them from Ames. I was just an intermediary, steering Ames in the direction of rare finds. I didn't kill anyone." Rubbing his wounded leg, he said, "I need help. I'll bleed to death."

"No, you won't." Squinting in pain, CJ slipped off his jacket, draped one of the sleeves over Marquee's thigh, and said, "Tie it in a knot around your leg." The sound of fabric swishing drew another round from Steed as Marquee complied. When CJ heard Steed insert a new clip into his weapon, he smiled and said, "Eight rounds and out. I know your ordnance limits now, Harry. Hope you're a fast reloader."

Nudging Marquee in the ribs with a hard knee, CJ yelled, "Marquee's giving you up over here, Harry. The rarest of the rare. Isn't that what you said I should be collecting when you gave me that line of bullshit about buyers and sellers and specialists? And staging that break-in at your store to get me and the cops focused on Marquee. Real nice touch. So was the phantom Suburban you planted in Marquee's garage. I should've realized all along that whoever killed Wiley and Chin was somebody looking to inhale rarefied air."

He turned his attention back to Marquee. "You should check out your garage more often, friend. Now what about Chin? Just a pigeon, I'm guessing?"

"Yeah," said Marquee, puzzled by the garage reference and shivering from blood loss. "Harry had me get Chin there that morning hoping a double homicide might send the cops scampering in the wrong direction. I made sure Chin showed up with a box of stolen seashells so he'd think the meeting was part of his and Ames's normal fencing scam. Harry even ran off with the shells."

"Then he killed Chin for no damn reason at all?"

"Oh, he had a reason." Marquee glanced back at the Packard. "The license plates on these cars."

Stone-cold killer, CJ thought, shaking his head in disgust as images of some of the combat-nurtured American GI psychos he'd run across in Vietnam resurfaced. The war had turned some men into nutcases just as capable of killing a fellow soldier over a carton of cigarettes or a night with some Saigon whore as they were of killing the enemy. He had no idea what had pushed Harry Steed to that point. Perhaps it had been *his* war. A war that had taught him to be a wheeler and a dealer, an insatiable hoarder of things, and, in the end, a killer. He guessed that if he'd looked long and hard enough, something he'd unfortunately never really done when it had come to Steed, he would have seen the soul-smoothing reflection of war in Steed's eyes. A look that Wiley Ames had once sworn to him he could see in the eyes of every man who'd been to war, including CJ.

When he heard what he thought was Steed moving toward them, he whispered to Marquee, "Be right back," and, duck-walking his way down the east side of the line of cars, moved to circle behind Steed. He'd reached the rear of the Nash Rambler when Steed popped out from behind the right front fender of the '55 Chevy and squeezed off two rounds. Uncertain whether it was the poor lighting or the slightly cockeyed, out-of-line Rambler that spoiled Steed's aim, CJ fired back, clipping Steed in the left cheek. Startled, with blood streaming down his cheek and his .45 dangling momentarily at his side, Steed took the full brunt of CJ's bull rush. A forearm to the chin and full-steam charge drove Steed into the floor, slamming his head into the concrete. As CJ crawled on top of the unconscious pawnshop owner, the doors to the Quonset hut rolled open and the headlights of a Littleton police car, responding to a report from a terrified-sounding Grant Ranch sales agent that someone in a Jeep was trespassing on the ranch property, flooded the inside of the Quonset hut.

A boyish-looking patrolman stepped out of the car. When he saw three men down on the floor, he drew his service revolver and shouted, "Nobody move! Arms in the air—everybody!"

Semiconscious and slumped face forward, Gaylord Marquee barely heard the command. Harry Steed, who was flat on his back and out cold with a hole in his cheek that was oozing blood, couldn't respond. Only CJ, who was staring down the barrel of a .38 police special, obliged and raised his hands.

In one way, Steed and Marquee fared better than CJ. Whisked off to Swedish Hospital for medical attention, they were spared the midnight police grilling that CJ was forced to endure in a drafty Littleton precinct substation while his shoulder screamed in pain.

Luckily, his interrogator, a graying, pudgy, clearly in-charge detective sergeant who had been called to the scene of the break-in by the two beat cops, was a seasoned cop with the investigative smarts to realize that the bizarre Quonset-hut scene, in which a verified Littleton resident and his companion, both white, had apparently been shot by a black intruder, wasn't quite what it seemed.

Five minutes into his interrogation, following a half-dozen attempts to comfortably adjust his pear-shaped body to an undersized, rickety wooden chair, Kip Manson, a twenty-year veteran of the Littleton police force, said, "Five and a half years is a long time to chase after a case. Even one as widely known in these parts as the GI Joe's killings, and especially if you're not a cop. Why so persistent, Floyd?"

"Just something I promised myself I'd do. I've said too much already. Don't think I'll say anything else without my lawyer here."

"Suit yourself," said Manson. "But I can tell you this. You haven't left yourself a whole lot of wiggle room, friend. You trespassed on private property, broke into a locked building, and shot two men."

"Two men who tried to kill me!"

"It'll be your word against theirs."

Unwilling to bite his tongue and aware that he just might be digging himself a deeper hole, CJ said, "What about those license plates I mentioned? They're stolen. They belonged to Wilcy Ames, like I've already said, or to his estate, at least. Steed killed Ames over them. The plates on the cars in that Quonset hut are first-of-state issues from every state in the Rocky Mountain West. Altogether they're worth sixty or seventy grand, easy."

"Seems like an awfully strange reason to kill two men," said Manson. "But then again, I'm no license-plate aficionado. Now, just for the record, if I were someone on the outside looking in, I'd say a more likely scenario is that you're the one who was willing to kill for those license plates."

CJ rubbed his injured shoulder and sighed as Manson glanced down at the two pages of notes he'd jotted on a yellow tablet. Flipping back one of the pages, Manson said, "You said Ames was a World War II vet and that Chin, the other guy killed that morning at GI Joe's, was a concert cellist."

"Yes."

"Odd sorta ducks to be hanging out together, don't you think?"

"Chin was just in the wrong place at the wrong time. Gaylord Marquee, that other guy they carted off to the hospital, told me so himself."

"The guy you shot."

"He tried to kill me, damn it. Steed had Marquee lure Chin to GI Joe's the morning of the killings, and Steed popped him along with Ames, hoping to get people like you looking in the wrong direction. Send you chasing after anything and anybody but them."

"Hope for your sake you're telling the truth, Floyd, and for the record once again, it wasn't us Littleton cops who spent years looking the wrong way. For the moment, though, let's forget about the GI Joe's killings and get back to why you're here. Maybe instead of the way you're saying things went down at that Quonset hut, they really unfolded like this. After five and a half years of dogging a case, you finally nail down all the ins and outs, and you decide to grab those first-of-state license plates for yourself and eliminate two other people who also knew their true value."

Looking frustrated, CJ said, "Talk to Gaylord Marquee if you want the truth. I've told you, he's the one who lured Chin to GI Joe's the morning of those killings, and I don't think he'll want to do Harry Steed's time for him."

"Okay," Manson said, stroking his chin thoughtfully. "Just tell me why, in all this time, Steed hasn't done away with Marquee? From what you're saying, the man clearly knew too much."

"Beats me. Maybe Steed was paying Marquee to keep quiet. Right now I'm thinking maybe I'll just shut up and wait for my lawyer."

"Your choice, Floyd. Perhaps you weren't out to steal those plates. Could be you, or maybe you and Marquee, were planning on stealing a couple of those vintage cars instead. Maybe Marquee got cold feet and you decided to get rid of him and score everything for yourself."

Still silent, CJ glanced toward the room's metal door, wondering why Ike's lawyer, Sam Guterro, hadn't yet appeared. Moments later the door edged open, and a plainclothes cop who'd been in the room when the interrogation had started stuck his head into the room and beckoned to Manson. Manson said with a wink, "Back in a sec." The two men whispered to one another with the door half open for a good thirty seconds before Manson returned. *They're setting me up,* CJ thought as Manson, scratching his head theatrically, retook his seat. "Got a couple of new wrinkles for you, Floyd. We've done some checking on you. Two tours of Vietnam as a patrol-boat machine gunner. A Navy Cross to your credit and enough skirmishes with the Denver cops since coming home from 'Nam to make your name pop on our computers like you're kin to Orville Redenbacher. War duty like that can make a man real hard inside. Make him think less about the price he might have to pay for starting something and shooting someone."

"You're headed down the wrong road, Sergeant."

"Maybe, maybe not. I'm just a simple-minded suburban cop from outside your big city who's stumbled face first into the real reason for a couple of five-and-a-half-year-old murders. You said earlier that Ames and Chin were killed with a .44 Mag."

"There's never really been any question about that."

Manson beamed. "Well, stepcousins that we are to Denver out here in the 'burbs, we nonetheless try our best to be thorough. My partner, the man I just talked to, had someone get a judge out of bed to issue a search warrant for that Quonset hut you broke into, and lo and behold, do you know what my people found during that search?"

"Beats me."

"A bunch more license plates packed up in boxes. Plates that I'm guessing must be pretty rare. They also found a .44 Mag semiautomatic tucked away in one of the boxes. Somehow I've got a feeling that gun isn't yours, Floyd."

"So why tell me?" CJ asked, suspecting that he'd all of a sudden become a bargaining chip.

"Oh, I think we both know why, Floyd. You and I, well, we're both, when you come right down to it—now, how do they say it?—little cogs. If that .44 is a murder weapon, and if it belongs to either Marquee or Steed, things will move pretty swiftly from here. Brew yourself up a mixture of media types looking to milk a story and politicians jockeying for position, and guess what? You've got electioneering news for months."

Surprised by Manson's forthrightness and looking confused, CJ asked, "What the hell gives, Sergeant?"

Manson smiled. It was the confident smile of a man with inside dope. "Let's just say somebody I don't see eye to eye with, somebody who wants to be Colorado's next governor, could be looking to ride your horse to glory, Floyd. That is, of course, if you're telling the truth, and if that .44 we found turns out to be a murder weapon. Bottom line here is that whether I like it or not, and whether or not the person I'm talking about ends up hating our guts, we'll all be sitting on the same side of the table in the end."

"And if the .44 doesn't turn out to be Marquee's or Steed's, what then?"

"Then that lawyer of yours who hasn't shown up should be doing his best to whittle down the time on your prison term. Like I said, we're bargaining chips, Floyd. Got another piece of news for you," Manson said, finally relaxing back in his chair.

"Which is?"

The look on Manson's face turned positively serious. "I did a couple of years in the navy myself. No Navy Cross, of course. Did my time in Korea, 1952 and '53. Got mixed up in what some political types still like to call a *conflict* instead of a *war*. Guess that's the reason I can't stomach politicians. Wanna guess what I babysat on the high-speed transport I served aboard?"

"Couldn't hazard a guess," said CJ, knowing very well where the pudgy police sergeant was headed with the question. "But I'm betting she was a lot bigger than my .50-caliber."

"Much bigger. A 40-millimeter cannon, to be exact, one of three on the old *Horace Bass*. Called her Harriet. What about you?"

The sounds and smells of the Mekong River Delta reached up and grabbed CJ by the throat as he whispered, "Bertha."

"Never really goes away, does it?" said Manson, noting the strange lost look on CJ's face.

Recalling what Wiley Ames had said to him the first time they'd met and feeling a strange, mission-accomplished sense of relief, CJ said, "Not really. But like a friend of mine once told me, you move on."

Chapter

30

CJ had never liked Sam Guterro—his holier-than-thou aloofness, his overly macho, manufactured courtroom stage presence, his arrogance, or his third grade pettiness. In all the years he'd known the man who'd been Ike's lawyer, he'd barely been able to endure more than a few minutes of Guterro's personality or his rancid-smelling breath.

He'd never understood why Ike had kept a man like Guterro around. Word on the street was that Guterro had once kept Ike from going to prison for nearly killing a man who had gotten too frisky with Marguerite in a bar one night, but Ike had never confirmed that rumor, and Willis Sundee, the only man CJ suspected knew the truth, had always been evasive or downright mum on the subject.

Guterro was his typical condescending, abrasive self the night he talked to CJ in private, lawyer-to-client fashion, following Sergeant Manson's interrogation. In his dressing down of CJ, he implied that CJ was either naive or stupid to have talked to Manson at all.

Instead of cold-cocking the dish-faced, redheaded barrister on the spot, CJ bit back his anger, swallowed his medicine, and, expecting that he would be bonded out of jail by late the next day, went off to jail, shoulder separation and all. Now he was having trouble controlling his temper as he stood outside the Arapahoe County Courthouse, free on a seventy-five-thousand-dollar bond, talking to Sam. CJ was angry over the fact that because of Sam's dawdling, and very likely his arrogance, he'd had to spend two nights in jail rather than one.

Henry Bales, recognizing the bad blood between the two men and trying his best to keep from being showered by Guterro's excuse-laced spittle or bowled over by his bad breath, stood several feet away, looking toward the courthouse doorway, where he expected Rosie Weeks, his and CJ's ride home, to appear any second.

Guterro, unwilling to back down, seemed intent on pushing CJ's buttons. "You keep your trap shut from now on, you hear me? That's what the hell delayed things. And never bet yourself that a cop like that Manson won't be there to put a spear in your ass if he gets the chance. Big-town cops, small-town cops, it doesn't matter. They're all the same. Didn't Ike teach you anything?"

CJ swallowed hard, thought briefly about his and Manson's shared experiences, and remained silent.

Guterro continued, "Best thing you have going for you is that Suburban the cops impounded from that Quonset hut. It's unregistered, but it's Steed's all right according to people in the know, and it pretty much ties him to the Petey Greene murder.

That's one thing in your overly loquacious favor, at least. Be certain that I'll milk that connection for all it's worth. The problem will be getting Marquee to roll on Steed."

"Nice to be blessed with small things," said CJ.

Guterro looked offended. "Listen up, Calvin, because for some reason you still seem to be missing the goddamn point. You're on the hook for trying to kill a couple of men. And to make matters worse, you've got some real damaging post-Vietnam stress history that won't be hard to hang out there. If I were you, I'd jettison the smugness. From this point forward, your job is to sit in the wings and keep quiet. I'll make the necessary connections between Steed and Marquee. I'll force Marquee's hand and get him to roll on Steed, and I'll use my ins at the Arapahoe County DA's office to move this thing away from where it could blow your goddamn head off. Got it?"

Looking fed up, CJ glanced at Henry and said, "Wanna step over here for a sec, Bull Tamer?"

Henry shrugged and stepped close to CJ and Sam.

CJ smiled. "Sam here just finished telling me how a smart lawyer like him can wrap up the case against Steed and Marquee in a tight little penitentiary-bound bow. Even outlined his strategy for me. Right, Sam?"

"Pretty much," said Guterro, looking puzzled.

"So I need a witness who can attest to the fact that I'm not stealing any of Sam's intellectual property from him when I do what I'm about to do." Looking Sam squarely in the eye, he said, "You're fired, asshole. Have your secretary send me a bill."

"You're not serious."

"Afraid so. Now, shuffle on off to Buffalo or Podunk, or wherever in the hell jerks like you feed your egos, and get outa my face. I just spent an extra night in jail because of your sorry ass, and in all the time I've talked to you since my release, you've never once asked me about Ike."

"You'll end up doing time," Sam said angrily.

CJ winked at Henry. "We've done time before, right, Bull Tamer?"

"The hardest kind," Henry said, catching a glimpse of Rosie's imposing figure as it filled the courthouse doorway.

"I kept Ike from going to prison for attempted murder," Sam protested.

"So I've heard," said CJ. "And you know what? I'm thinking you'll have to take that up with him. Adios, jackass." CJ turned and headed for the courthouse door.

"Didn't leave yourself much room for reconciliation," said Henry, matching him stride for stride.

"Didn't plan to," CJ said, looping his uninjured arm over Henry's shoulders. "Sometimes there's just no room for reconciliation between the North and the South. You and I both know that."

Epilogue

"Never keep a gun you killed somebody with or a Suburban you ran somebody down with around," Rosie Weeks said, looking past CJ and west from Ike Floyd's gravesite toward the Rockies. "Poor Petey."

"One other thing," said CJ, who was kneeling next to Ike's headstone, adjusting the huge bouquet of black-eyed Susans, Ike's favorite flower, that Marguerite had sent with him to the cemetery. "Try not to brag to anyone about all the guns you've got protecting your store."

He paused to stare down from Ike's hillside grave onto row after row of headstones below. "Doesn't seem like we buried him almost two months ago," CJ said haltingly.

"He was the best," Rosie said reassuringly.

Silent now, CJ glanced skyward toward a bank of flying-saucer-shaped clouds. Shifting his weight to one knee and standing, he asked, "Do you think we end up anywhere but in the dirt when it's all said and done, Red?"

"We better. Otherwise Etta Lee's gonna be one pissed-off lady," Rosie said, hoping his lighthearted response would keep CJ from slipping back down the mountain of sorrow he'd been trying his best to scale for months. "How's the shoulder, by the way?"

Rolling his injured left shoulder over and back, CJ said, "Fine. But it's gonna be a legal problem for me here real soon."

"How's that?"

"Remember me telling you about that Arapahoe County DA, the Cuban-cigar-smoking little rat terrier with political ambitions that Sergeant Manson warned me about?"

"Yeah. You've told me about him and Manson. Isn't he the guy who got you out from under breaking-and-entering and attempted-murder charges?"

"Yep. He's the wonderful one," CJ said sarcastically.

"So what's he want?"

"His pound of flesh. He and the Denver DA are tag-teaming Harry Steed. They want me to testify against Steed in his murder trial and do a repeat performance when Marquee's trial comes up. They're going after Marquee as an accessory to murder even though he rolled on Steed, and even after Steed tried to set Marquee up for Petey's murder by stashing that second damaged white Suburban in Marquee's garage."

"So how's the shoulder fit in?"

"Mr. Rat Terrier DA says that in both cases the defense will try to impugn my testimony by characterizing me as nothing more than a trigger-happy Vietnam-vet wacko and car thief. He claims they'll not only introduce my medical records to show how I injured my shoulder but that they'll also bring in a string of witnesses who'll claim I've had a hard time adjusting to life after the war. That new lawyer I replaced Sam Guterro with agrees."

"That's damn sure stretchin' the shit outa the truth. What

war did any of those lyin' lawyer bastards ever fight in? You ask me, they need to put Steed under the jail and Marquee right there with him."

"It's America, Rosie. Innocent until proven guilty, remember?"

"My ass. That crazy-ass, license-plate-hoarding miser took away three people's lives just so he could slap a bunch of rare license plates on a few old cars, go out to some metal barn hidden away in the woods, and cream in his pants while he's lookin' at his prizes like he's at some strip joint droolin' over naked women. Whacked-out son of a bitch, if you ask me."

CJ laughed. "Don't blow a gasket, Red. Think of it like this: there're plenty of folks out there who are crazier."

"Guess so," Rosie said, stretching out his already wide-legged stance on the hillside. "Anybody saying why Marquee kept his mouth shut all those years about Steed killin' Ames and that Chinaman?"

"Money. What else? But not in the way of cold, hard cash. From what I'm hearing, two of the eight cars that were in that Quonset hut had their titles transferred from Steed to Marquee several years back, and that means that thirty or forty grand floated Marquee's way without any cash ever changing hands."

"Slick way of launderin' hush money," said Rosie.

"But not slick enough. All that goes around comes around," said CJ, smiling as he used one of Ike's favorite phrases. "The Denver DA's got Cheryl Goldsby in line to testify against Steed and Marquee as well. She's being primed to spill her guts about how Marquee sold off a bunch of her uncle's other rare license plates for her. Plates that Steed never got his hands on when he stole most of Wiley's collection. Plates that Marquee bought from Goldsby for a song and then resold. I ended up with one of them, that rare 1909 Monte Vista municipal tag I told you about. It's what started my whole investigation rolling, really."

Nodding, Rosie said, "How long before they go to trial?"

"Four to six months, I've been told. It'll take the prosecution that long to build their case and to cement the link between Chin and Steed. There's no question that Molly Burgess, that cellist girlfriend of Goldsby's, can prove Steed knew Chin, so that's a start. Turns out Marquee and Chin really were also moving stolen seashells through GI Joe's with Harry Steed's 10 percent cut of a blessing. Another nice little financial plum for Marquee. Now, here's an eye-opener for you. The reason Burgess knew Chin, and why she can prove a Chin to Steed connection, is because before she hooked up with Cheryl Goldsby and came out of the closet; she was Chin's girlfriend. That's why she avoided me all those times I tried to get in touch with her. She didn't know what I was after, and she didn't want her straight-world past catching up with her gay-world future and maybe wrecking her relationship with Goldsby."

"What a frickin' double-dealin' mess. And all of it endin' up in a murder trial that'll cost us taxpayers a bundle. They're all passengers on a goddamn perverted ship of fools, you ask me. No matter, though," Rosie said, scratching his head. "As long as Steed and Marquee end up gettin' theirs in the end, Steed for killin' Ames, Chin, and poor old Petey and Marquee for helpin' him do it, I'm okay. As for love havin' anything to do with it, straight or gay, I'm guessin' we all best grab on to that when we can. Think I've told you that before, though, my man."

Aware of where Rosie was headed, CJ simply nodded.

Wagging his index finger at CJ, Rosie said, "I'm only gonna say this once. You choose bad, you end up sad. I'd be gettin' my ducks in order with Mavis if I were you and forgettin' the hell about DeeAnn."

"I've heard the sermon before, Rosie."

"Yeah, but you evidently ain't been listenin'. Every time I look up these days, you got DeeAnn hangin' on your arm. Now, don't get me wrong. She's a decent enough person, and God knows she can turn heads, but trust me, CJ, she ain't in Mavis's class."

Hoping to avoid getting into an argument with his best friend, CJ said, "It's a rough time for me right now, Red. I've got estate problems pulling at me every day, a rocky business to keep afloat, and a seventy-five-thousand-dollar bond secured by everything I own in the world. A bond that lets me keep walking the streets and earning a living instead of twiddling away my days in jail."

"Okay, I'll cut you some slack. Just remember, when all the fog lifts, don't make the mistake of choosin' DeeAnn over Mavis."

CJ stared down at Ike's dirt-covered gravesite and the few new blades of grass that had nosed their way up out of the soil and found himself thinking about what Ike had said about his own failures when it came to love. "Mavis is out of my league, Red."

"Bullshit. You're just lookin' for some excuse to keep from risin' above yourself. No matter. Mavis'll be home from school in a few weeks. You'll have time enough to think about where the two of you are headed." Rosie dusted off his hands, indicating that he was done with the subject. "You gonna bring another bail bondsman in with you?"

"Not right now. Too stretched. Like I said, I had to put the Victorian up as collateral for my bond. Good thing Ike had the title to the place in joint tenancy."

"He was lookin' out for you."

"Yeah." CJ watched the bouquet of black-eyed Susans sway in the breeze. "He always was." Staring off into the distance, misty-eyed, he said, "You ready to go?"

"Whenever you are."

"Then let's head out." CJ stooped and fluffed up the flowers. Eyeing the headstone, he silently read, *Isaac Tremaine Floyd, 1923–1977*. For a brief second he thought the headstone was too plain, but as he glanced over his shoulder, face to the wind, and read the quotation near the tombstone's bottom—*Keep it simple: one, two, three*—he realized that it was perfect.